D1498466

GODDESS GIRLS

PERSEPHONE THE PHONY

CREATED BY
JOAN HOLUB &
SUZANNE WILLIAMS
ADAPTED BY DAVID CAMPITI

✳

ILLUSTRATED BY EDUARDO GARCIA
AT GLASS HOUSE GRAPHICS

Aladdin
New York   London   Toronto   Sydney   New Delhi

ALADDIN

An imprint of Simon & Schuster Children's Publishing Division
1230 Avenue of the Americas, New York, New York 10020
First Aladdin edition February 2022
Text copyright © 2022 by Joan Holub and Suzanne Williams
Cover illustration by João Zod
Illustrations copyright © 2022 by Glass House Graphics
Art by Eduardo Garcia. Additional art by João Zod, Marcos Cortez, and Noza.
Lettering by Marcos Inoue. Art services by Glass House Graphics.
All rights reserved, including the right of reproduction in whole or in part in any form.
ALADDIN and related logo are registered trademarks of Simon & Schuster, Inc. For information about special discounts for bulk purchases, please contact Simon & Schuster Special Sales at 1-866-506-1949 or business@simonandschuster.com. The Simon & Schuster Speakers Bureau can bring authors to your live event. For more information or to book an event contact the Simon & Schuster Speakers Bureau at 1-866-248-3049 or visit our website at www.simonspeakers.com.
The illustrations for this book were rendered digitally.
The text of this book was set in Font Anime Ace 2.0 BB at 6.5 points over
7.5 point leading and SteinAntik at 10 points over 11 point leading.
Manufactured in China 1121 SCP
2 4 6 8 10 9 7 5 3 1
Library of Congress Control Number 2021937700
ISBN 978-1-5344-7390-4 (hc)
ISBN 978-1-5344-7389-8 (pbk)
ISBN 978-1-5344-7391-1 (ebook)

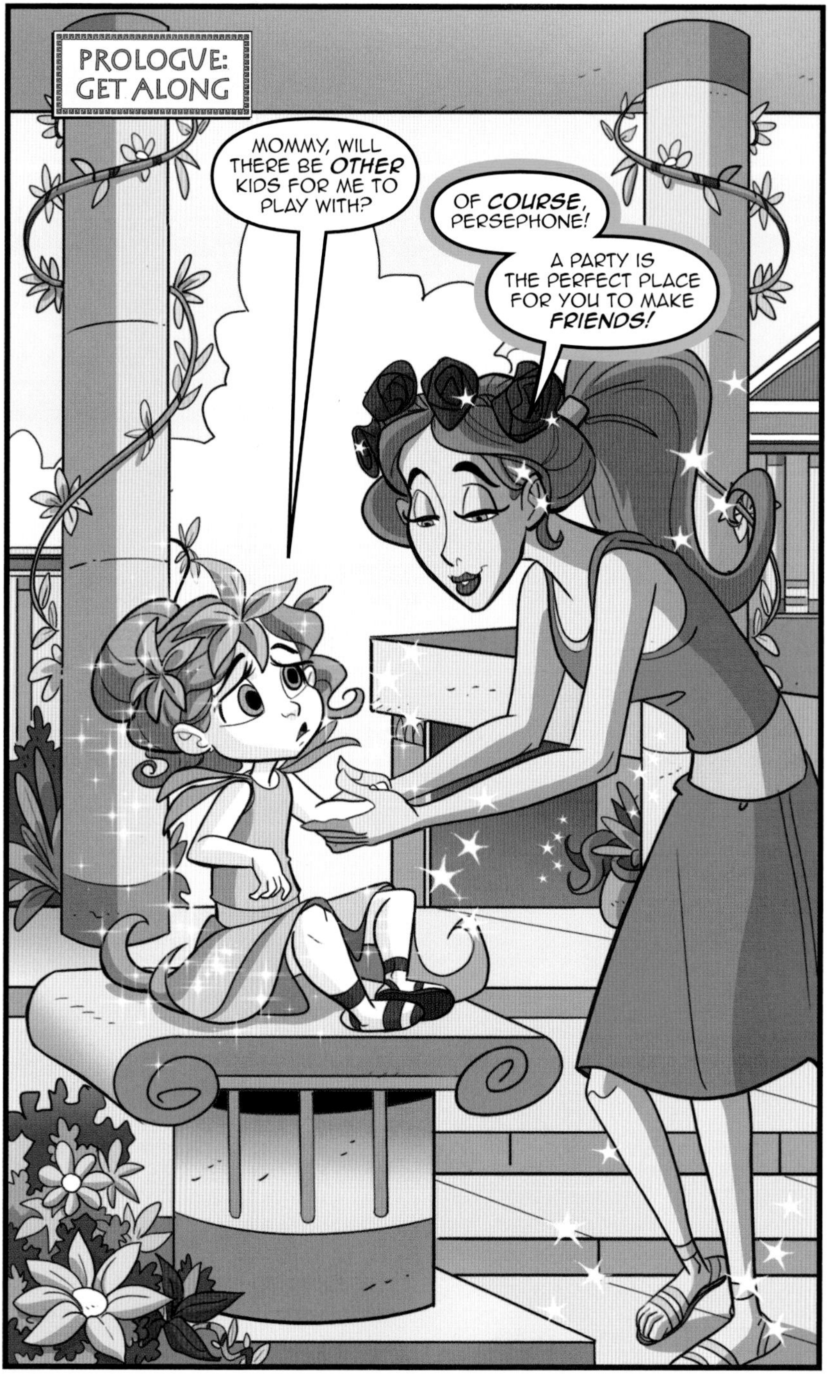
PROLOGUE: GET ALONG
MOMMY, WILL THERE BE OTHER KIDS FOR ME TO PLAY WITH?
OF COURSE, PERSEPHONE!
A PARTY IS THE PERFECT PLACE FOR YOU TO MAKE FRIENDS!

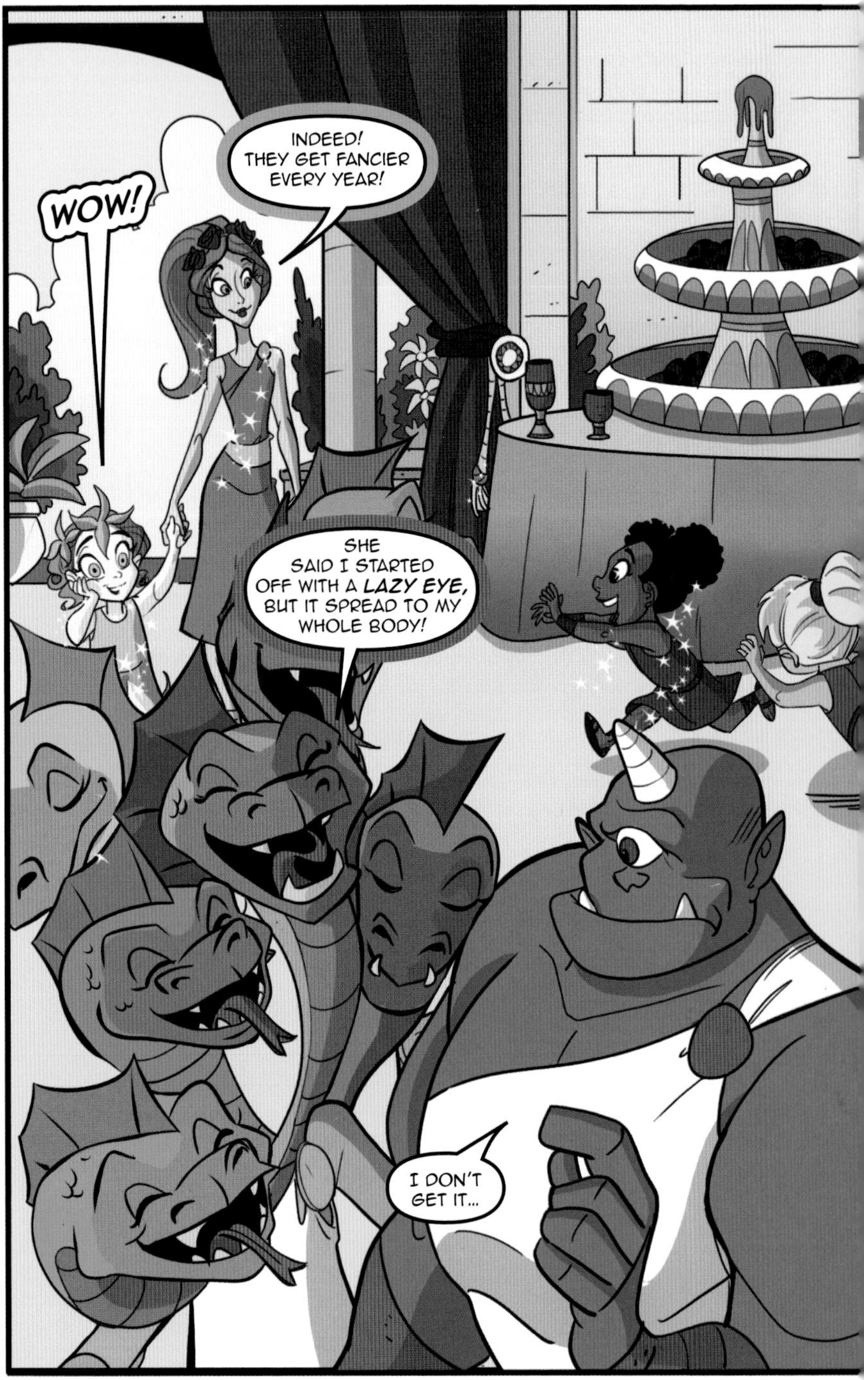
WOW!
INDEED! THEY GET FANCIER EVERY YEAR!
SHE SAID I STARTED OFF WITH A *LAZY EYE,* BUT IT SPREAD TO MY WHOLE BODY!
I DON'T GET IT...

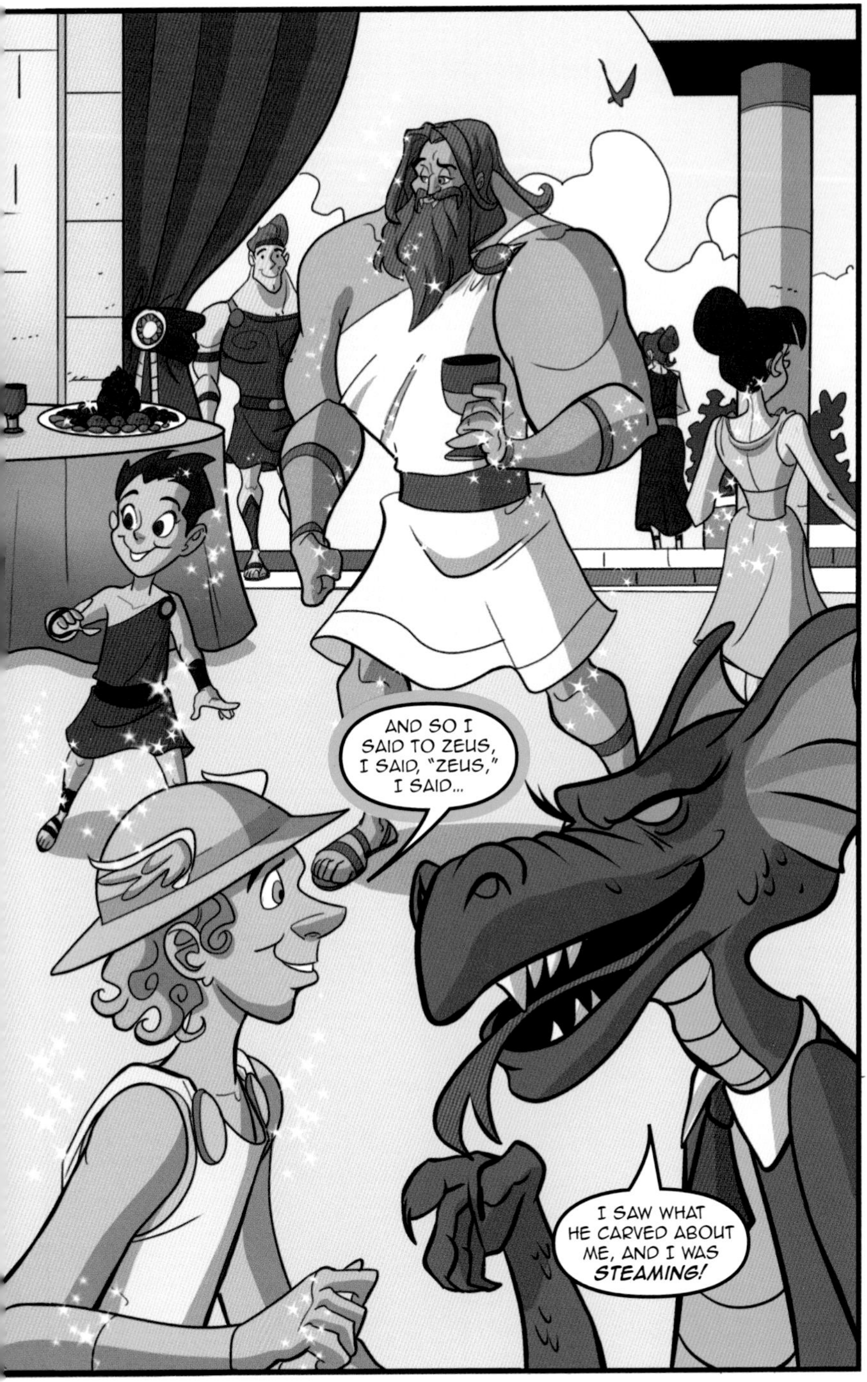
AND SO I SAID TO ZEUS, I SAID, "ZEUS," I SAID...
I SAW WHAT HE CARVED ABOUT ME, AND I WAS *STEAMING!*

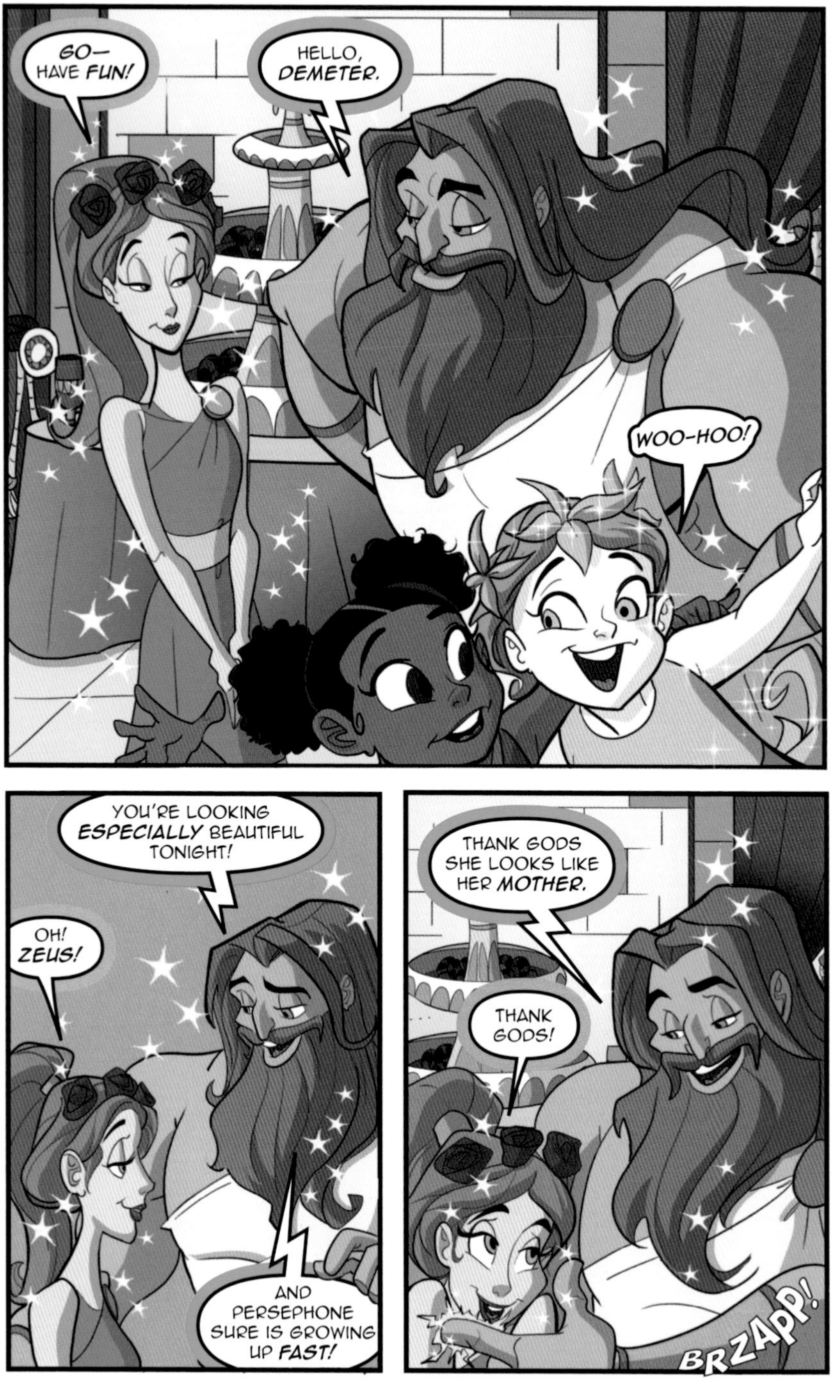
GO— HAVE FUN!
HELLO, DEMETER.
WOO-HOO!
YOU'RE LOOKING ESPECIALLY BEAUTIFUL TONIGHT!
OH! ZEUS!
AND PERSEPHONE SURE IS GROWING UP FAST!
THANK GODS SHE LOOKS LIKE HER MOTHER.
THANK GODS!
BRZAPP!

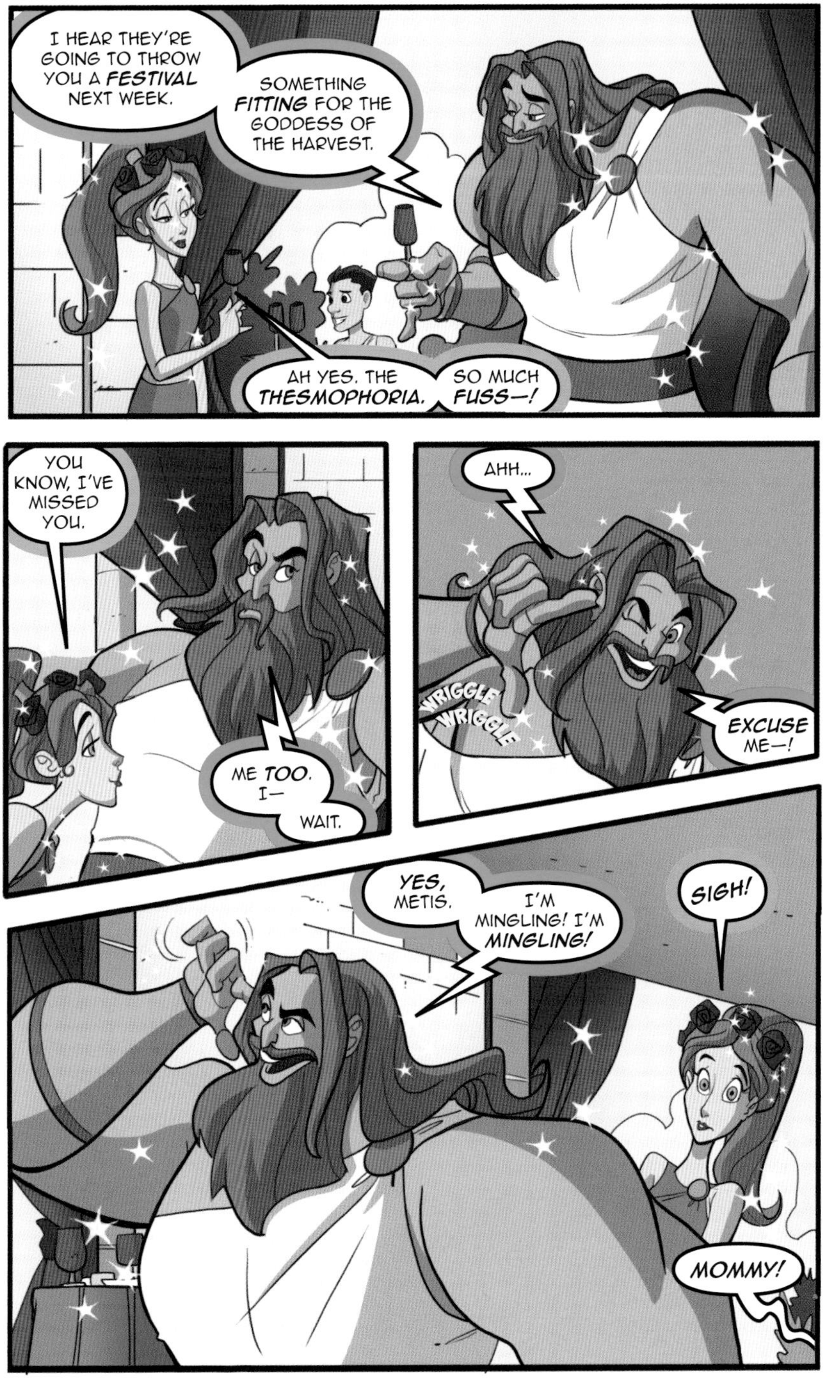
I HEAR THEY'RE GOING TO THROW YOU A FESTIVAL NEXT WEEK.
SOMETHING FITTING FOR THE GODDESS OF THE HARVEST.
AH YES. THE THESMOPHORIA.
SO MUCH FUSS—!
YOU KNOW, I'VE MISSED YOU.
ME TOO. I—
WAIT.
AHH...
WRIGGLE WRIGGLE
EXCUSE ME—!
YES, METIS.
I'M MINGLING! I'M MINGLING!
SIGH!
MOMMY!

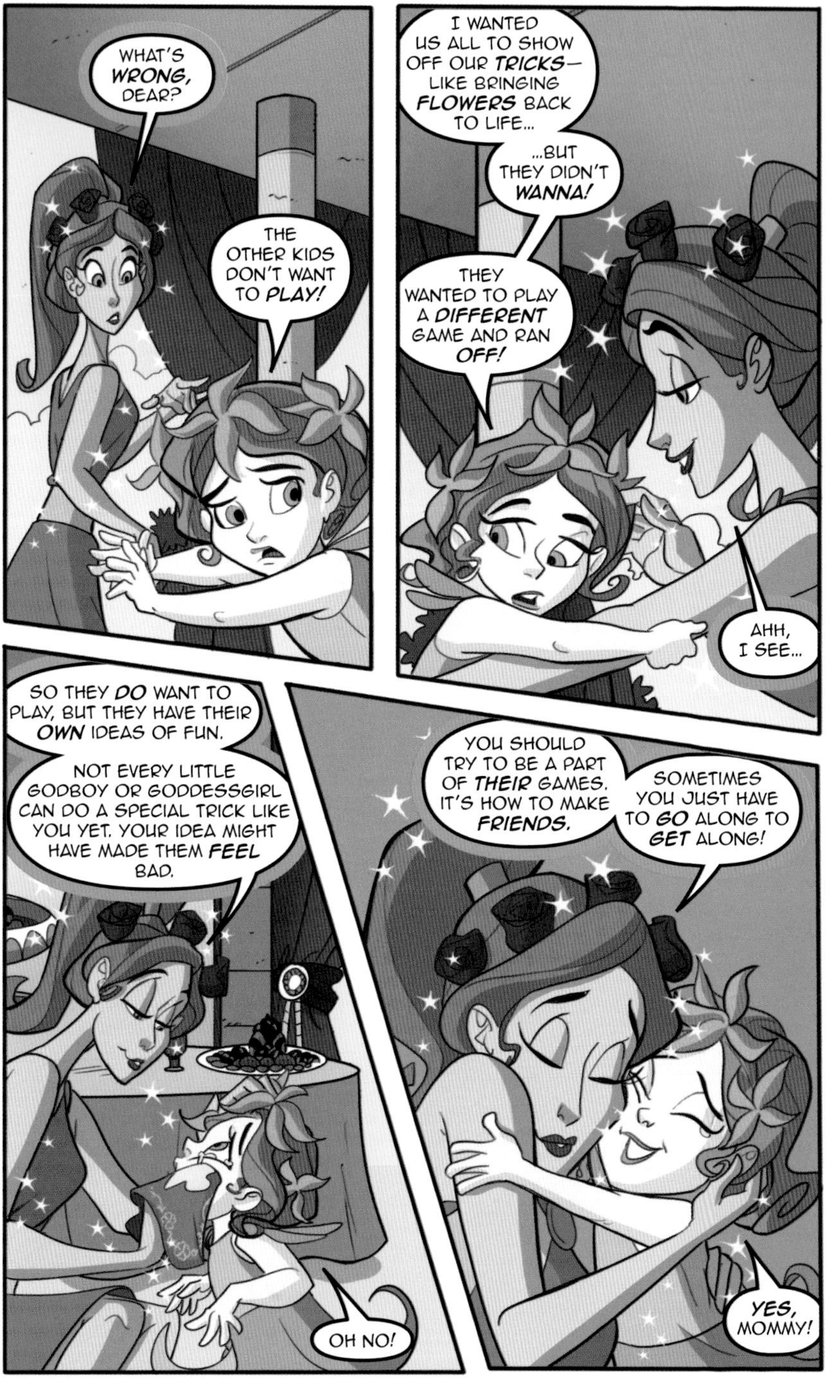
WHAT'S *WRONG,* DEAR?
THE OTHER KIDS DON'T WANT TO *PLAY!*
I WANTED US ALL TO SHOW OFF OUR *TRICKS*— LIKE BRINGING *FLOWERS* BACK TO LIFE...
...BUT THEY DIDN'T *WANNA!*
THEY WANTED TO PLAY A *DIFFERENT* GAME AND RAN *OFF!*
AHH, I SEE...
SO THEY *DO* WANT TO PLAY, BUT THEY HAVE THEIR *OWN* IDEAS OF FUN.
NOT EVERY LITTLE GODBOY OR GODDESSGIRL CAN DO A SPECIAL TRICK LIKE YOU YET. YOUR IDEA MIGHT HAVE MADE THEM *FEEL* BAD.
OH NO!
YOU SHOULD TRY TO BE A PART OF *THEIR* GAMES. IT'S HOW TO MAKE *FRIENDS.*
SOMETIMES YOU JUST HAVE TO *GO* ALONG TO *GET* ALONG!
YES, MOMMY!

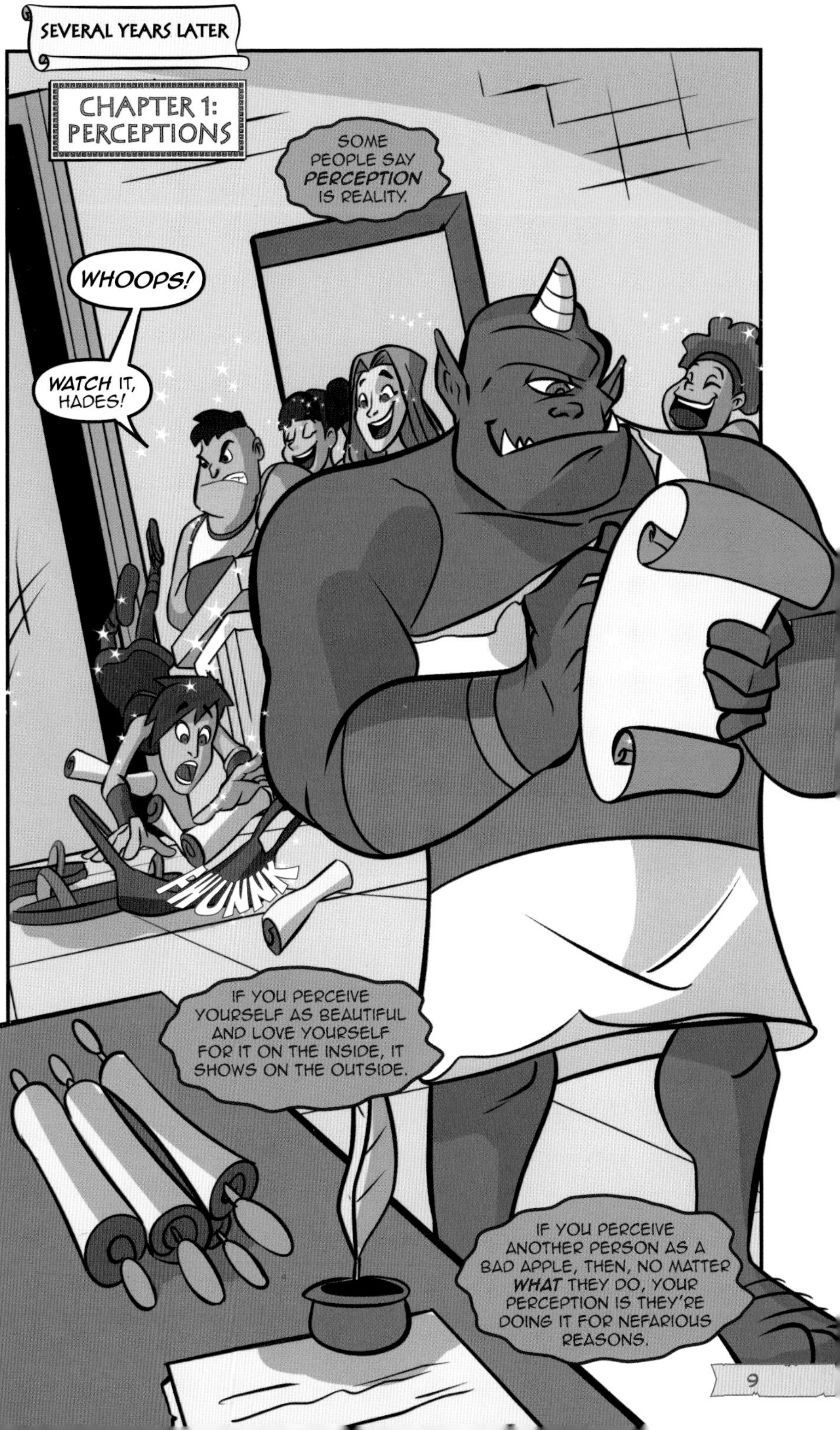
SEVERAL YEARS LATER
CHAPTER 1: PERCEPTIONS
SOME PEOPLE SAY *PERCEPTION* IS REALITY.
WHOOPS!
WATCH IT, HADES!
THUNNK
IF YOU PERCEIVE YOURSELF AS BEAUTIFUL AND LOVE YOURSELF FOR IT ON THE INSIDE, IT SHOWS ON THE OUTSIDE.
IF YOU PERCEIVE ANOTHER PERSON AS A BAD APPLE, THEN, NO MATTER *WHAT* THEY DO, YOUR PERCEPTION IS THEY'RE DOING IT FOR NEFARIOUS REASONS.

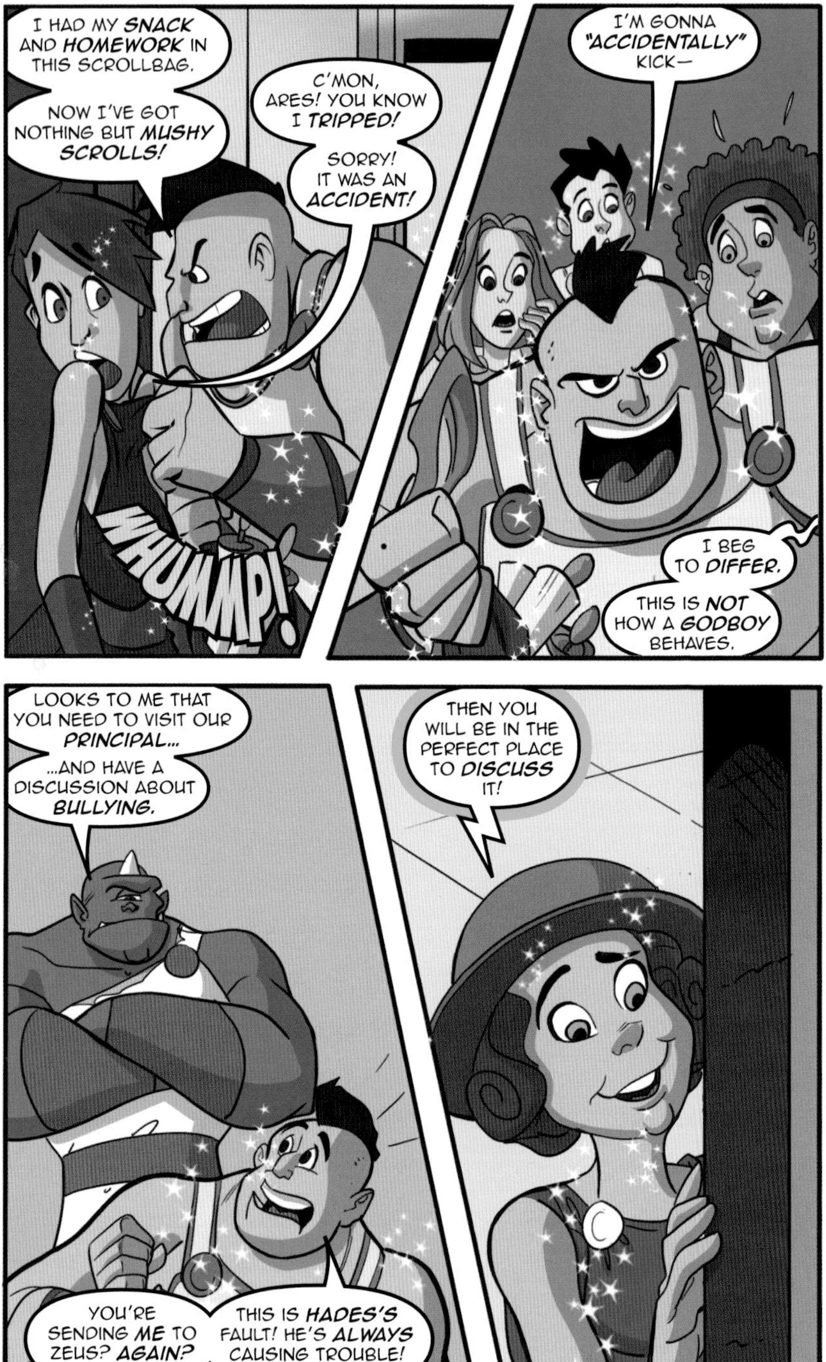
I HAD MY SNACK AND HOMEWORK IN THIS SCROLLBAG.
NOW I'VE GOT NOTHING BUT MUSHY SCROLLS!
C'MON, ARES! YOU KNOW I TRIPPED!
SORRY! IT WAS AN ACCIDENT!
WHUMMP!
I'M GONNA "ACCIDENTALLY" KICK—
I BEG TO DIFFER.
THIS IS NOT HOW A GODBOY BEHAVES.
LOOKS TO ME THAT YOU NEED TO VISIT OUR PRINCIPAL...
...AND HAVE A DISCUSSION ABOUT BULLYING.
YOU'RE SENDING ME TO ZEUS? AGAIN?
THIS IS HADES'S FAULT! HE'S ALWAYS CAUSING TROUBLE!
THEN YOU WILL BE IN THE PERFECT PLACE TO DISCUSS IT!

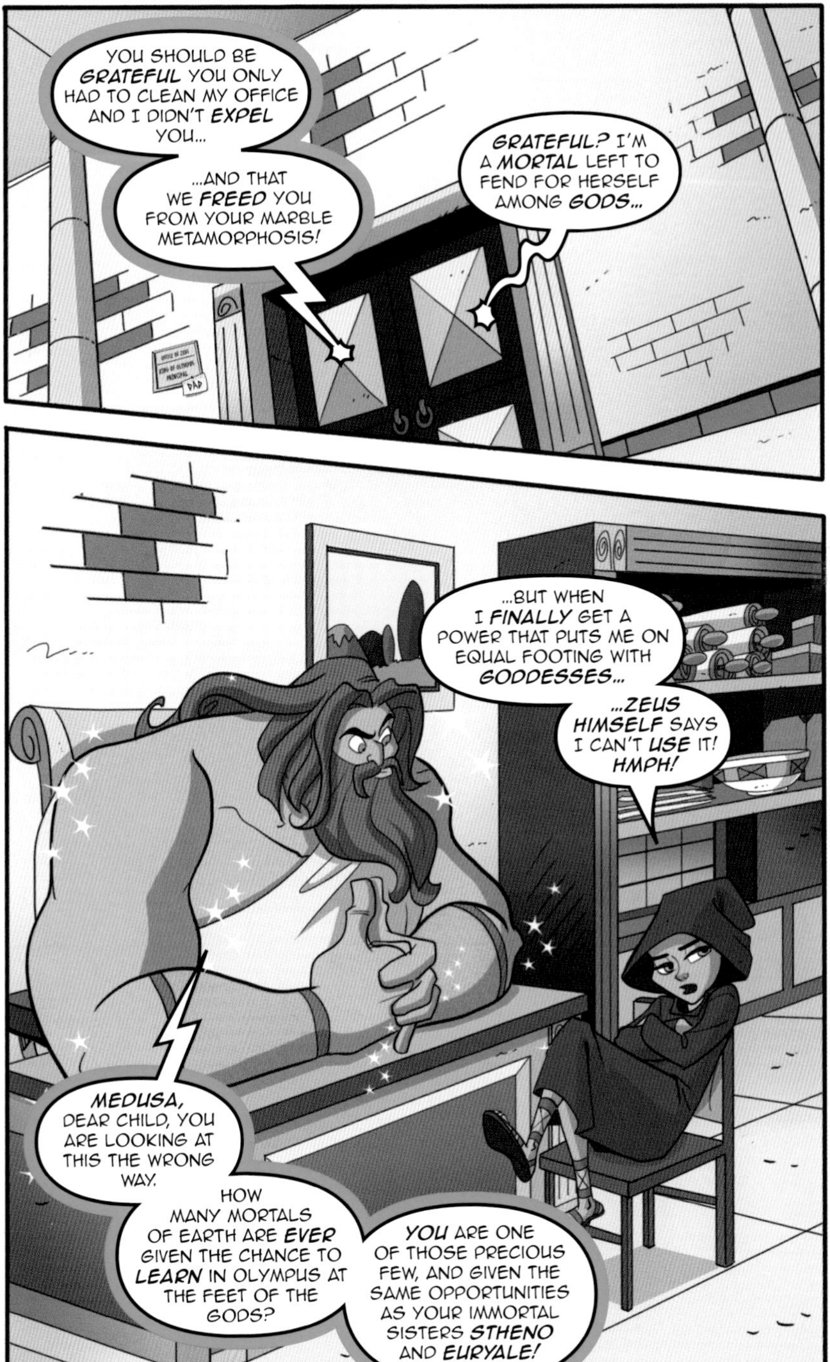
YOU SHOULD BE *GRATEFUL* YOU ONLY HAD TO CLEAN MY OFFICE AND I DIDN'T *EXPEL* YOU...
...AND THAT WE *FREED* YOU FROM YOUR MARBLE METAMORPHOSIS!
GRATEFUL? I'M A *MORTAL* LEFT TO FEND FOR HERSELF AMONG *GODS*...
DAD
...BUT WHEN I *FINALLY* GET A POWER THAT PUTS ME ON EQUAL FOOTING WITH *GODDESSES*...
...*ZEUS HIMSELF* SAYS I CAN'T *USE* IT! *HMPH!*
MEDUSA, DEAR CHILD, YOU ARE LOOKING AT THIS THE WRONG WAY.
HOW MANY MORTALS OF EARTH ARE *EVER* GIVEN THE CHANCE TO *LEARN* IN OLYMPUS AT THE FEET OF THE GODS?
YOU ARE ONE OF THOSE PRECIOUS FEW, AND GIVEN THE SAME OPPORTUNITIES AS YOUR IMMORTAL SISTERS *STHENO* AND *EURYALE!*

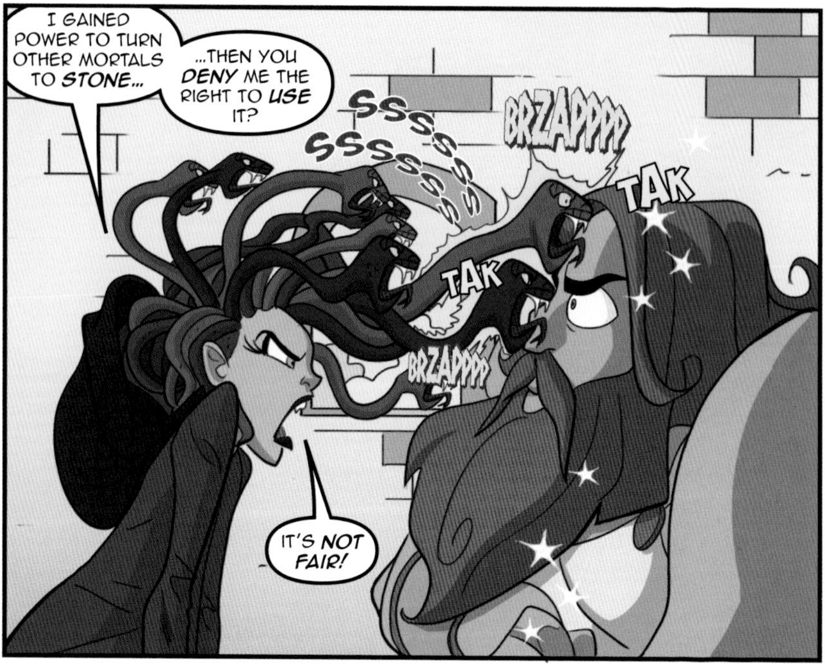
I GAINED POWER TO TURN OTHER MORTALS TO STONE...
...THEN YOU DENY ME THE RIGHT TO USE IT?
SSSSSSSSSSS
BRZAPPPP
TAK
TAK
BRZAPPPP
IT'S NOT FAIR!

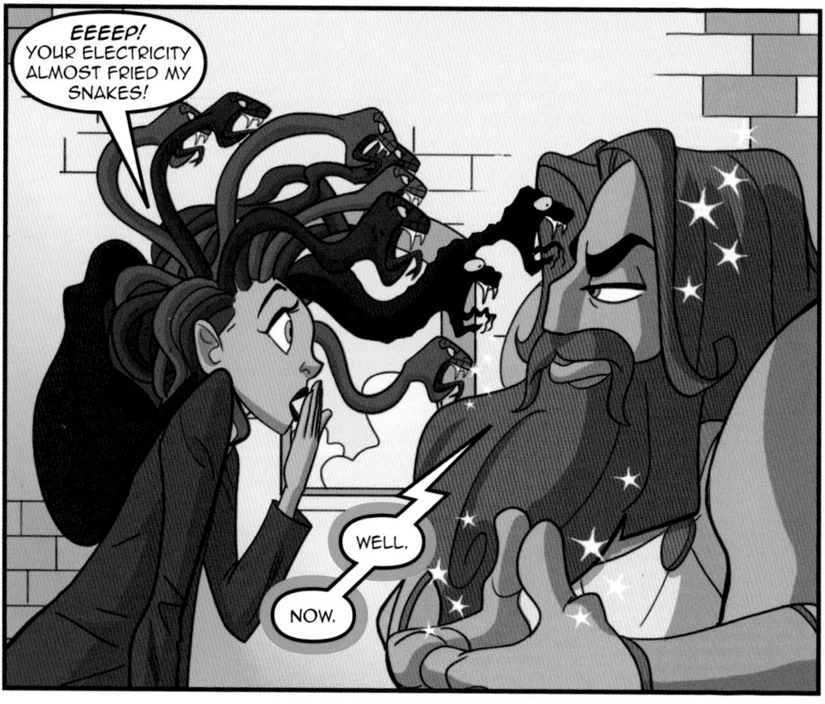
EEEEP! YOUR ELECTRICITY ALMOST FRIED MY SNAKES!
WELL.
NOW.

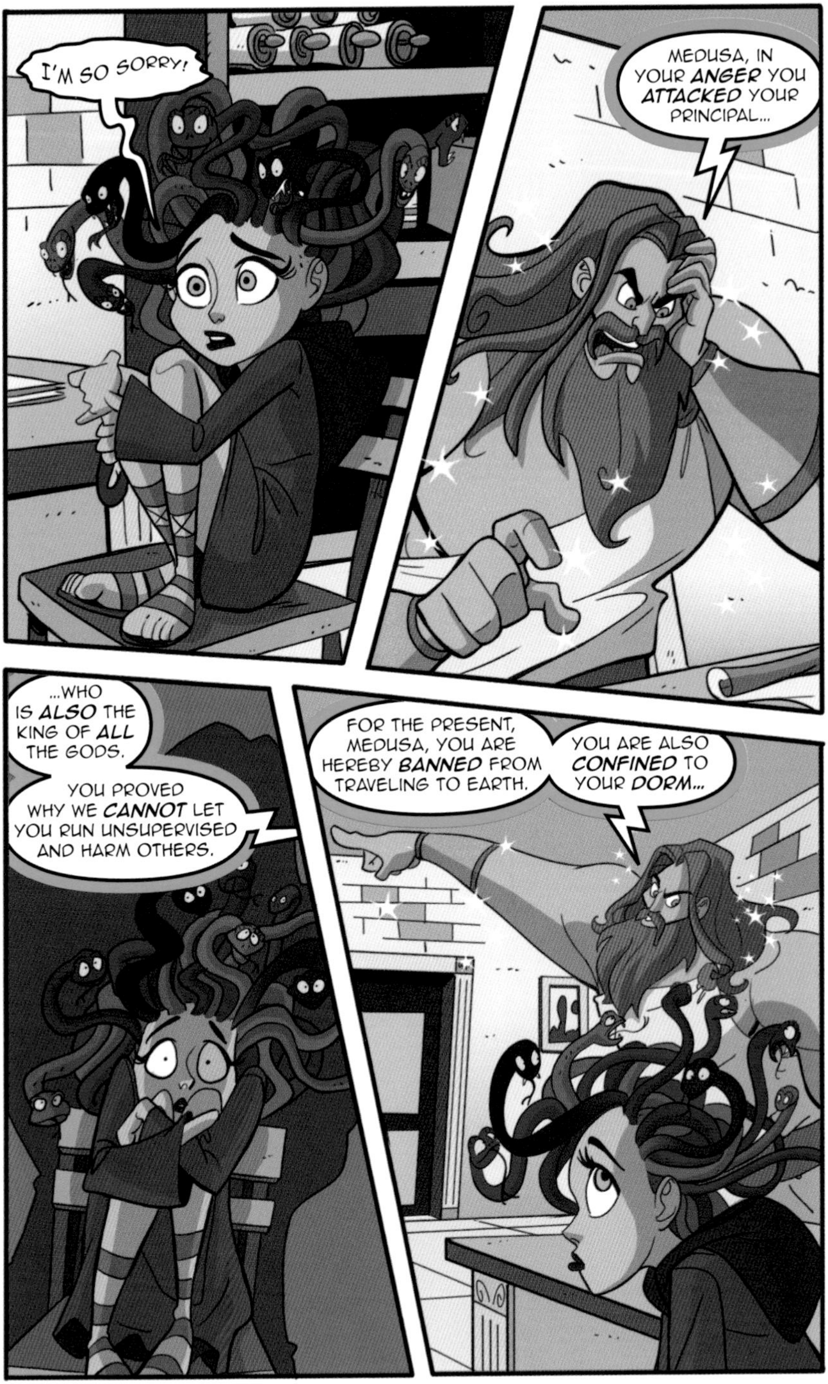
I'M SO SORRY!
MEDUSA, IN YOUR ANGER YOU ATTACKED YOUR PRINCIPAL...
...WHO IS ALSO THE KING OF ALL THE GODS.
YOU PROVED WHY WE CANNOT LET YOU RUN UNSUPERVISED AND HARM OTHERS.
FOR THE PRESENT, MEDUSA, YOU ARE HEREBY BANNED FROM TRAVELING TO EARTH.
YOU ARE ALSO CONFINED TO YOUR DORM...

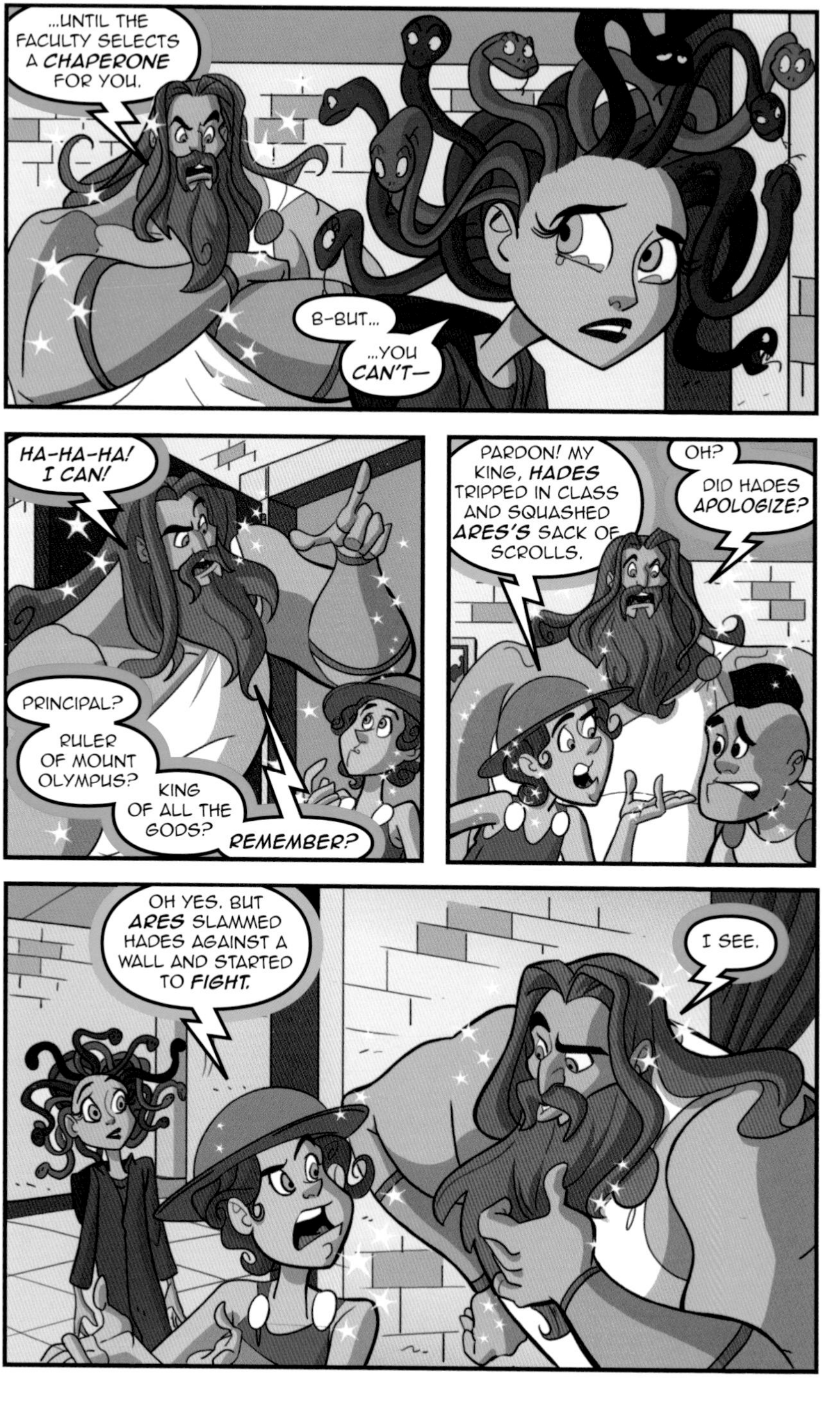
...UNTIL THE FACULTY SELECTS A *CHAPERONE* FOR YOU.
B-BUT...
...YOU *CAN'T—*
HA-HA-HA! I CAN!
PRINCIPAL?
RULER OF MOUNT OLYMPUS?
KING OF ALL THE GODS?
REMEMBER?
PARDON! MY KING, *HADES* TRIPPED IN CLASS AND SQUASHED *ARES'S* SACK OF SCROLLS.
OH?
DID HADES *APOLOGIZE?*
OH YES. BUT *ARES* SLAMMED HADES AGAINST A WALL AND STARTED TO *FIGHT.*
I SEE.

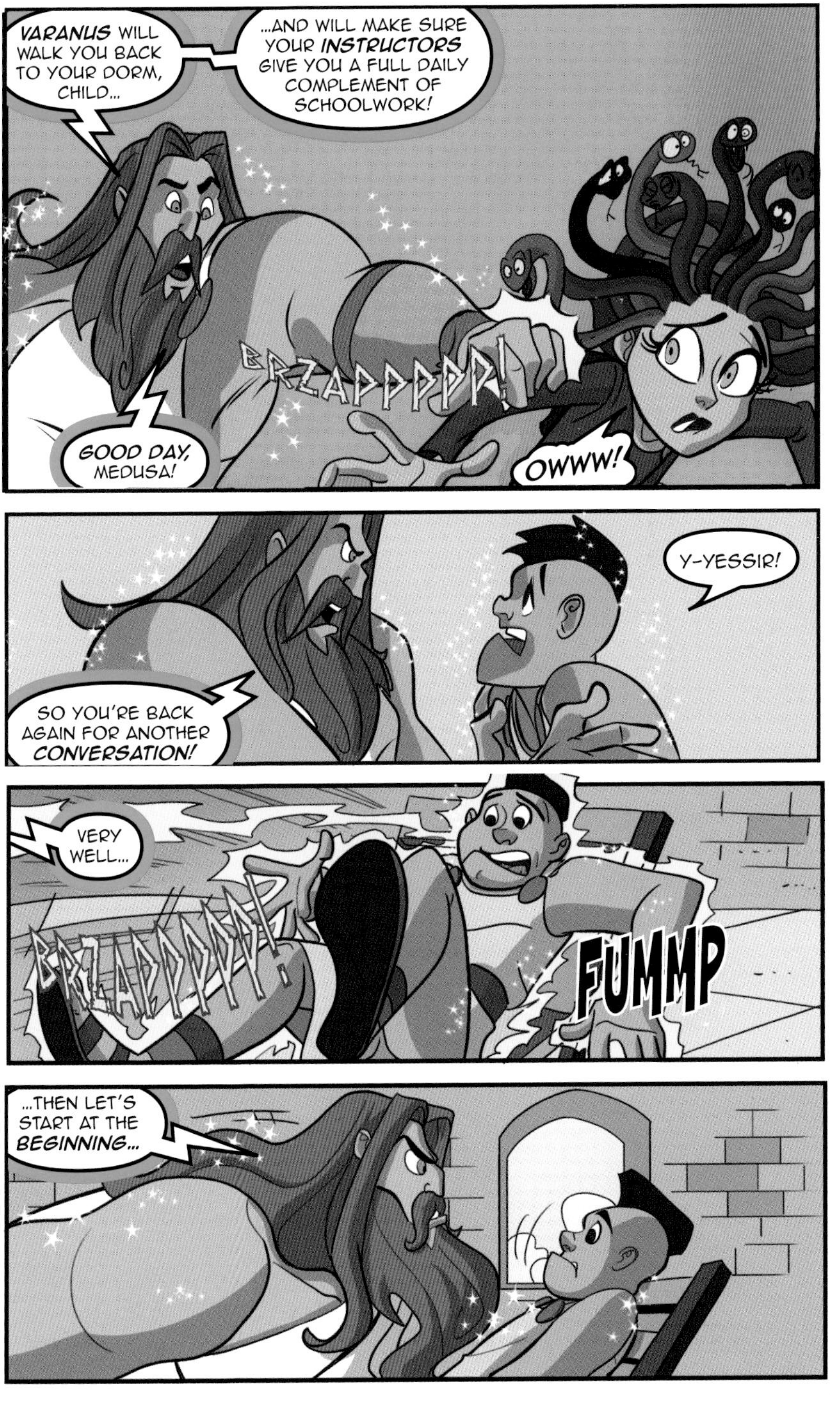
VARANUS WILL WALK YOU BACK TO YOUR DORM, CHILD...
...AND WILL MAKE SURE YOUR INSTRUCTORS GIVE YOU A FULL DAILY COMPLEMENT OF SCHOOLWORK!
BRZAPPPPPP!
GOOD DAY, MEDUSA!
OWWW!
Y-YESSIR!
SO YOU'RE BACK AGAIN FOR ANOTHER CONVERSATION!
VERY WELL...
BRZAPPPPPP!
FUMMP
...THEN LET'S START AT THE BEGINNING...

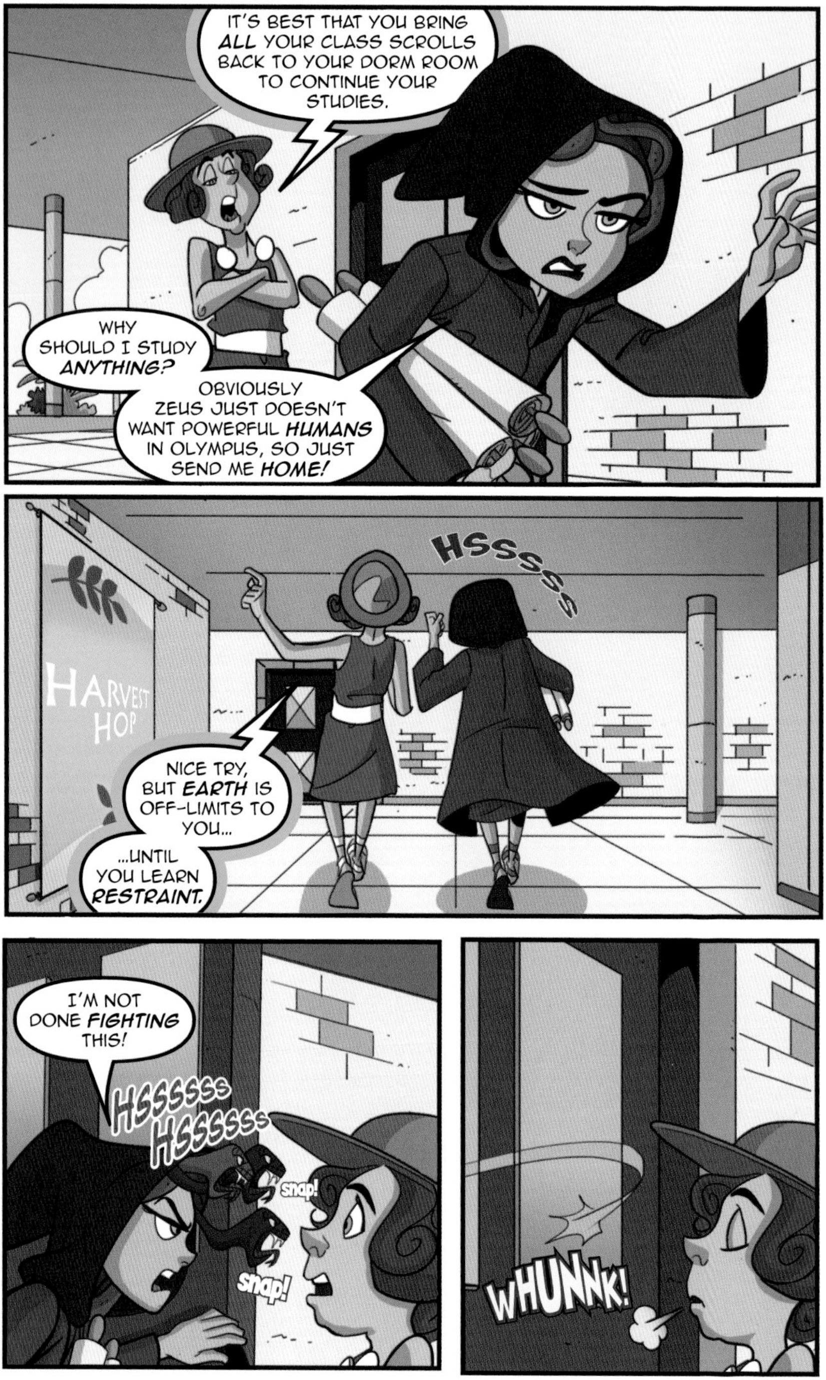

IT'S BEST THAT YOU BRING ALL YOUR CLASS SCROLLS BACK TO YOUR DORM ROOM TO CONTINUE YOUR STUDIES.
WHY SHOULD I STUDY ANYTHING?
OBVIOUSLY ZEUS JUST DOESN'T WANT POWERFUL HUMANS IN OLYMPUS, SO JUST SEND ME HOME!
HSSSSS
HARVEST HOP
NICE TRY, BUT EARTH IS OFF-LIMITS TO YOU...
...UNTIL YOU LEARN RESTRAINT.
I'M NOT DONE FIGHTING THIS!
HSSSSSS HSSSSSS
snap!
snap!
WHUNNK!

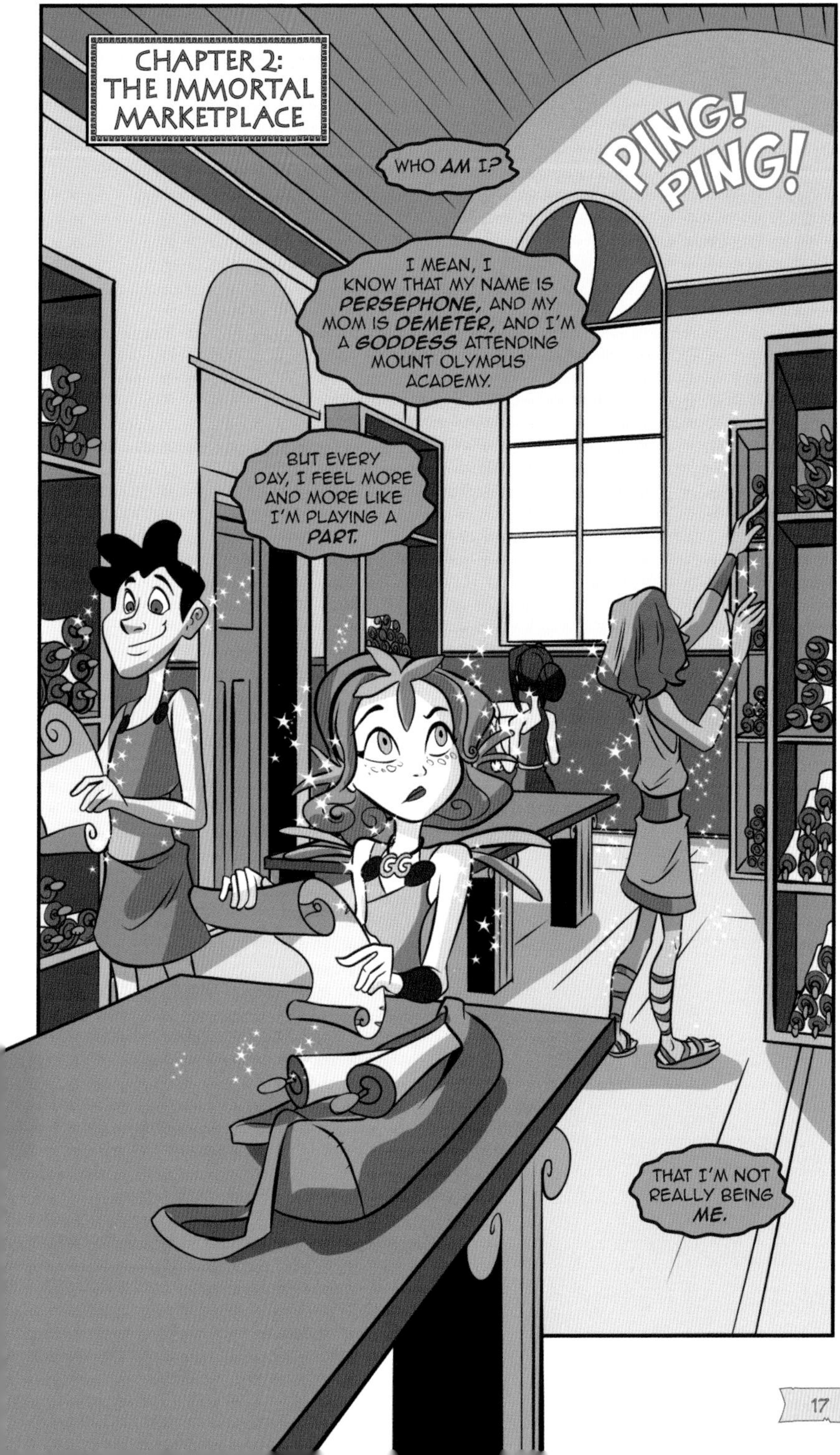
CHAPTER 2:
THE IMMORTAL
MARKETPLACE
WHO AM I?
PING!
PING!
I MEAN, I KNOW THAT MY NAME IS PERSEPHONE, AND MY MOM IS DEMETER, AND I'M A GODDESS ATTENDING MOUNT OLYMPUS ACADEMY.
BUT EVERY DAY, I FEEL MORE AND MORE LIKE I'M PLAYING A PART.
THAT I'M NOT REALLY BEING ME.

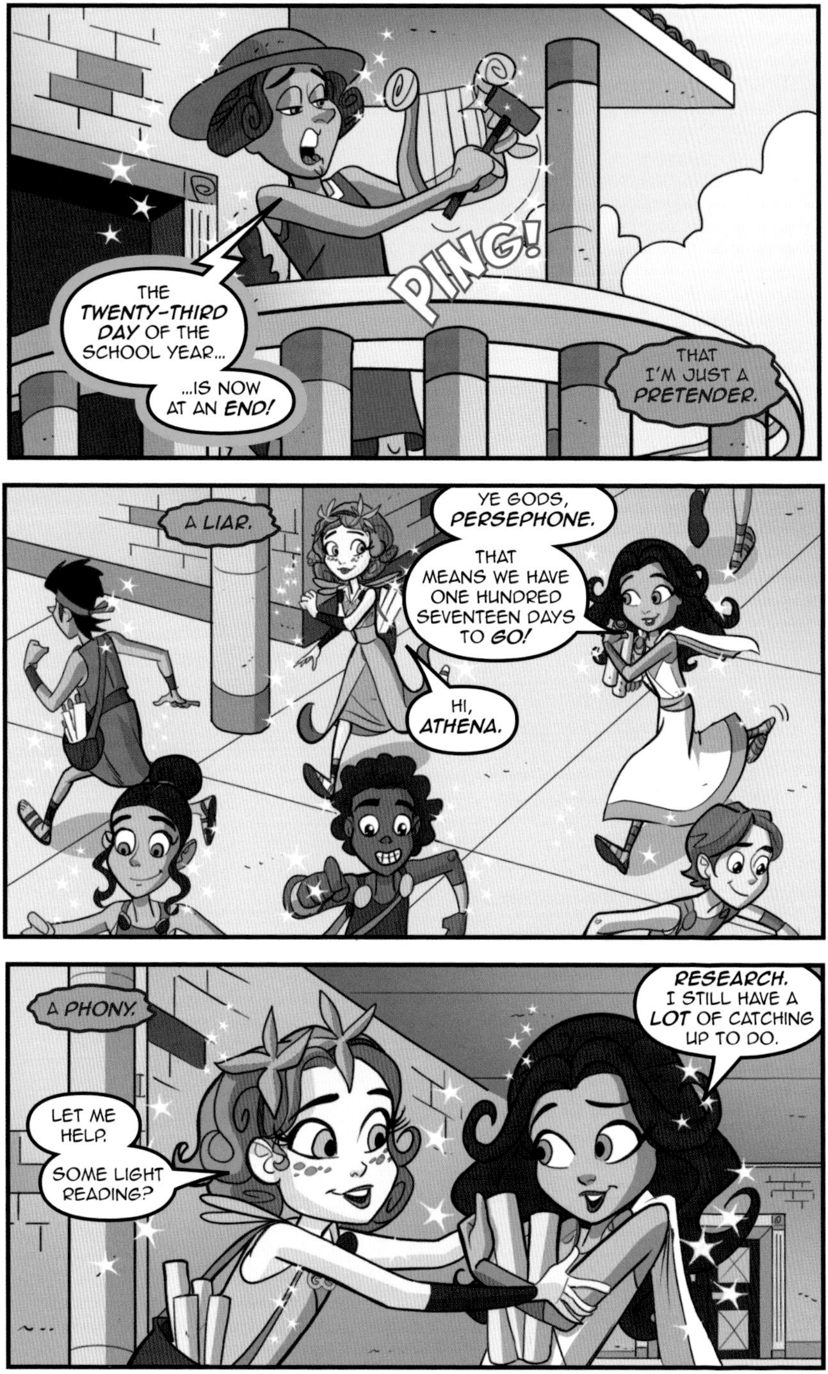

THE TWENTY-THIRD DAY OF THE SCHOOL YEAR...
...IS NOW AT AN END!
PING!
THAT I'M JUST A PRETENDER.
A LIAR.
YE GODS, PERSEPHONE.
THAT MEANS WE HAVE ONE HUNDRED SEVENTEEN DAYS TO GO!
HI, ATHENA.
A PHONY.
RESEARCH. I STILL HAVE A LOT OF CATCHING UP TO DO.
LET ME HELP.
SOME LIGHT READING?

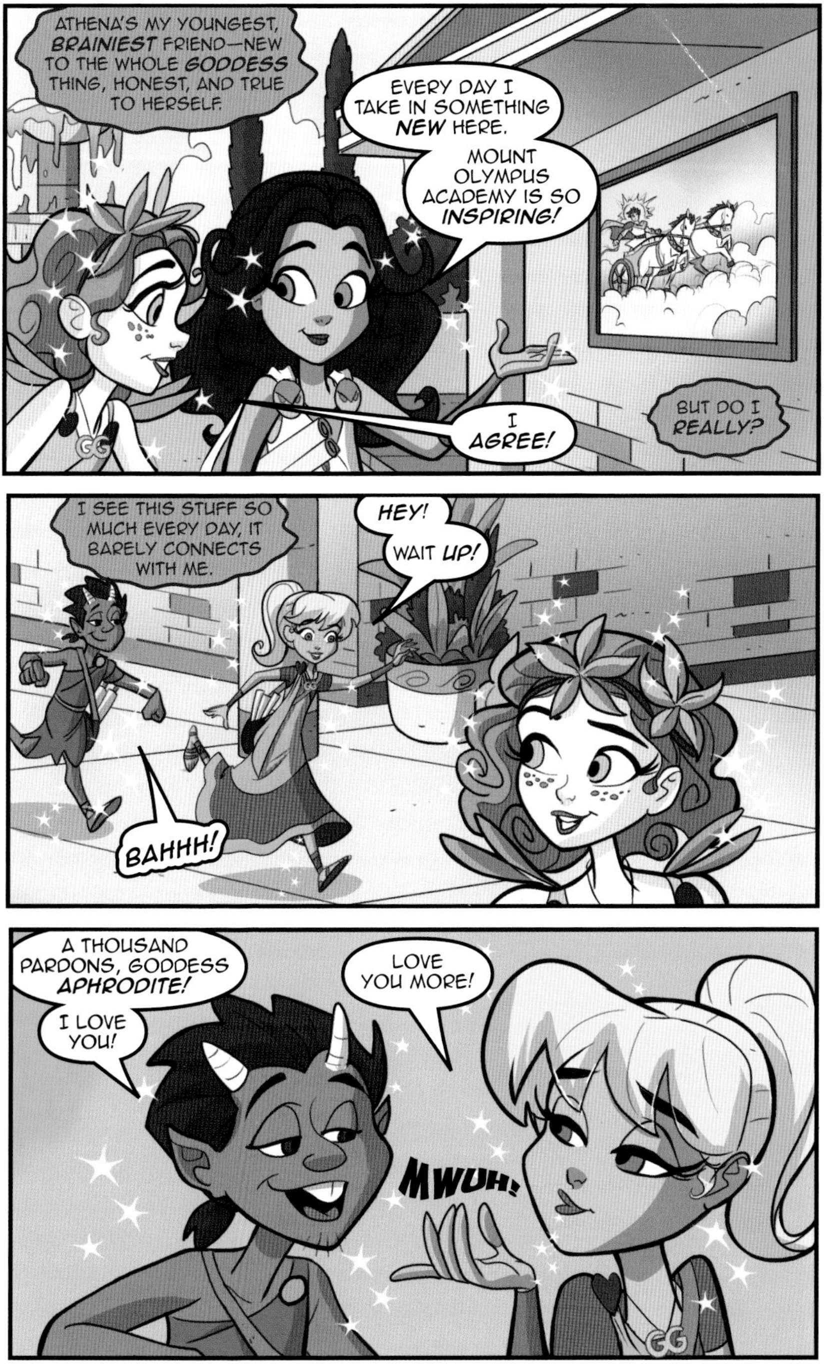
ATHENA'S MY YOUNGEST, BRAINIEST FRIEND—NEW TO THE WHOLE GODDESS THING, HONEST, AND TRUE TO HERSELF.
EVERY DAY I TAKE IN SOMETHING NEW HERE.
MOUNT OLYMPUS ACADEMY IS SO INSPIRING!
I AGREE!
BUT DO I REALLY?
I SEE THIS STUFF SO MUCH EVERY DAY, IT BARELY CONNECTS WITH ME.
HEY!
WAIT UP!
BAHHH!
A THOUSAND PARDONS, GODDESS APHRODITE!
I LOVE YOU!
LOVE YOU MORE!
MWUH!

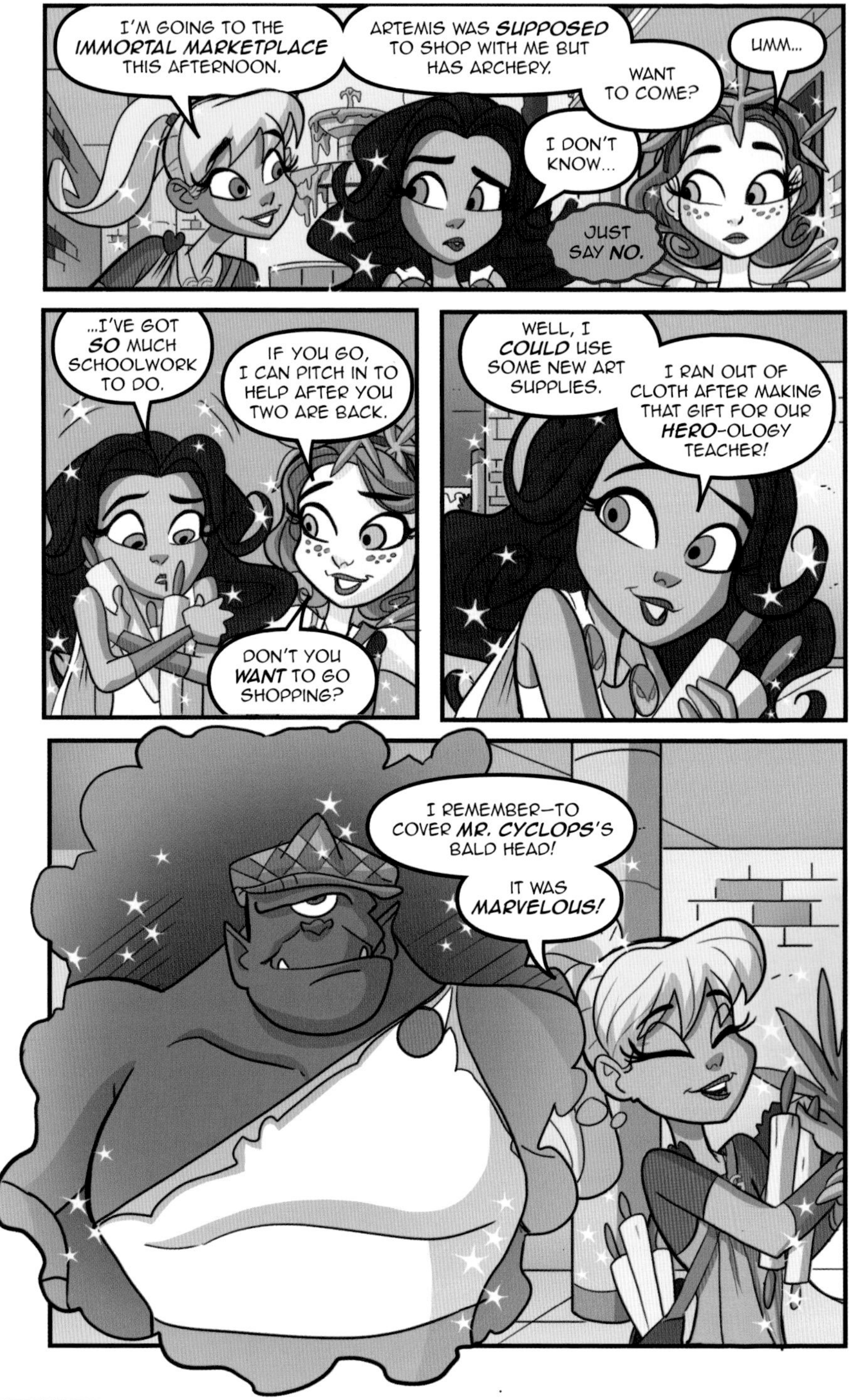
I'M GOING TO THE IMMORTAL MARKETPLACE THIS AFTERNOON.
ARTEMIS WAS SUPPOSED TO SHOP WITH ME BUT HAS ARCHERY.
WANT TO COME?
UMM...
I DON'T KNOW...
JUST SAY NO.
...I'VE GOT SO MUCH SCHOOLWORK TO DO.
IF YOU GO, I CAN PITCH IN TO HELP AFTER YOU TWO ARE BACK.
DON'T YOU WANT TO GO SHOPPING?
WELL, I COULD USE SOME NEW ART SUPPLIES.
I RAN OUT OF CLOTH AFTER MAKING THAT GIFT FOR OUR HERO-OLOGY TEACHER!
I REMEMBER—TO COVER MR. CYCLOPS'S BALD HEAD!
IT WAS MARVELOUS!

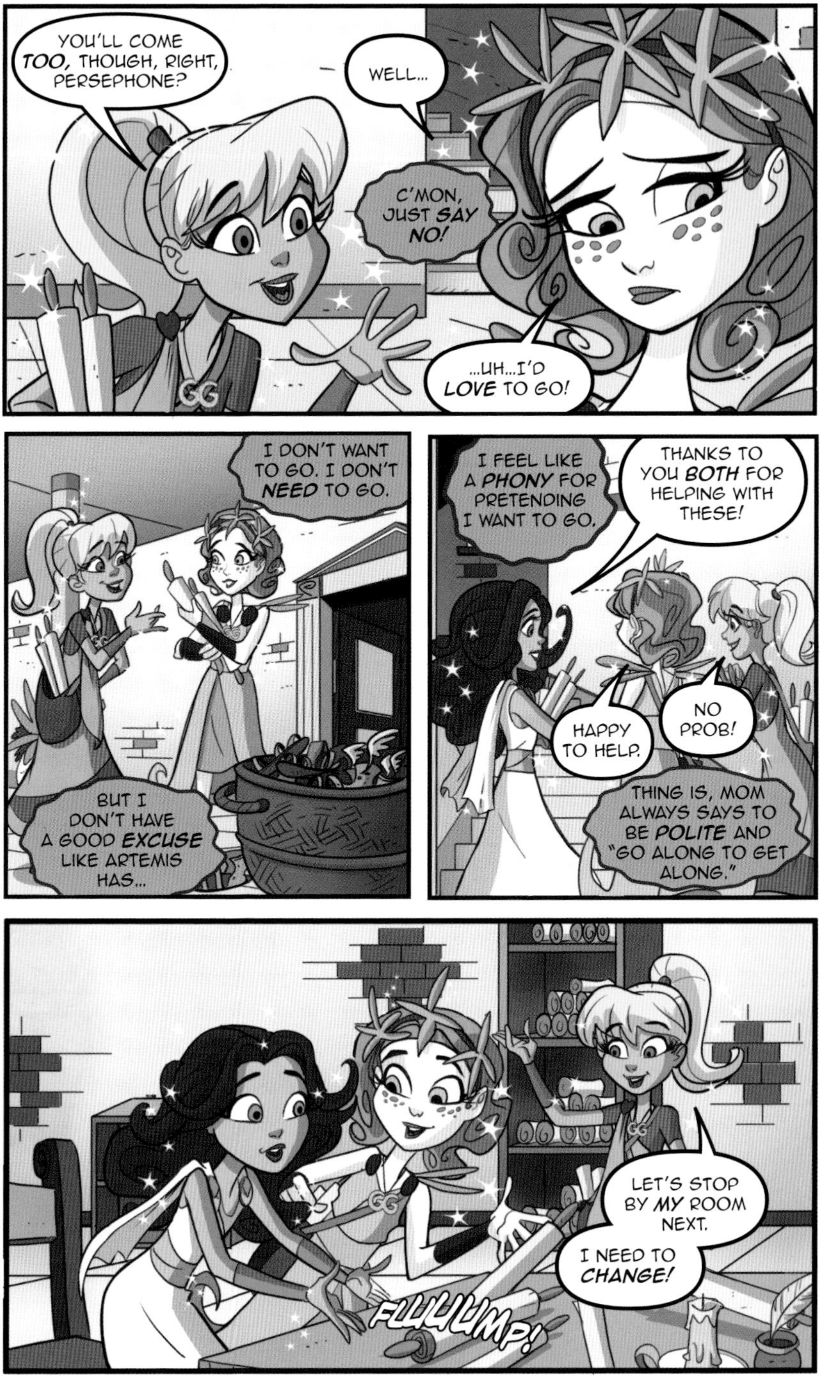

YOU'LL COME TOO, THOUGH, RIGHT, PERSEPHONE?
WELL...
C'MON, JUST SAY NO!
...UH...I'D LOVE TO GO!
I DON'T WANT TO GO. I DON'T NEED TO GO.
BUT I DON'T HAVE A GOOD EXCUSE LIKE ARTEMIS HAS...
I FEEL LIKE A PHONY FOR PRETENDING I WANT TO GO.
THANKS TO YOU BOTH FOR HELPING WITH THESE!
HAPPY TO HELP.
NO PROB!
THING IS, MOM ALWAYS SAYS TO BE POLITE AND "GO ALONG TO GET ALONG."
LET'S STOP BY MY ROOM NEXT.
I NEED TO CHANGE!
FLUUUMP!

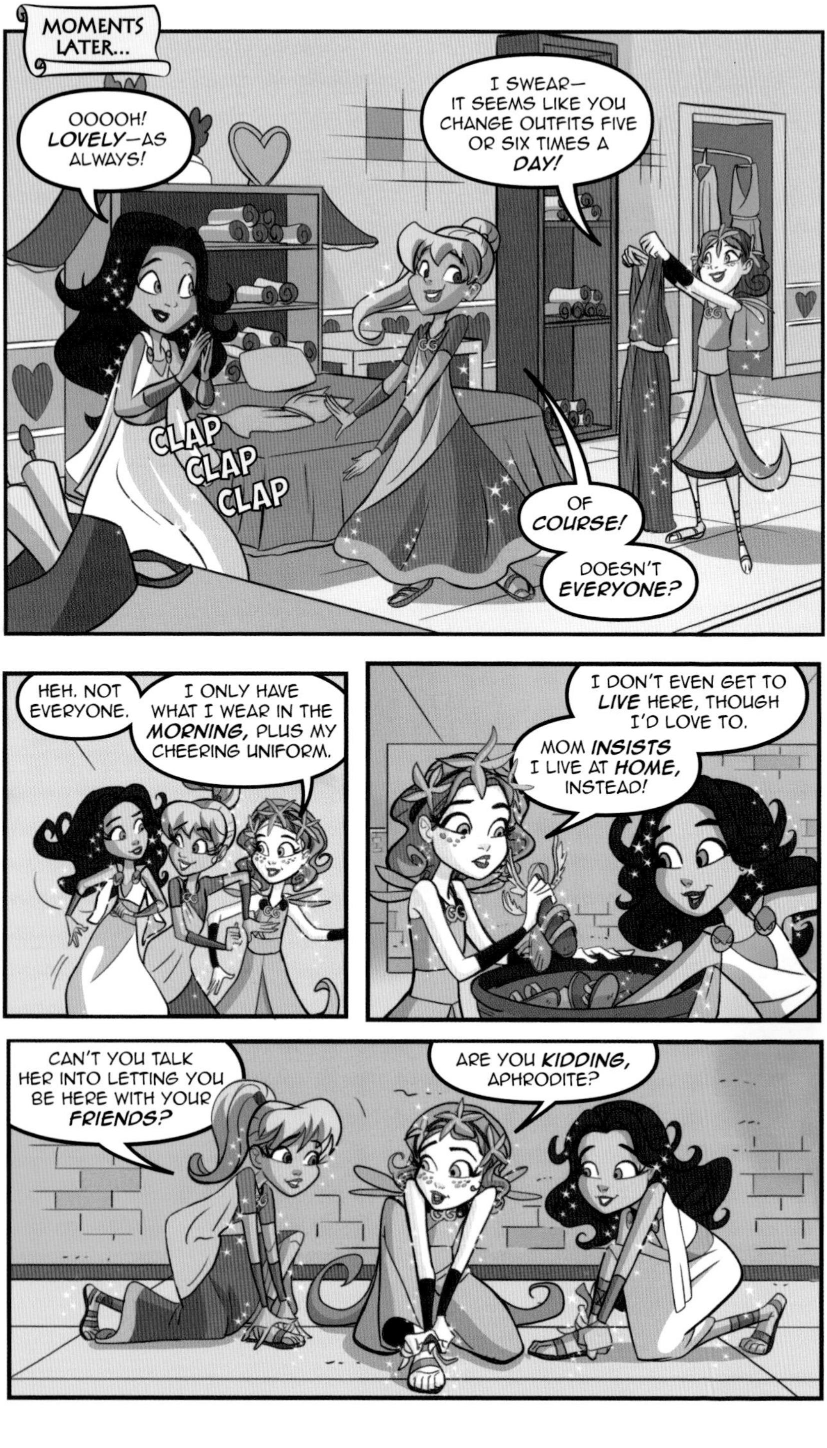
MOMENTS LATER...
OOOOH! LOVELY—AS ALWAYS!
I SWEAR— IT SEEMS LIKE YOU CHANGE OUTFITS FIVE OR SIX TIMES A DAY!
CLAP CLAP CLAP
OF COURSE!
DOESN'T EVERYONE?
HEH. NOT EVERYONE.
I ONLY HAVE WHAT I WEAR IN THE MORNING, PLUS MY CHEERING UNIFORM.
I DON'T EVEN GET TO LIVE HERE, THOUGH I'D LOVE TO.
MOM INSISTS I LIVE AT HOME, INSTEAD!
CAN'T YOU TALK HER INTO LETTING YOU BE HERE WITH YOUR FRIENDS?
ARE YOU KIDDING, APHRODITE?

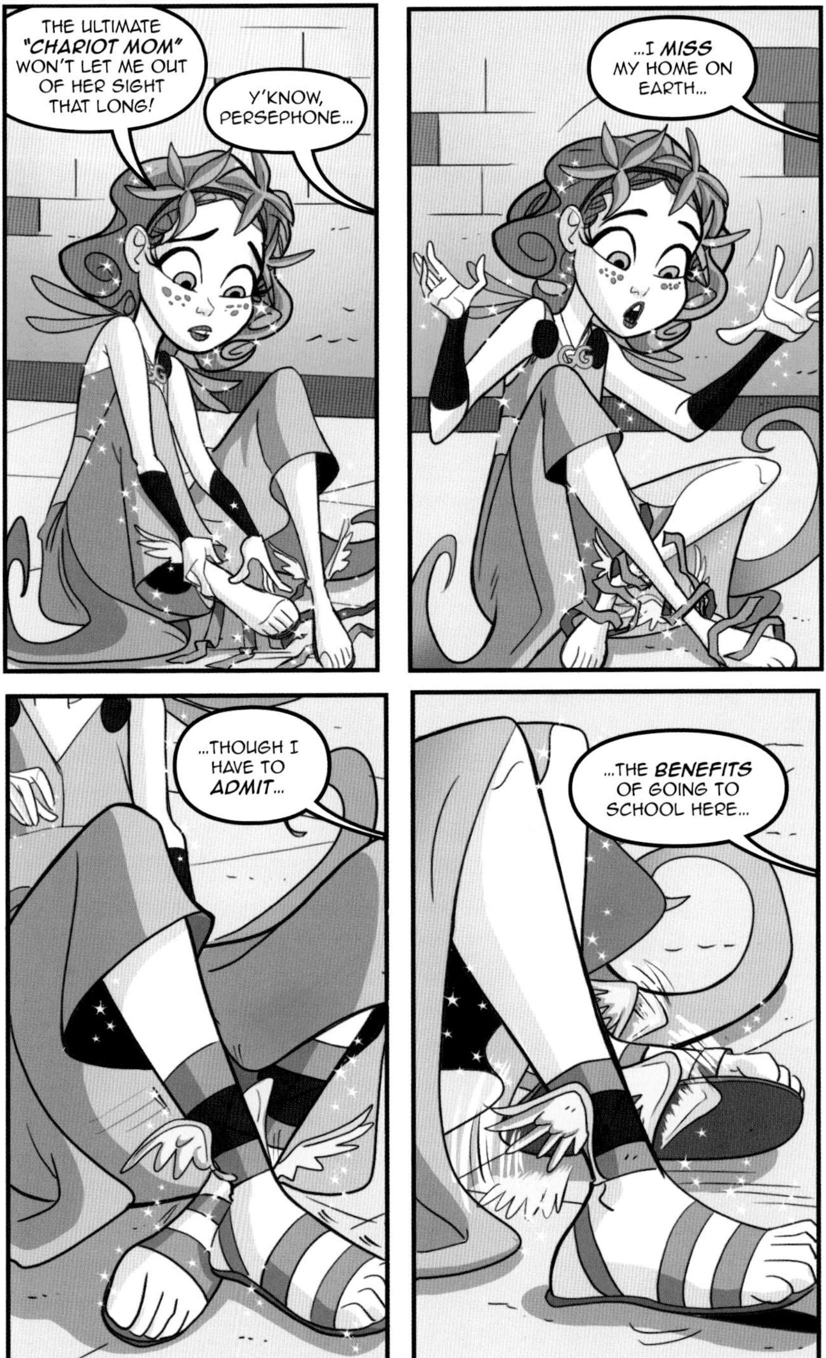
THE ULTIMATE "CHARIOT MOM" WON'T LET ME OUT OF HER SIGHT THAT LONG!
Y'KNOW, PERSEPHONE...
...I MISS MY HOME ON EARTH...
...THOUGH I HAVE TO ADMIT...
...THE BENEFITS OF GOING TO SCHOOL HERE...

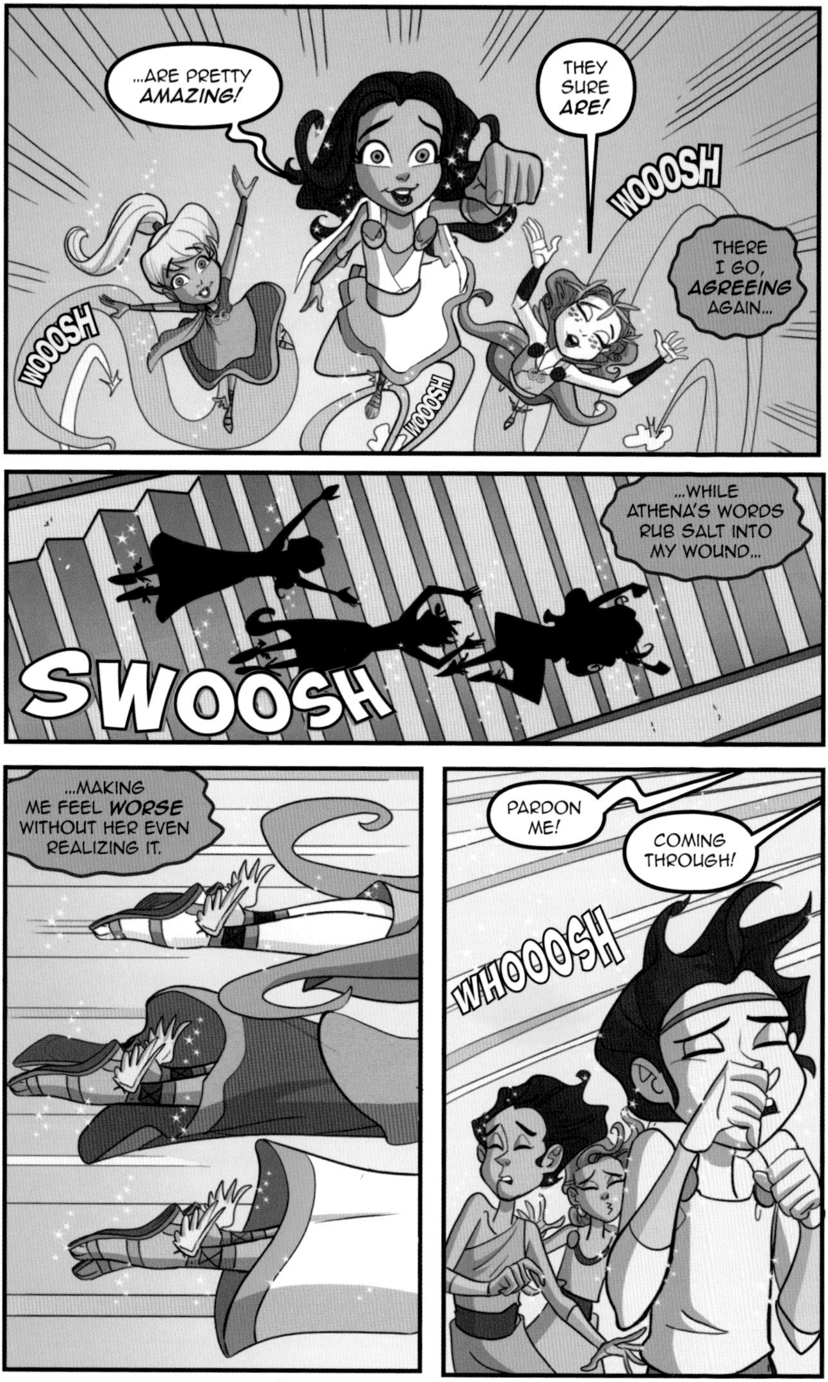
...ARE PRETTY AMAZING!
THEY SURE ARE!
WOOOSH
THERE I GO, AGREEING AGAIN...
WOOOSH
WOOOSH
...WHILE ATHENA'S WORDS RUB SALT INTO MY WOUND...
SWOOSH
...MAKING ME FEEL WORSE WITHOUT HER EVEN REALIZING IT.
PARDON ME!
COMING THROUGH!
WHOOOSH

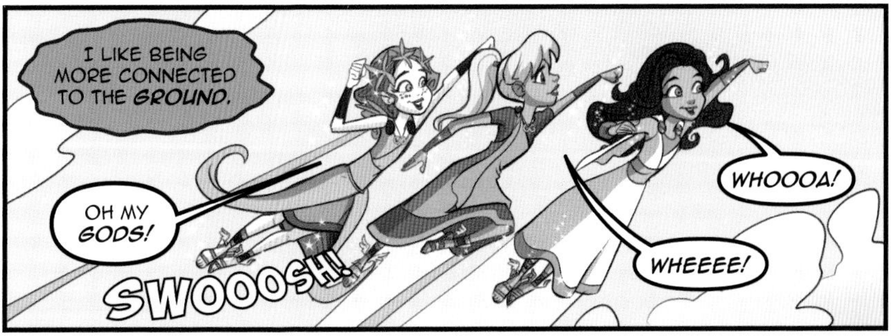
I LIKE BEING MORE CONNECTED TO THE **GROUND.**
OH MY **GODS!**
SWOOOSH!
WHOOOA!
WHEEEE!

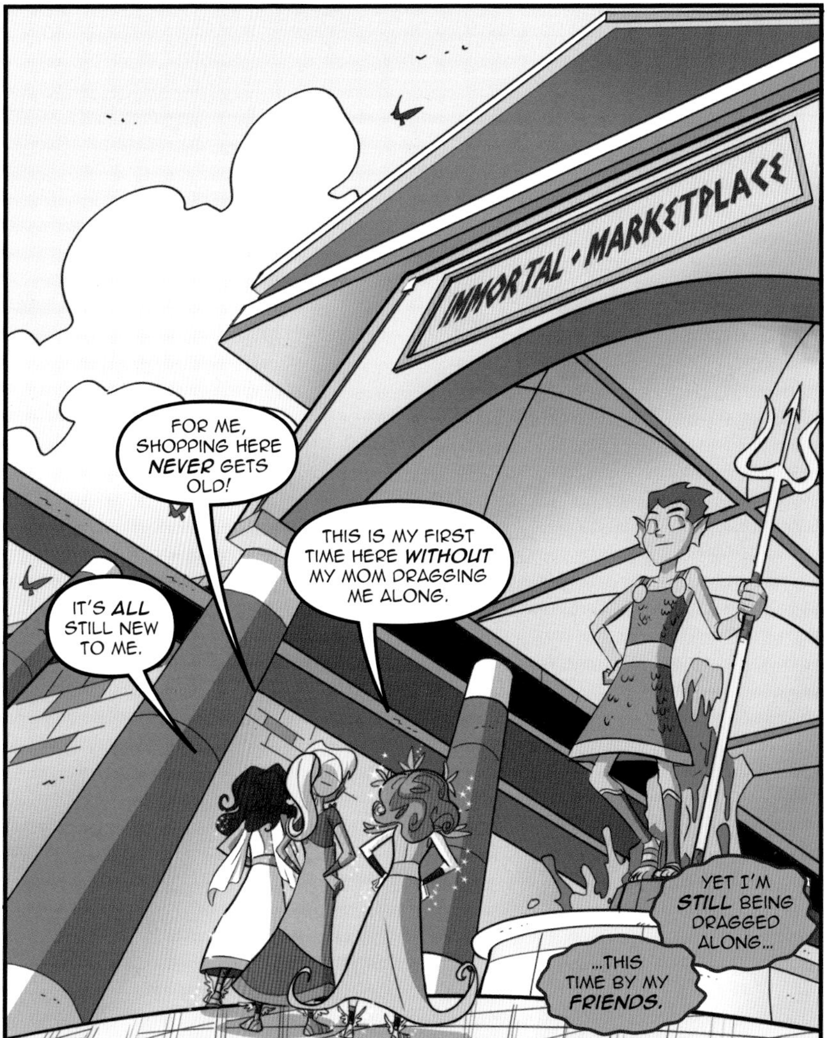
IMMORTAL • MARKETPLACE
FOR ME, SHOPPING HERE ***NEVER*** GETS OLD!
IT'S ***ALL*** STILL NEW TO ME.
THIS IS MY FIRST TIME HERE ***WITHOUT*** MY MOM DRAGGING ME ALONG.
YET I'M ***STILL*** BEING DRAGGED ALONG...
...THIS TIME BY MY ***FRIENDS.***

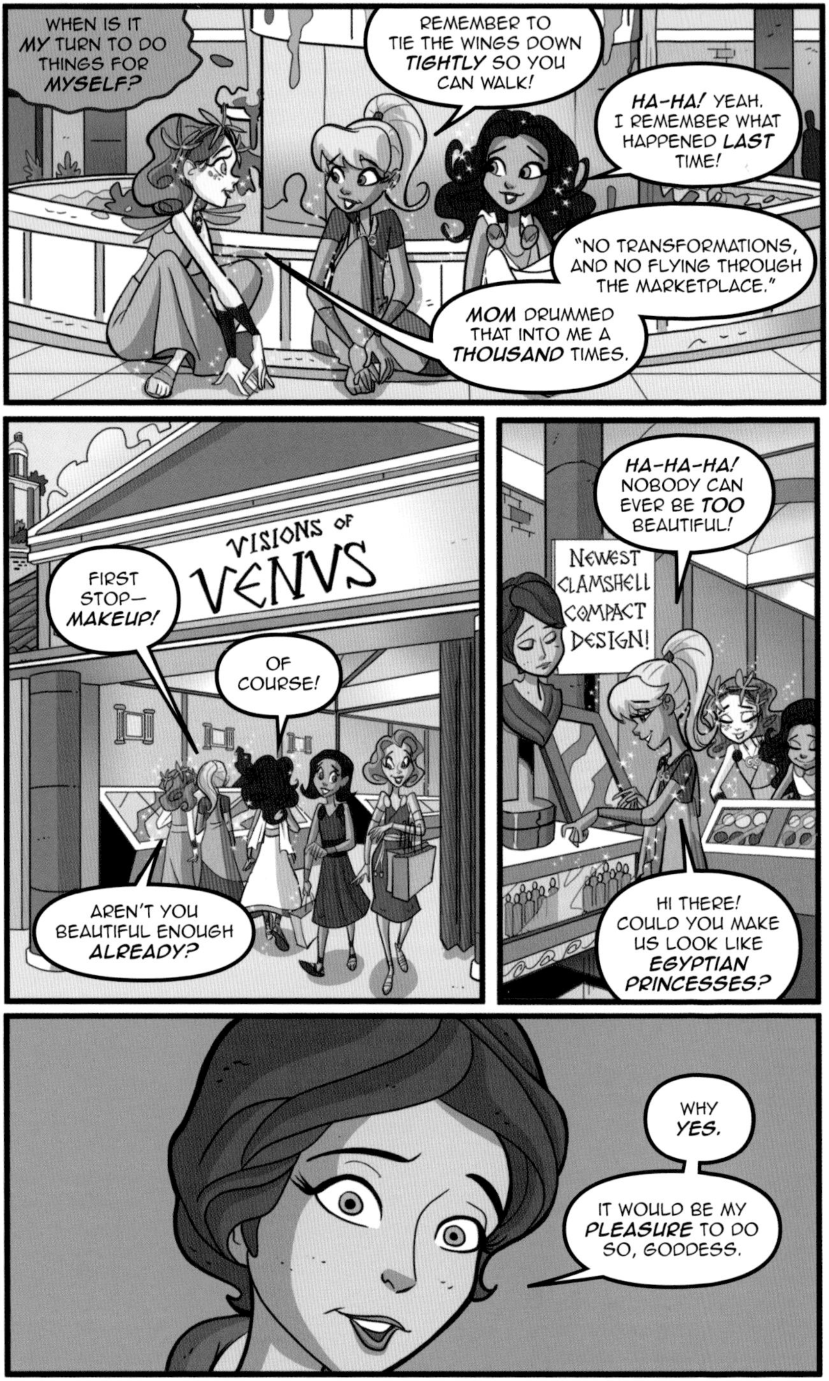

WHEN IS IT *MY* TURN TO DO THINGS FOR *MYSELF?*
REMEMBER TO TIE THE WINGS DOWN *TIGHTLY* SO YOU CAN WALK!
HA-HA! YEAH. I REMEMBER WHAT HAPPENED *LAST* TIME!
"NO TRANSFORMATIONS, AND NO FLYING THROUGH THE MARKETPLACE."
MOM DRUMMED THAT INTO ME A *THOUSAND* TIMES.
VISIONS OF VENUS
FIRST STOP— *MAKEUP!*
OF COURSE!
AREN'T YOU BEAUTIFUL ENOUGH *ALREADY?*
HA-HA-HA! NOBODY CAN EVER BE *TOO* BEAUTIFUL!
NEWEST CLAMSHELL COMPACT DESIGN!
HI THERE! COULD YOU MAKE US LOOK LIKE *EGYPTIAN PRINCESSES?*
WHY *YES.*
IT WOULD BE MY *PLEASURE* TO DO SO, GODDESS.

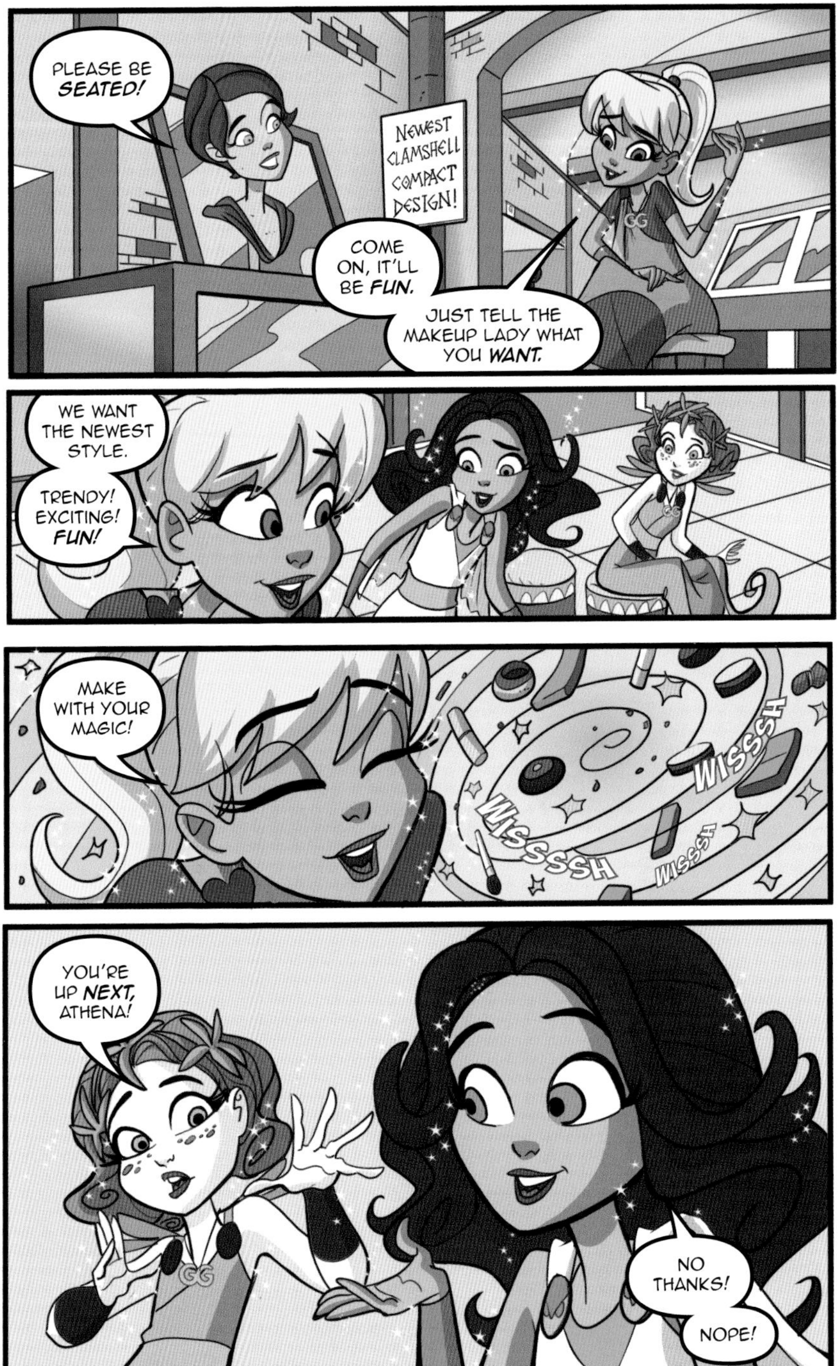
PLEASE BE SEATED!
NEWEST CLAMSHELL COMPACT DESIGN!
COME ON, IT'LL BE FUN.
JUST TELL THE MAKEUP LADY WHAT YOU WANT.
WE WANT THE NEWEST STYLE.
TRENDY! EXCITING! FUN!
MAKE WITH YOUR MAGIC!
WISSSSSH
WISSSH
WISSSH
YOU'RE UP NEXT, ATHENA!
NO THANKS!
NOPE!

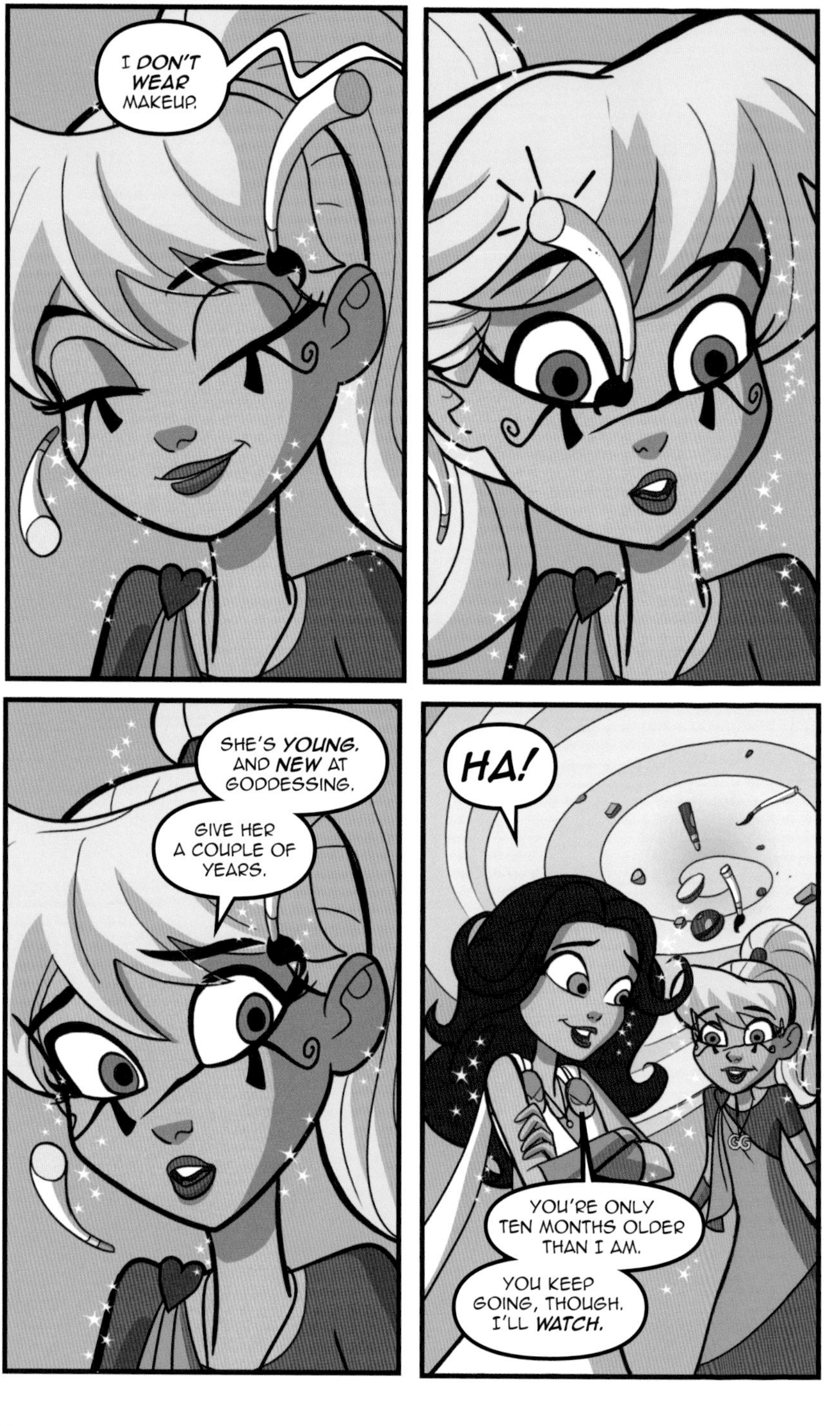
I DON'T WEAR MAKEUP.
SHE'S YOUNG. AND NEW AT GODDESSING.
GIVE HER A COUPLE OF YEARS.
HA!
YOU'RE ONLY TEN MONTHS OLDER THAN I AM.
YOU KEEP GOING, THOUGH. I'LL WATCH.

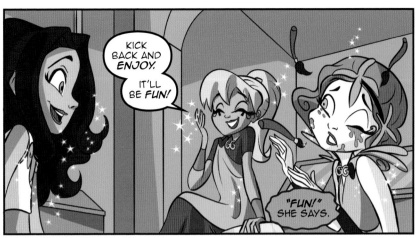

KICK BACK AND *ENJOY.*

IT'LL BE *FUN!*

"FUN!" SHE SAYS.

SOON...

WHAT'LL WE DO *NEXT?*

THAT WAS SO GREAT!

KNITTING SUPPLIES!

SURE.

WHY DID I EVEN *BUY* THAT EYELINER? JUST BECAUSE *APHRODITE* WANTED ME TO?

HEY, LOOK— IT'S POSEIDON'S *AWARD* FROM THE INVENTION FAIR!

CHISELED IN ROCK, HE LOOKS ALMOST AS GOOD AS IN PERSON...

...AND WITH *YOUR* ALABASTER SKIN TONE, PERSEPHONE!

I *KNOW* I'M AS WHITE AS MARBLE...

AND AGAINST MY SUPER-PALE SKIN, THIS RACCOON-STYLE EYELINER MAKES ME LOOK POSITIVELY *PASTY!*

OR WORSE... *HIDEOUS!*

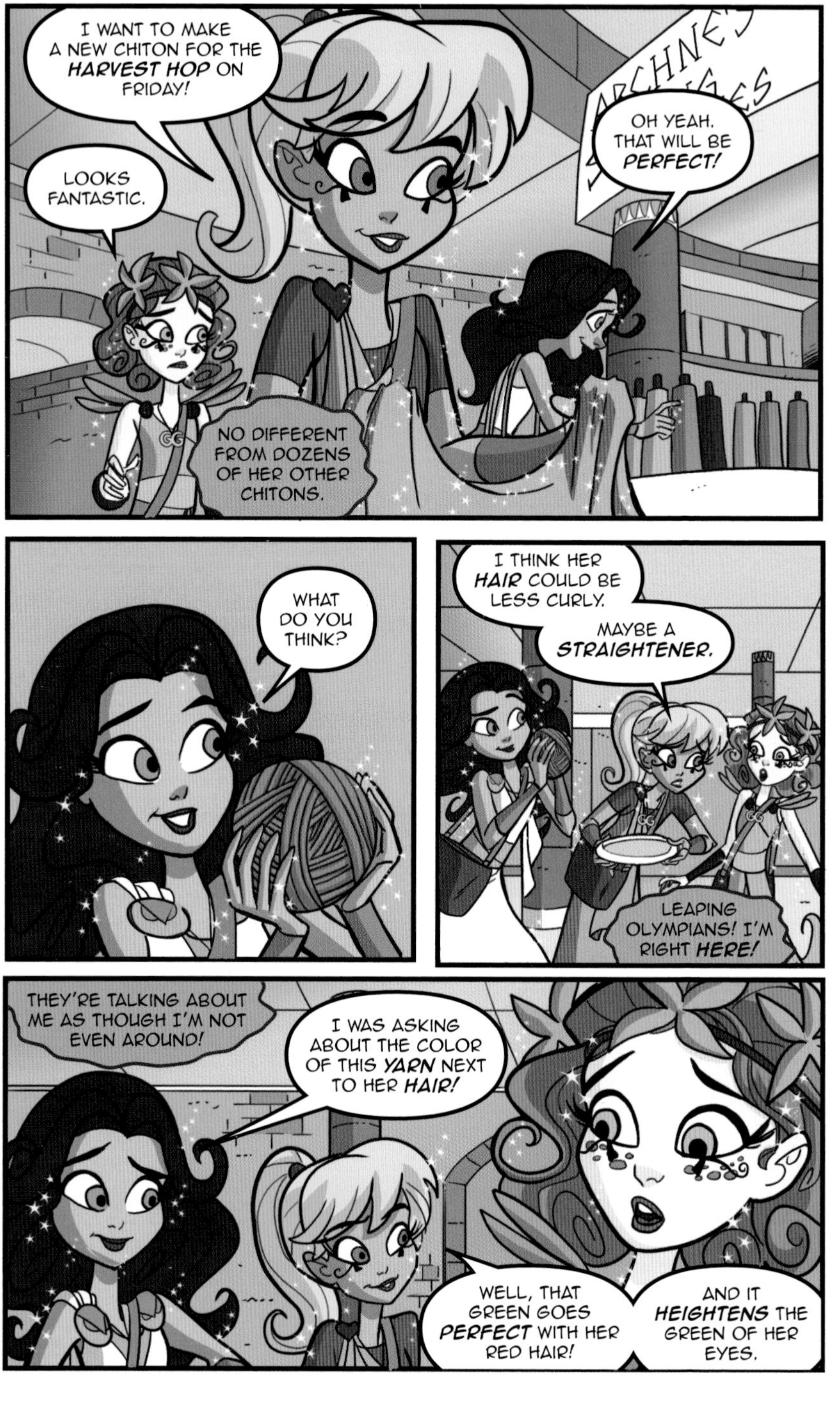
I WANT TO MAKE A NEW CHITON FOR THE HARVEST HOP ON FRIDAY!
LOOKS FANTASTIC.
OH YEAH. THAT WILL BE PERFECT!
NO DIFFERENT FROM DOZENS OF HER OTHER CHITONS.
WHAT DO YOU THINK?
I THINK HER HAIR COULD BE LESS CURLY.
MAYBE A STRAIGHTENER.
LEAPING OLYMPIANS! I'M RIGHT HERE!
THEY'RE TALKING ABOUT ME AS THOUGH I'M NOT EVEN AROUND!
I WAS ASKING ABOUT THE COLOR OF THIS YARN NEXT TO HER HAIR!
WELL, THAT GREEN GOES PERFECT WITH HER RED HAIR!
AND IT HEIGHTENS THE GREEN OF HER EYES.

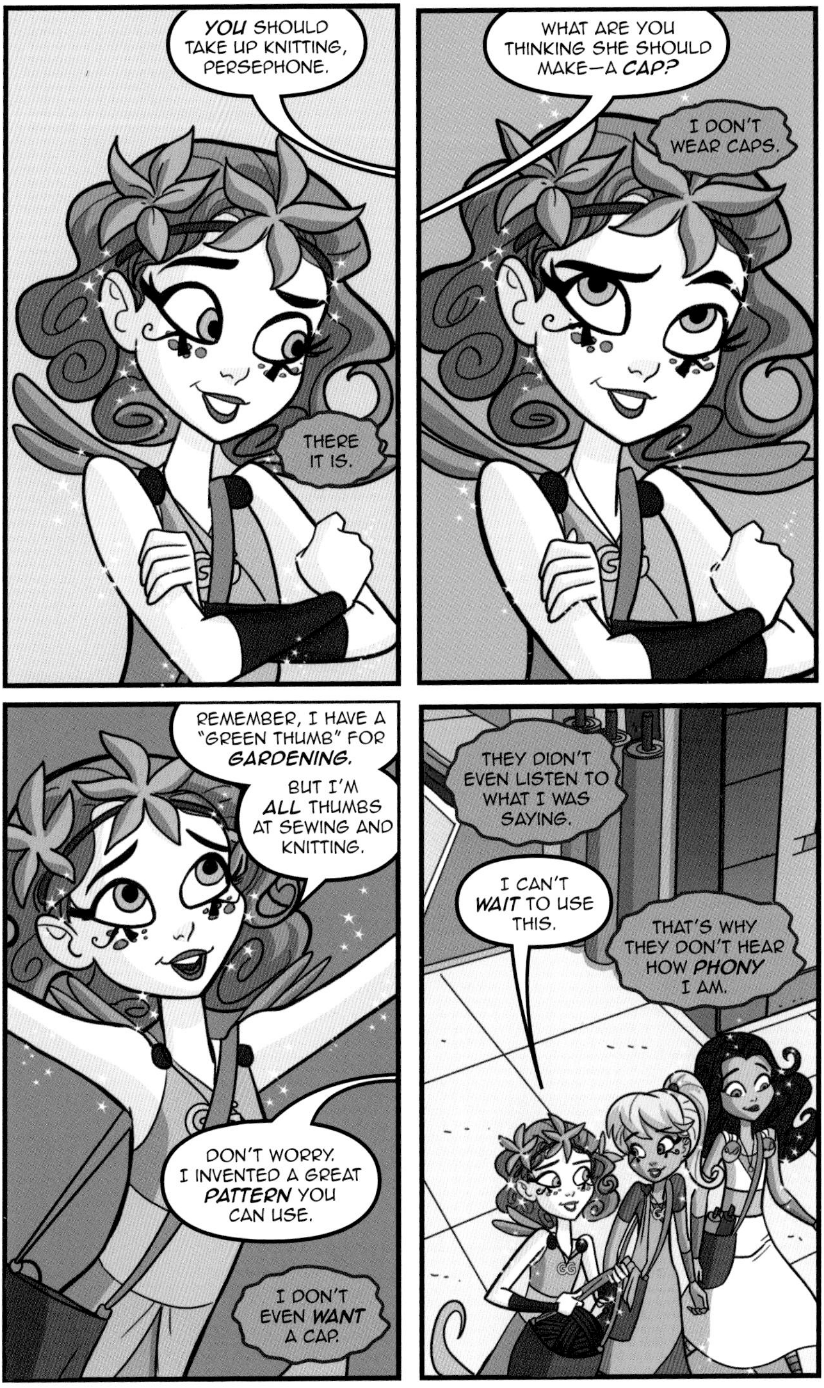
YOU SHOULD TAKE UP KNITTING, PERSEPHONE.
THERE IT IS.
WHAT ARE YOU THINKING SHE SHOULD MAKE—A CAP?
I DON'T WEAR CAPS.
REMEMBER, I HAVE A "GREEN THUMB" FOR GARDENING.
BUT I'M ALL THUMBS AT SEWING AND KNITTING.
DON'T WORRY. I INVENTED A GREAT PATTERN YOU CAN USE.
I DON'T EVEN WANT A CAP.
THEY DIDN'T EVEN LISTEN TO WHAT I WAS SAYING.
I CAN'T WAIT TO USE THIS.
THAT'S WHY THEY DON'T HEAR HOW PHONY I AM.

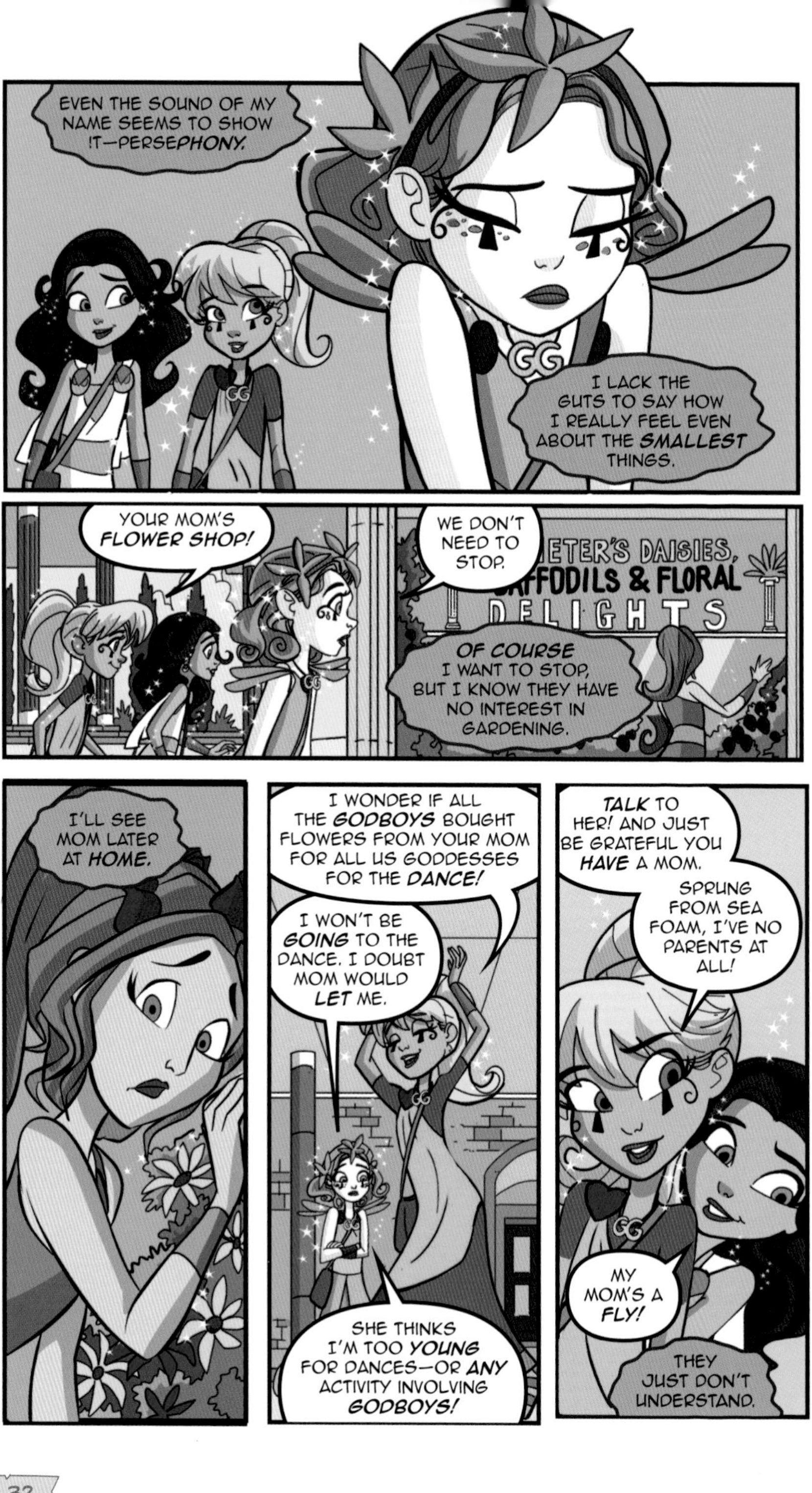

EVEN THE SOUND OF MY NAME SEEMS TO SHOW IT—PERSEPHONY.
I LACK THE GUTS TO SAY HOW I REALLY FEEL EVEN ABOUT THE SMALLEST THINGS.
YOUR MOM'S FLOWER SHOP!
WE DON'T NEED TO STOP.
ETER'S DAISIES, AFFODILS & FLORAL DELIGHTS
OF COURSE I WANT TO STOP, BUT I KNOW THEY HAVE NO INTEREST IN GARDENING.
I'LL SEE MOM LATER AT HOME.
I WONDER IF ALL THE GODBOYS BOUGHT FLOWERS FROM YOUR MOM FOR ALL US GODDESSES FOR THE DANCE!
I WON'T BE GOING TO THE DANCE. I DOUBT MOM WOULD LET ME.
SHE THINKS I'M TOO YOUNG FOR DANCES—OR ANY ACTIVITY INVOLVING GODBOYS!
TALK TO HER! AND JUST BE GRATEFUL YOU HAVE A MOM.
SPRUNG FROM SEA FOAM, I'VE NO PARENTS AT ALL!
MY MOM'S A FLY!
THEY JUST DON'T UNDERSTAND.

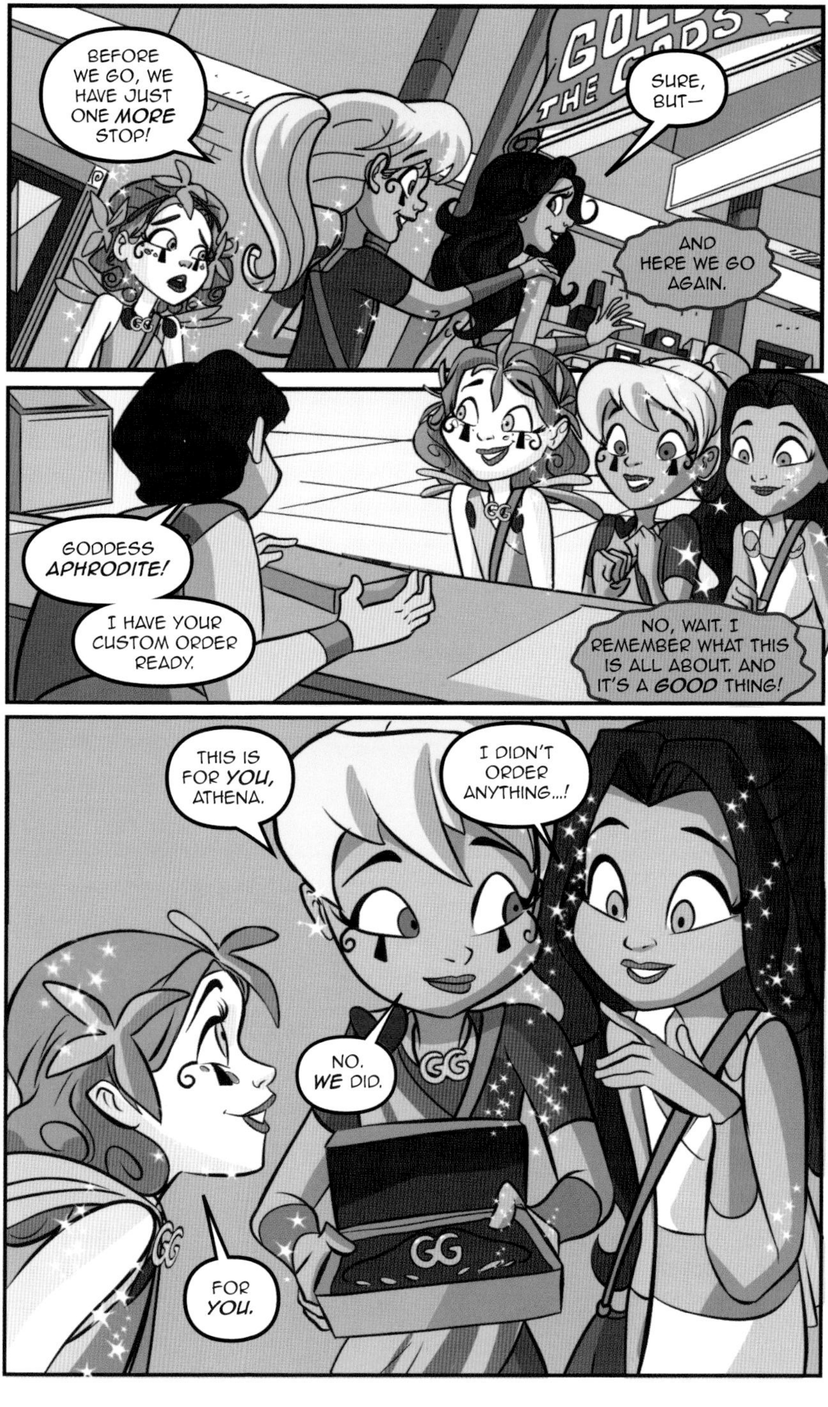
GOLD THE GODS
BEFORE WE GO, WE HAVE JUST ONE *MORE* STOP!
SURE, BUT—
AND HERE WE GO AGAIN.
GODDESS *APHRODITE!*
I HAVE YOUR CUSTOM ORDER READY.
NO, WAIT. I REMEMBER WHAT THIS IS ALL ABOUT. AND IT'S A *GOOD* THING!
THIS IS FOR *YOU,* ATHENA.
I DIDN'T ORDER ANYTHING...!
NO. *WE* DID.
FOR *YOU.*

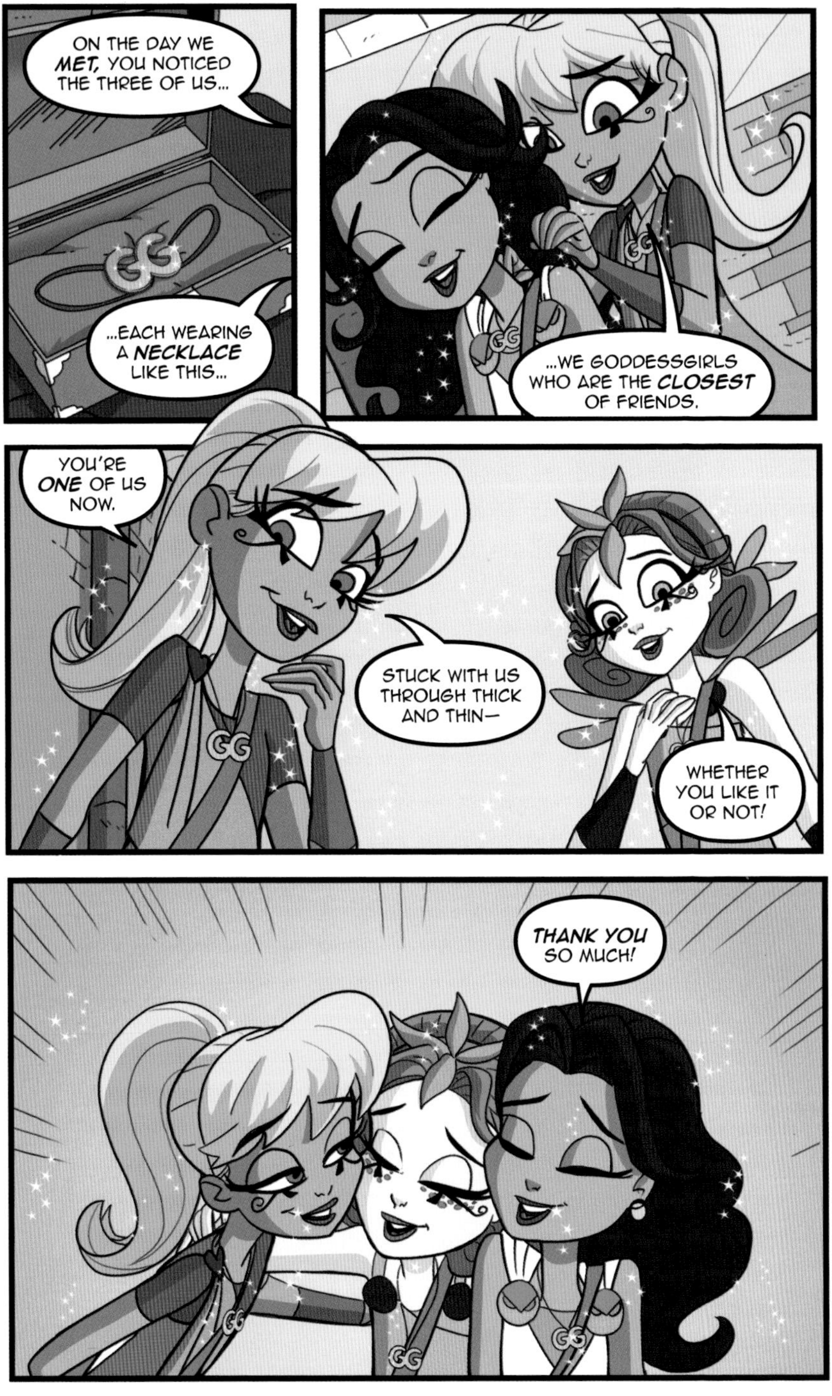
ON THE DAY WE MET, YOU NOTICED THE THREE OF US...
...EACH WEARING A NECKLACE LIKE THIS...
...WE GODDESSGIRLS WHO ARE THE CLOSEST OF FRIENDS.
YOU'RE ONE OF US NOW.
STUCK WITH US THROUGH THICK AND THIN—
WHETHER YOU LIKE IT OR NOT!
THANK YOU SO MUCH!

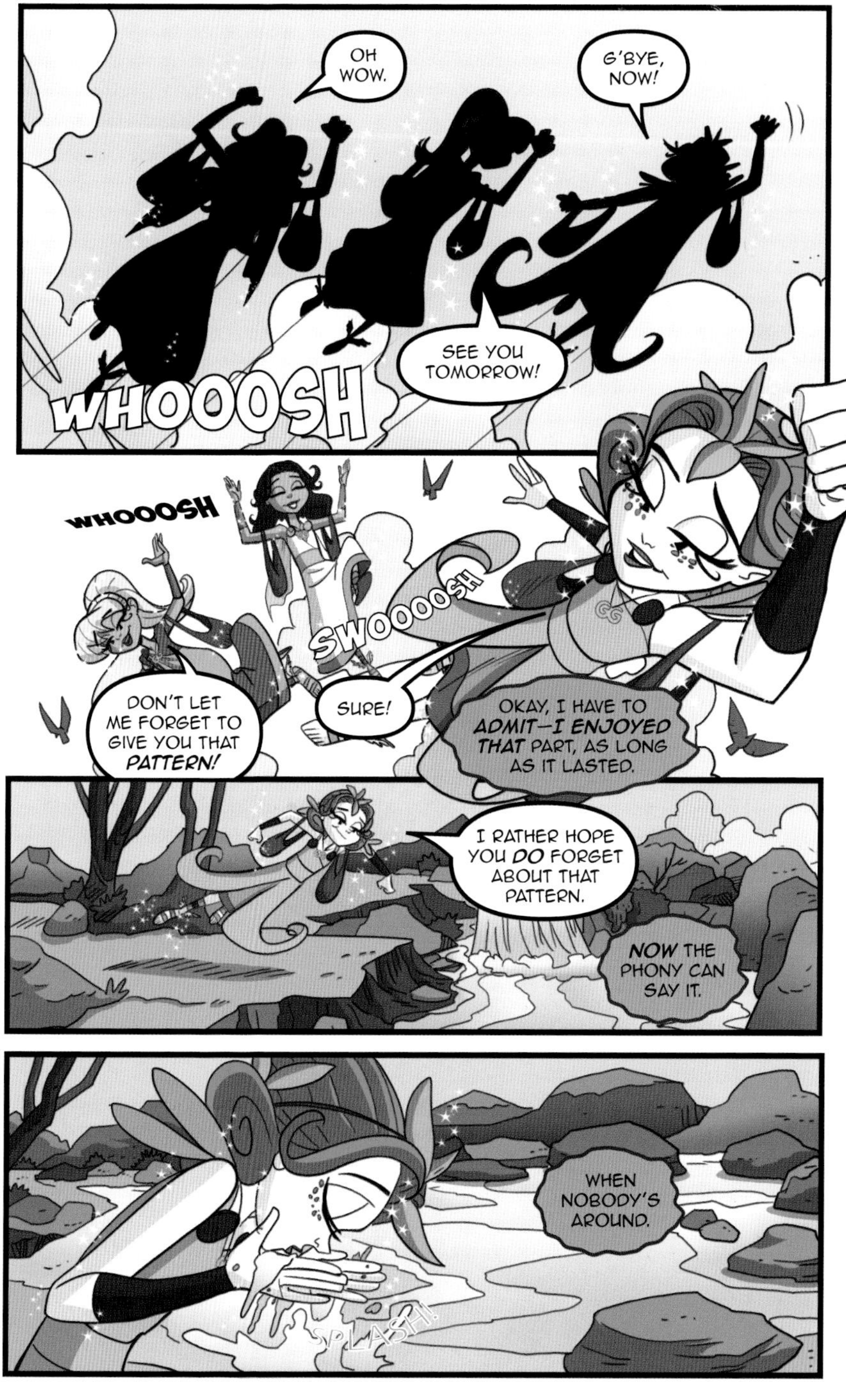
OH WOW.
G'BYE, NOW!
SEE YOU TOMORROW!
WHOOOSH
WHOOOSH
SWOOOOSH
DON'T LET ME FORGET TO GIVE YOU THAT *PATTERN!*
SURE!
OKAY, I HAVE TO *ADMIT—I ENJOYED THAT* PART, AS LONG AS IT LASTED.
I RATHER HOPE YOU *DO* FORGET ABOUT THAT PATTERN.
NOW THE PHONY CAN SAY IT.
WHEN NOBODY'S AROUND.
SPLASH!

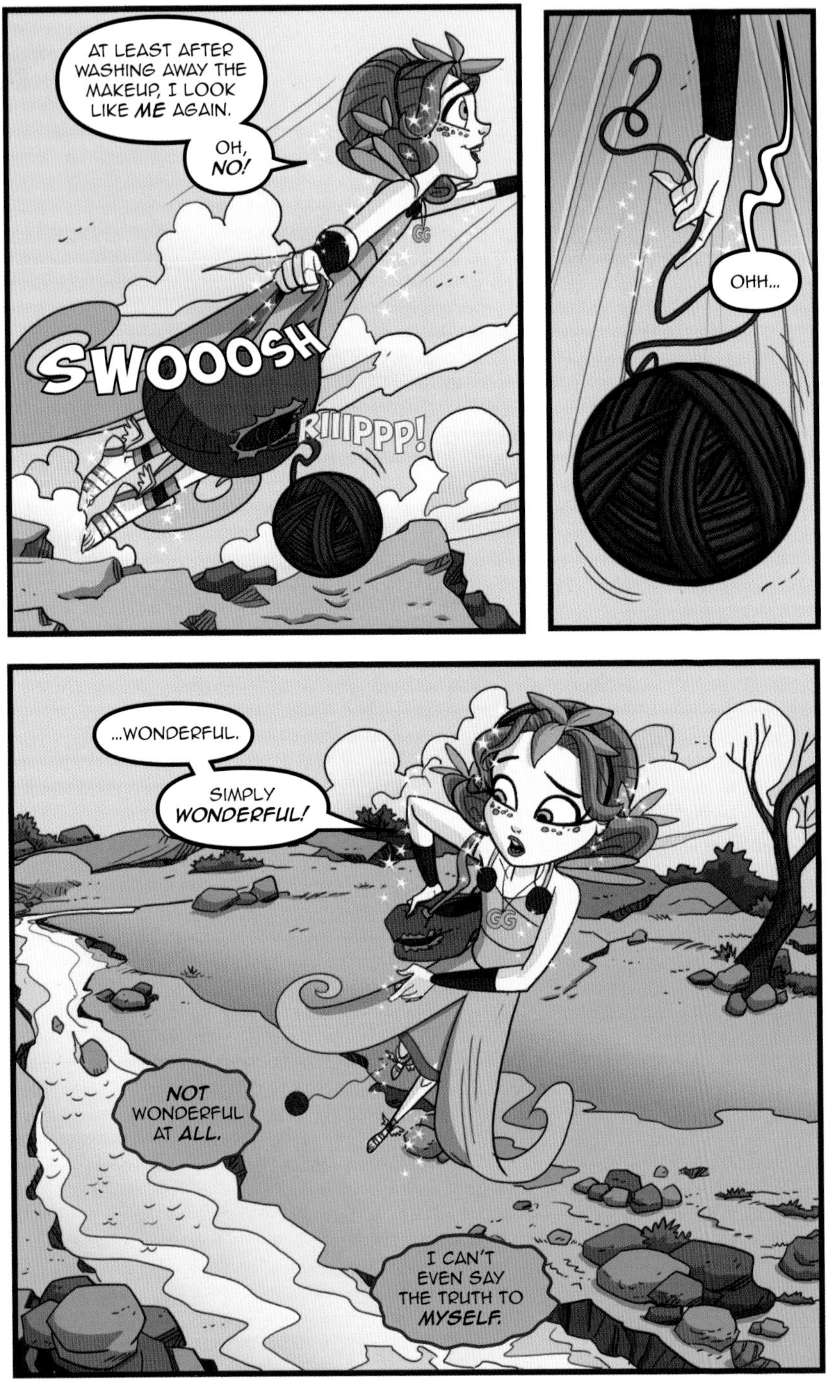
AT LEAST AFTER WASHING AWAY THE MAKEUP, I LOOK LIKE *ME* AGAIN.
OH, *NO!*
SWOOOSH
RIIIPPP!
OHH...
...WONDERFUL.
SIMPLY *WONDERFUL!*
NOT WONDERFUL AT *ALL*.
I CAN'T EVEN SAY THE TRUTH TO *MYSELF*.

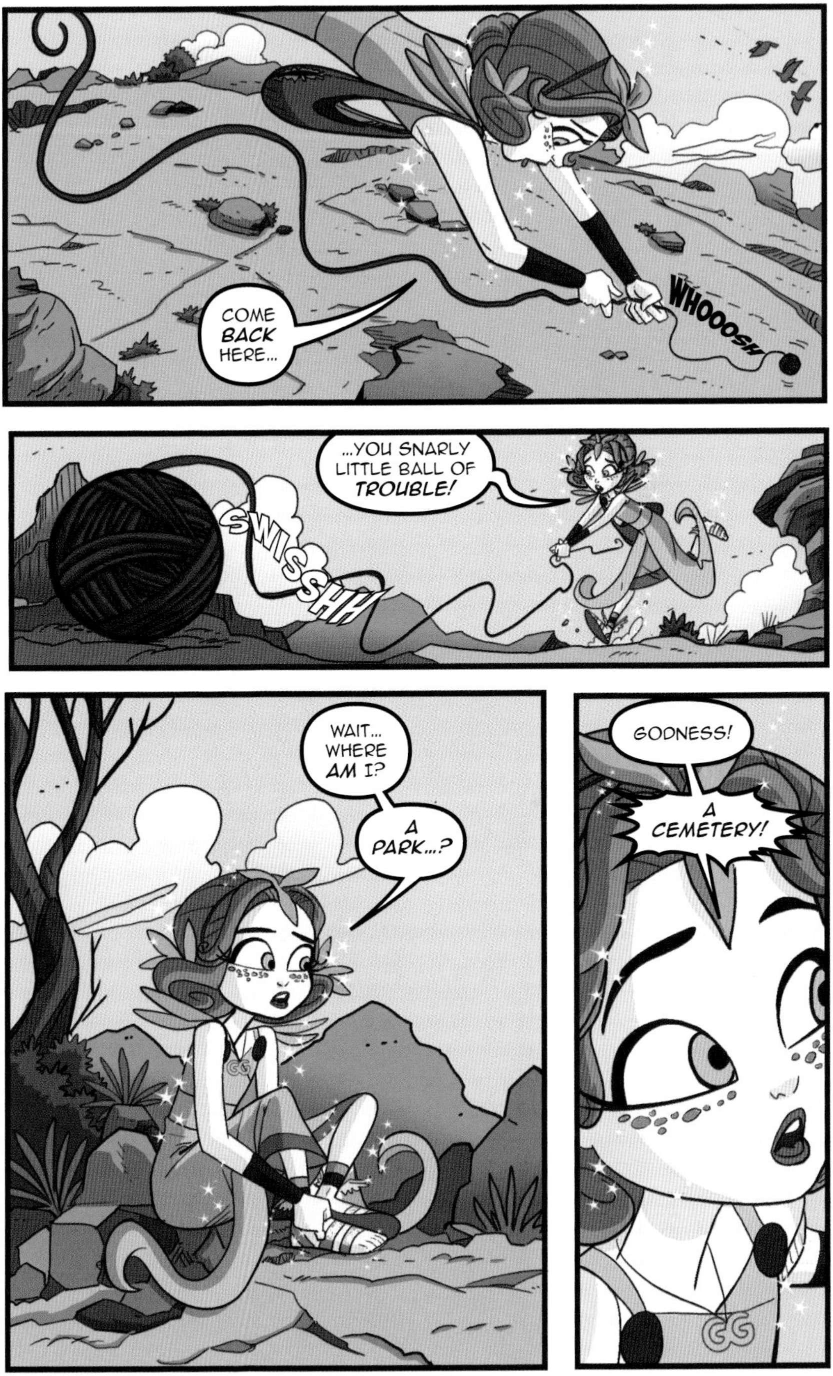
COME BACK HERE...
WHOOOSH
...YOU SNARLY LITTLE BALL OF TROUBLE!
SWISSHH
WAIT... WHERE AM I?
A PARK...?
GODNESS!
A CEMETERY!

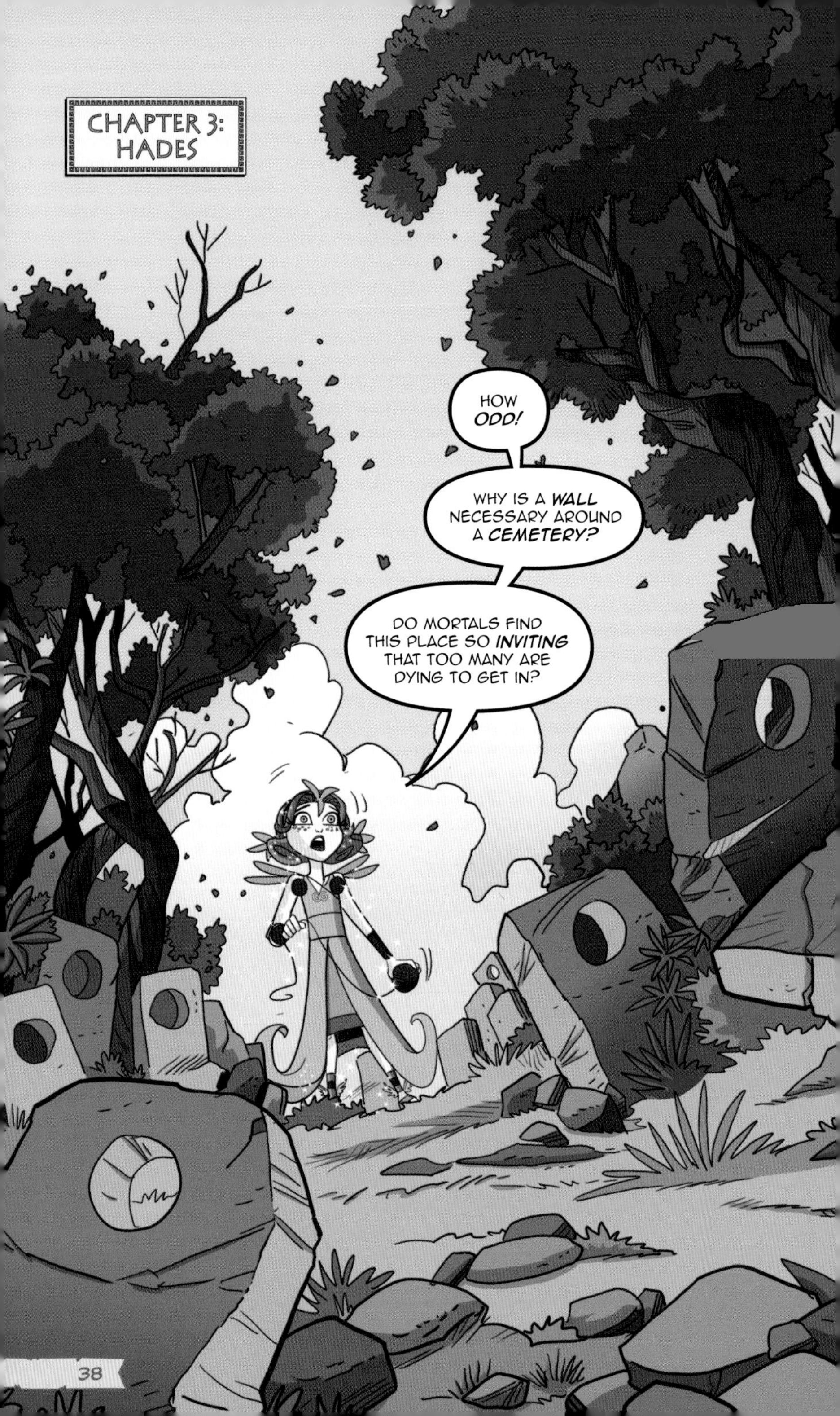

CHAPTER 3:
HADES
HOW ODD!
WHY IS A WALL NECESSARY AROUND A CEMETERY?
DO MORTALS FIND THIS PLACE SO INVITING THAT TOO MANY ARE DYING TO GET IN?

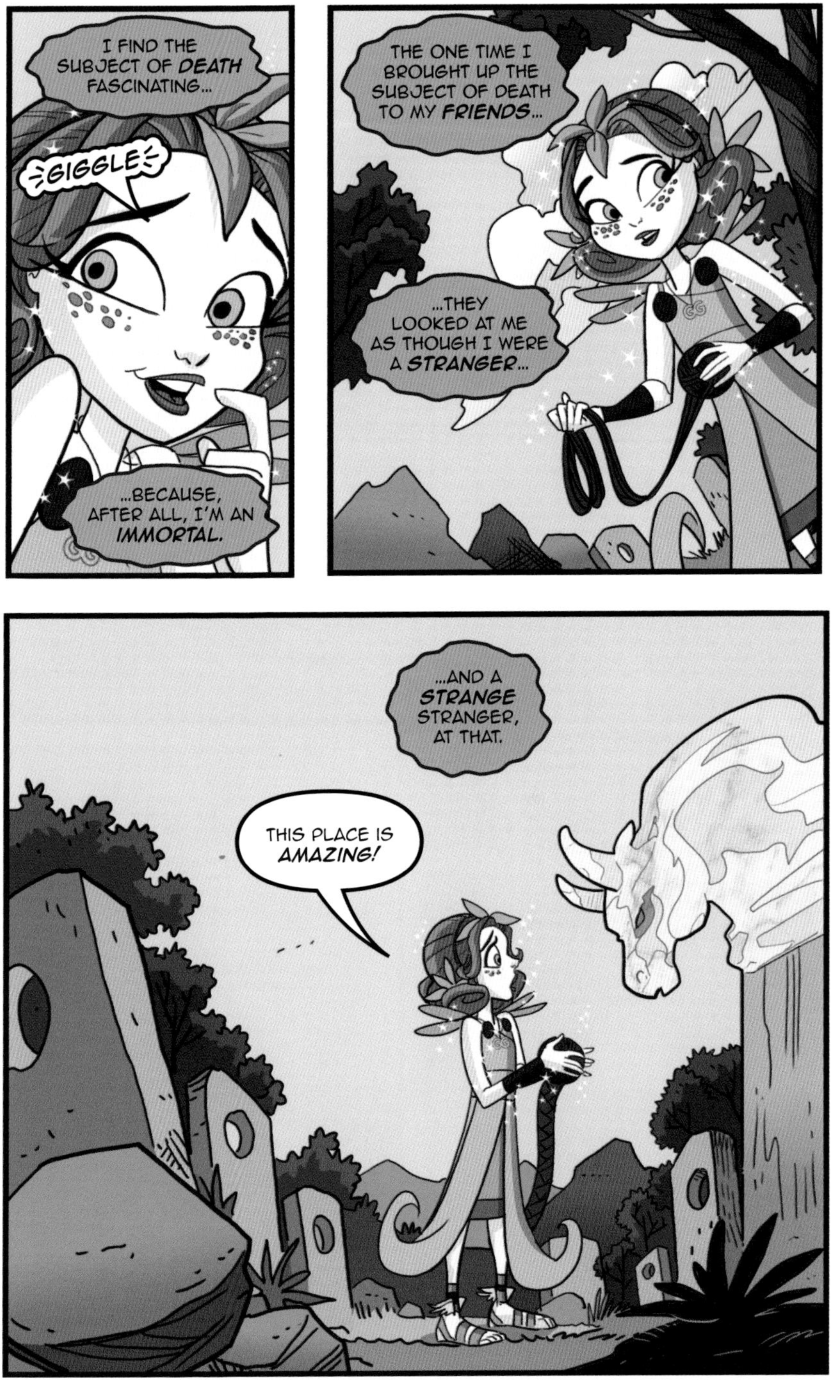
I FIND THE SUBJECT OF DEATH FASCINATING...
GIGGLE
...BECAUSE, AFTER ALL, I'M AN IMMORTAL.
THE ONE TIME I BROUGHT UP THE SUBJECT OF DEATH TO MY FRIENDS...
...THEY LOOKED AT ME AS THOUGH I WERE A STRANGER...
...AND A STRANGE STRANGER, AT THAT.
THIS PLACE IS AMAZING!

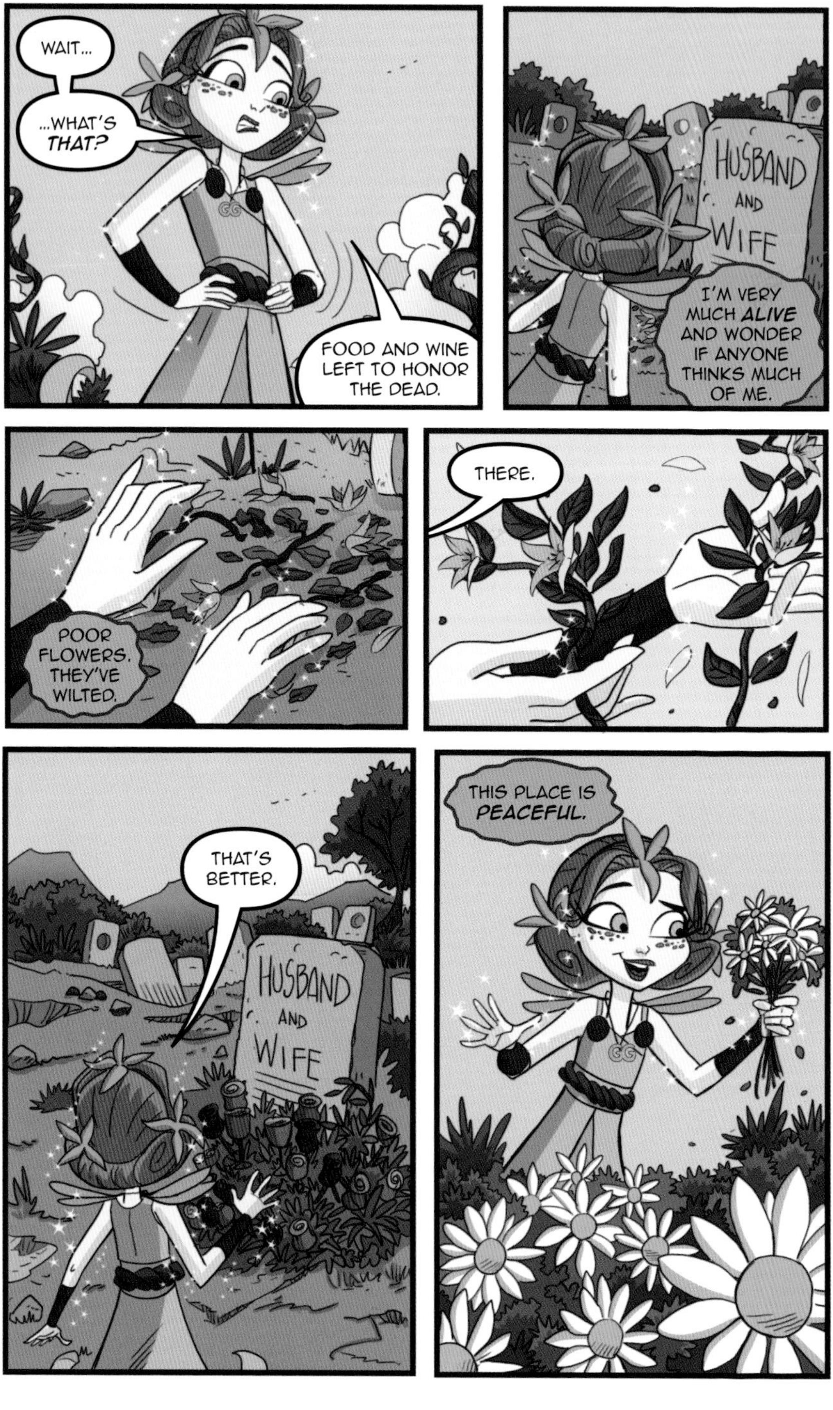
WAIT...
...WHAT'S THAT?
FOOD AND WINE LEFT TO HONOR THE DEAD.
HUSBAND AND WIFE
I'M VERY MUCH ALIVE AND WONDER IF ANYONE THINKS MUCH OF ME.
POOR FLOWERS. THEY'VE WILTED.
THERE.
THAT'S BETTER.
HUSBAND AND WIFE
THIS PLACE IS PEACEFUL.

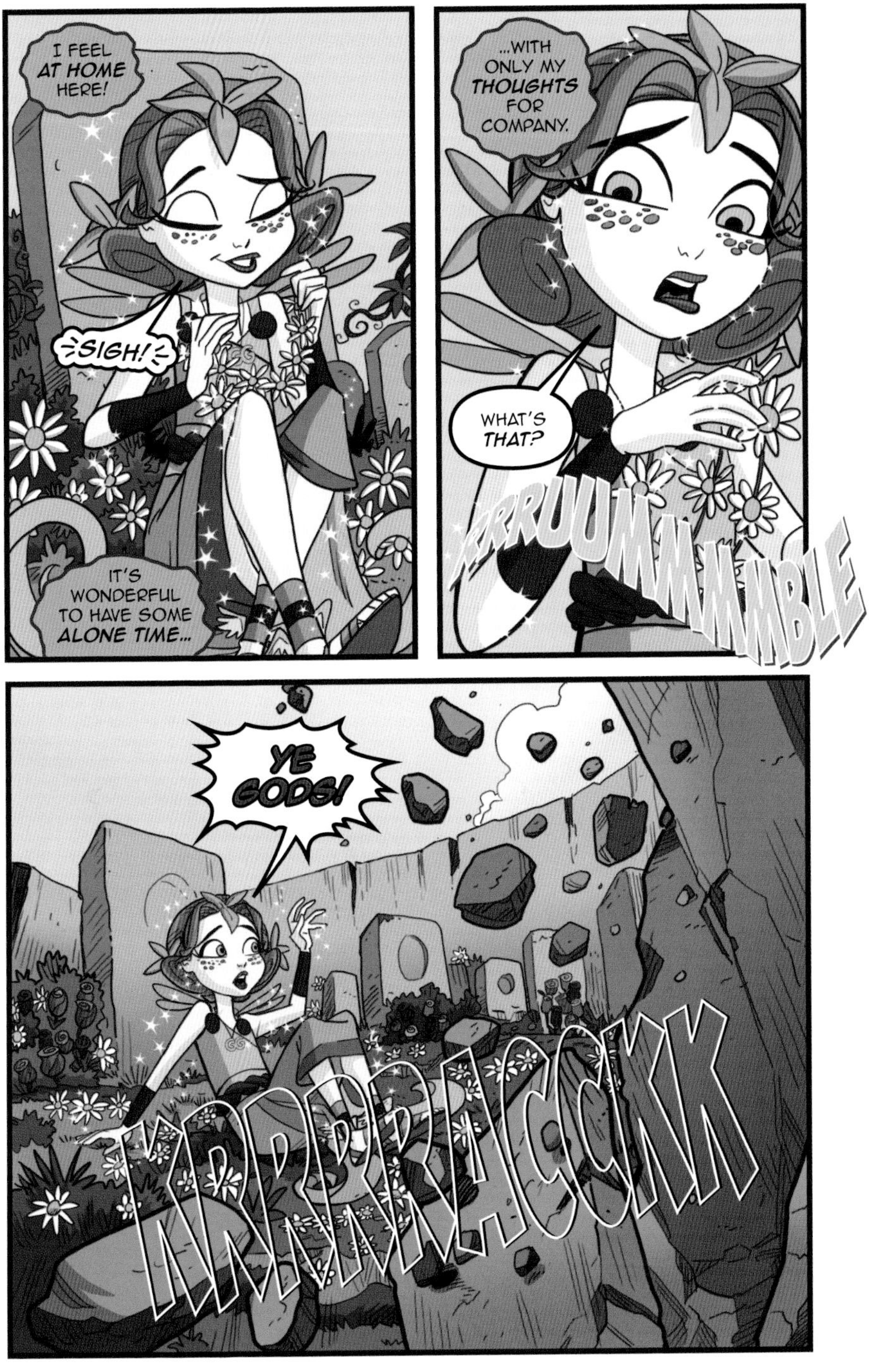
I FEEL AT HOME HERE!
SIGH!
IT'S WONDERFUL TO HAVE SOME ALONE TIME...
...WITH ONLY MY THOUGHTS FOR COMPANY.
WHAT'S THAT?
KRRRUUMMMMMBLE
YE GODS!
KRRRRACCCKK

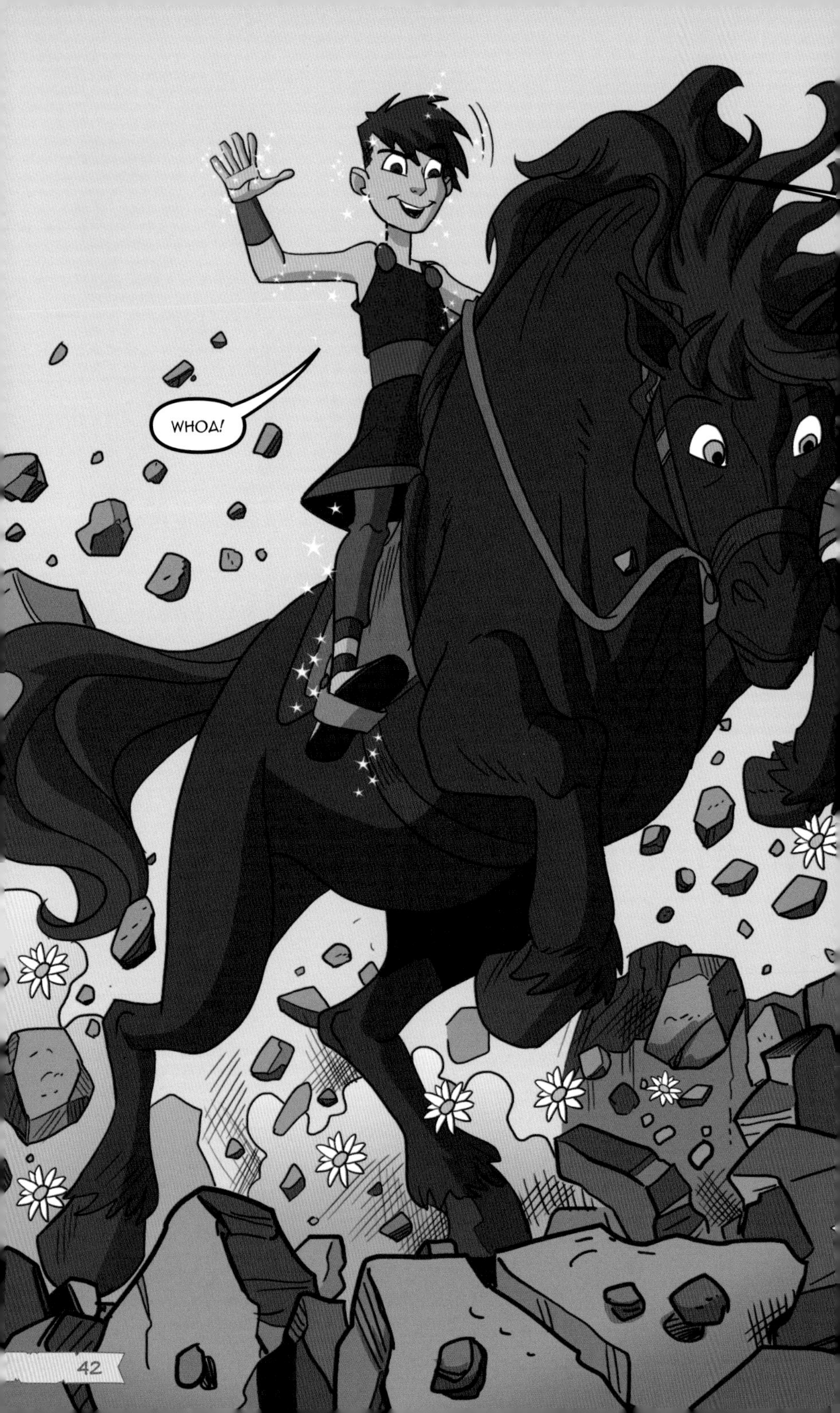
WHOA!

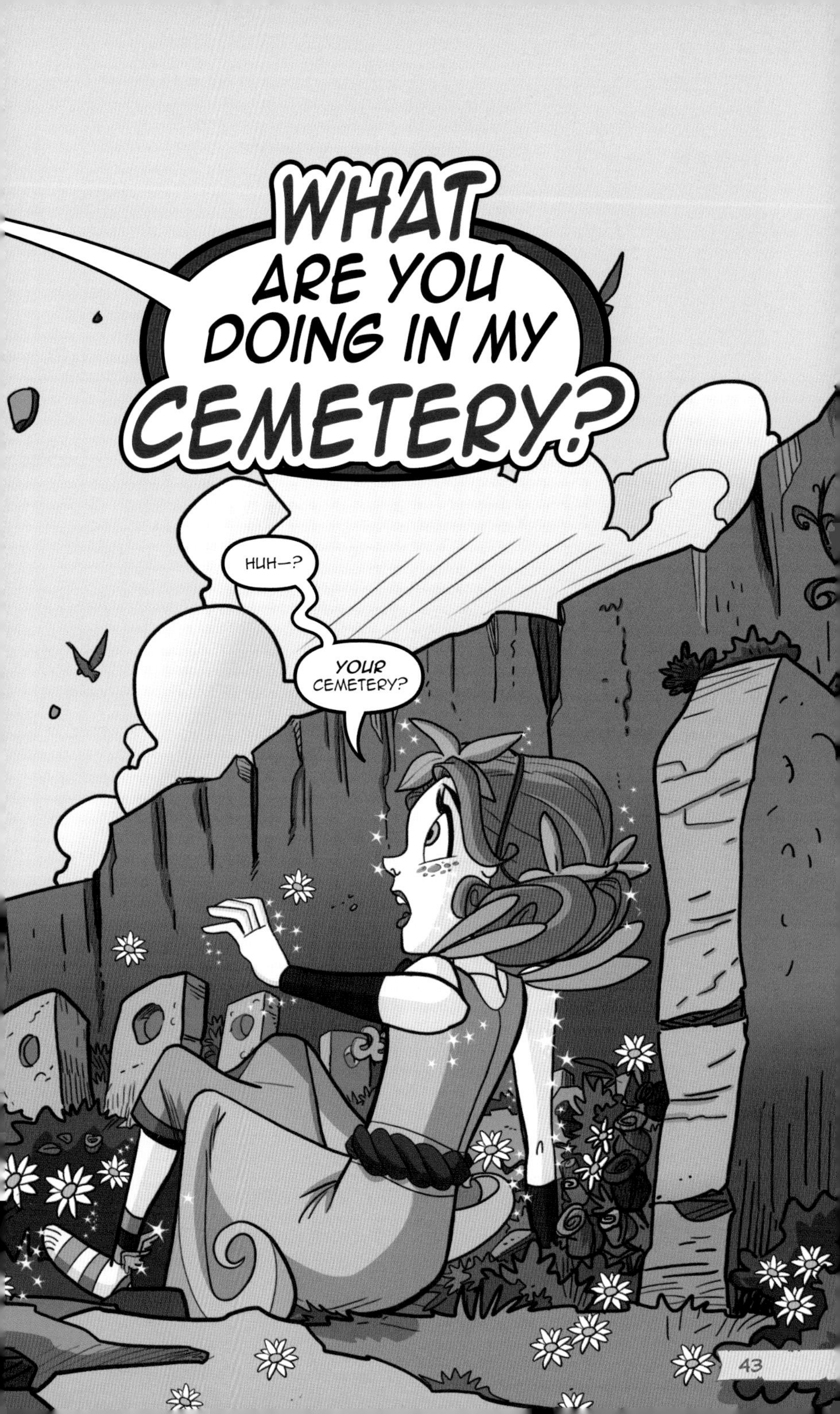
WHAT ARE YOU DOING IN MY CEMETERY?
HUH—?
YOUR CEMETERY?

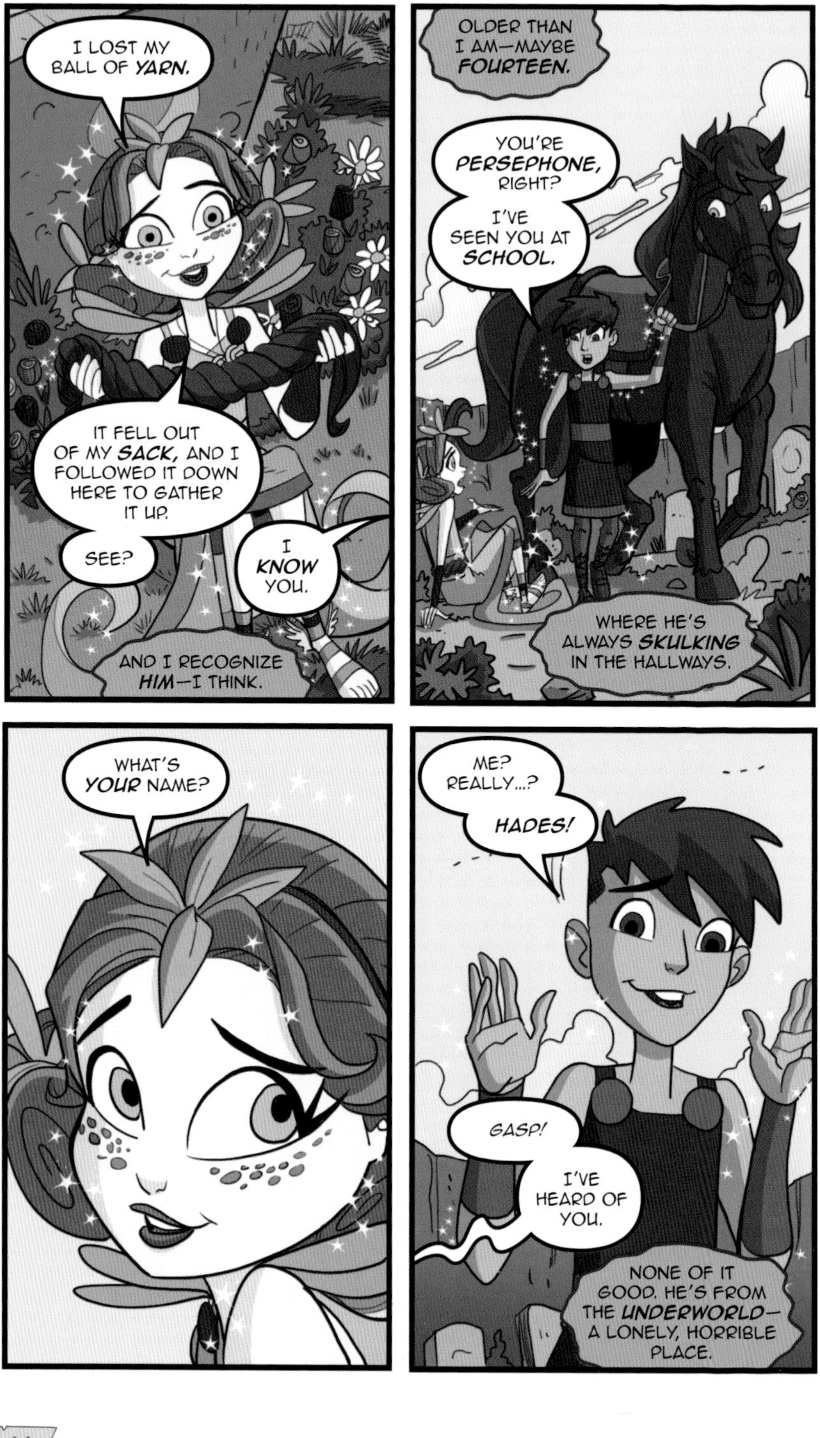
I LOST MY BALL OF YARN.
IT FELL OUT OF MY SACK, AND I FOLLOWED IT DOWN HERE TO GATHER IT UP.
SEE?
I KNOW YOU.
AND I RECOGNIZE HIM—I THINK.
OLDER THAN I AM—MAYBE FOURTEEN.
YOU'RE PERSEPHONE, RIGHT?
I'VE SEEN YOU AT SCHOOL.
WHERE HE'S ALWAYS SKULKING IN THE HALLWAYS.
WHAT'S YOUR NAME?
ME? REALLY...?
HADES!
GASP!
I'VE HEARD OF YOU.
NONE OF IT GOOD. HE'S FROM THE UNDERWORLD—A LONELY, HORRIBLE PLACE.

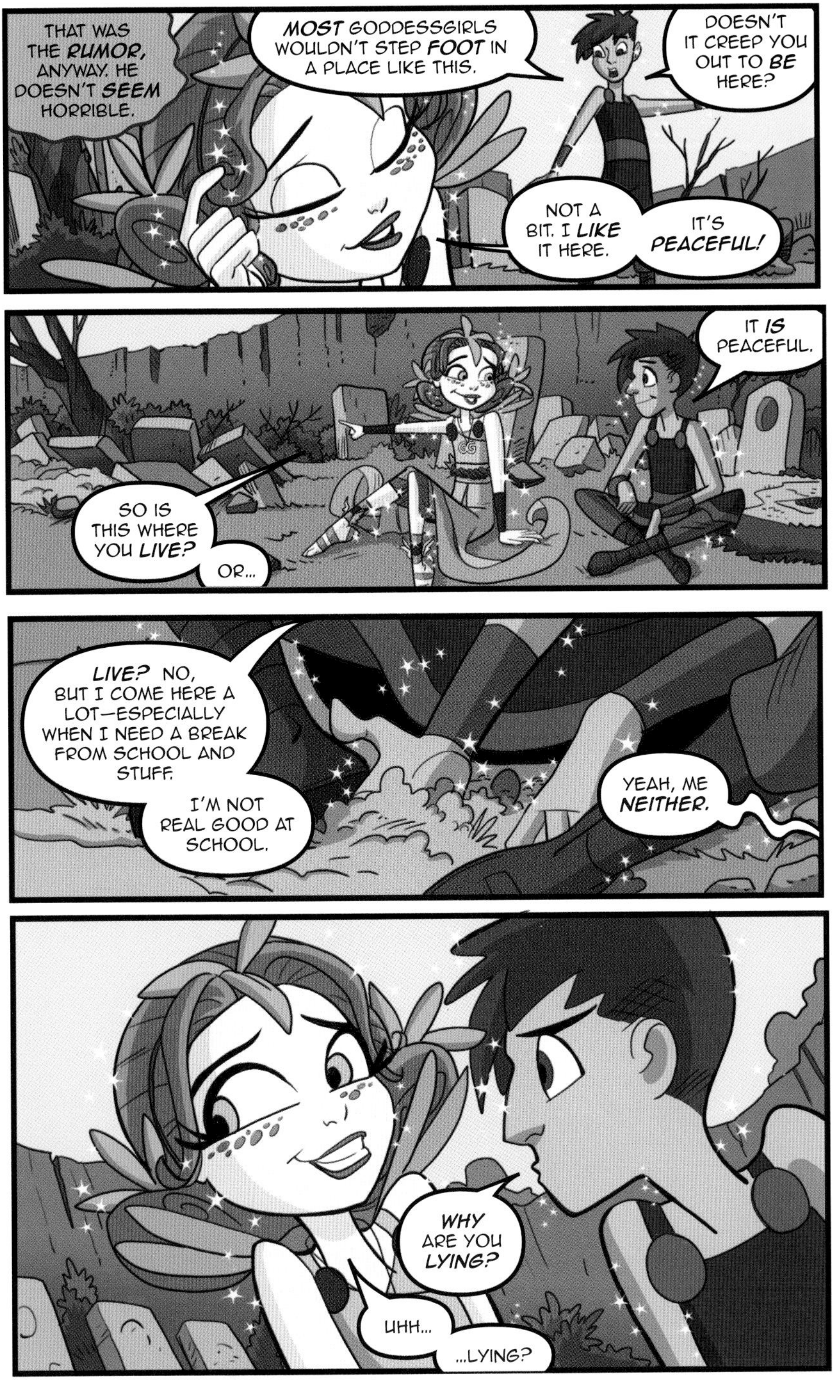

THAT WAS THE *RUMOR*, ANYWAY. HE DOESN'T *SEEM* HORRIBLE.
MOST GODDESSGIRLS WOULDN'T STEP *FOOT* IN A PLACE LIKE THIS.
DOESN'T IT CREEP YOU OUT TO *BE* HERE?
NOT A BIT. I *LIKE* IT HERE.
IT'S *PEACEFUL!*
IT *IS* PEACEFUL.
SO IS THIS WHERE YOU *LIVE?*
OR...
LIVE? NO, BUT I COME HERE A LOT—ESPECIALLY WHEN I NEED A BREAK FROM SCHOOL AND STUFF.
I'M NOT REAL GOOD AT SCHOOL.
YEAH, ME *NEITHER.*
WHY ARE YOU *LYING?*
UHH...
...LYING?

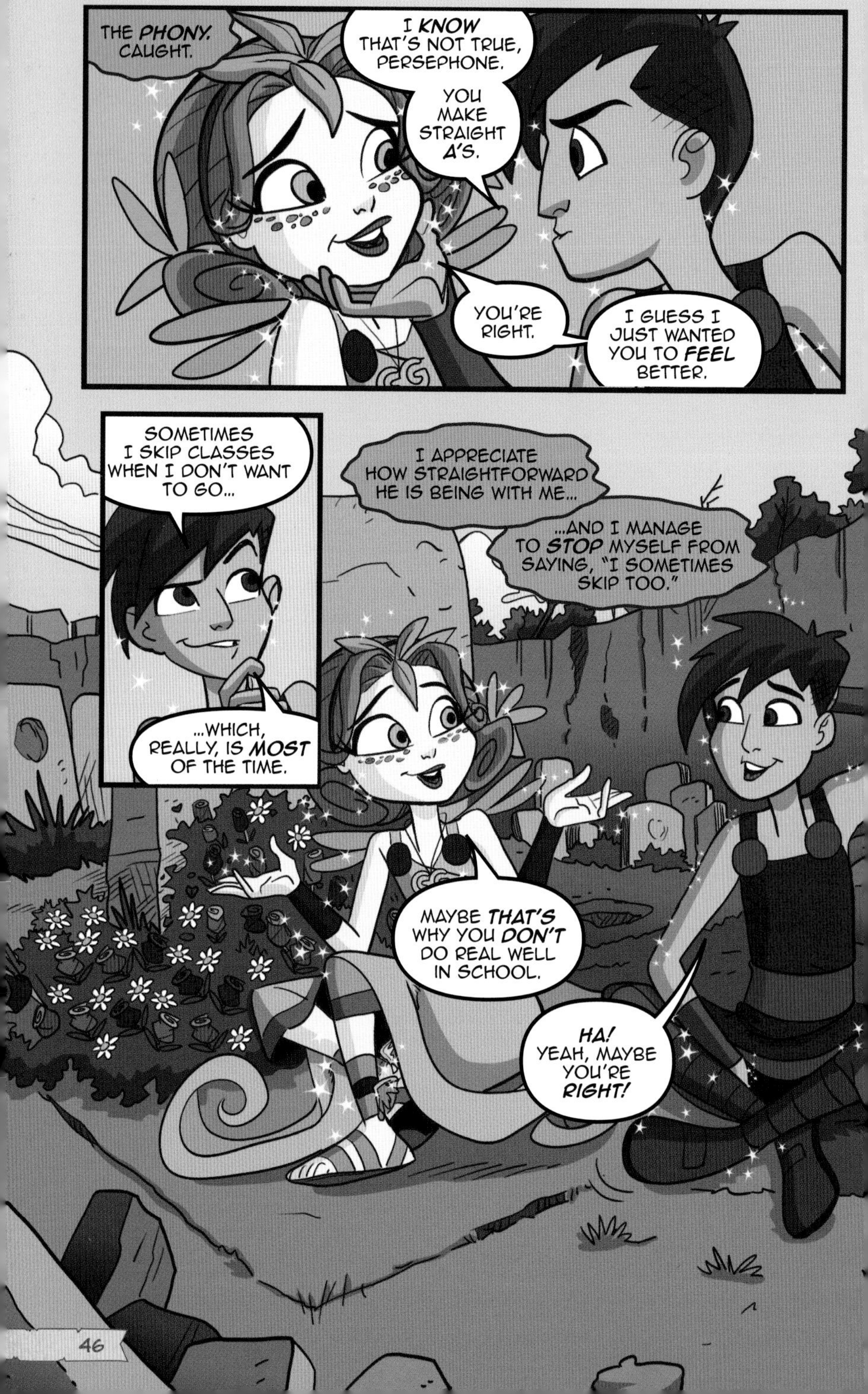

THE PHONY. CAUGHT.
I KNOW THAT'S NOT TRUE, PERSEPHONE.
YOU MAKE STRAIGHT A'S.
YOU'RE RIGHT.
I GUESS I JUST WANTED YOU TO FEEL BETTER.
SOMETIMES I SKIP CLASSES WHEN I DON'T WANT TO GO...
...WHICH, REALLY, IS MOST OF THE TIME.
I APPRECIATE HOW STRAIGHTFORWARD HE IS BEING WITH ME...
...AND I MANAGE TO STOP MYSELF FROM SAYING, "I SOMETIMES SKIP TOO."
MAYBE THAT'S WHY YOU DON'T DO REAL WELL IN SCHOOL.
HA! YEAH, MAYBE YOU'RE RIGHT!

DO YOU HAVE ANY CLASSES WITH *MR. CYCLOPS?*

OH, YES. I HAVE HIM FOR MY LAST CLASS OF THE DAY.

DOES HE WALK AROUND BAREFOOT IN YOUR CLASS TOO?

YES! AND HE LEAVES HIS *SANDALS* LYING AROUND FOR EVERYONE TO *TRIP* OVER.

THOSE THINGS ARE AS BIG AS *BOATS!*

IT'S BECOME A *GAME* TO *HIDE* THEM!

HAVE *YOU* EVER DONE THAT?

NO, BUT MY FRIENDS *ATHENA* AND *APHRODITE* ONCE DECORATED THEM WITH GLITTERY STARS AND HUNG THEM FROM THE CEILING!

I'VE SEEN YOU *WITH* THEM. YOUR FRIENDS.

...REALLY?

SO WHO DO *YOU* HANG OUT WITH?

I'M... KIND OF A *LONER.*

TELL ME MORE ABOUT *YOUR* FRIENDS.

ATHENA IS SO SMART—SHE INVENTED THE *OLIVE!*

NOBODY KNOWS *FASHION* BETTER THAN *APHRODITE.*

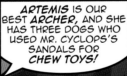

ARTEMIS IS OUR BEST *ARCHER,* AND SHE HAS THREE DOGS WHO USED MR. CYCLOPS'S SANDALS FOR *CHEW TOYS!*

HA-HA-HA! I *SAW* THAT!

WHAT A *DROOLY MESS!*

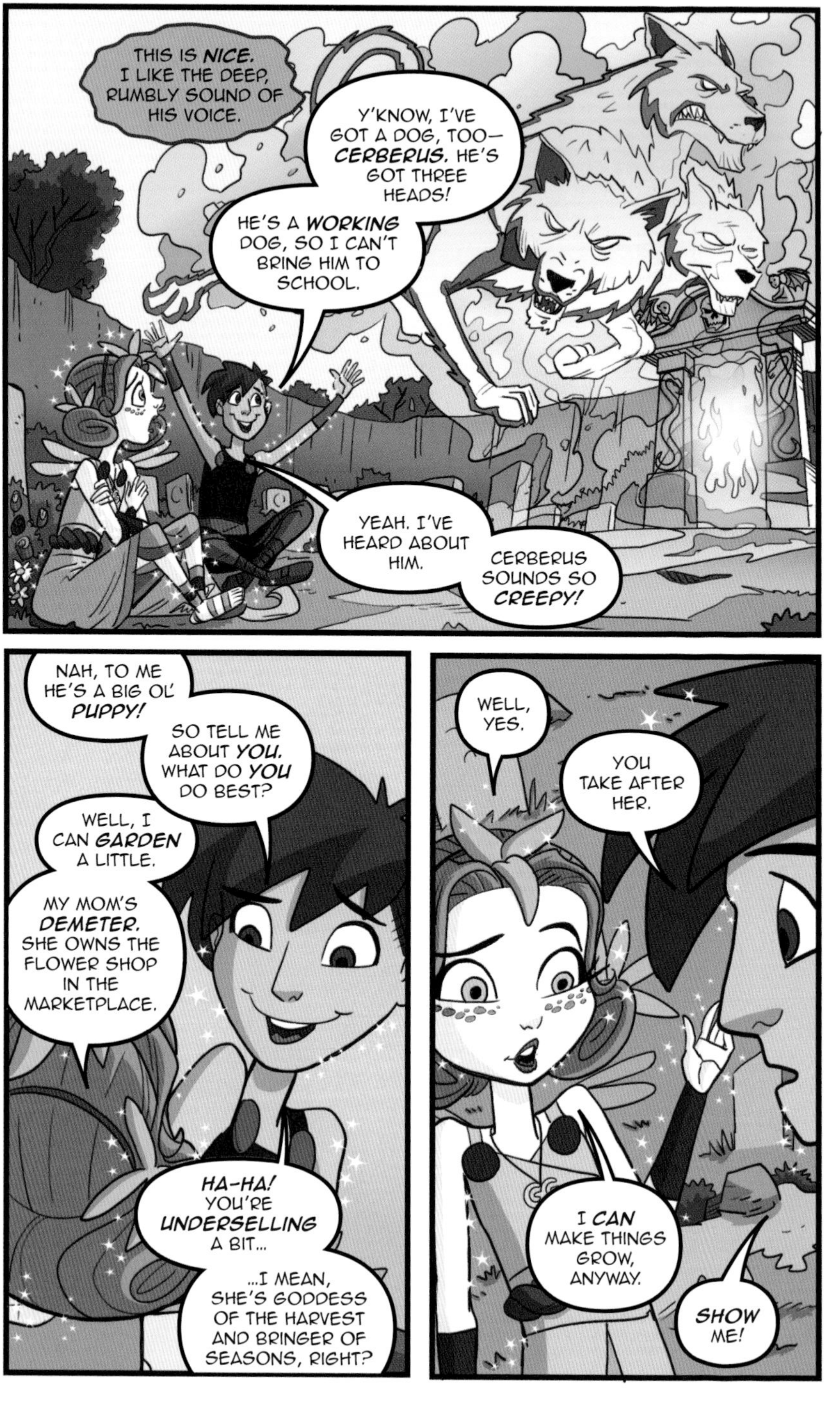
THIS IS NICE. I LIKE THE DEEP, RUMBLY SOUND OF HIS VOICE.
Y'KNOW, I'VE GOT A DOG, TOO—CERBERUS. HE'S GOT THREE HEADS!
HE'S A WORKING DOG, SO I CAN'T BRING HIM TO SCHOOL.
YEAH. I'VE HEARD ABOUT HIM.
CERBERUS SOUNDS SO CREEPY!
NAH, TO ME HE'S A BIG OL' PUPPY!
SO TELL ME ABOUT YOU. WHAT DO YOU DO BEST?
WELL, I CAN GARDEN A LITTLE.
MY MOM'S DEMETER. SHE OWNS THE FLOWER SHOP IN THE MARKETPLACE.
HA-HA! YOU'RE UNDERSELLING A BIT...
...I MEAN, SHE'S GODDESS OF THE HARVEST AND BRINGER OF SEASONS, RIGHT?
WELL, YES.
YOU TAKE AFTER HER.
I CAN MAKE THINGS GROW, ANYWAY.
SHOW ME!

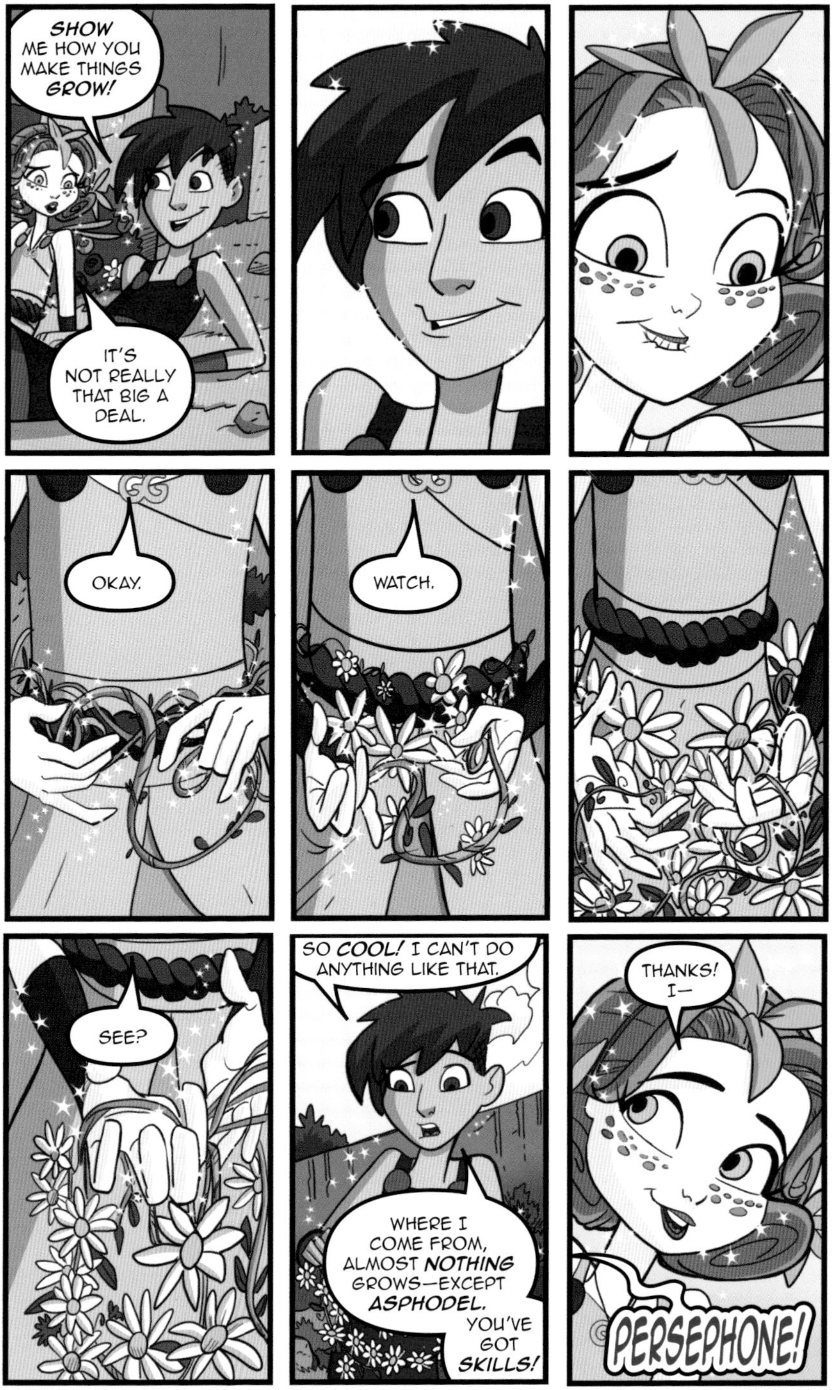
SHOW ME HOW YOU MAKE THINGS GROW!
IT'S NOT REALLY THAT BIG A DEAL.
OKAY.
WATCH.
SEE?
SO COOL! I CAN'T DO ANYTHING LIKE THAT.
WHERE I COME FROM, ALMOST NOTHING GROWS—EXCEPT ASPHODEL.
YOU'VE GOT SKILLS!
THANKS! I—
PERSEPHONE!

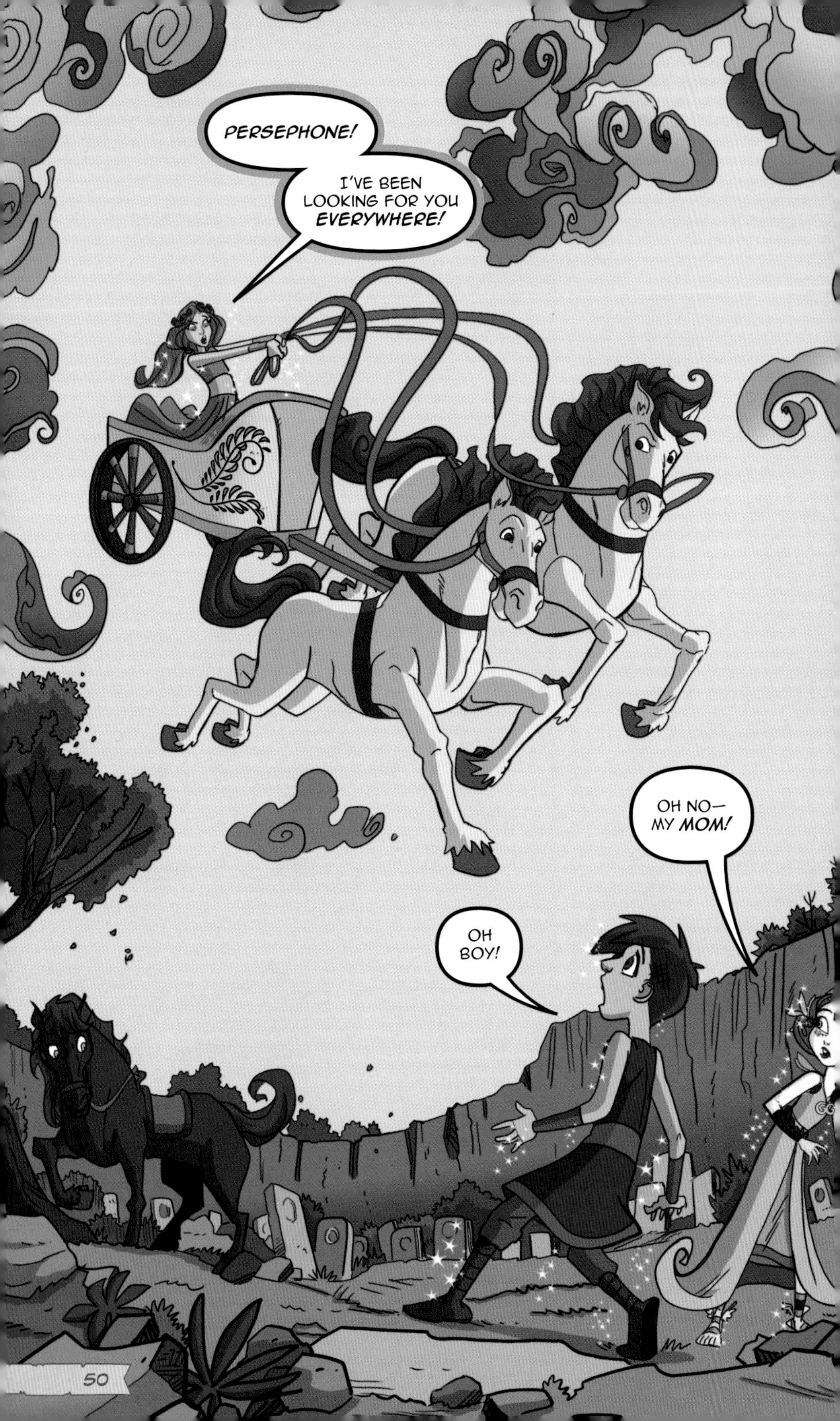
PERSEPHONE!
I'VE BEEN LOOKING FOR YOU *EVERYWHERE!*
OH NO— MY *MOM!*
OH BOY!

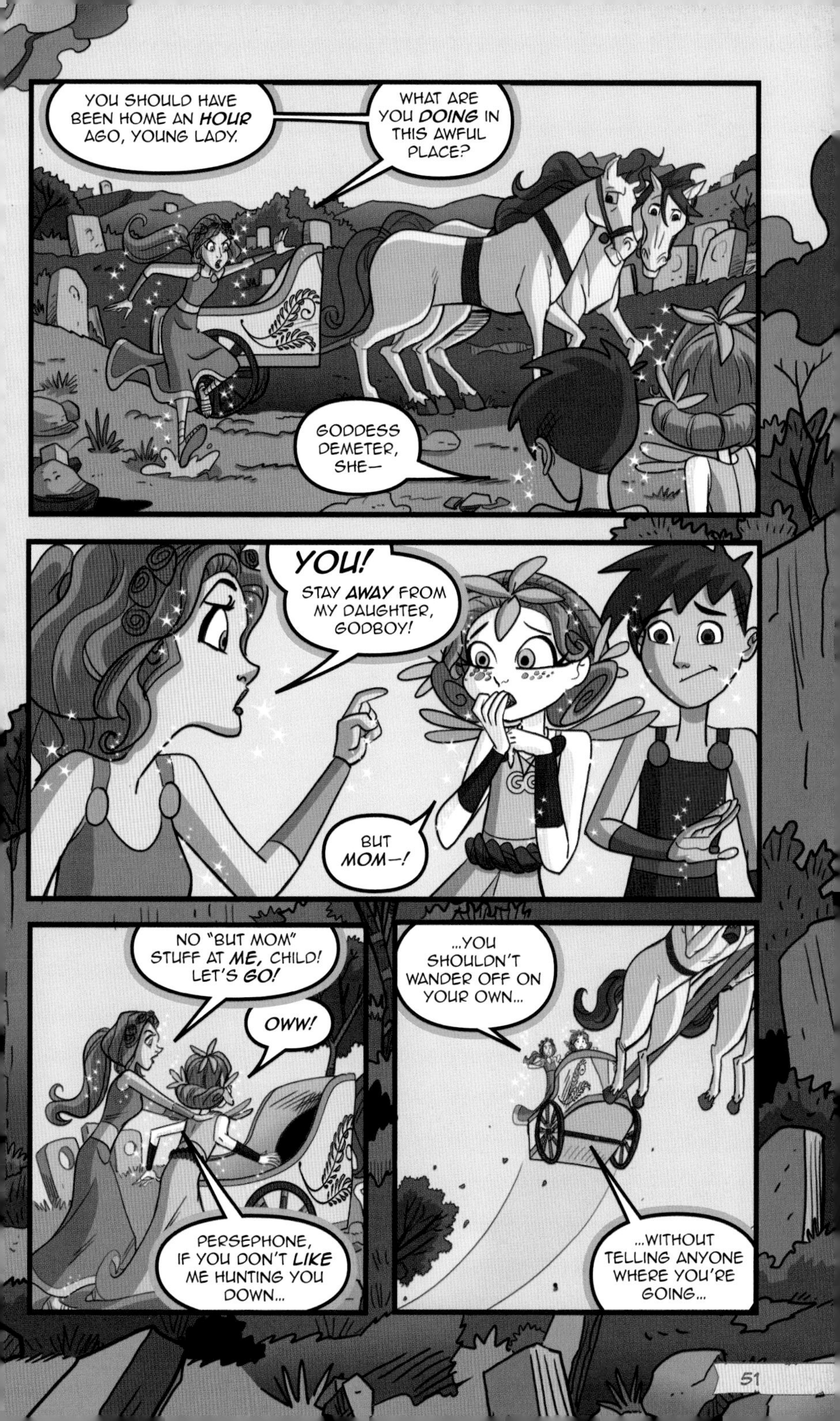
YOU SHOULD HAVE BEEN HOME AN HOUR AGO, YOUNG LADY.
WHAT ARE YOU DOING IN THIS AWFUL PLACE?
GODDESS DEMETER, SHE—
YOU! STAY AWAY FROM MY DAUGHTER, GODBOY!
BUT MOM—!
NO "BUT MOM" STUFF AT ME, CHILD! LET'S GO!
OWW!
PERSEPHONE, IF YOU DON'T LIKE ME HUNTING YOU DOWN...
...YOU SHOULDN'T WANDER OFF ON YOUR OWN...
...WITHOUT TELLING ANYONE WHERE YOU'RE GOING...

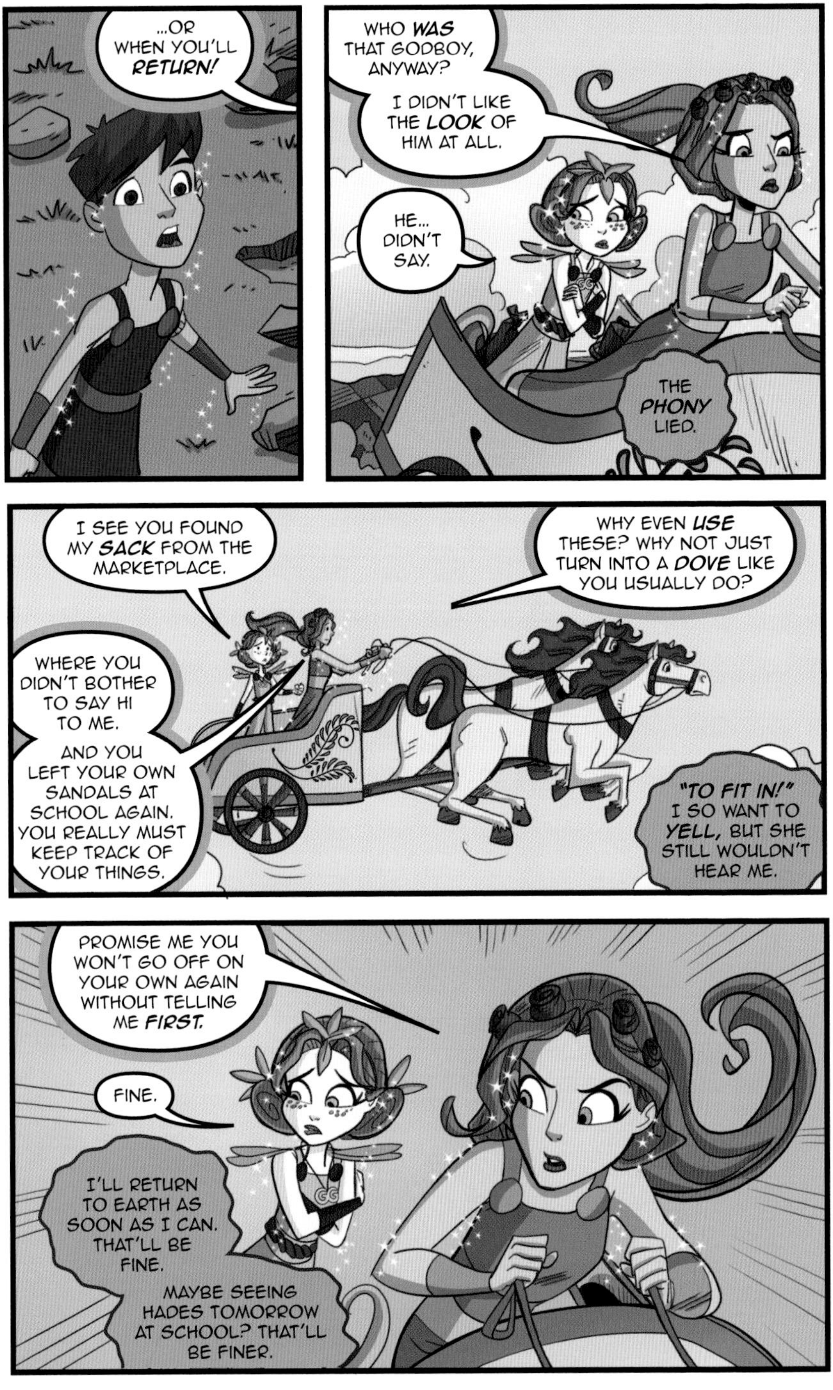
...OR WHEN YOU'LL *RETURN!*
WHO *WAS* THAT GODBOY, ANYWAY?
I DIDN'T LIKE THE *LOOK* OF HIM AT ALL.
HE... DIDN'T SAY.
THE *PHONY* LIED.
I SEE YOU FOUND MY *SACK* FROM THE MARKETPLACE.
WHERE YOU DIDN'T BOTHER TO SAY HI TO ME.
AND YOU LEFT YOUR OWN SANDALS AT SCHOOL AGAIN. YOU REALLY MUST KEEP TRACK OF YOUR THINGS.
WHY EVEN *USE* THESE? WHY NOT JUST TURN INTO A *DOVE* LIKE YOU USUALLY DO?
"TO FIT IN!" I SO WANT TO *YELL,* BUT SHE STILL WOULDN'T HEAR ME.
PROMISE ME YOU WON'T GO OFF ON YOUR OWN AGAIN WITHOUT TELLING ME *FIRST.*
FINE.
I'LL RETURN TO EARTH AS SOON AS I CAN. THAT'LL BE FINE.
MAYBE SEEING HADES TOMORROW AT SCHOOL? THAT'LL BE FINER.

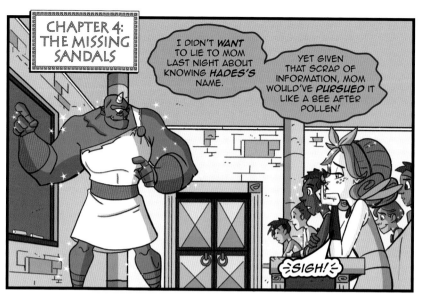

CHAPTER 4: THE MISSING SANDALS

I DIDN'T *WANT* TO LIE TO MOM LAST NIGHT ABOUT KNOWING *HADES'S* NAME.

YET GIVEN THAT SCRAP OF INFORMATION, MOM WOULD'VE *PURSUED* IT LIKE A BEE AFTER POLLEN!

⊰SIGH!⊱

IN *HER* VIEW APHRODITE IS TOO *OBSESSED* WITH HER LOOKS.

ATHENA IS TOO *SMART* FOR HER OWN GOOD.

AND ARTEMIS SPENDS TOO MUCH TIME TRAIPSING ABOUT IN THE *WOODS* WITH HER DOGS.

IT'S A *MIRACLE* MOM EVEN *ALLOWS* ME TO HAVE FRIENDS!

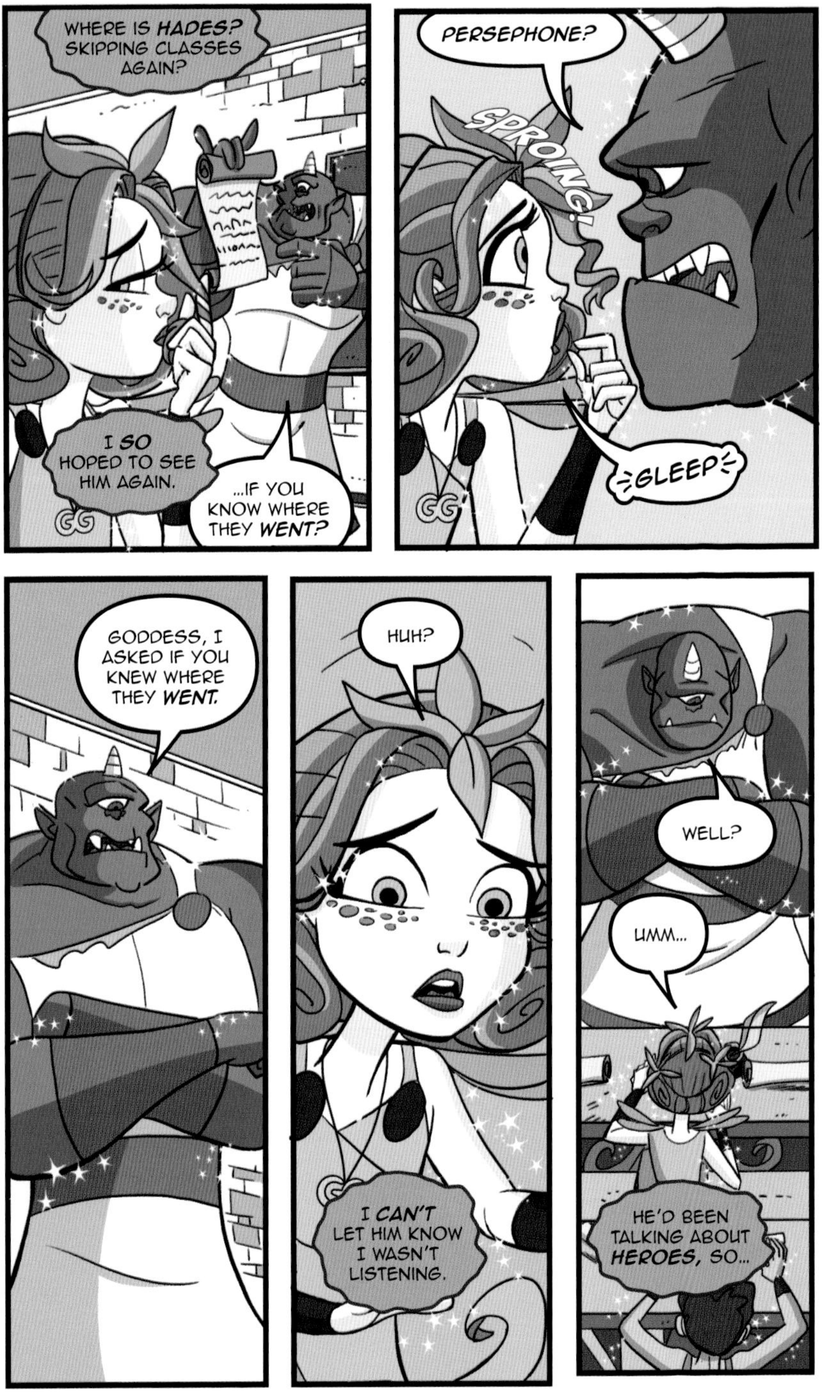
WHERE IS HADES? SKIPPING CLASSES AGAIN?
I SO HOPED TO SEE HIM AGAIN.
...IF YOU KNOW WHERE THEY WENT?
PERSEPHONE?
SPROING!
GLEEP
GODDESS, I ASKED IF YOU KNEW WHERE THEY WENT.
HUH?
I CAN'T LET HIM KNOW I WASN'T LISTENING.
WELL?
UMM...
HE'D BEEN TALKING ABOUT HEROES, SO...

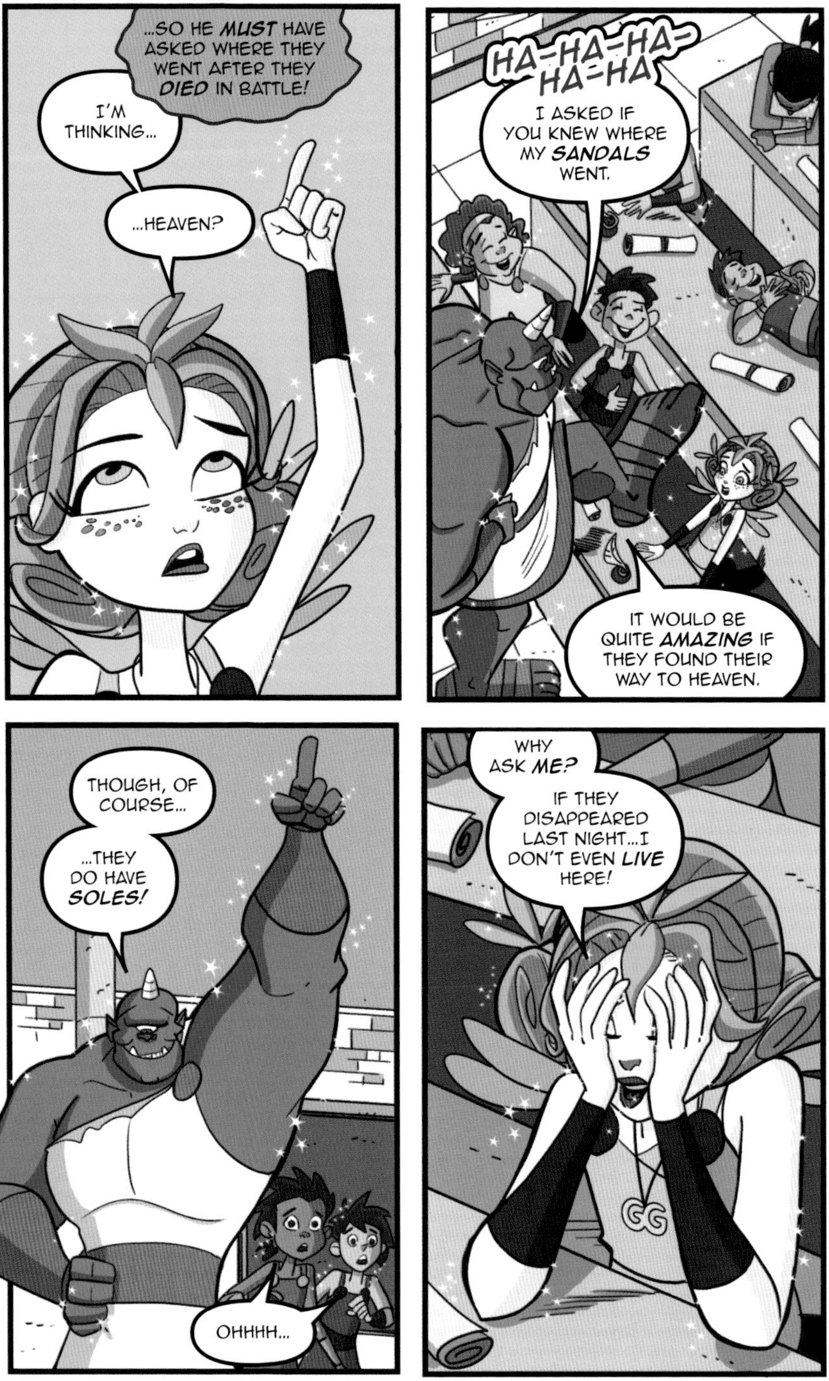
...SO HE MUST HAVE ASKED WHERE THEY WENT AFTER THEY DIED IN BATTLE!
I'M THINKING...
...HEAVEN?
HA-HA-HA-HA-HA
I ASKED IF YOU KNEW WHERE MY SANDALS WENT.
IT WOULD BE QUITE AMAZING IF THEY FOUND THEIR WAY TO HEAVEN.
THOUGH, OF COURSE...
...THEY DO HAVE SOLES!
OHHHH...
WHY ASK ME?
IF THEY DISAPPEARED LAST NIGHT...I DON'T EVEN LIVE HERE!

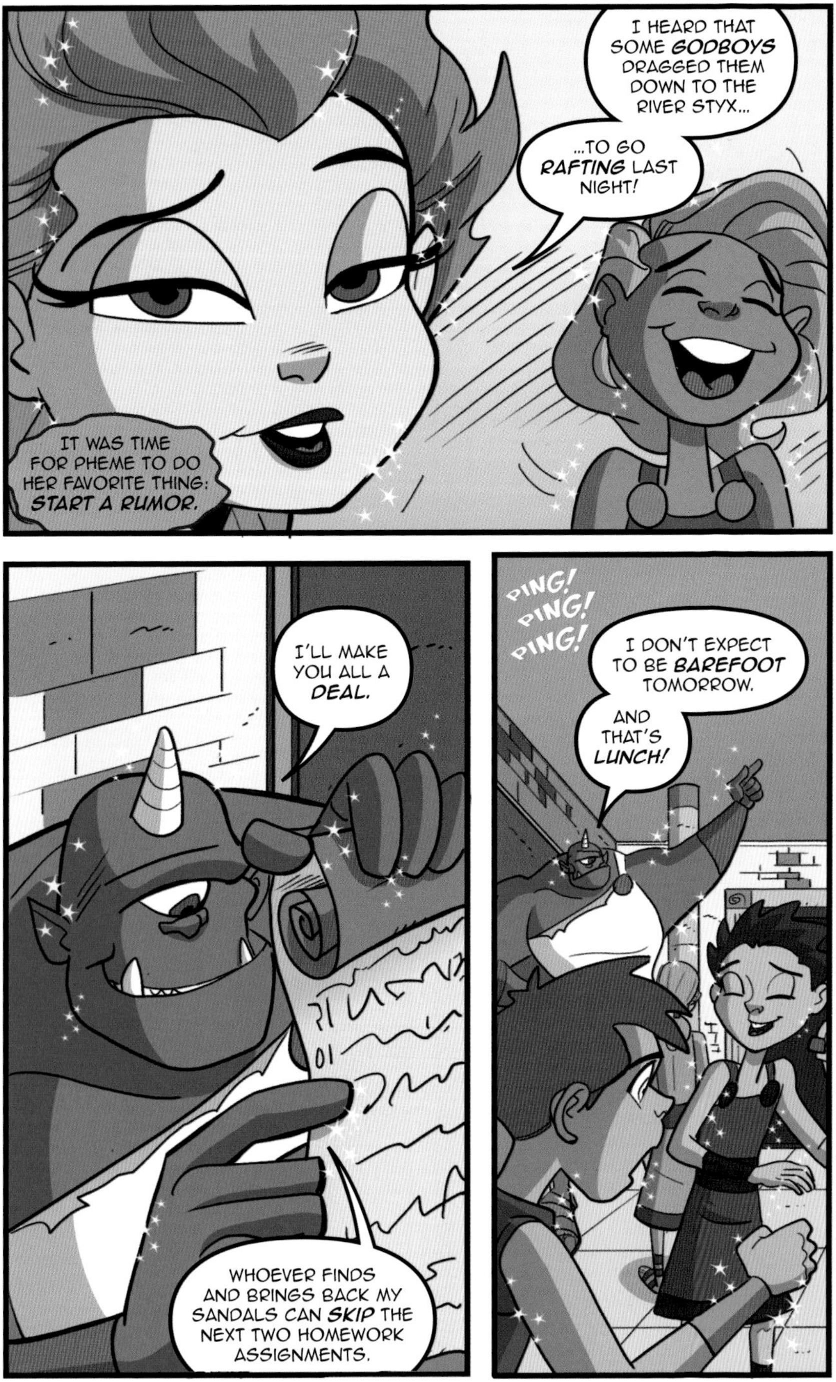
IT WAS TIME FOR PHEME TO DO HER FAVORITE THING: START A RUMOR.
I HEARD THAT SOME GODBOYS DRAGGED THEM DOWN TO THE RIVER STYX...
...TO GO RAFTING LAST NIGHT!
I'LL MAKE YOU ALL A DEAL.
WHOEVER FINDS AND BRINGS BACK MY SANDALS CAN SKIP THE NEXT TWO HOMEWORK ASSIGNMENTS.
PING! PING! PING!
I DON'T EXPECT TO BE BAREFOOT TOMORROW.
AND THAT'S LUNCH!

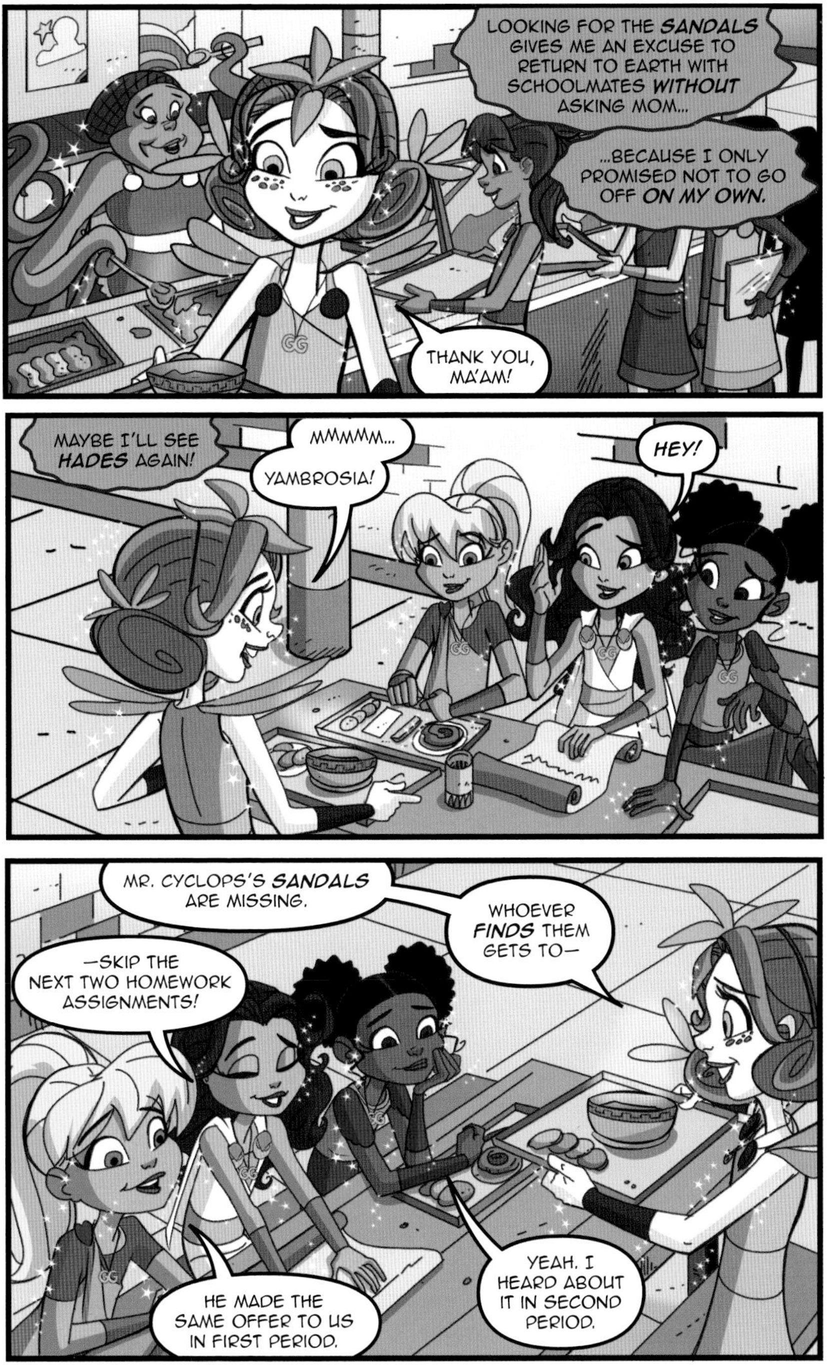
LOOKING FOR THE SANDALS GIVES ME AN EXCUSE TO RETURN TO EARTH WITH SCHOOLMATES WITHOUT ASKING MOM...
...BECAUSE I ONLY PROMISED NOT TO GO OFF ON MY OWN.
THANK YOU, MA'AM!
MAYBE I'LL SEE HADES AGAIN!
MMMMM...
YAMBROSIA!
HEY!
MR. CYCLOPS'S SANDALS ARE MISSING.
WHOEVER FINDS THEM GETS TO—
—SKIP THE NEXT TWO HOMEWORK ASSIGNMENTS!
HE MADE THE SAME OFFER TO US IN FIRST PERIOD.
YEAH. I HEARD ABOUT IT IN SECOND PERIOD.

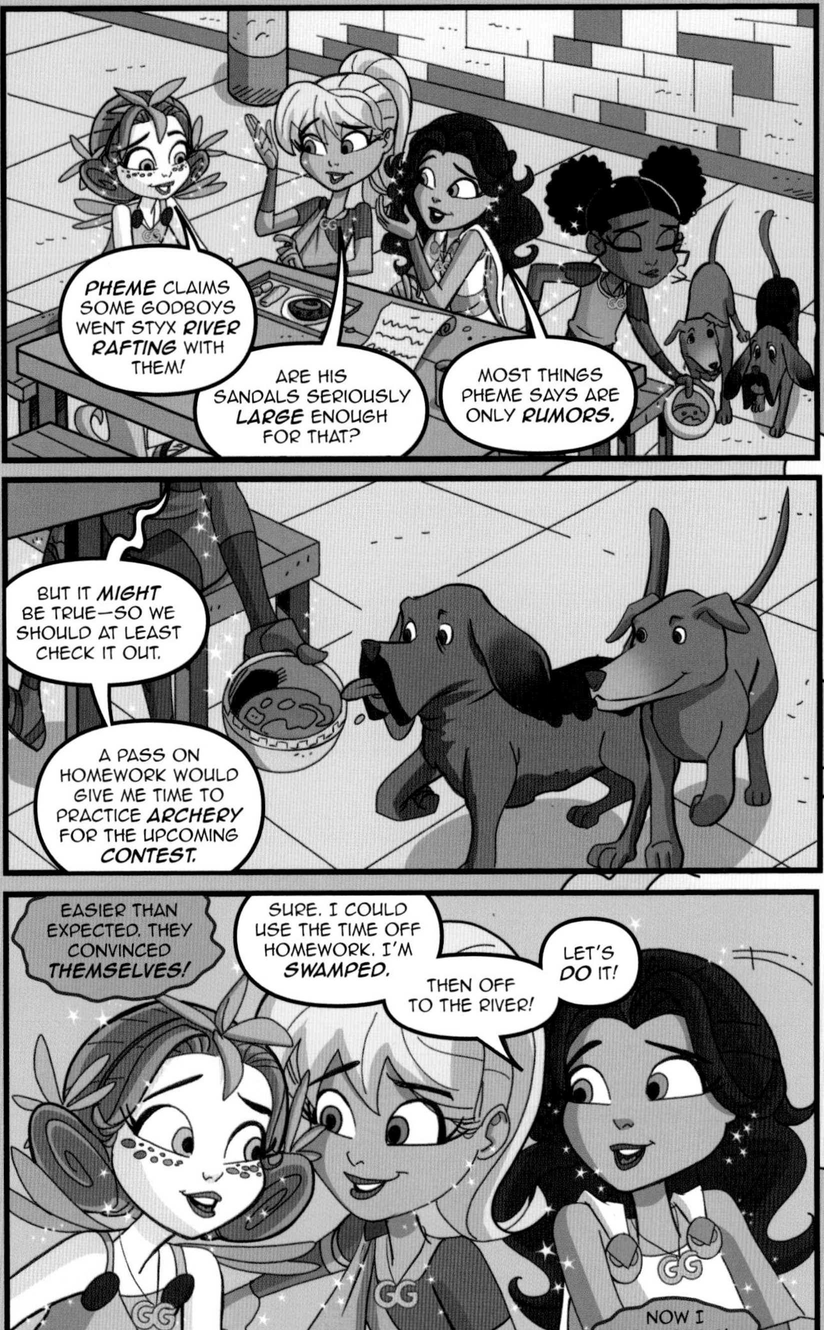
PHEME CLAIMS SOME GODBOYS WENT STYX RIVER RAFTING WITH THEM!
ARE HIS SANDALS SERIOUSLY LARGE ENOUGH FOR THAT?
MOST THINGS PHEME SAYS ARE ONLY RUMORS.
BUT IT MIGHT BE TRUE—SO WE SHOULD AT LEAST CHECK IT OUT.
A PASS ON HOMEWORK WOULD GIVE ME TIME TO PRACTICE ARCHERY FOR THE UPCOMING CONTEST.
EASIER THAN EXPECTED. THEY CONVINCED THEMSELVES!
SURE. I COULD USE THE TIME OFF HOMEWORK. I'M SWAMPED.
THEN OFF TO THE RIVER!
LET'S DO IT!
NOW I JUST HOPE I'LL SEE HADES!

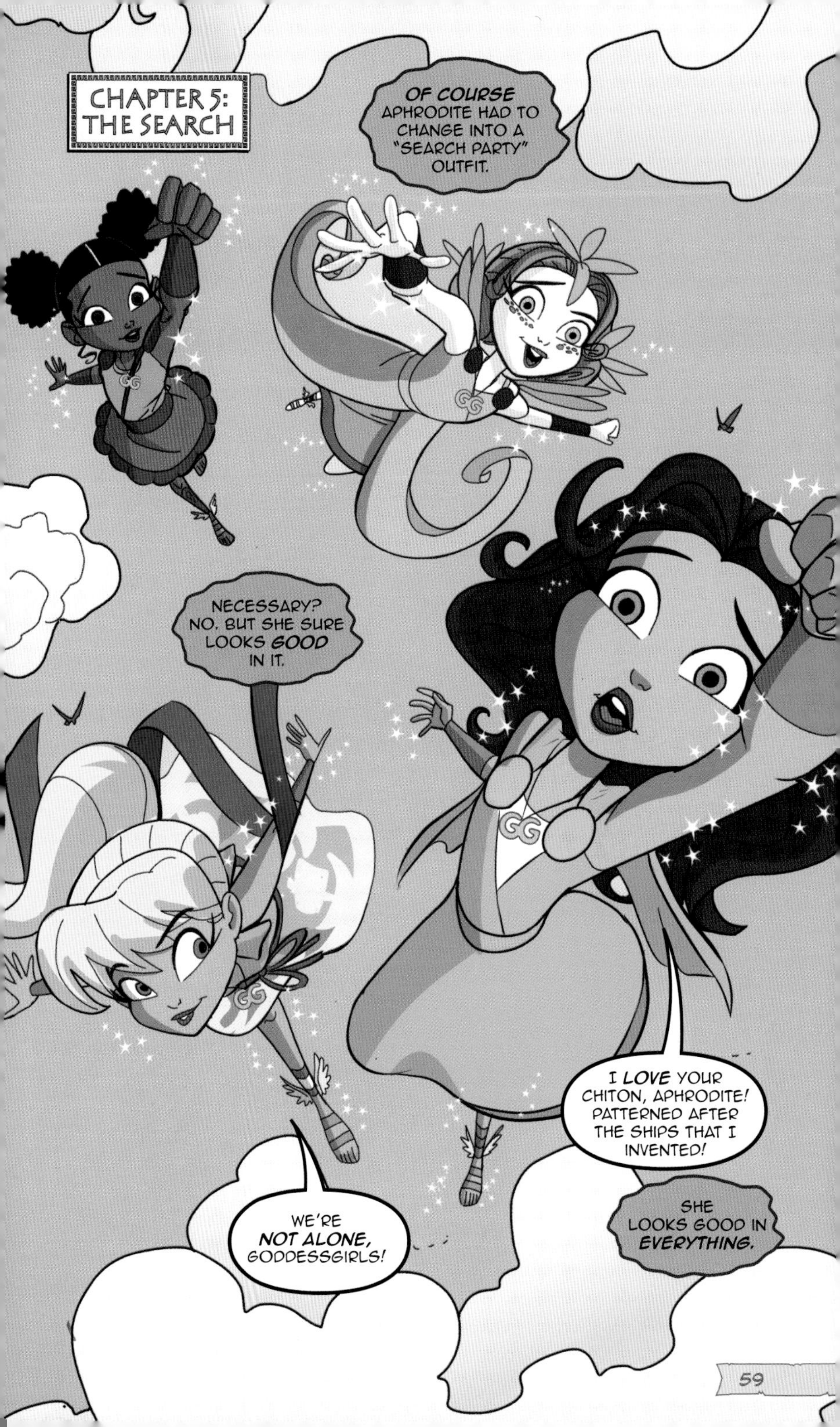
CHAPTER 5: THE SEARCH
OF COURSE APHRODITE HAD TO CHANGE INTO A "SEARCH PARTY" OUTFIT.
NECESSARY? NO. BUT SHE SURE LOOKS GOOD IN IT.
I LOVE YOUR CHITON, APHRODITE! PATTERNED AFTER THE SHIPS THAT I INVENTED!
SHE LOOKS GOOD IN EVERYTHING.
WE'RE NOT ALONE, GODDESSGIRLS!

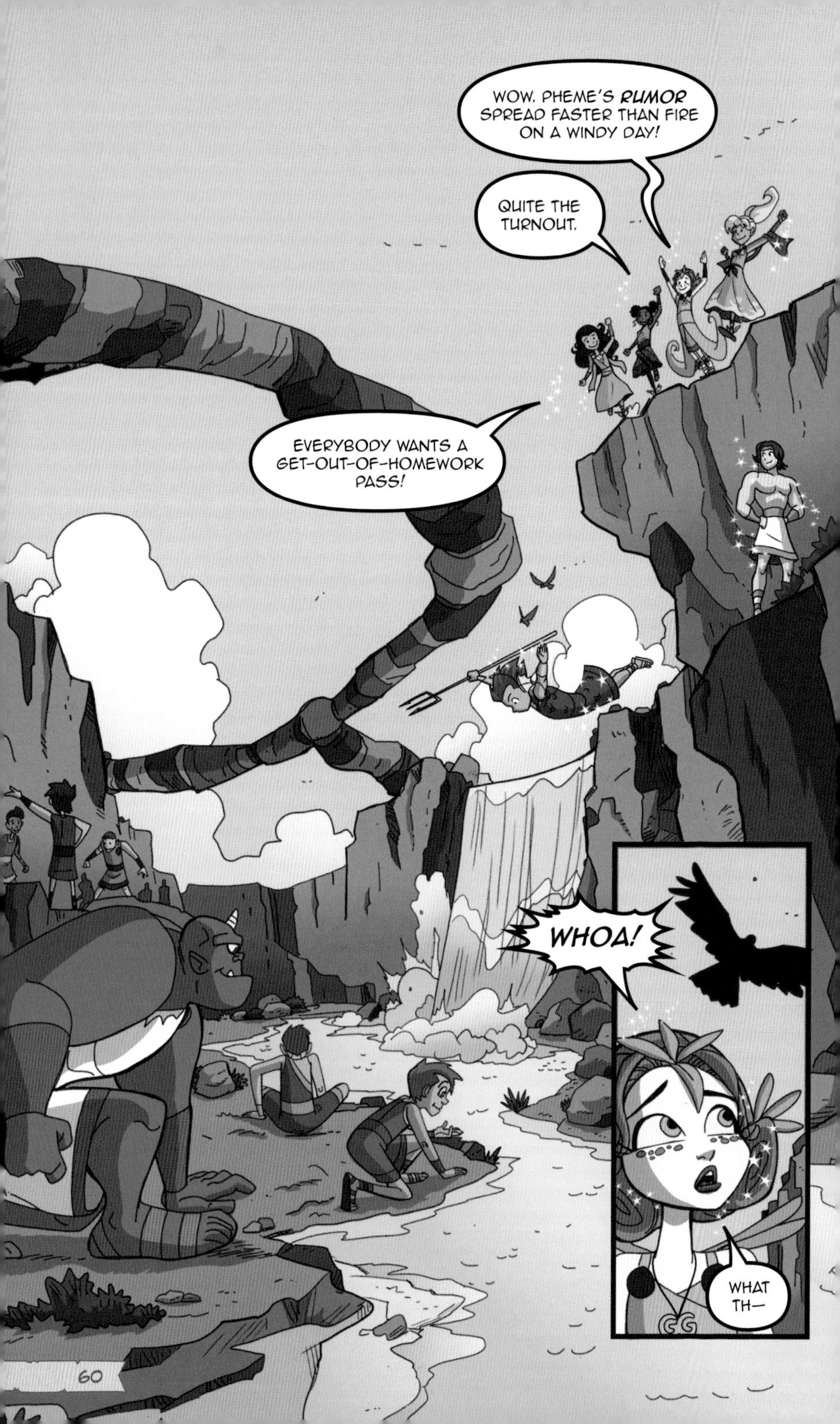

WOW. PHEME'S **RUMOR** SPREAD FASTER THAN FIRE ON A WINDY DAY!
QUITE THE TURNOUT.
EVERYBODY WANTS A GET-OUT-OF-HOMEWORK PASS!
WHOA!
WHAT TH—
GG

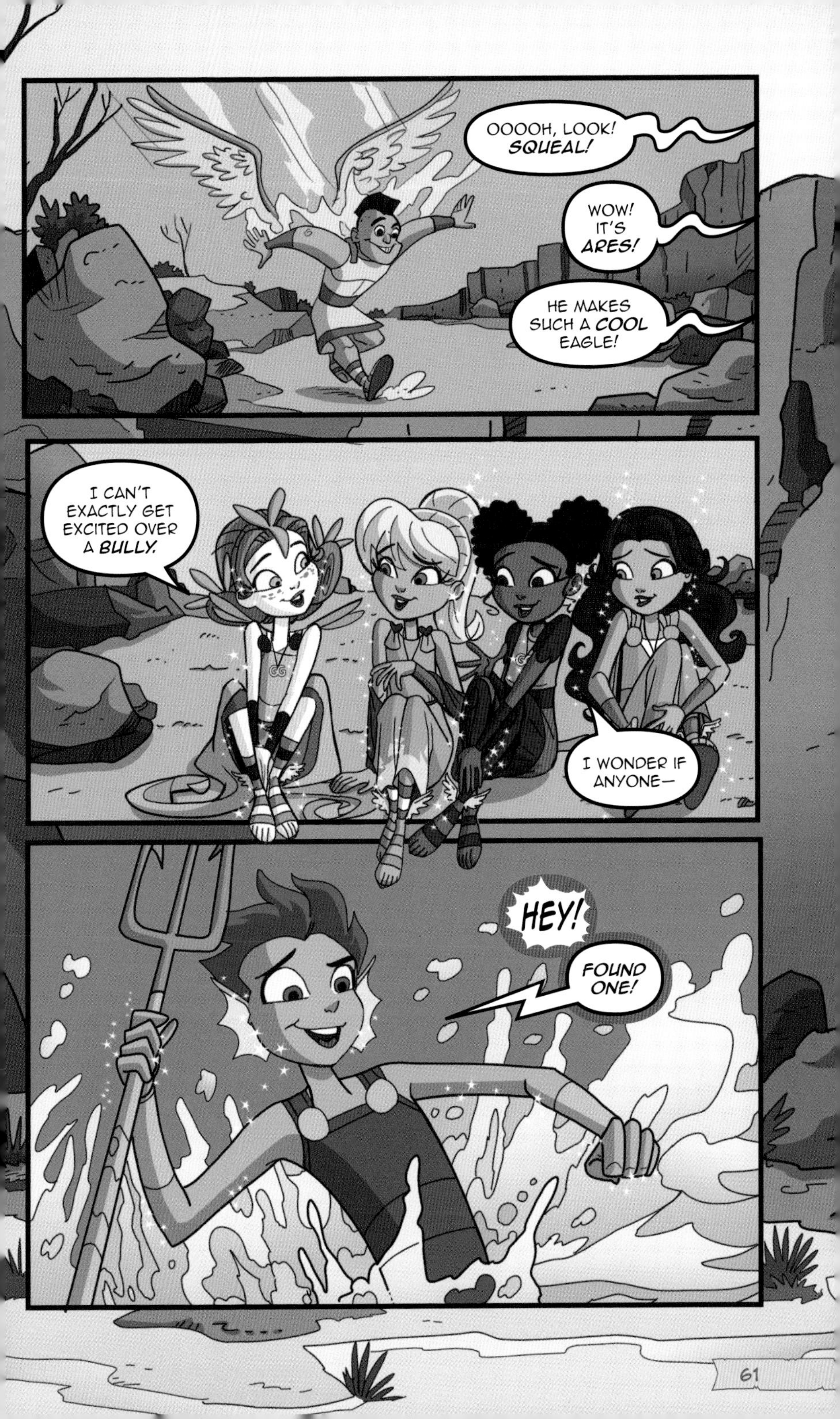
OOOOH, LOOK! SQUEAL!
WOW! IT'S ARES!
HE MAKES SUCH A COOL EAGLE!
I CAN'T EXACTLY GET EXCITED OVER A BULLY.
I WONDER IF ANYONE—
HEY!
FOUND ONE!

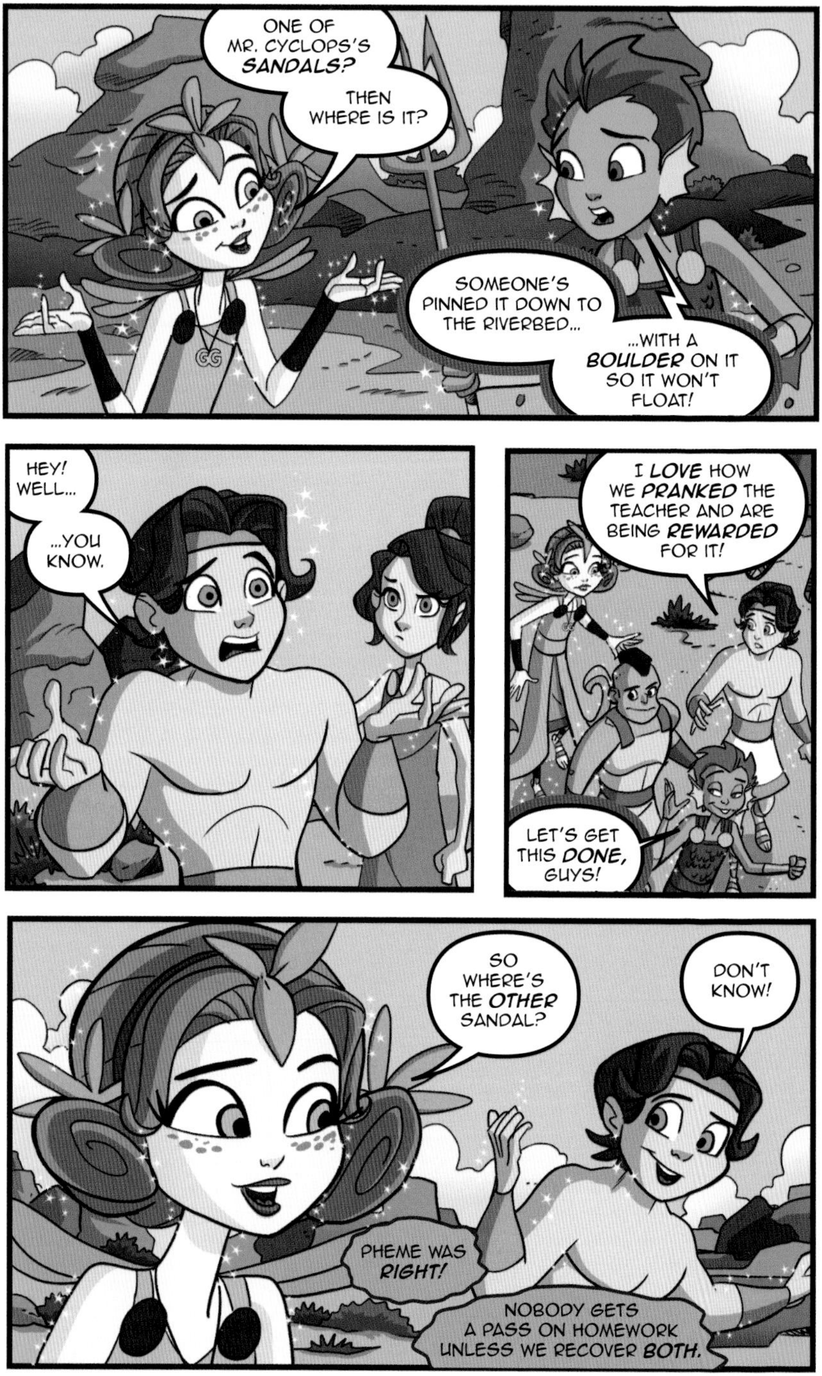
ONE OF MR. CYCLOPS'S *SANDALS?*
THEN WHERE IS IT?
SOMEONE'S PINNED IT DOWN TO THE RIVERBED...
...WITH A *BOULDER* ON IT SO IT WON'T FLOAT!
HEY! WELL...
...YOU KNOW.
I *LOVE* HOW WE *PRANKED* THE TEACHER AND ARE BEING *REWARDED* FOR IT!
LET'S GET THIS *DONE,* GUYS!
SO WHERE'S THE *OTHER* SANDAL?
DON'T KNOW!
PHEME WAS *RIGHT!*
NOBODY GETS A PASS ON HOMEWORK UNLESS WE RECOVER *BOTH.*

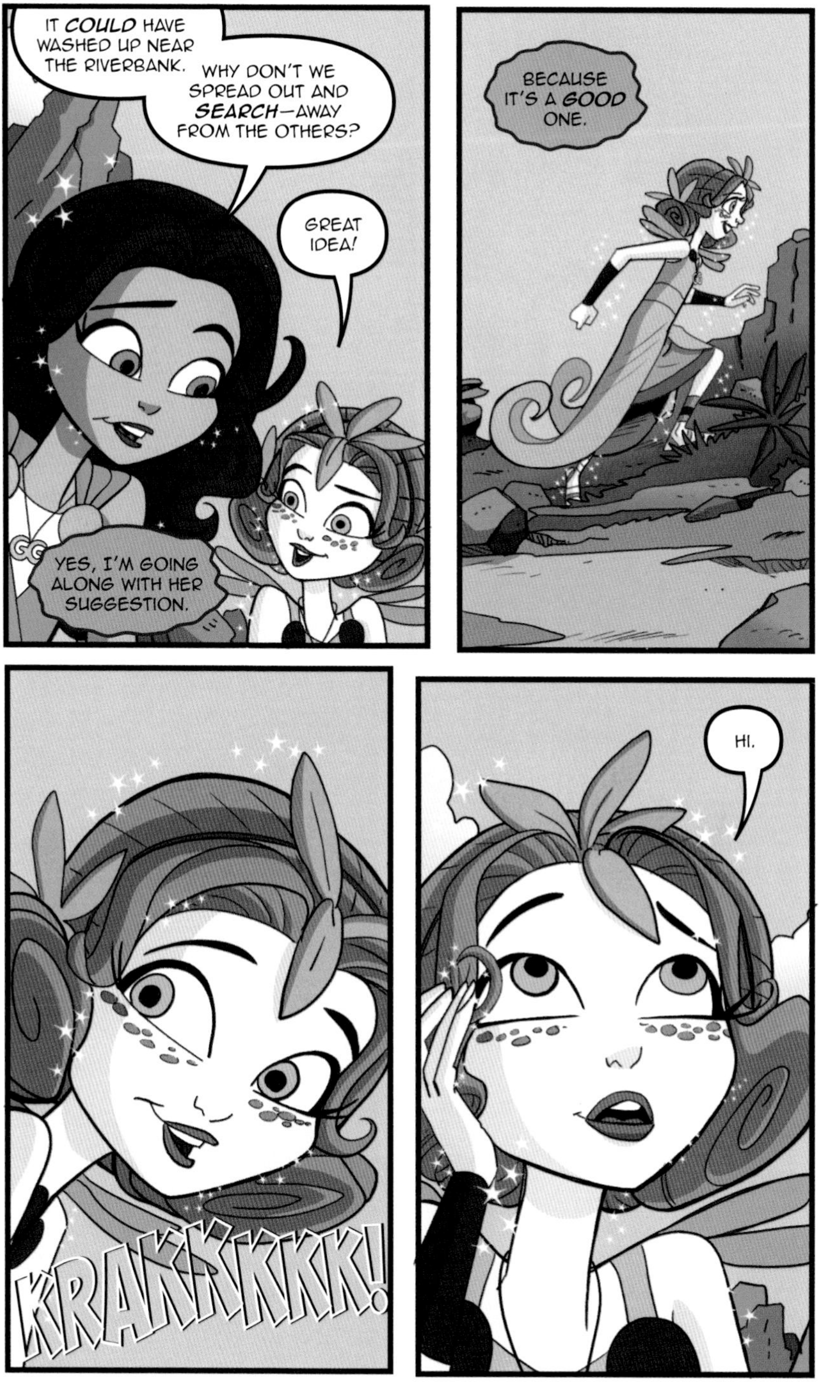
IT COULD HAVE WASHED UP NEAR THE RIVERBANK.
WHY DON'T WE SPREAD OUT AND SEARCH—AWAY FROM THE OTHERS?
GREAT IDEA!
YES, I'M GOING ALONG WITH HER SUGGESTION.
BECAUSE IT'S A GOOD ONE.
KRAKKKKKK!
HI.

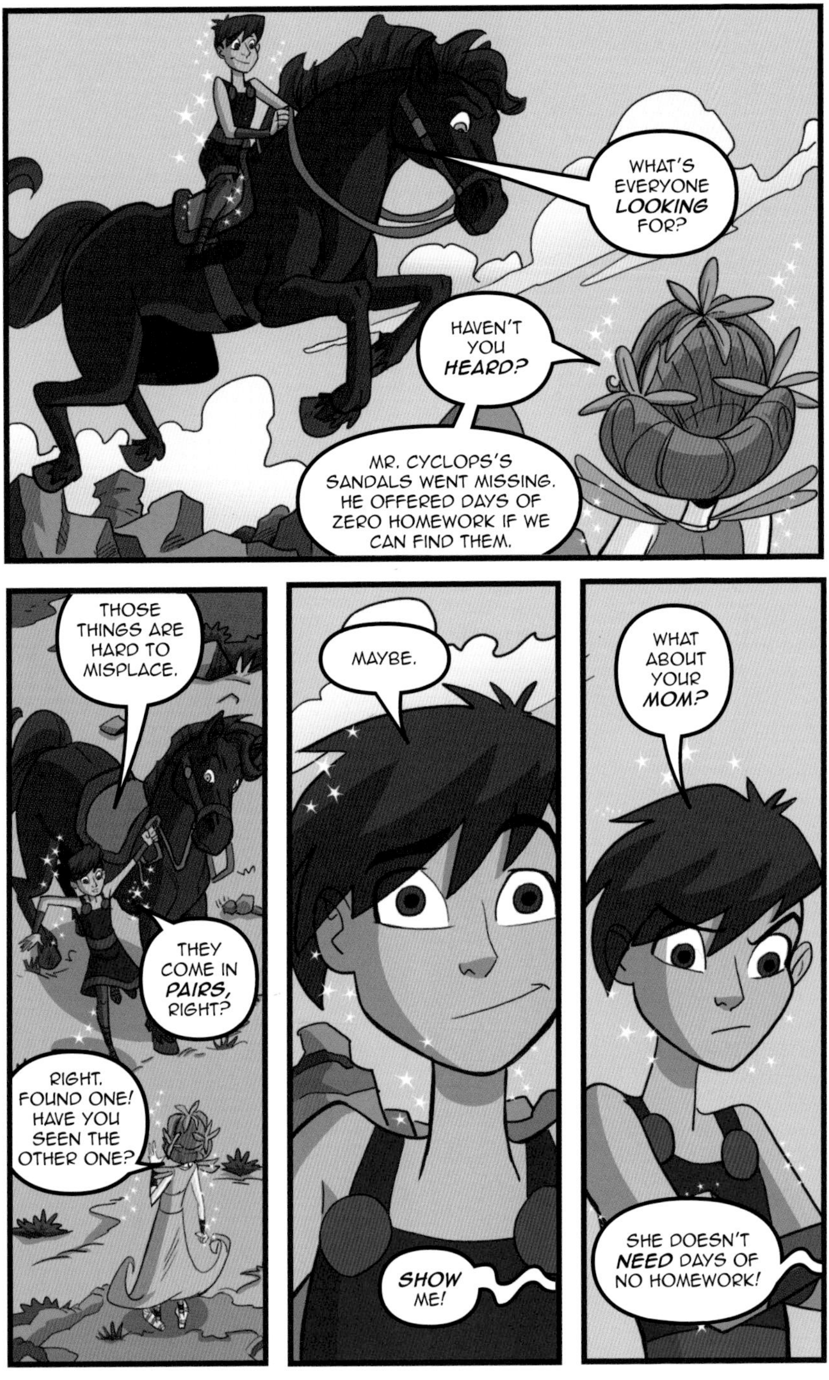

WHAT'S EVERYONE LOOKING FOR?
HAVEN'T YOU HEARD?
MR. CYCLOPS'S SANDALS WENT MISSING. HE OFFERED DAYS OF ZERO HOMEWORK IF WE CAN FIND THEM.
THOSE THINGS ARE HARD TO MISPLACE.
THEY COME IN PAIRS, RIGHT?
RIGHT. FOUND ONE! HAVE YOU SEEN THE OTHER ONE?
MAYBE.
SHOW ME!
WHAT ABOUT YOUR MOM?
SHE DOESN'T NEED DAYS OF NO HOMEWORK!

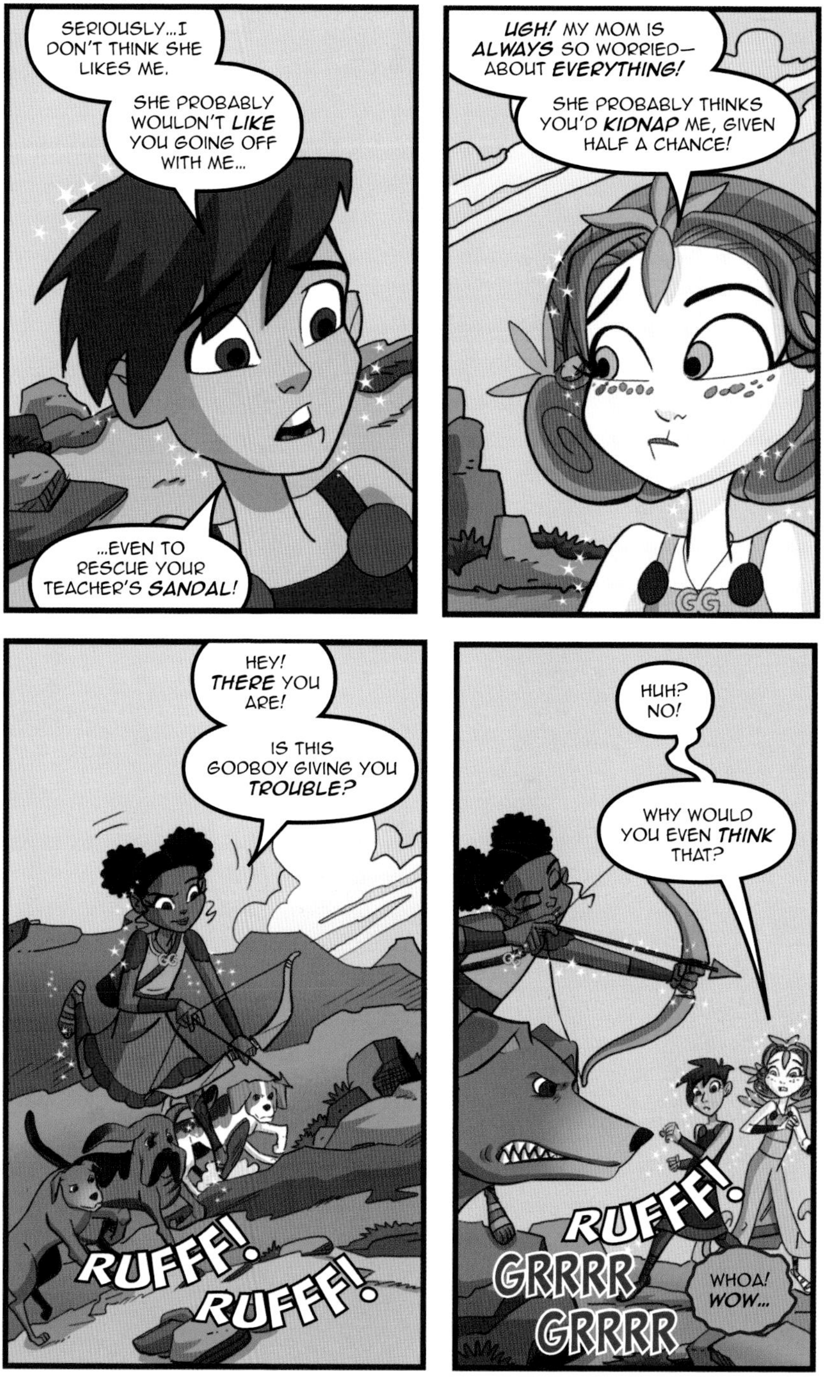
SERIOUSLY...I DON'T THINK SHE LIKES ME.
SHE PROBABLY WOULDN'T LIKE YOU GOING OFF WITH ME...
...EVEN TO RESCUE YOUR TEACHER'S SANDAL!
UGH! MY MOM IS ALWAYS SO WORRIED—ABOUT EVERYTHING!
SHE PROBABLY THINKS YOU'D KIDNAP ME, GIVEN HALF A CHANCE!
HEY! THERE YOU ARE!
IS THIS GODBOY GIVING YOU TROUBLE?
RUFFF!
RUFFF!
HUH? NO!
WHY WOULD YOU EVEN THINK THAT?
RUFFF!
GRRRR
GRRRR
WHOA! WOW...

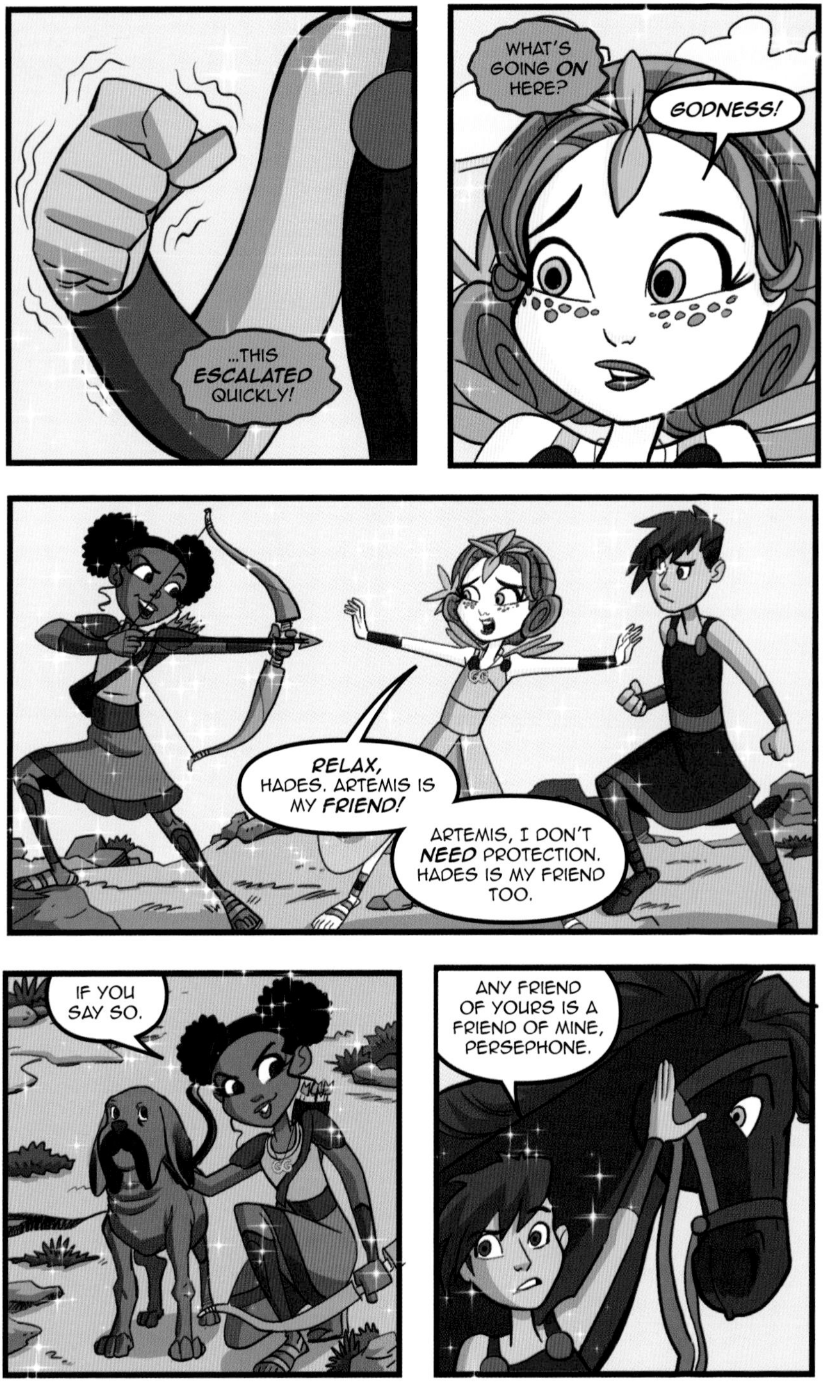
...THIS ESCALATED QUICKLY!
WHAT'S GOING ON HERE?
GODNESS!
RELAX, HADES. ARTEMIS IS MY FRIEND!
ARTEMIS, I DON'T NEED PROTECTION. HADES IS MY FRIEND TOO.
IF YOU SAY SO.
ANY FRIEND OF YOURS IS A FRIEND OF MINE, PERSEPHONE.

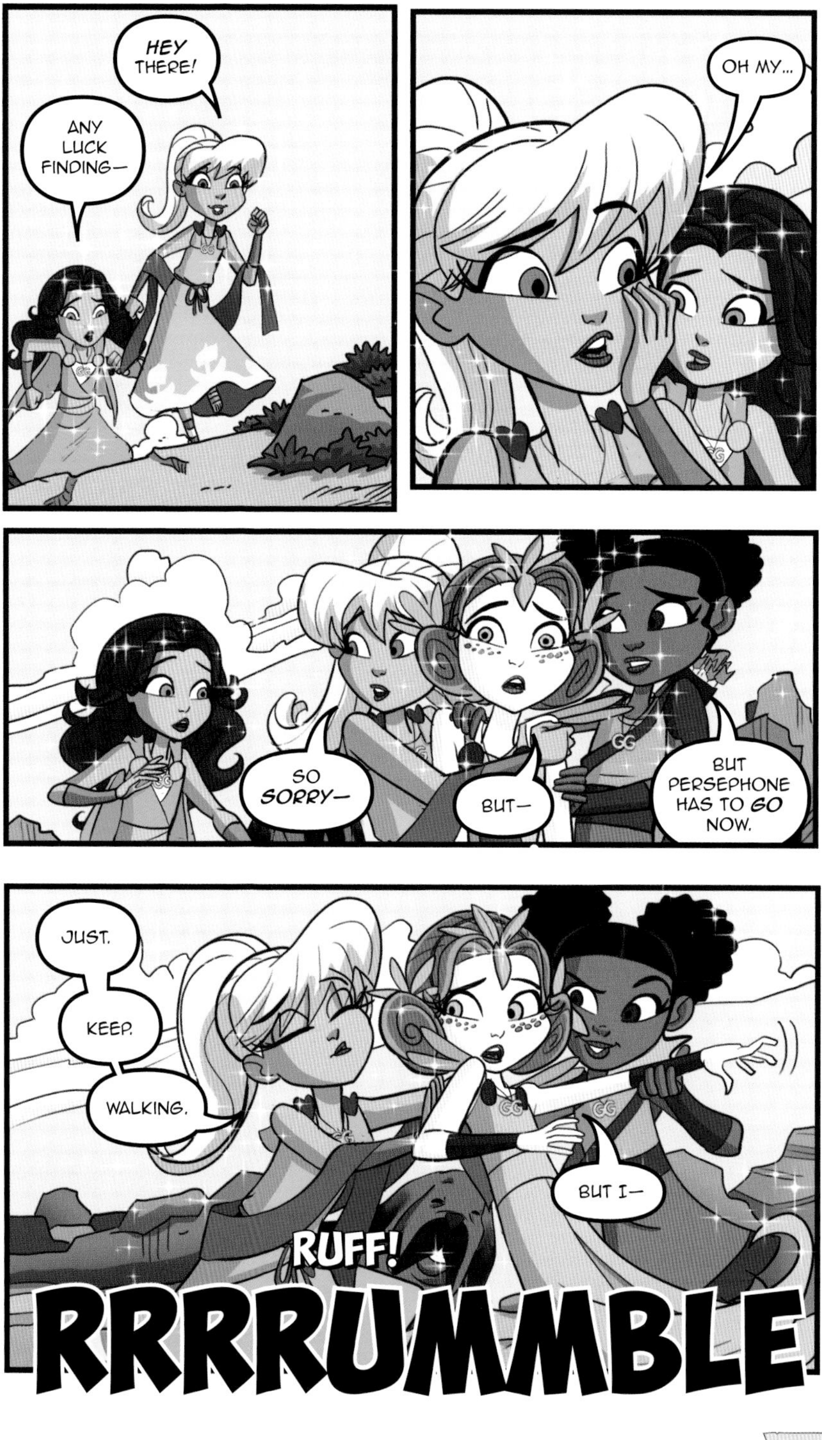
ANY LUCK FINDING—
HEY THERE!
OH MY...
SO SORRY—
BUT—
BUT PERSEPHONE HAS TO GO NOW.
JUST.
KEEP.
WALKING.
BUT I—
RUFF!
RRRRUMMBLE

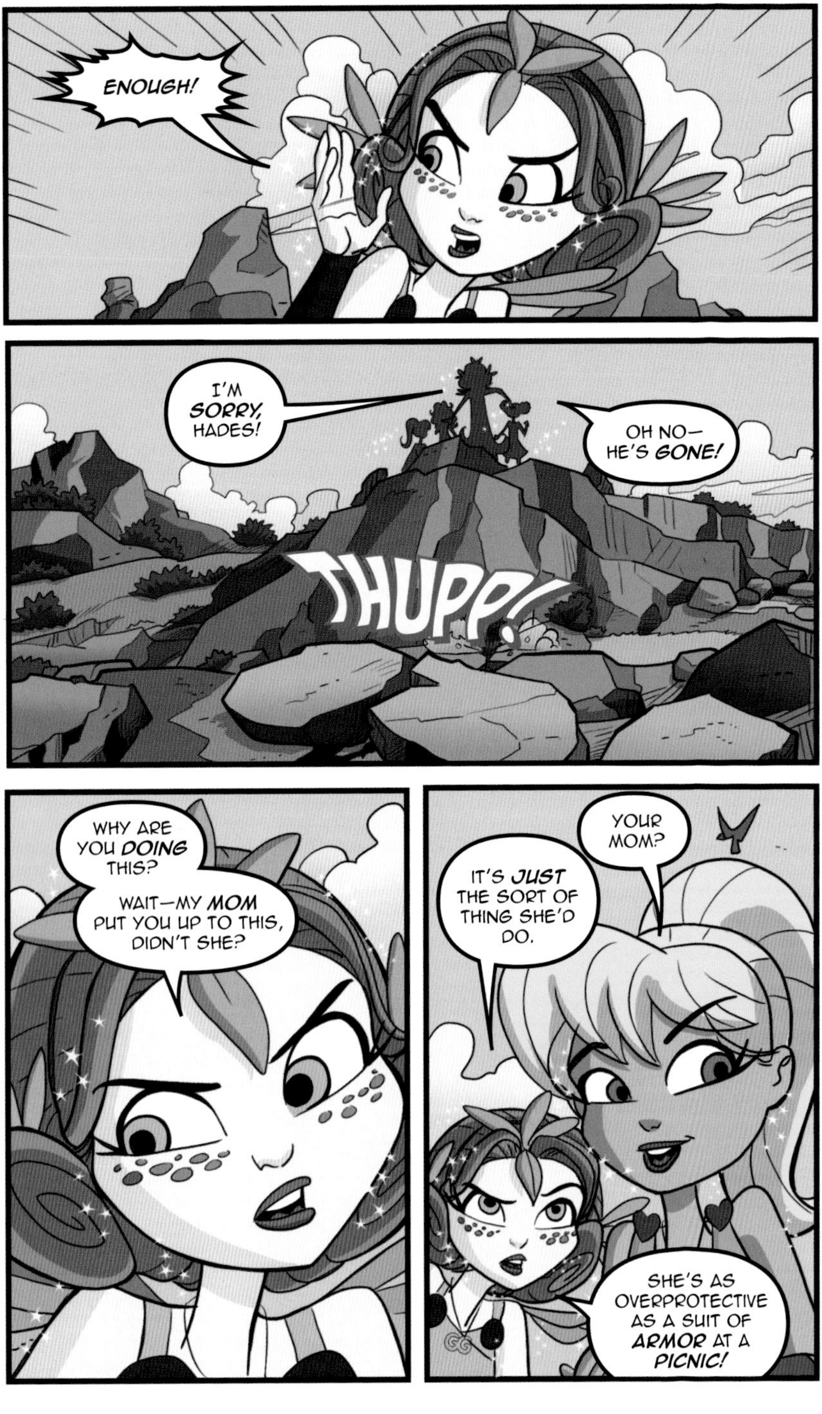
ENOUGH!
I'M SORRY, HADES!
OH NO— HE'S GONE!
THUPP!
WHY ARE YOU DOING THIS?
WAIT—MY MOM PUT YOU UP TO THIS, DIDN'T SHE?
IT'S JUST THE SORT OF THING SHE'D DO.
YOUR MOM?
SHE'S AS OVERPROTECTIVE AS A SUIT OF ARMOR AT A PICNIC!

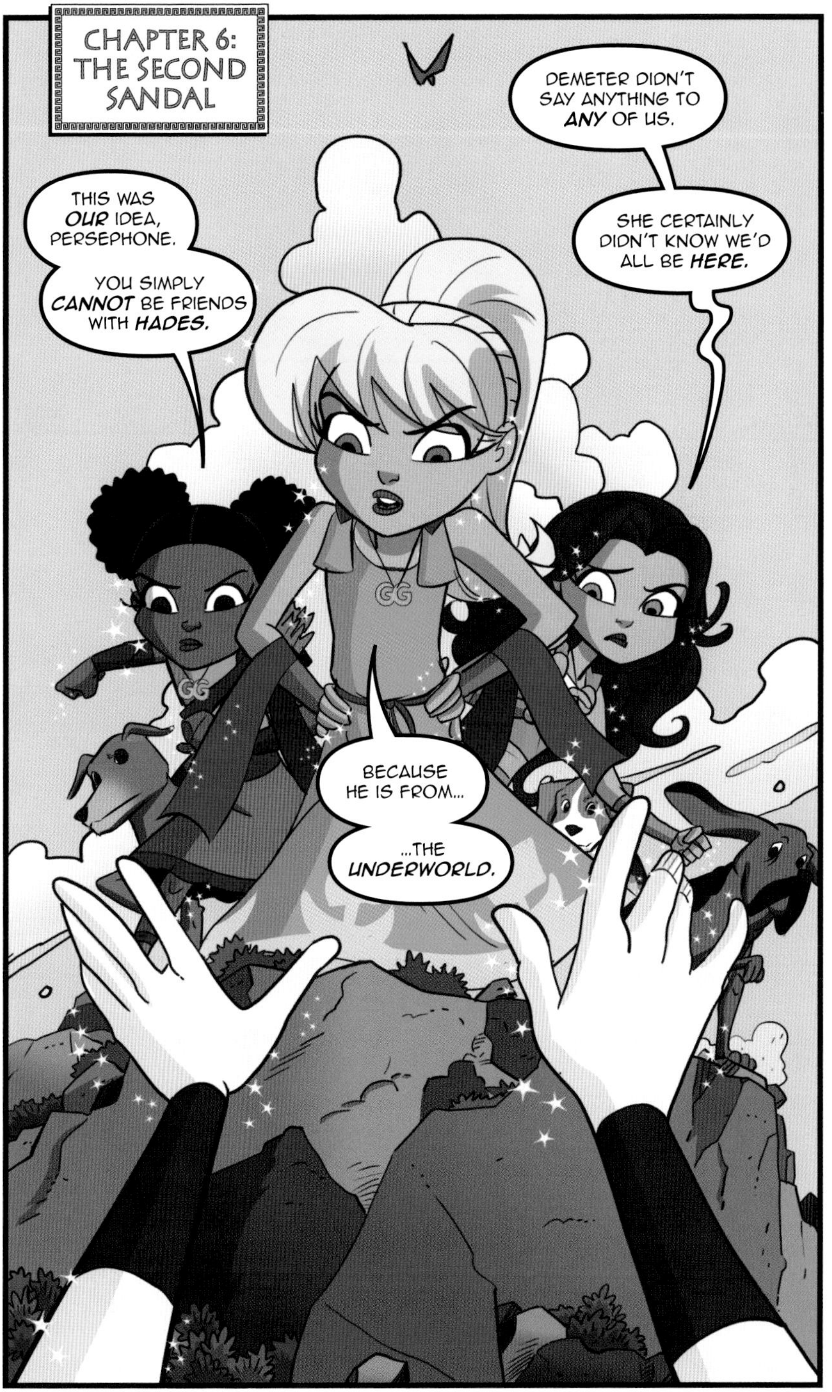
CHAPTER 6: THE SECOND SANDAL
THIS WAS OUR IDEA, PERSEPHONE.
YOU SIMPLY CANNOT BE FRIENDS WITH HADES.
DEMETER DIDN'T SAY ANYTHING TO ANY OF US.
SHE CERTAINLY DIDN'T KNOW WE'D ALL BE HERE.
BECAUSE HE IS FROM...
...THE UNDERWORLD.

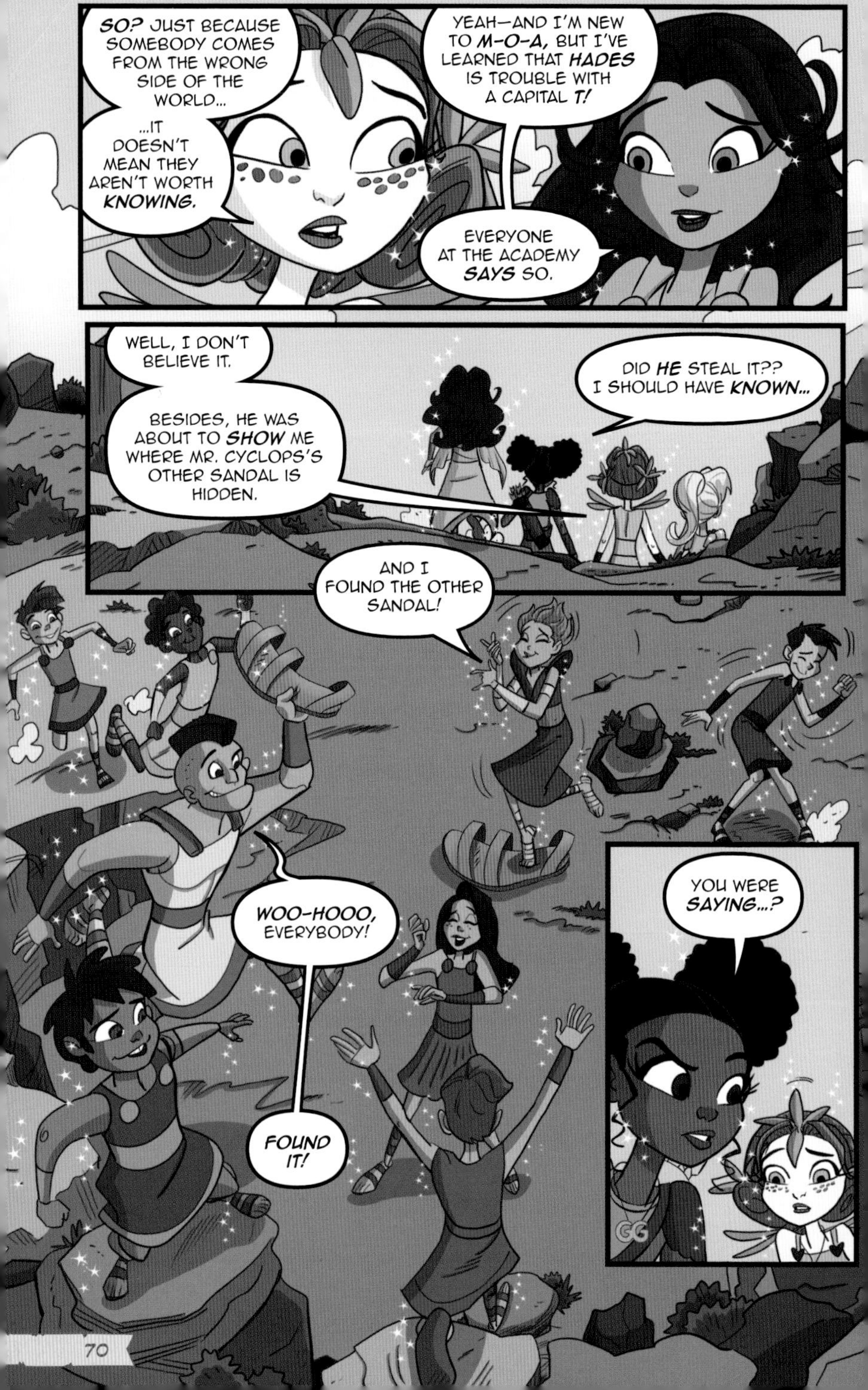
SO? JUST BECAUSE SOMEBODY COMES FROM THE WRONG SIDE OF THE WORLD...
...IT DOESN'T MEAN THEY AREN'T WORTH KNOWING.
YEAH—AND I'M NEW TO M-O-A, BUT I'VE LEARNED THAT HADES IS TROUBLE WITH A CAPITAL T!
EVERYONE AT THE ACADEMY SAYS SO.
WELL, I DON'T BELIEVE IT.
BESIDES, HE WAS ABOUT TO SHOW ME WHERE MR. CYCLOPS'S OTHER SANDAL IS HIDDEN.
DID HE STEAL IT?? I SHOULD HAVE KNOWN...
AND I FOUND THE OTHER SANDAL!
WOO-HOOO, EVERYBODY!
FOUND IT!
YOU WERE SAYING...?
GG

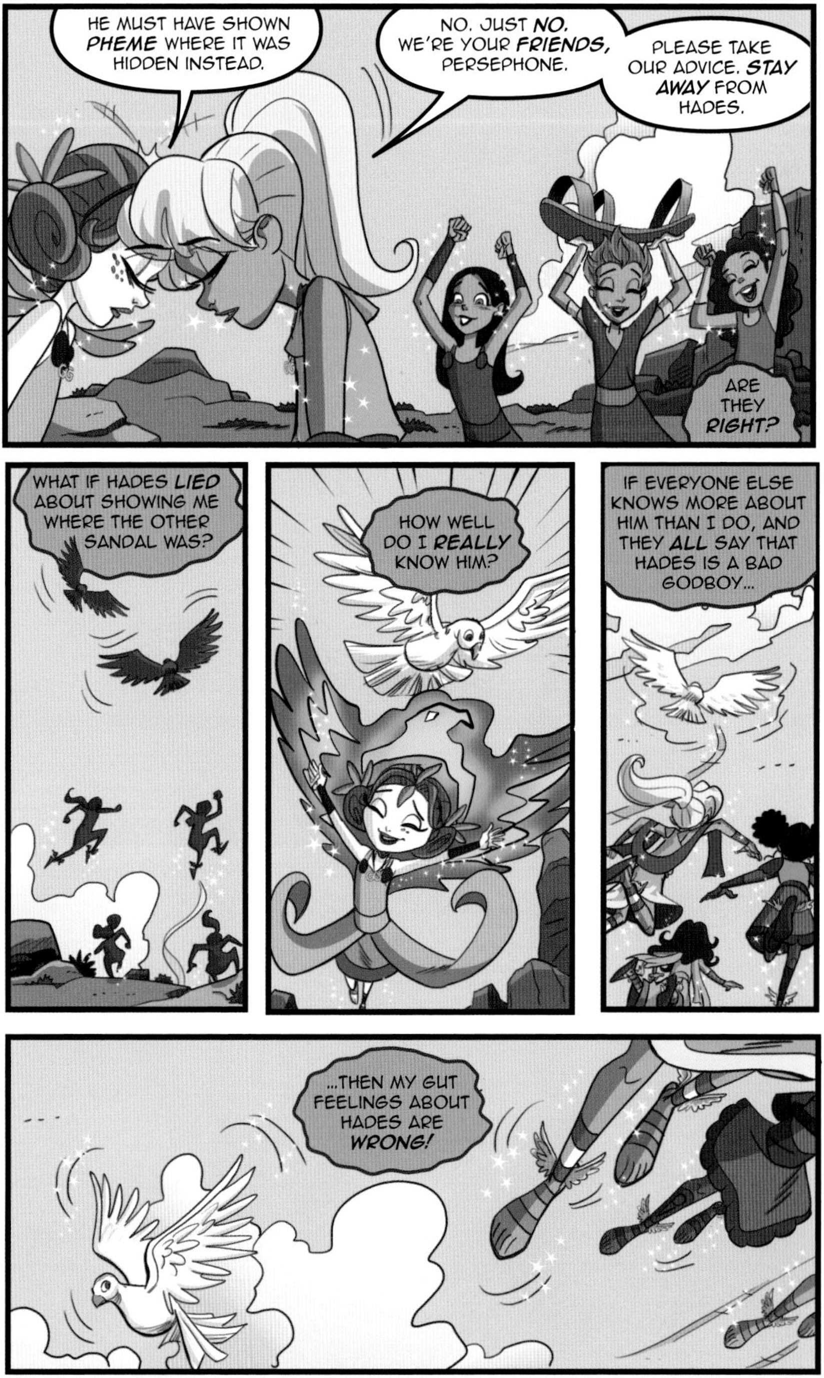
HE MUST HAVE SHOWN PHEME WHERE IT WAS HIDDEN INSTEAD.
NO. JUST NO. WE'RE YOUR FRIENDS, PERSEPHONE.
PLEASE TAKE OUR ADVICE. STAY AWAY FROM HADES.
ARE THEY RIGHT?
WHAT IF HADES LIED ABOUT SHOWING ME WHERE THE OTHER SANDAL WAS?
HOW WELL DO I REALLY KNOW HIM?
IF EVERYONE ELSE KNOWS MORE ABOUT HIM THAN I DO, AND THEY ALL SAY THAT HADES IS A BAD GODBOY...
...THEN MY GUT FEELINGS ABOUT HADES ARE WRONG!

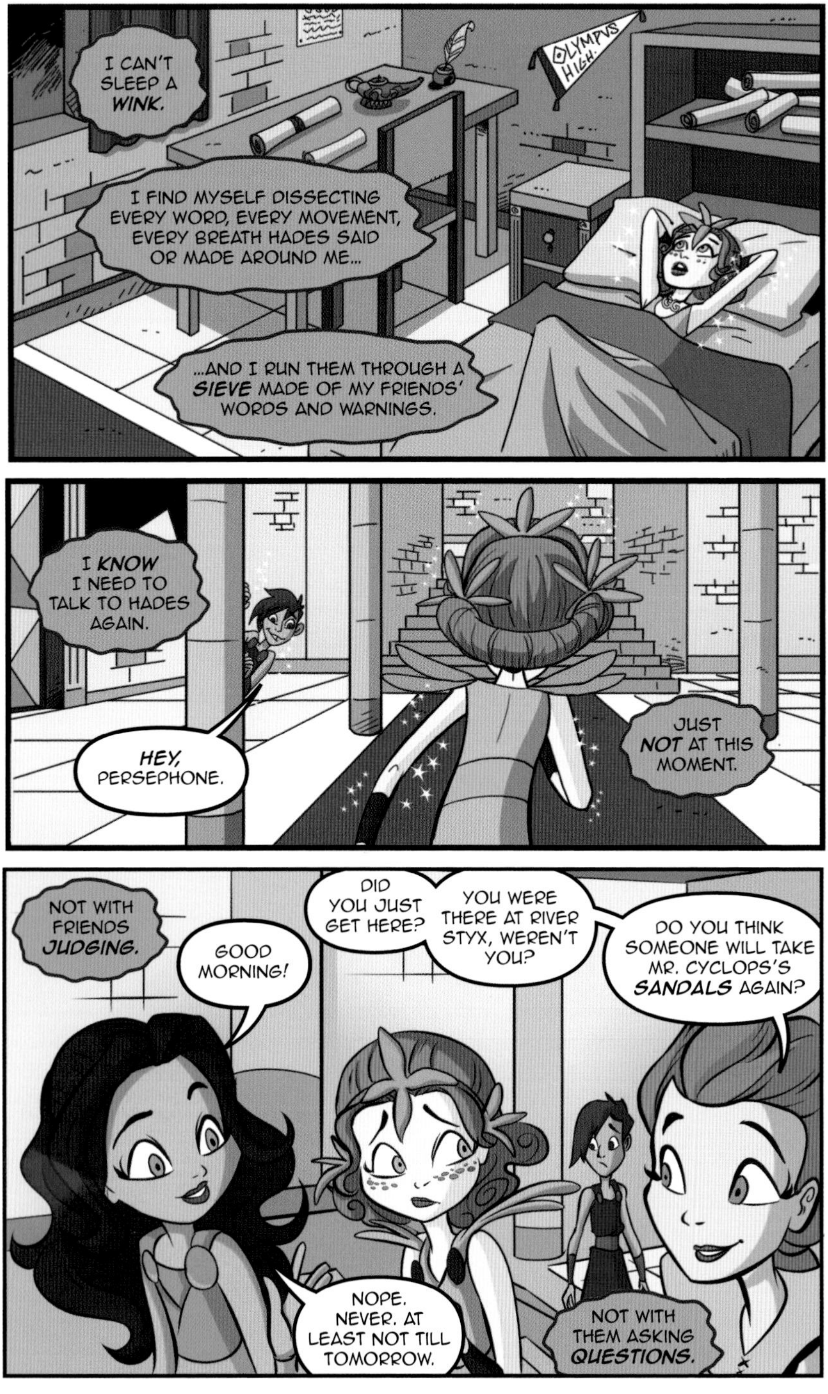
I CAN'T SLEEP A WINK.
OLYMPUS HIGH
I FIND MYSELF DISSECTING EVERY WORD, EVERY MOVEMENT, EVERY BREATH HADES SAID OR MADE AROUND ME...
...AND I RUN THEM THROUGH A SIEVE MADE OF MY FRIENDS' WORDS AND WARNINGS.
I KNOW I NEED TO TALK TO HADES AGAIN.
HEY, PERSEPHONE.
JUST NOT AT THIS MOMENT.
NOT WITH FRIENDS JUDGING.
GOOD MORNING!
DID YOU JUST GET HERE?
YOU WERE THERE AT RIVER STYX, WEREN'T YOU?
DO YOU THINK SOMEONE WILL TAKE MR. CYCLOPS'S SANDALS AGAIN?
NOPE. NEVER. AT LEAST NOT TILL TOMORROW.
NOT WITH THEM ASKING QUESTIONS.

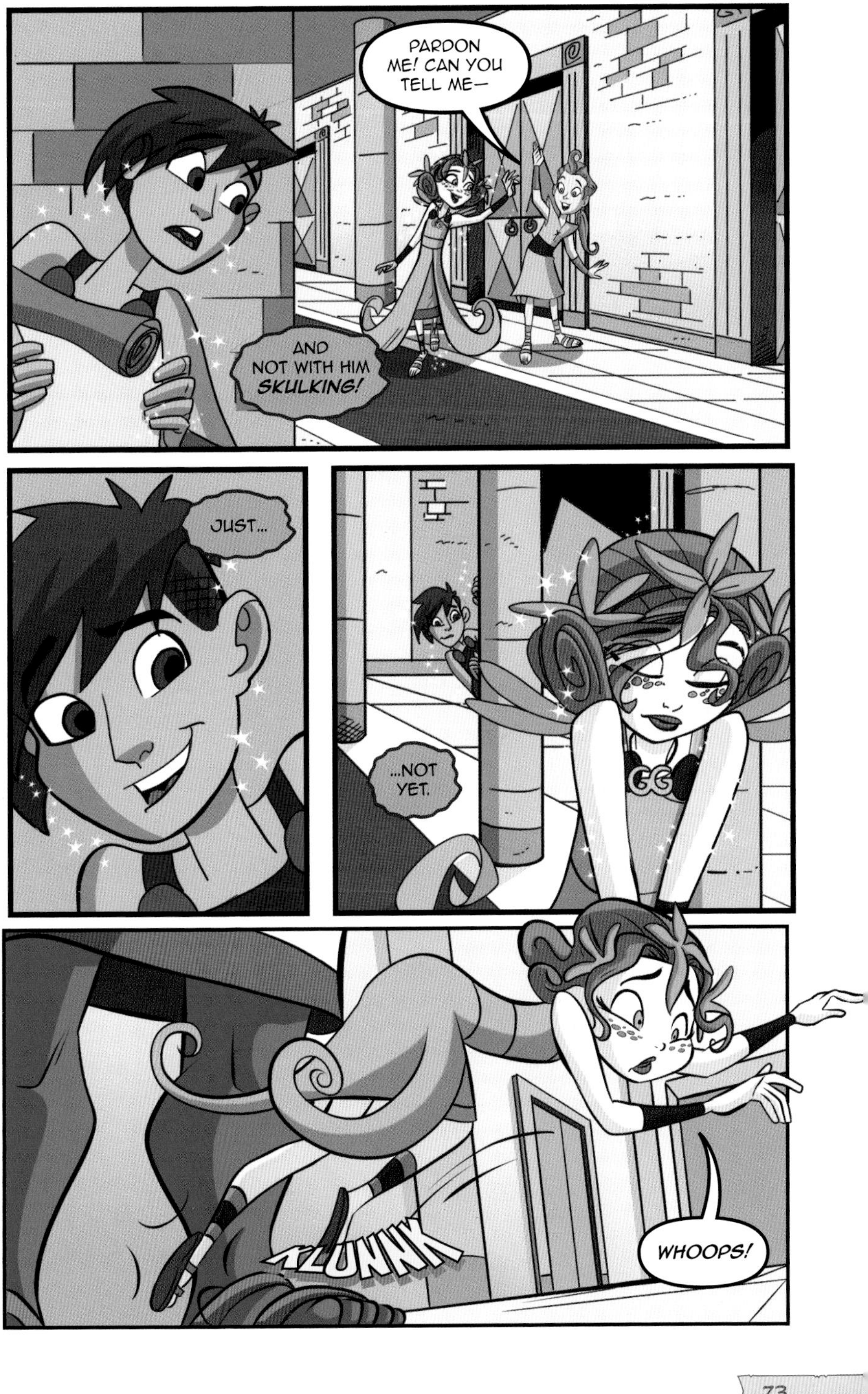
PARDON ME! CAN YOU TELL ME—
AND NOT WITH HIM SKULKING!
JUST...
...NOT YET.
KLUNNK
WHOOPS!

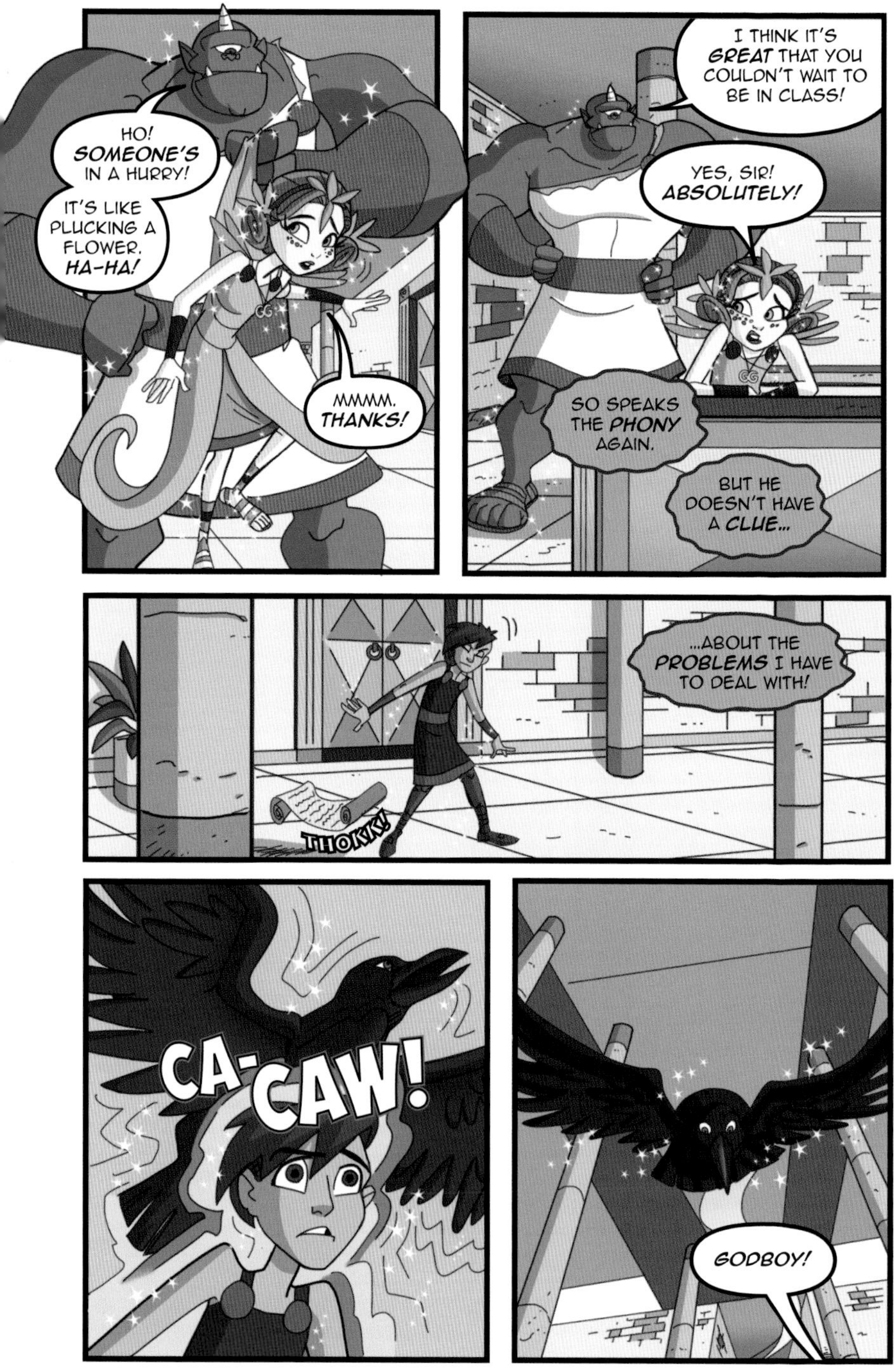
HO! SOMEONE'S IN A HURRY!
IT'S LIKE PLUCKING A FLOWER. HA-HA!
MMMM. THANKS!
I THINK IT'S GREAT THAT YOU COULDN'T WAIT TO BE IN CLASS!
YES, SIR! ABSOLUTELY!
SO SPEAKS THE PHONY AGAIN.
BUT HE DOESN'T HAVE A CLUE...
...ABOUT THE PROBLEMS I HAVE TO DEAL WITH!
THOKK!
CA-CAW!
GODBOY!

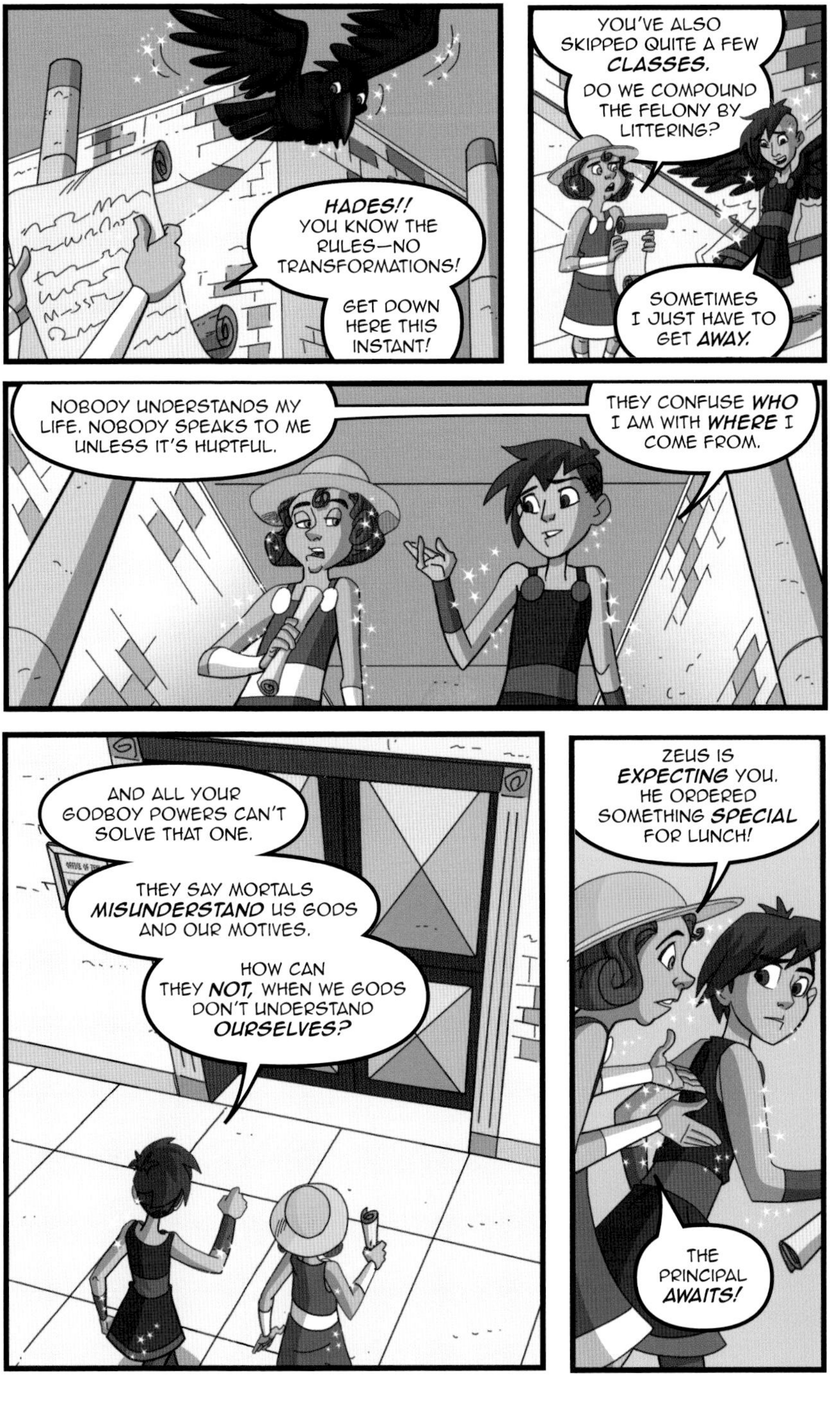
HADES!!
YOU KNOW THE RULES—NO TRANSFORMATIONS!
GET DOWN HERE THIS INSTANT!
YOU'VE ALSO SKIPPED QUITE A FEW CLASSES.
DO WE COMPOUND THE FELONY BY LITTERING?
SOMETIMES I JUST HAVE TO GET AWAY.
NOBODY UNDERSTANDS MY LIFE. NOBODY SPEAKS TO ME UNLESS IT'S HURTFUL.
THEY CONFUSE WHO I AM WITH WHERE I COME FROM.
AND ALL YOUR GODBOY POWERS CAN'T SOLVE THAT ONE.
THEY SAY MORTALS MISUNDERSTAND US GODS AND OUR MOTIVES.
HOW CAN THEY NOT, WHEN WE GODS DON'T UNDERSTAND OURSELVES?
ZEUS IS EXPECTING YOU. HE ORDERED SOMETHING SPECIAL FOR LUNCH!
THE PRINCIPAL AWAITS!

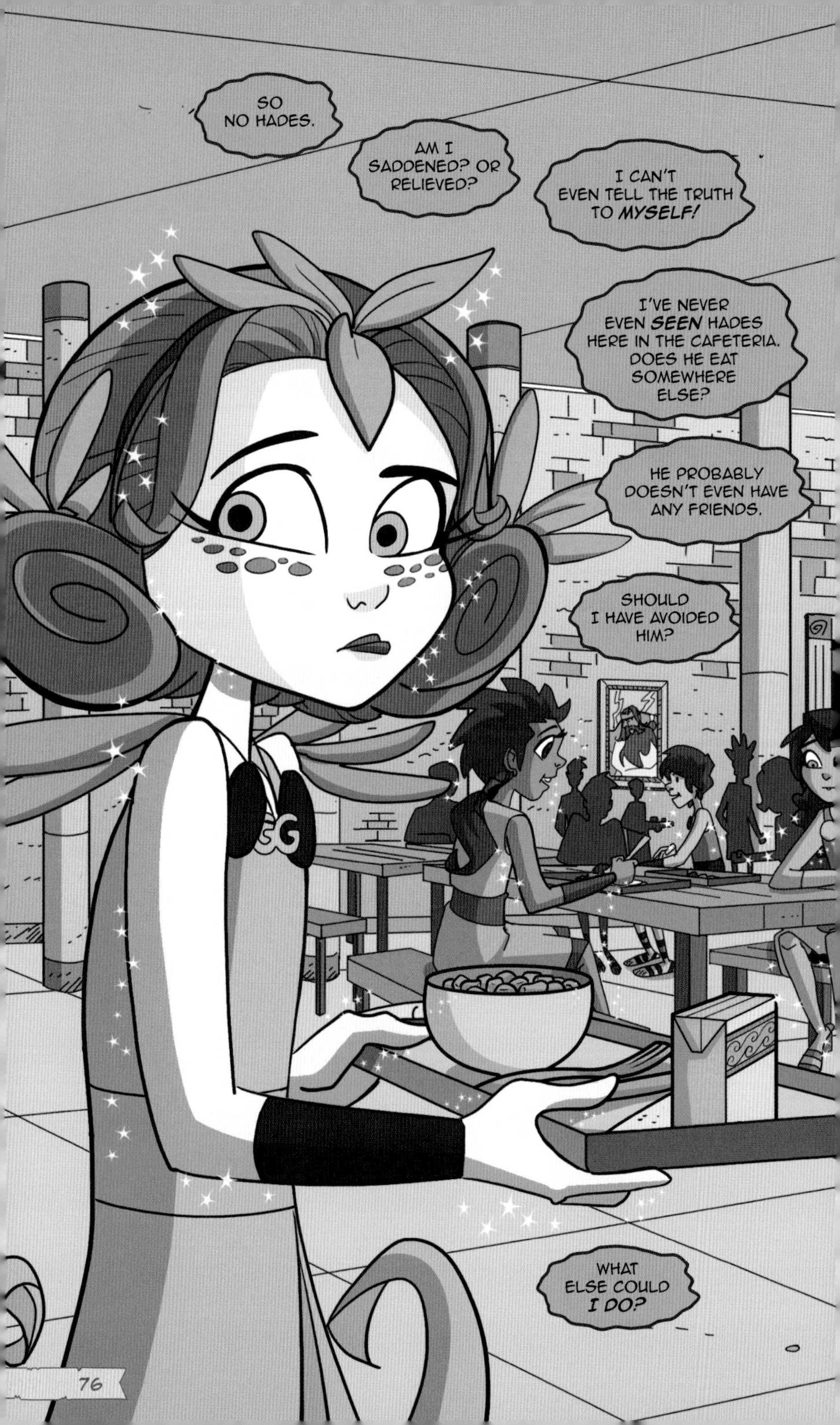
SO NO HADES.
AM I SADDENED? OR RELIEVED?
I CAN'T EVEN TELL THE TRUTH TO *MYSELF!*
I'VE NEVER EVEN *SEEN* HADES HERE IN THE CAFETERIA. DOES HE EAT SOMEWHERE ELSE?
HE PROBABLY DOESN'T EVEN HAVE ANY FRIENDS.
SHOULD I HAVE AVOIDED HIM?
WHAT ELSE COULD *I DO?*

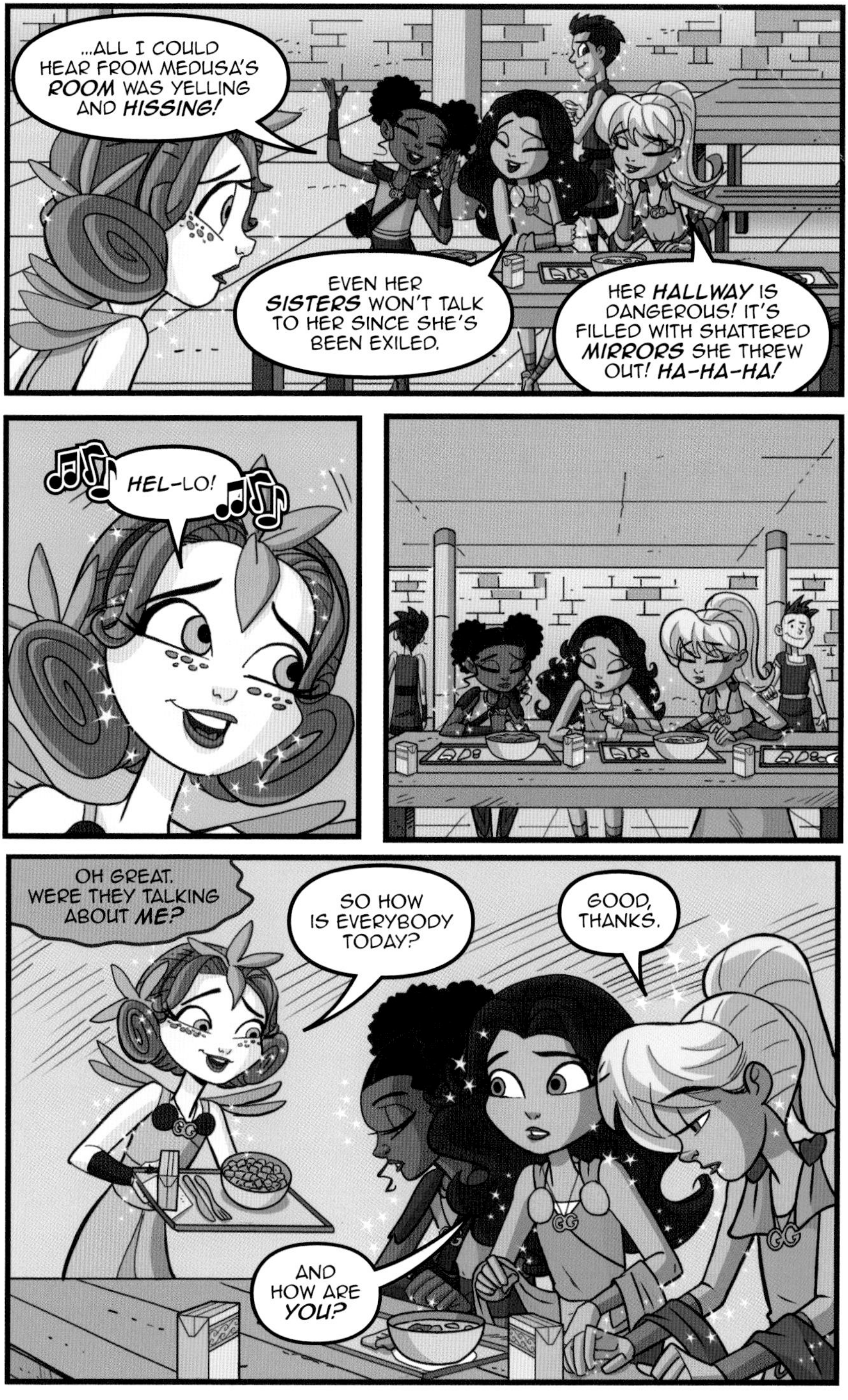
...ALL I COULD HEAR FROM MEDUSA'S ROOM WAS YELLING AND HISSING!
EVEN HER SISTERS WON'T TALK TO HER SINCE SHE'S BEEN EXILED.
HER HALLWAY IS DANGEROUS! IT'S FILLED WITH SHATTERED MIRRORS SHE THREW OUT! HA-HA-HA!
HEL-LO!
OH GREAT. WERE THEY TALKING ABOUT ME?
SO HOW IS EVERYBODY TODAY?
GOOD, THANKS.
AND HOW ARE YOU?

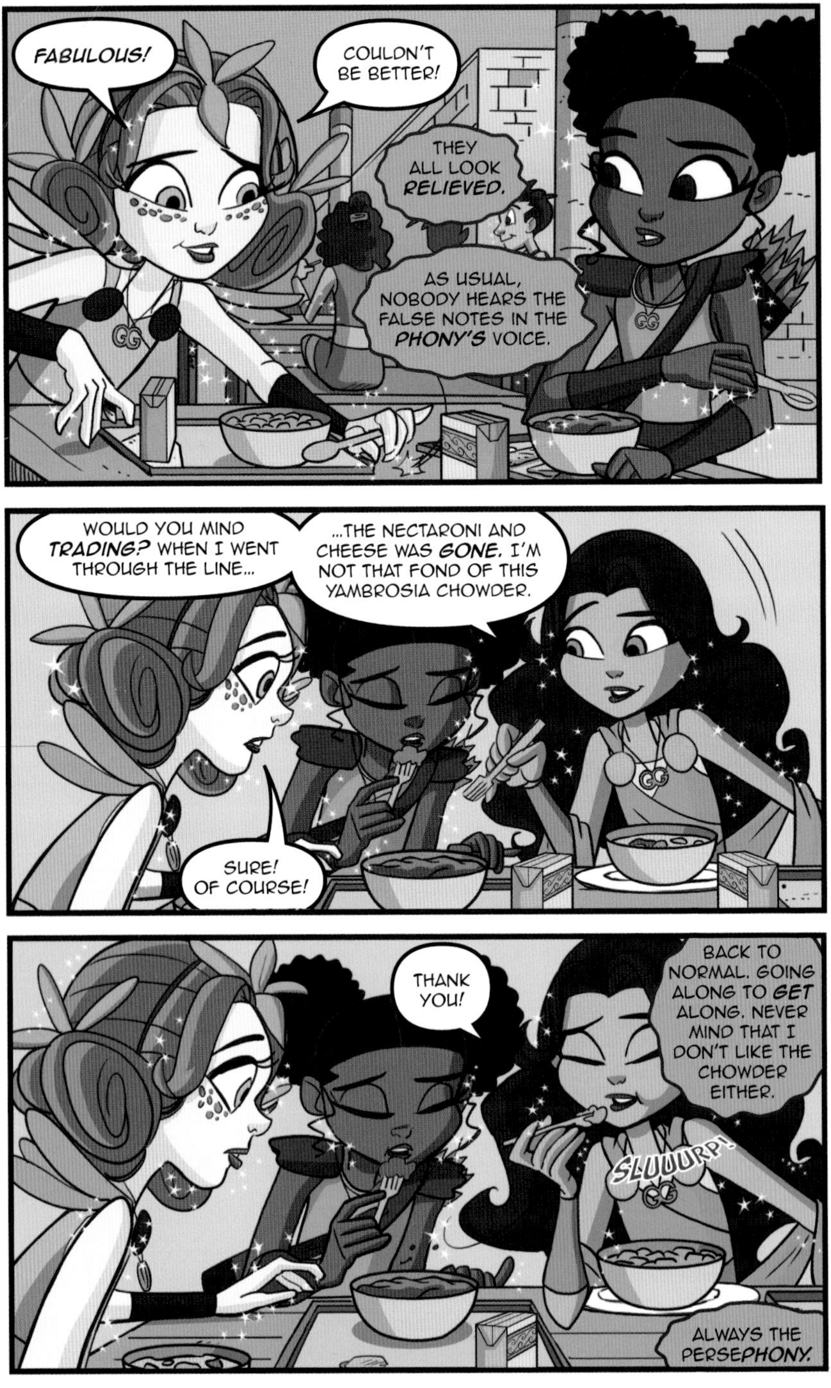
FABULOUS!
COULDN'T BE BETTER!
THEY ALL LOOK RELIEVED.
AS USUAL, NOBODY HEARS THE FALSE NOTES IN THE PHONY'S VOICE.
WOULD YOU MIND TRADING? WHEN I WENT THROUGH THE LINE...
...THE NECTARONI AND CHEESE WAS GONE. I'M NOT THAT FOND OF THIS YAMBROSIA CHOWDER.
SURE! OF COURSE!
THANK YOU!
BACK TO NORMAL. GOING ALONG TO GET ALONG. NEVER MIND THAT I DON'T LIKE THE CHOWDER EITHER.
SLUUURP!
ALWAYS THE PERSEPHONY.

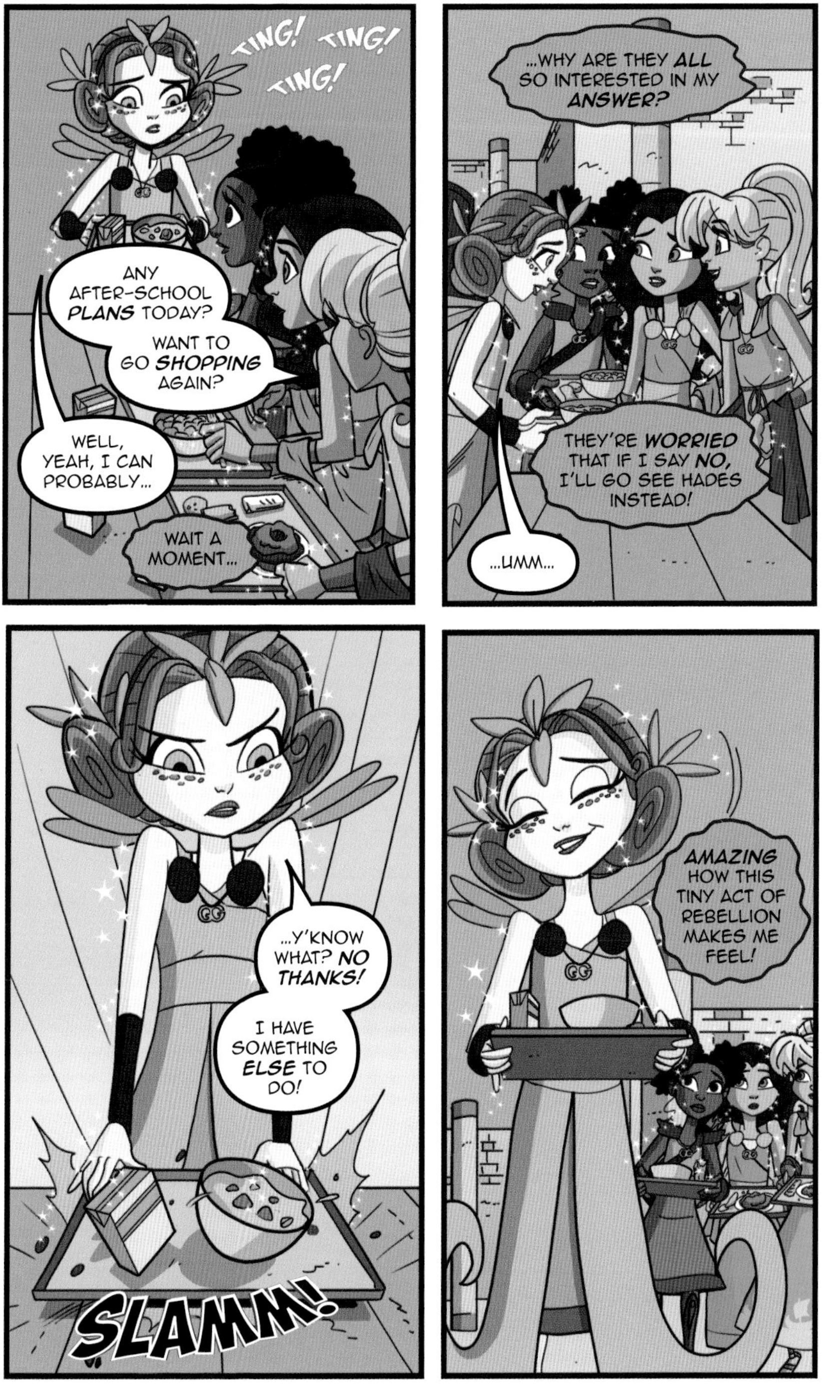
TING! TING!
TING!
ANY AFTER-SCHOOL PLANS TODAY?
WANT TO GO SHOPPING AGAIN?
WELL, YEAH, I CAN PROBABLY...
WAIT A MOMENT...
...WHY ARE THEY ALL SO INTERESTED IN MY ANSWER?
THEY'RE WORRIED THAT IF I SAY NO, I'LL GO SEE HADES INSTEAD!
...UMM...
...Y'KNOW WHAT? NO THANKS!
I HAVE SOMETHING ELSE TO DO!
SLAMM!
AMAZING HOW THIS TINY ACT OF REBELLION MAKES ME FEEL!

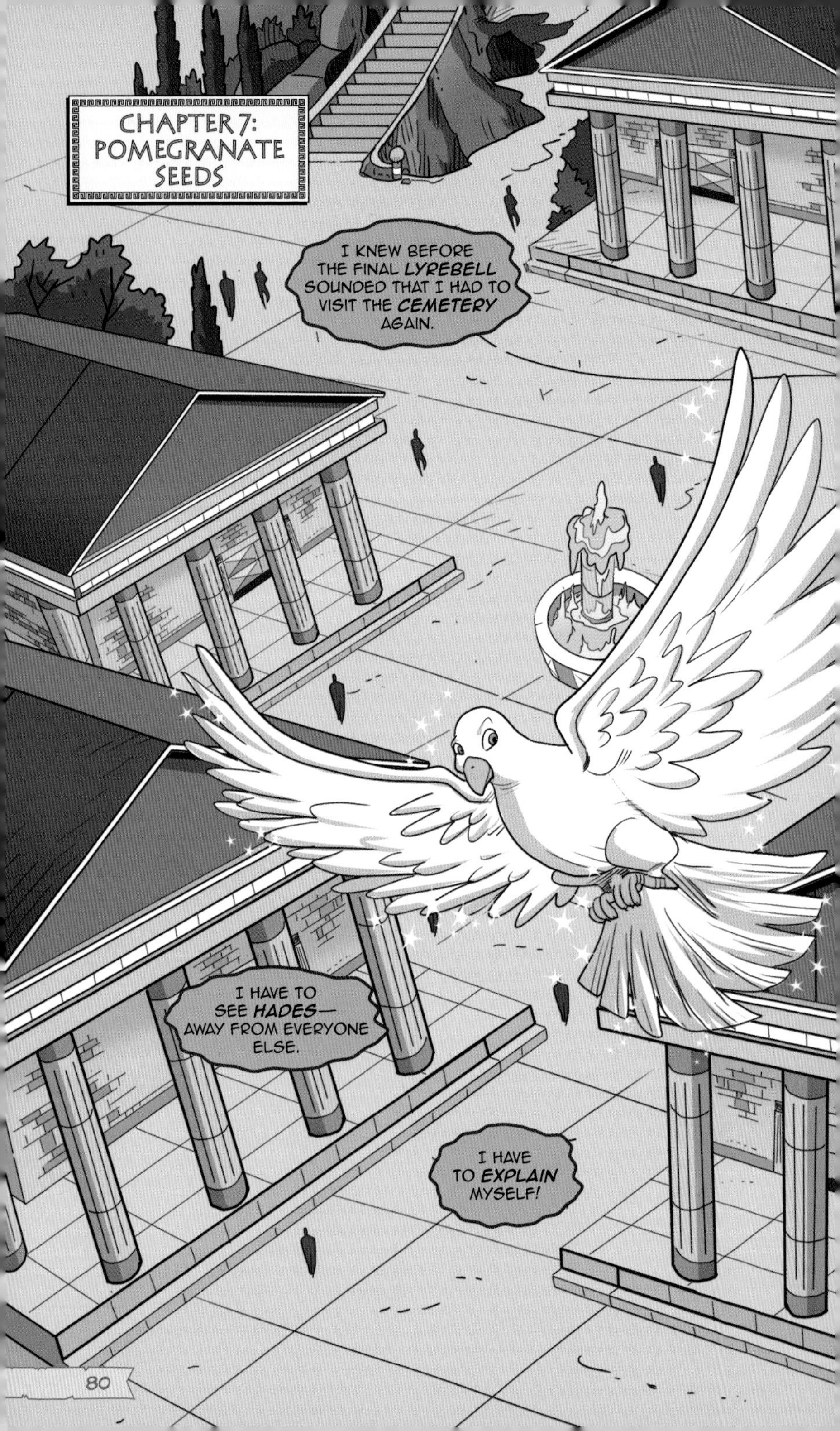

CHAPTER 7: POMEGRANATE SEEDS
I KNEW BEFORE THE FINAL LYREBELL SOUNDED THAT I HAD TO VISIT THE CEMETERY AGAIN.
I HAVE TO SEE HADES— AWAY FROM EVERYONE ELSE.
I HAVE TO EXPLAIN MYSELF!

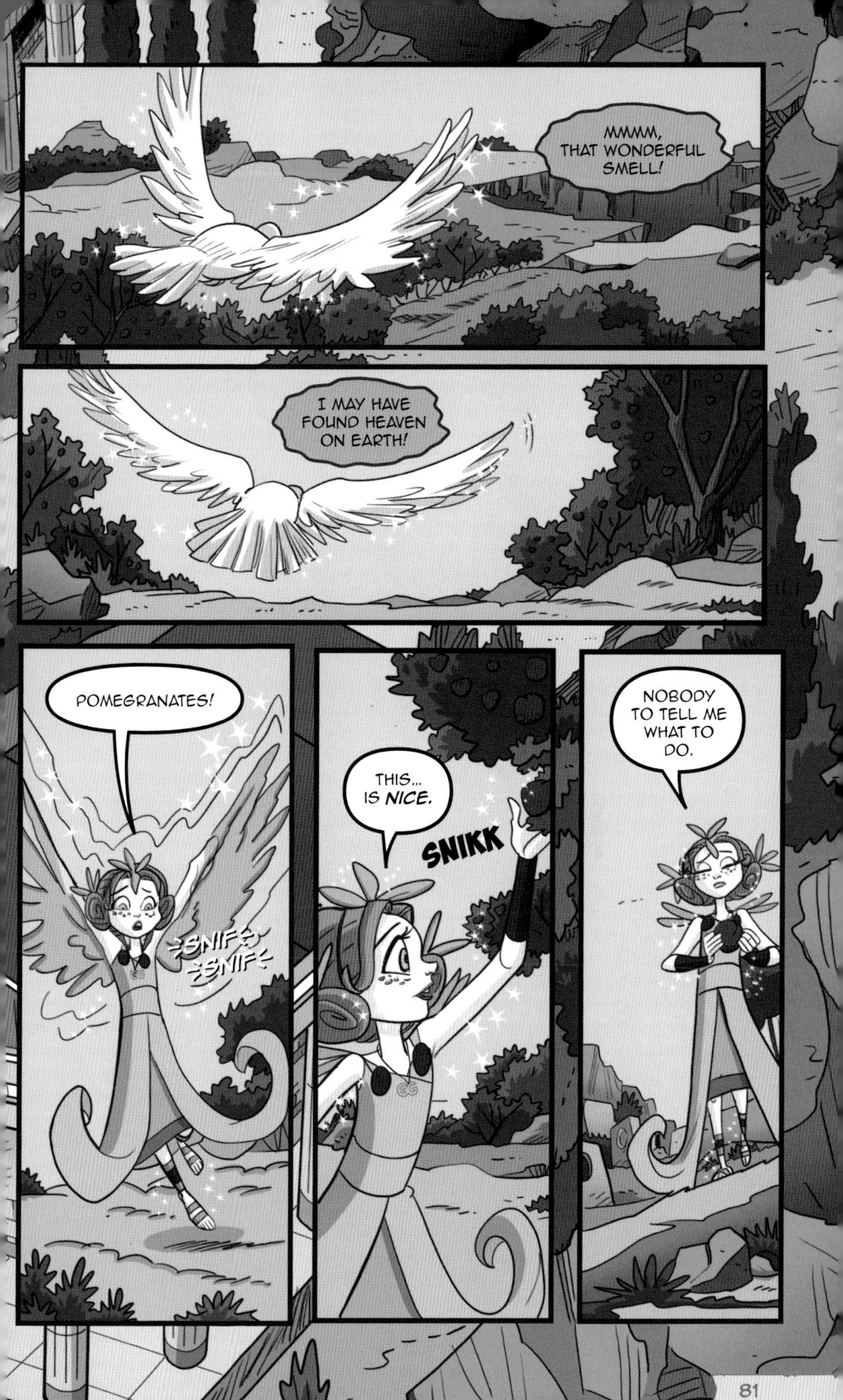
MMMM, THAT WONDERFUL SMELL!
I MAY HAVE FOUND HEAVEN ON EARTH!
POMEGRANATES!
SNIF SNIF
THIS... IS NICE.
SNIKK
NOBODY TO TELL ME WHAT TO DO.

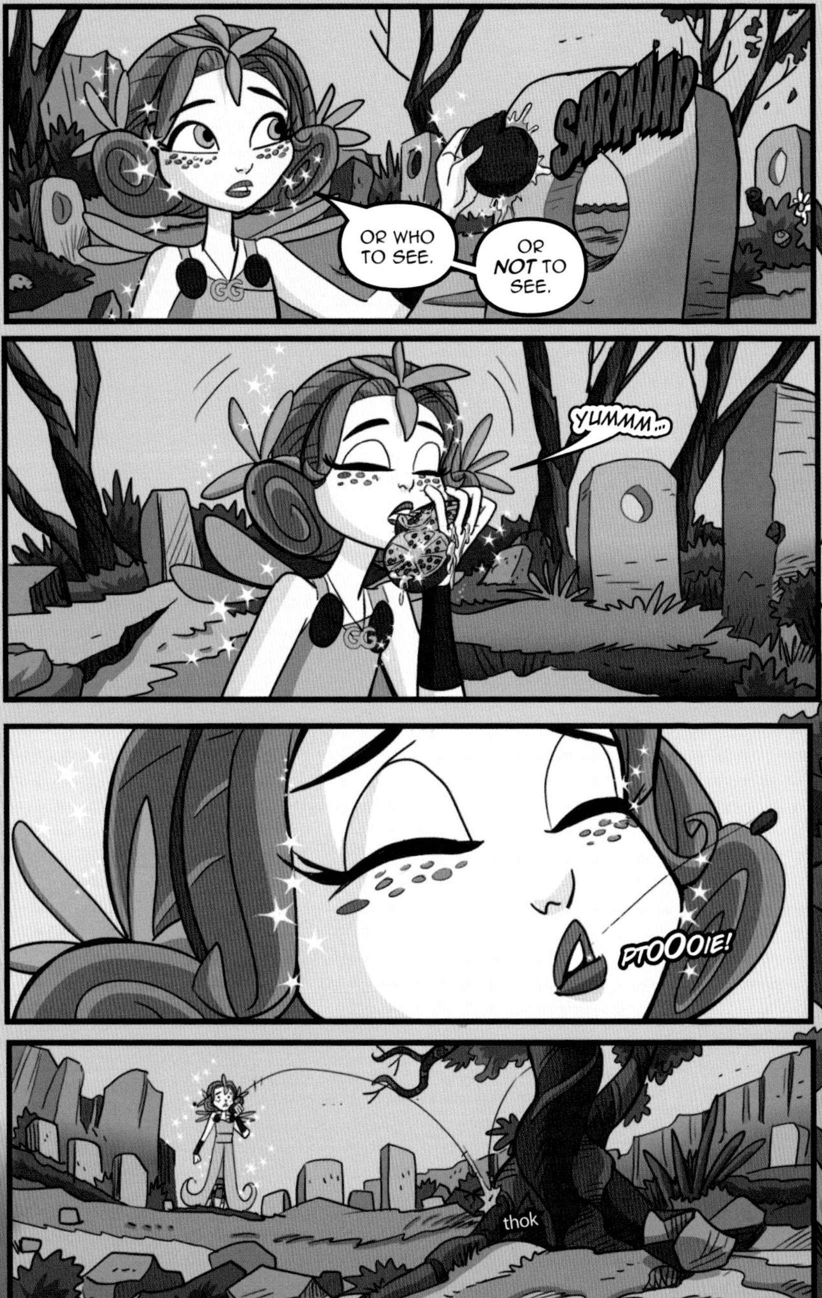
SHRAAAP
OR WHO TO SEE.
OR *NOT* TO SEE.
YUMMM...
PTOOOIE!
thok

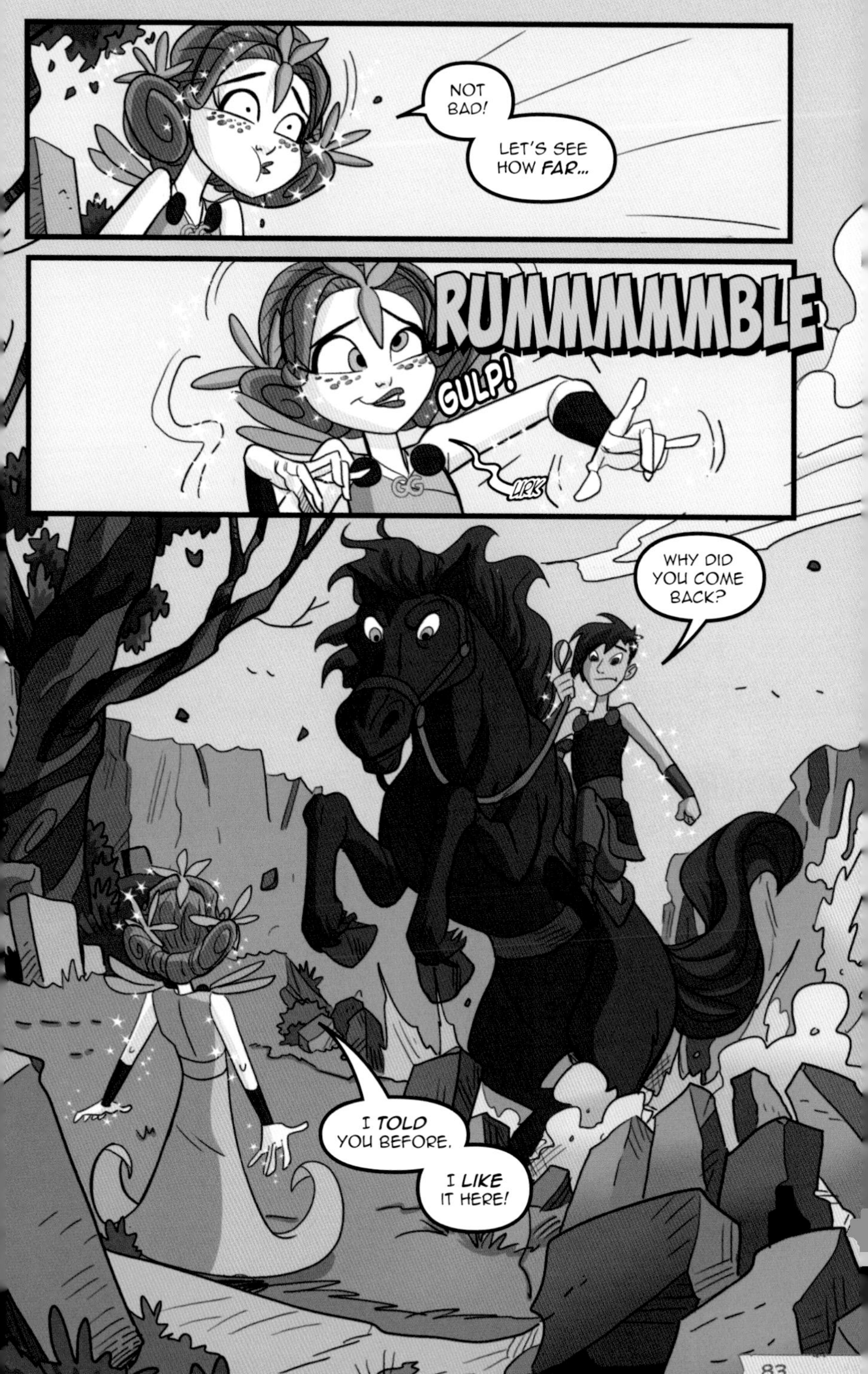

NOT BAD!
LET'S SEE HOW FAR...
RUMMMMMMBLE
GULP!
URK
WHY DID YOU COME BACK?
I TOLD YOU BEFORE.
I LIKE IT HERE!

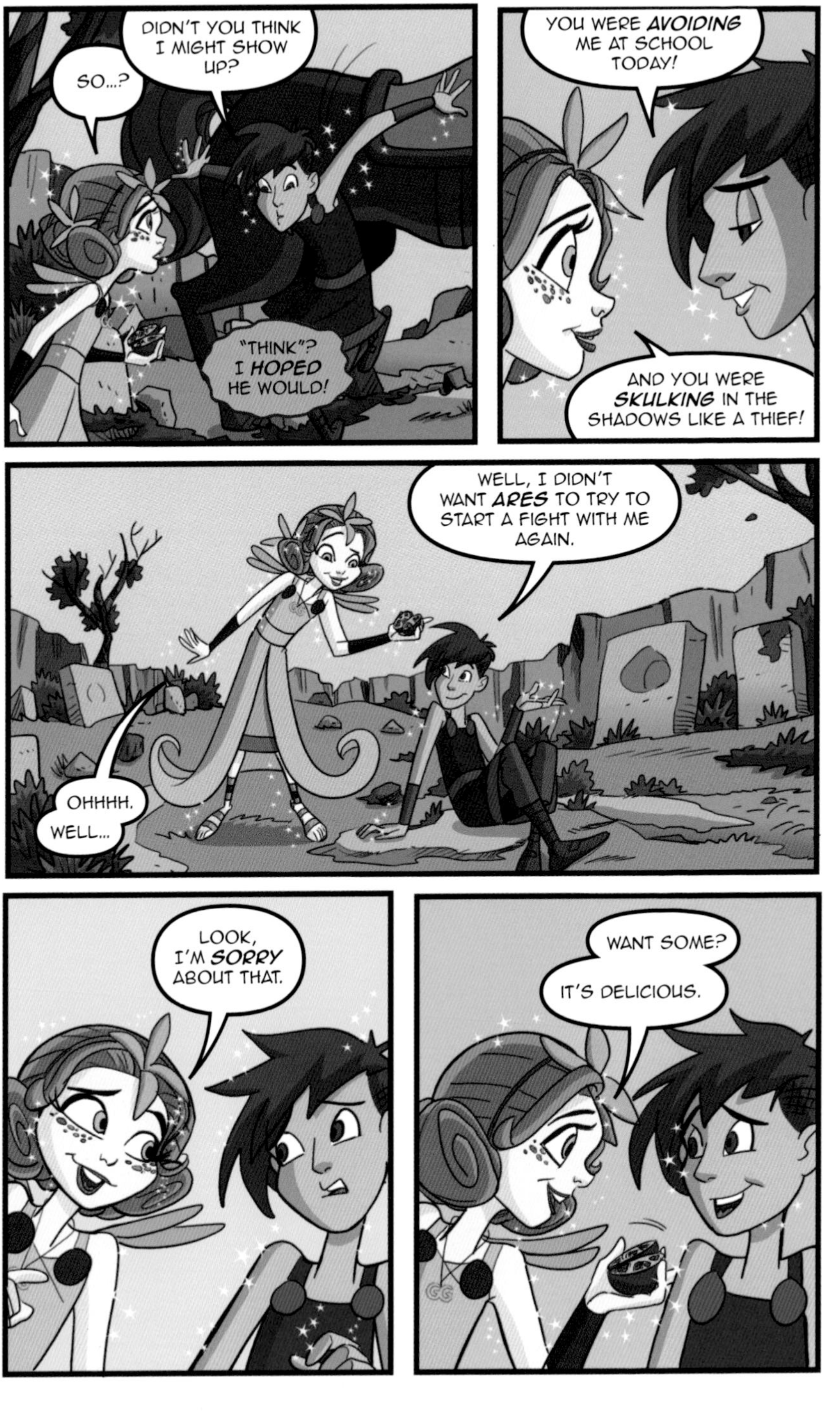
SO...?
DIDN'T YOU THINK I MIGHT SHOW UP?
"THINK"? I **HOPED** HE WOULD!
YOU WERE **AVOIDING** ME AT SCHOOL TODAY!
AND YOU WERE **SKULKING** IN THE SHADOWS LIKE A THIEF!
WELL, I DIDN'T WANT **ARES** TO TRY TO START A FIGHT WITH ME AGAIN.
OHHHH. WELL...
LOOK, I'M **SORRY** ABOUT THAT.
WANT SOME?
IT'S DELICIOUS.

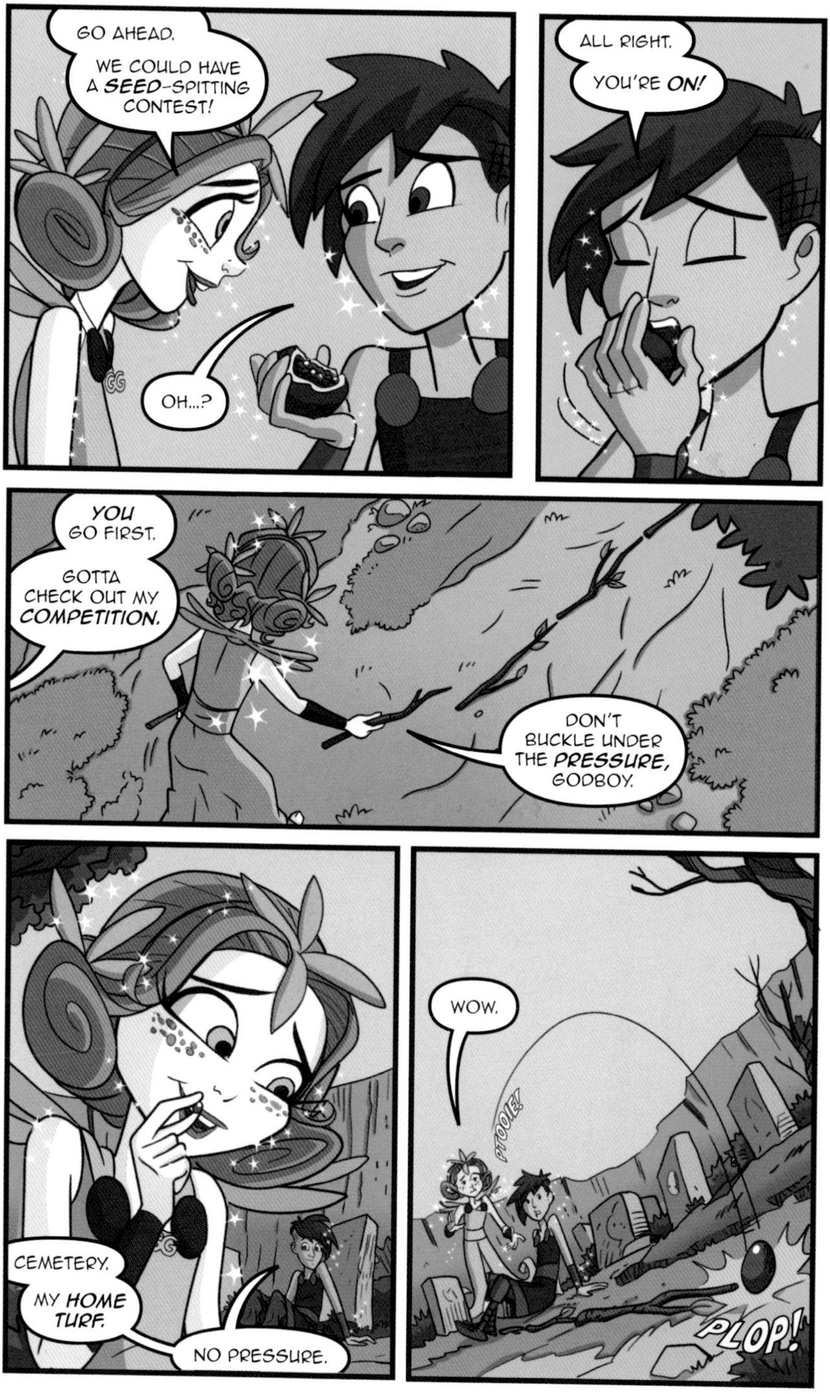

GO AHEAD.
WE COULD HAVE A SEED-SPITTING CONTEST!
OH...?
ALL RIGHT.
YOU'RE ON!
YOU GO FIRST.
GOTTA CHECK OUT MY COMPETITION.
DON'T BUCKLE UNDER THE PRESSURE, GODBOY.
CEMETERY.
MY HOME TURF.
NO PRESSURE.
WOW.
PTOOIE!
PLOP!

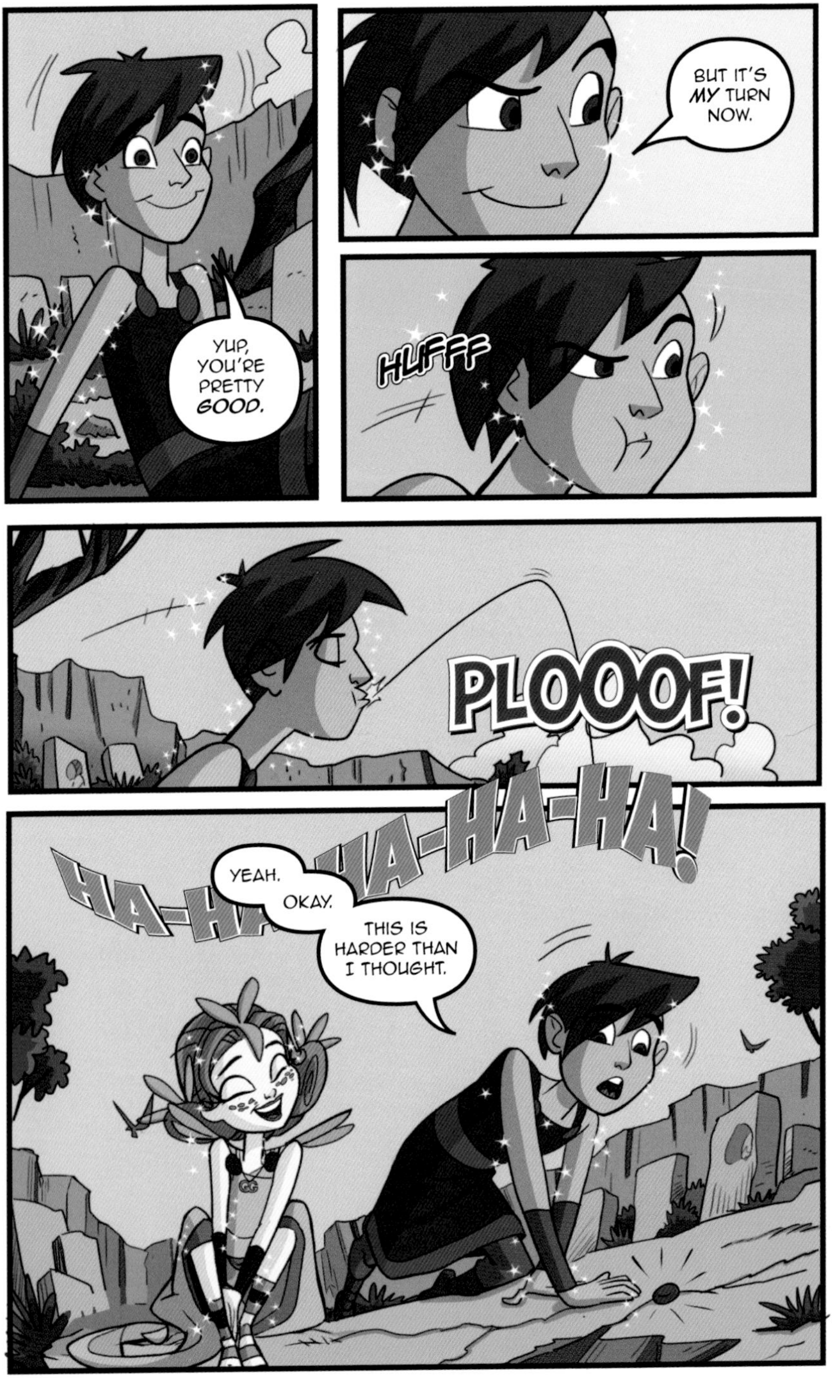
YUP, YOU'RE PRETTY GOOD.
BUT IT'S MY TURN NOW.
HUFFF
PLOOOF!
HA-HA-HA-HA-HA!
YEAH.
OKAY.
THIS IS HARDER THAN I THOUGHT.

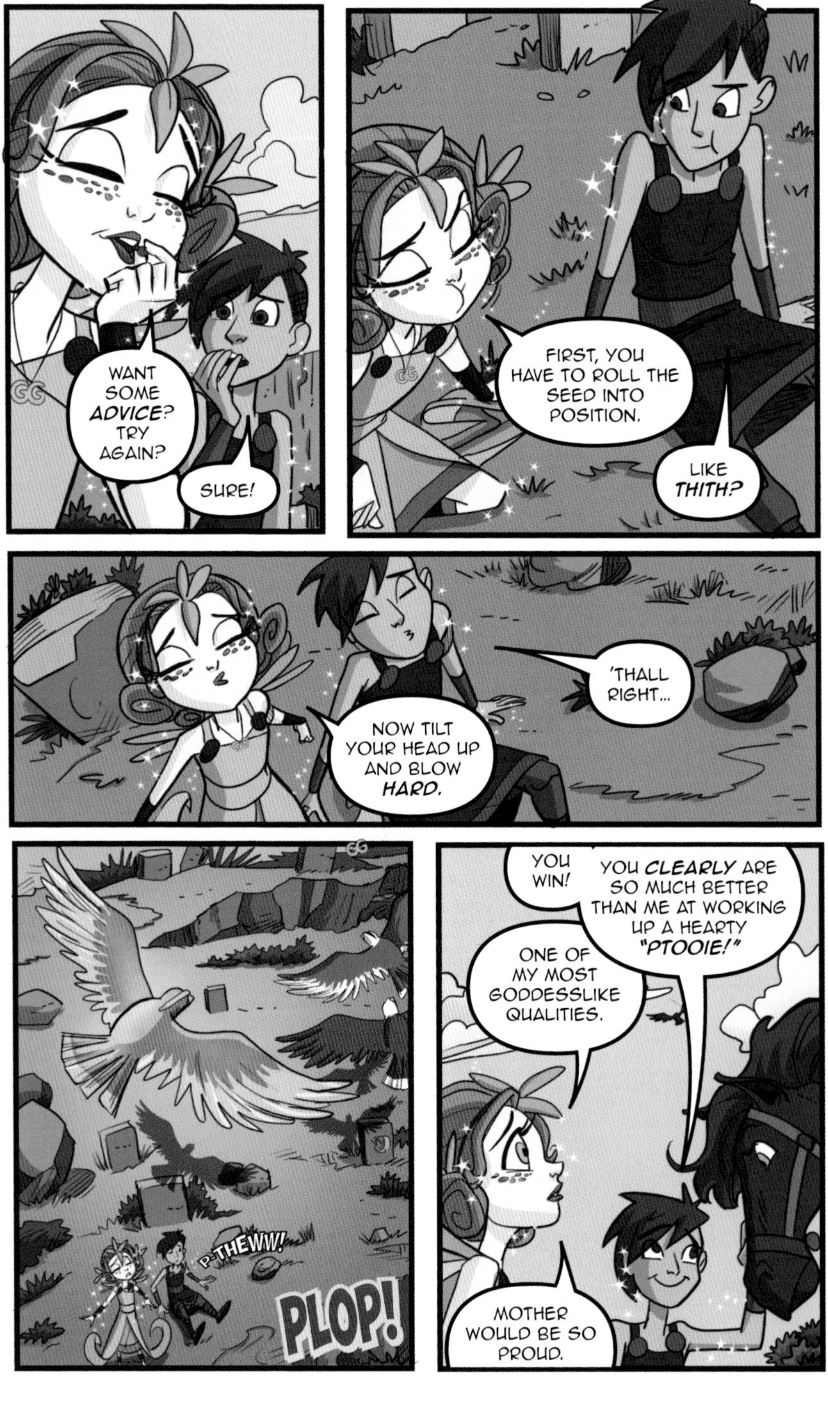
WANT SOME *ADVICE*? TRY AGAIN?
SURE!
FIRST, YOU HAVE TO ROLL THE SEED INTO POSITION.
LIKE *THITH?*
NOW TILT YOUR HEAD UP AND BLOW *HARD.*
'THALL RIGHT...
P-THEWW!
PLOP!
YOU WIN!
YOU *CLEARLY* ARE SO MUCH BETTER THAN ME AT WORKING UP A HEARTY *"PTOOIE!"*
ONE OF MY MOST GODDESSLIKE QUALITIES.
MOTHER WOULD BE SO PROUD.

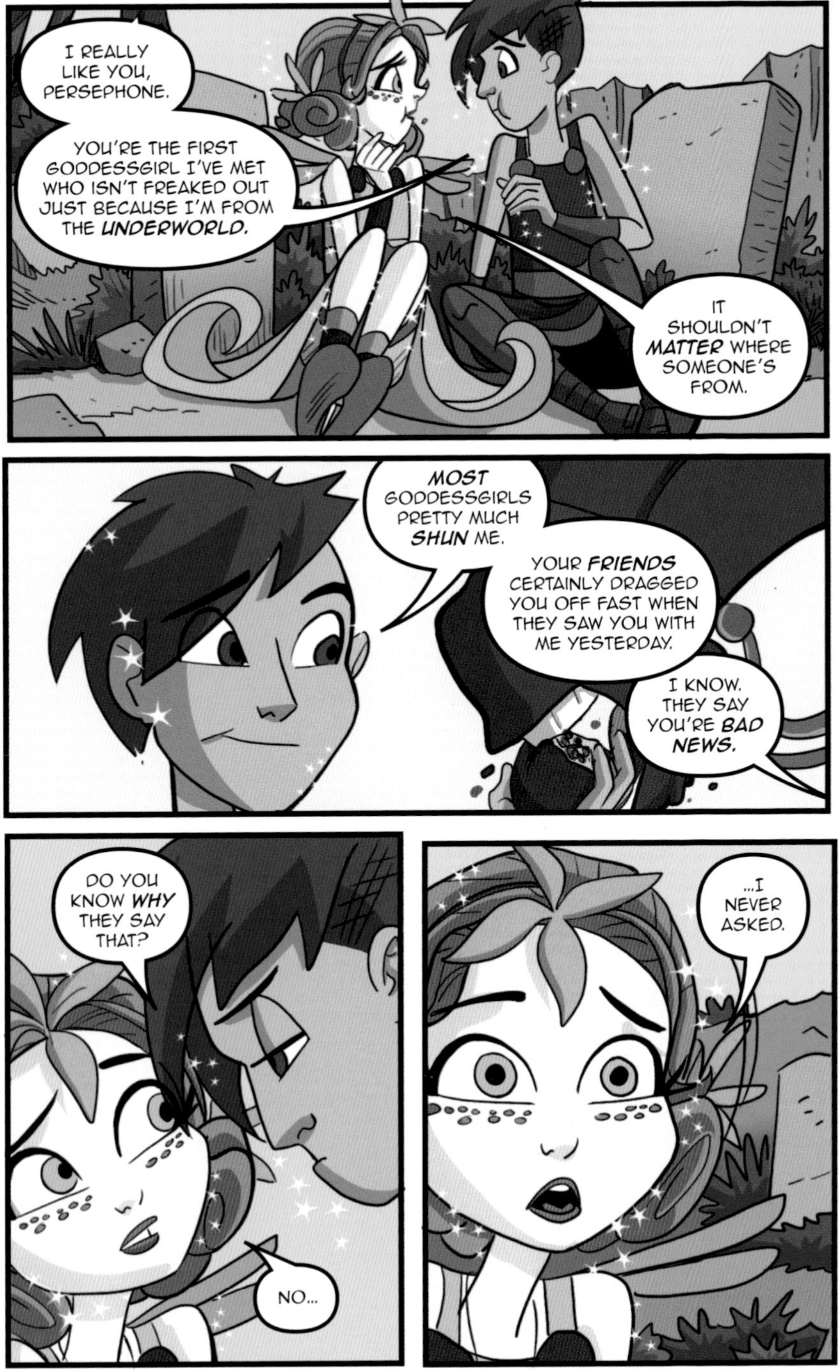
I REALLY LIKE YOU, PERSEPHONE.
YOU'RE THE FIRST GODDESSGIRL I'VE MET WHO ISN'T FREAKED OUT JUST BECAUSE I'M FROM THE UNDERWORLD.
IT SHOULDN'T MATTER WHERE SOMEONE'S FROM.
MOST GODDESSGIRLS PRETTY MUCH SHUN ME.
YOUR FRIENDS CERTAINLY DRAGGED YOU OFF FAST WHEN THEY SAW YOU WITH ME YESTERDAY.
I KNOW. THEY SAY YOU'RE BAD NEWS.
DO YOU KNOW WHY THEY SAY THAT?
NO...
...I NEVER ASKED.

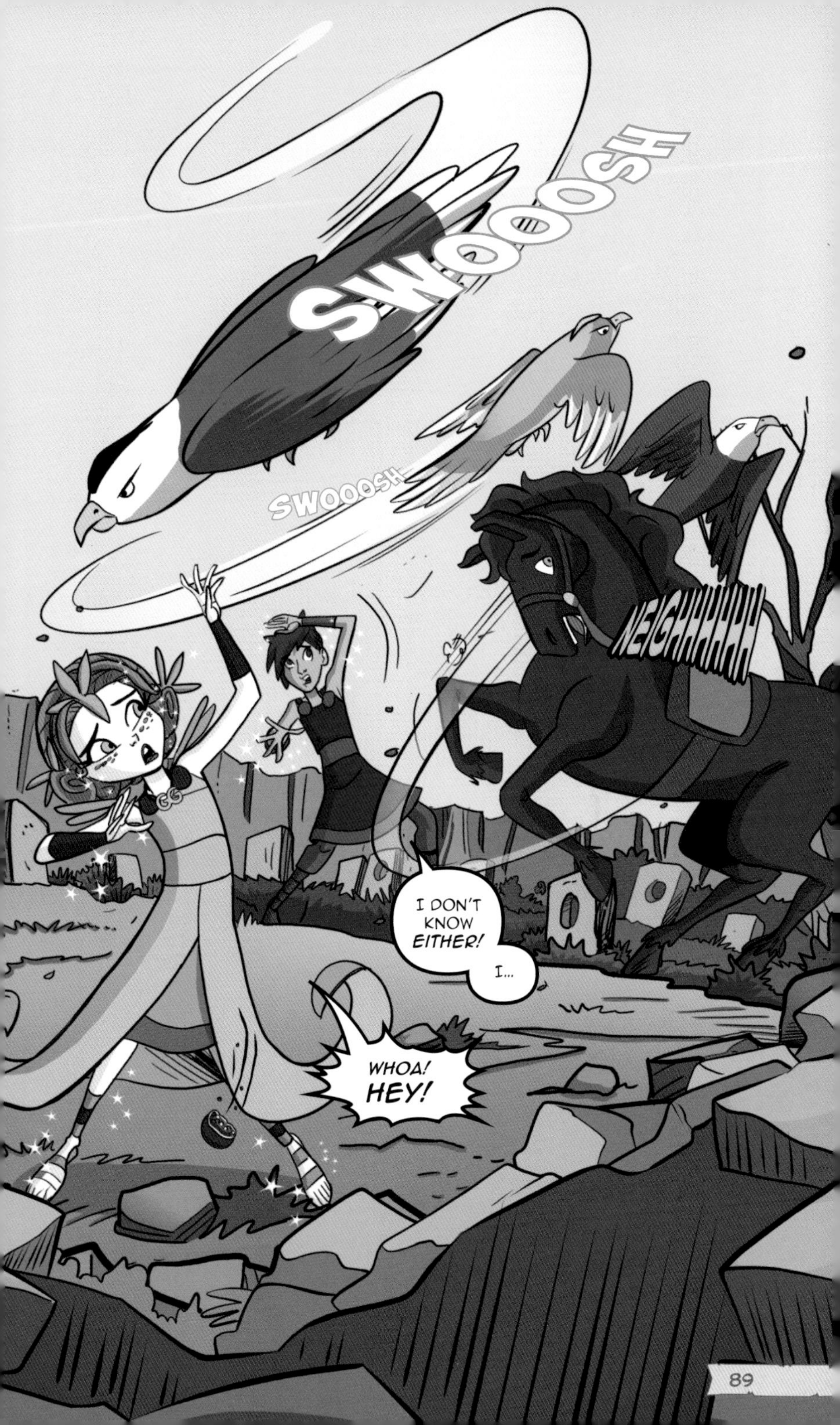
SWOOOSH
SWOOOSH
NEIGHHHHHH
I DON'T KNOW EITHER!
I...
WHOA! HEY!

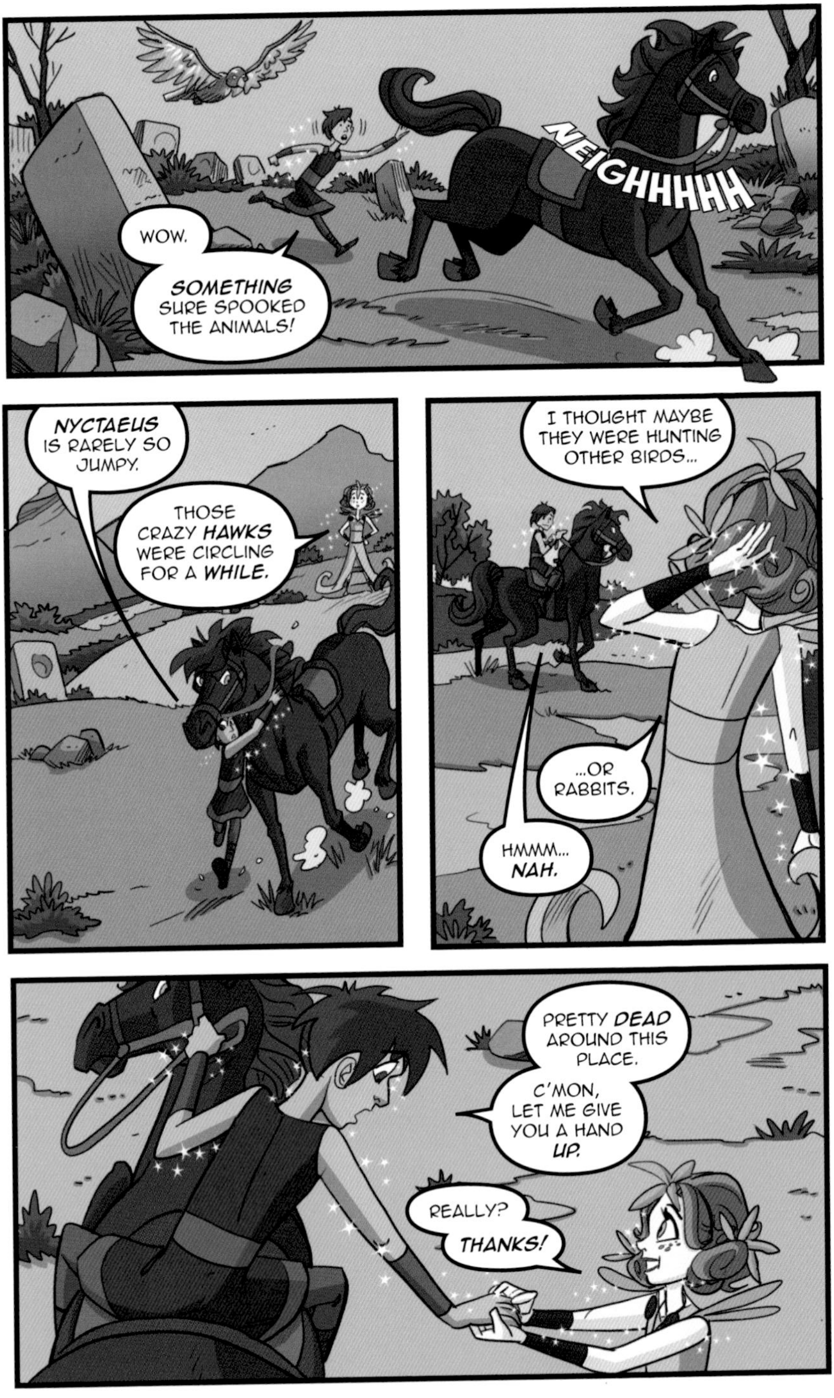
NEIGHHHHHH
WOW.
SOMETHING SURE SPOOKED THE ANIMALS!
NYCTAEUS IS RARELY SO JUMPY.
THOSE CRAZY HAWKS WERE CIRCLING FOR A WHILE.
I THOUGHT MAYBE THEY WERE HUNTING OTHER BIRDS...
...OR RABBITS.
HMMM... NAH.
PRETTY DEAD AROUND THIS PLACE.
C'MON, LET ME GIVE YOU A HAND UP.
REALLY? THANKS!

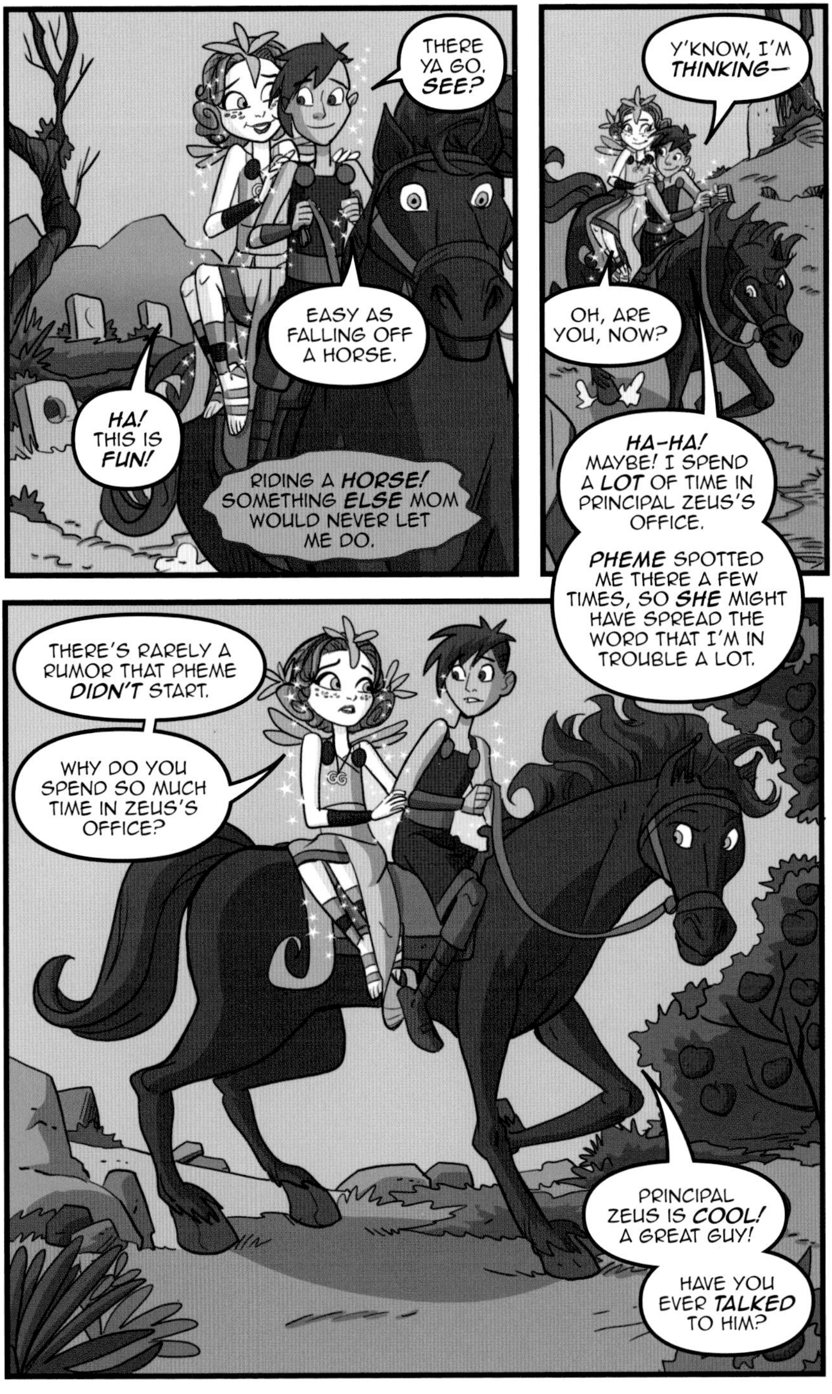
THERE YA GO. SEE?
EASY AS FALLING OFF A HORSE.
HA! THIS IS FUN!
RIDING A HORSE! SOMETHING ELSE MOM WOULD NEVER LET ME DO.
Y'KNOW, I'M THINKING—
OH, ARE YOU, NOW?
HA-HA! MAYBE! I SPEND A LOT OF TIME IN PRINCIPAL ZEUS'S OFFICE.
PHEME SPOTTED ME THERE A FEW TIMES, SO SHE MIGHT HAVE SPREAD THE WORD THAT I'M IN TROUBLE A LOT.
THERE'S RARELY A RUMOR THAT PHEME DIDN'T START.
WHY DO YOU SPEND SO MUCH TIME IN ZEUS'S OFFICE?
PRINCIPAL ZEUS IS COOL! A GREAT GUY!
HAVE YOU EVER TALKED TO HIM?

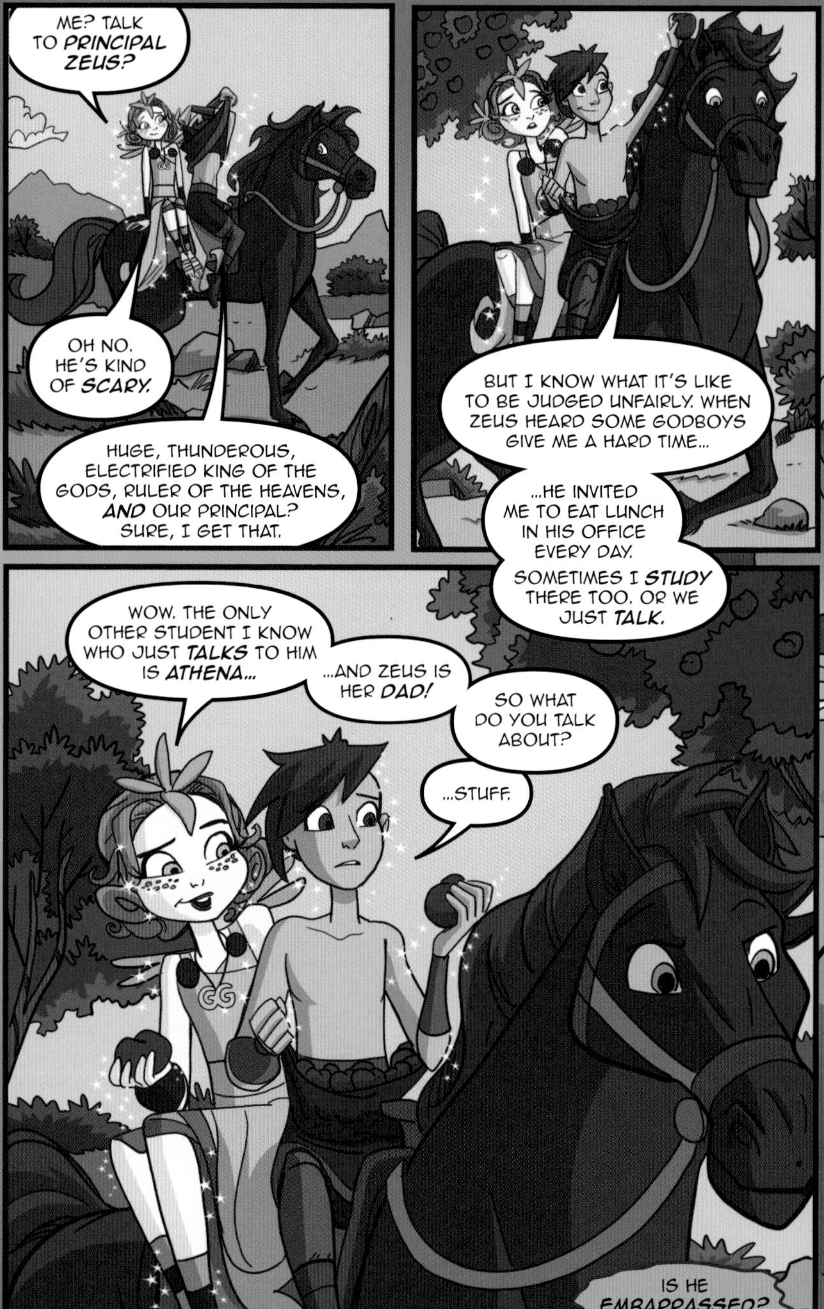
ME? TALK TO PRINCIPAL ZEUS?
OH NO. HE'S KIND OF SCARY.
HUGE, THUNDEROUS, ELECTRIFIED KING OF THE GODS, RULER OF THE HEAVENS, AND OUR PRINCIPAL? SURE, I GET THAT.
BUT I KNOW WHAT IT'S LIKE TO BE JUDGED UNFAIRLY. WHEN ZEUS HEARD SOME GODBOYS GIVE ME A HARD TIME...
...HE INVITED ME TO EAT LUNCH IN HIS OFFICE EVERY DAY.
SOMETIMES I STUDY THERE TOO. OR WE JUST TALK.
WOW. THE ONLY OTHER STUDENT I KNOW WHO JUST TALKS TO HIM IS ATHENA...
...AND ZEUS IS HER DAD!
SO WHAT DO YOU TALK ABOUT?
...STUFF.
IS HE EMBARRASSED?

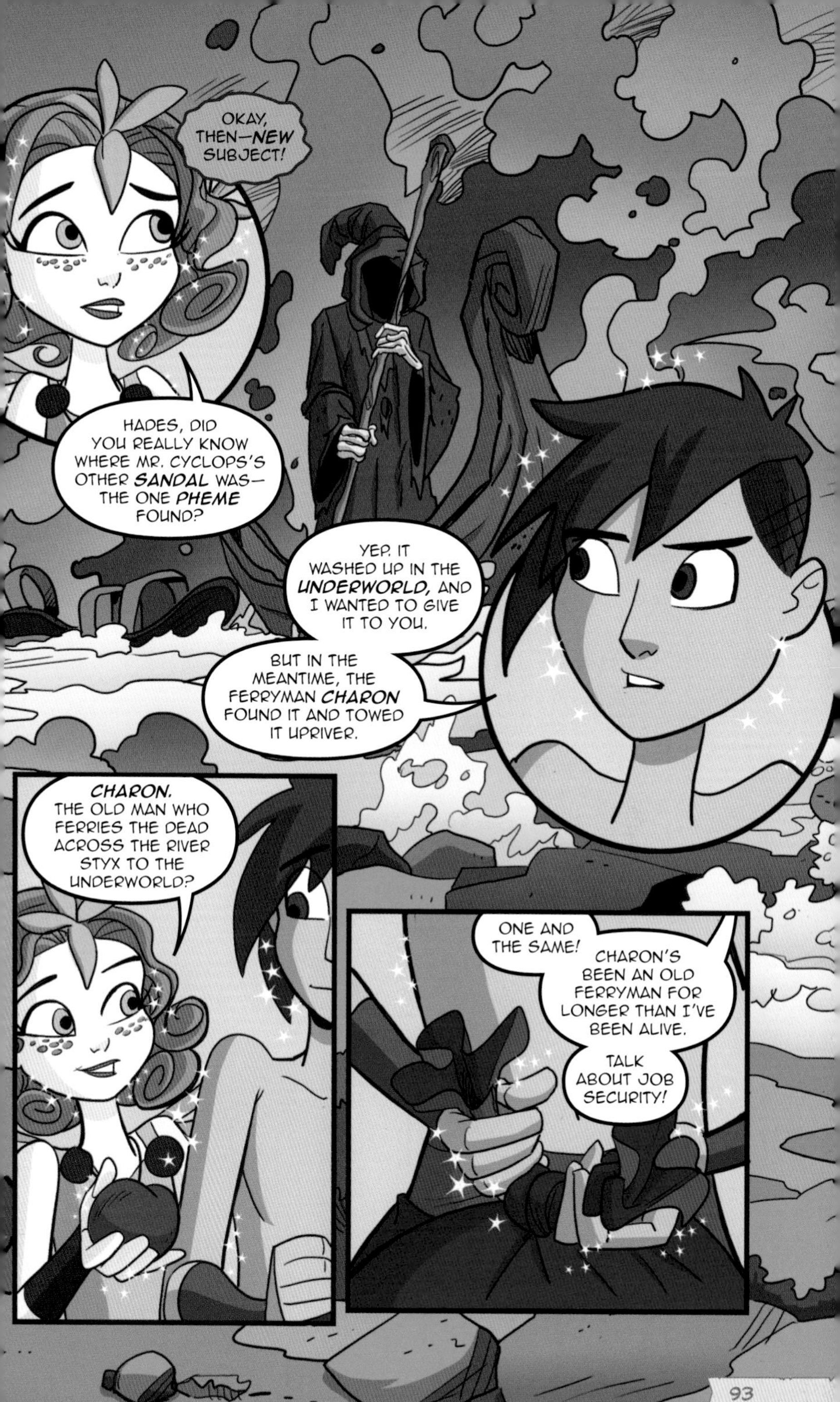

OKAY, THEN—NEW SUBJECT!
HADES, DID YOU REALLY KNOW WHERE MR. CYCLOPS'S OTHER SANDAL WAS— THE ONE PHEME FOUND?
YEP. IT WASHED UP IN THE UNDERWORLD, AND I WANTED TO GIVE IT TO YOU.
BUT IN THE MEANTIME, THE FERRYMAN CHARON FOUND IT AND TOWED IT UPRIVER.
CHARON. THE OLD MAN WHO FERRIES THE DEAD ACROSS THE RIVER STYX TO THE UNDERWORLD?
ONE AND THE SAME!
CHARON'S BEEN AN OLD FERRYMAN FOR LONGER THAN I'VE BEEN ALIVE.
TALK ABOUT JOB SECURITY!

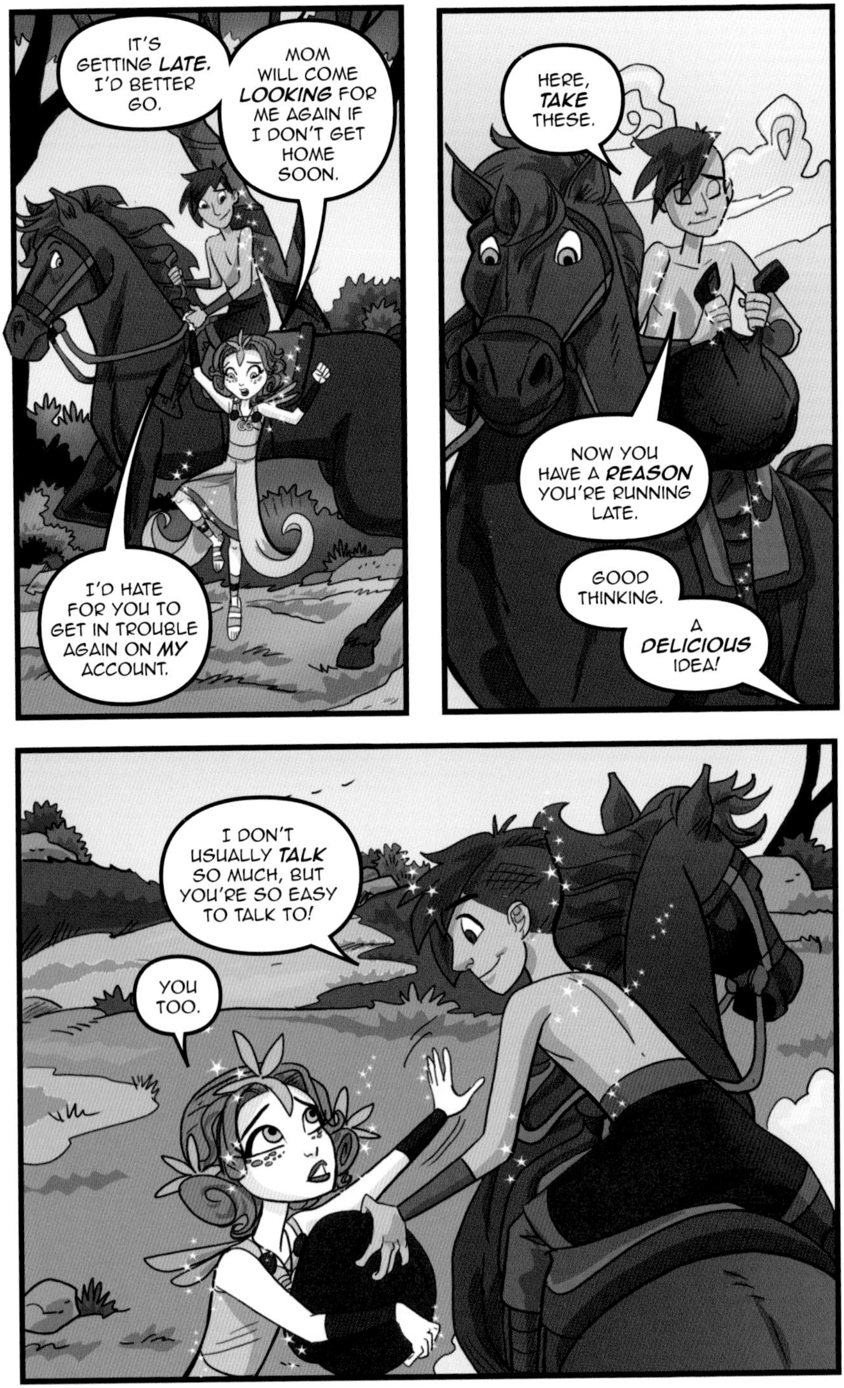
IT'S GETTING LATE. I'D BETTER GO.
MOM WILL COME LOOKING FOR ME AGAIN IF I DON'T GET HOME SOON.
I'D HATE FOR YOU TO GET IN TROUBLE AGAIN ON MY ACCOUNT.
HERE, TAKE THESE.
NOW YOU HAVE A REASON YOU'RE RUNNING LATE.
GOOD THINKING.
A DELICIOUS IDEA!
I DON'T USUALLY TALK SO MUCH, BUT YOU'RE SO EASY TO TALK TO!
YOU TOO.

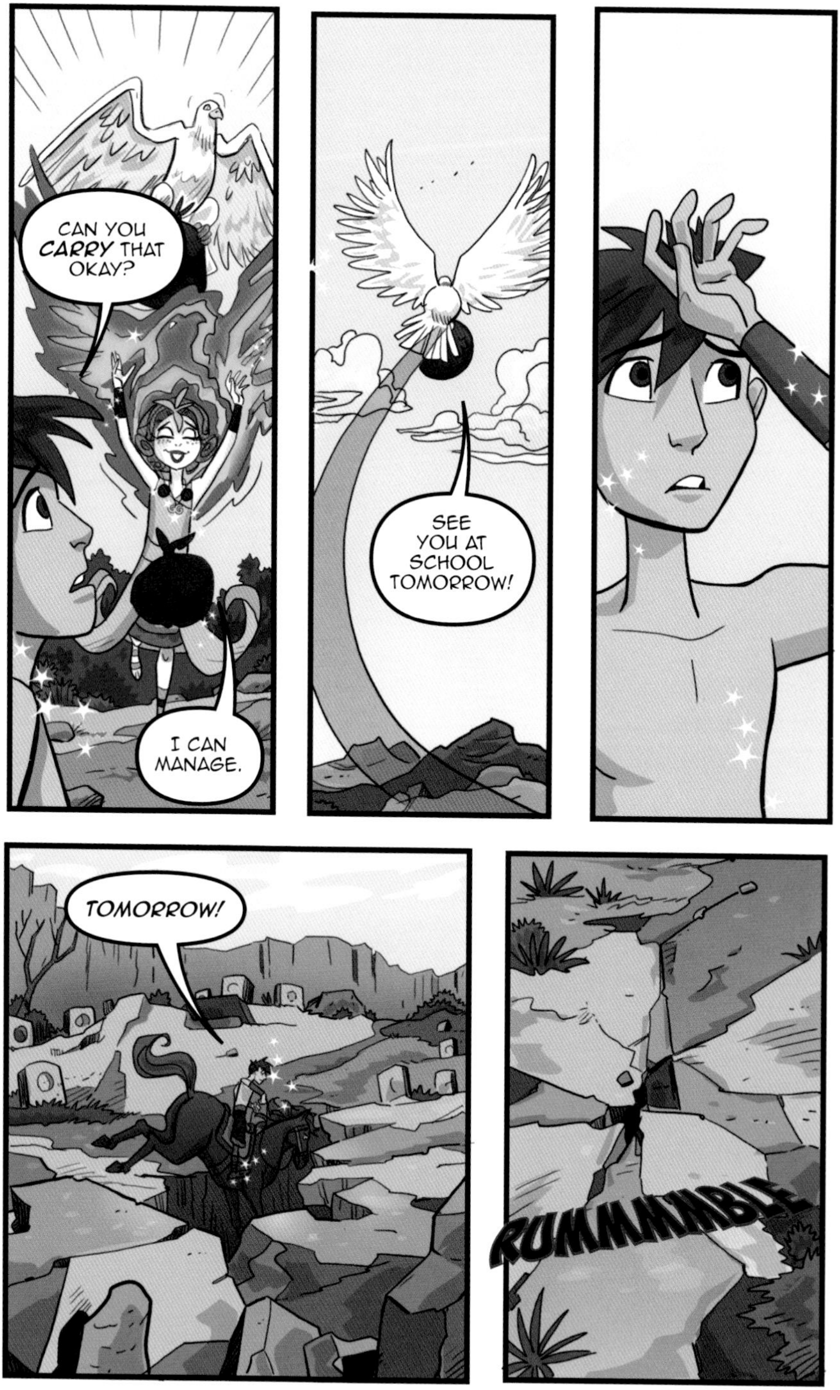
CAN YOU *CARRY* THAT OKAY?
I CAN MANAGE.
SEE YOU AT SCHOOL TOMORROW!
TOMORROW!
RUMMMMBLE

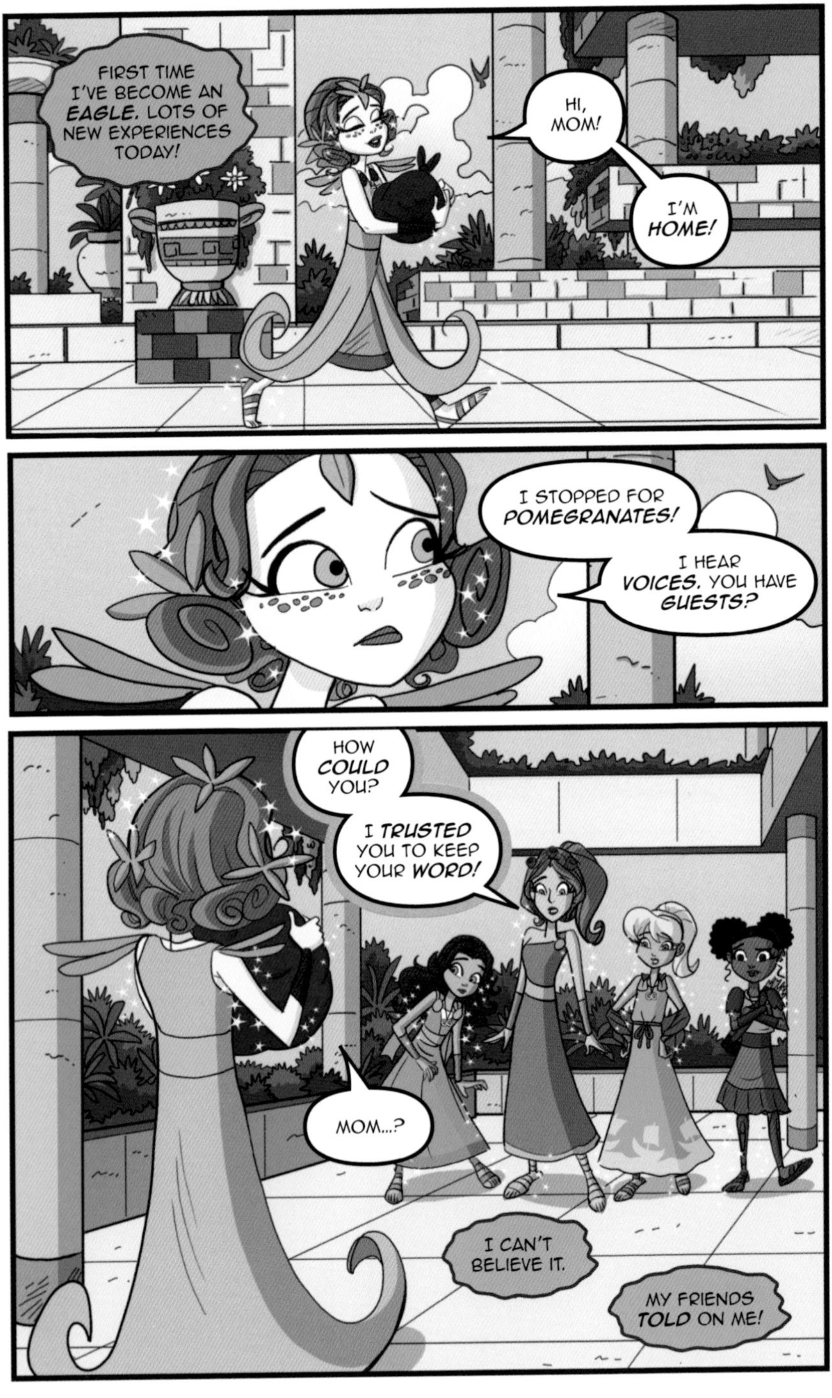
FIRST TIME I'VE BECOME AN EAGLE. LOTS OF NEW EXPERIENCES TODAY!
HI, MOM!
I'M HOME!
I STOPPED FOR POMEGRANATES!
I HEAR VOICES. YOU HAVE GUESTS?
HOW COULD YOU?
I TRUSTED YOU TO KEEP YOUR WORD!
MOM...?
I CAN'T BELIEVE IT.
MY FRIENDS TOLD ON ME!

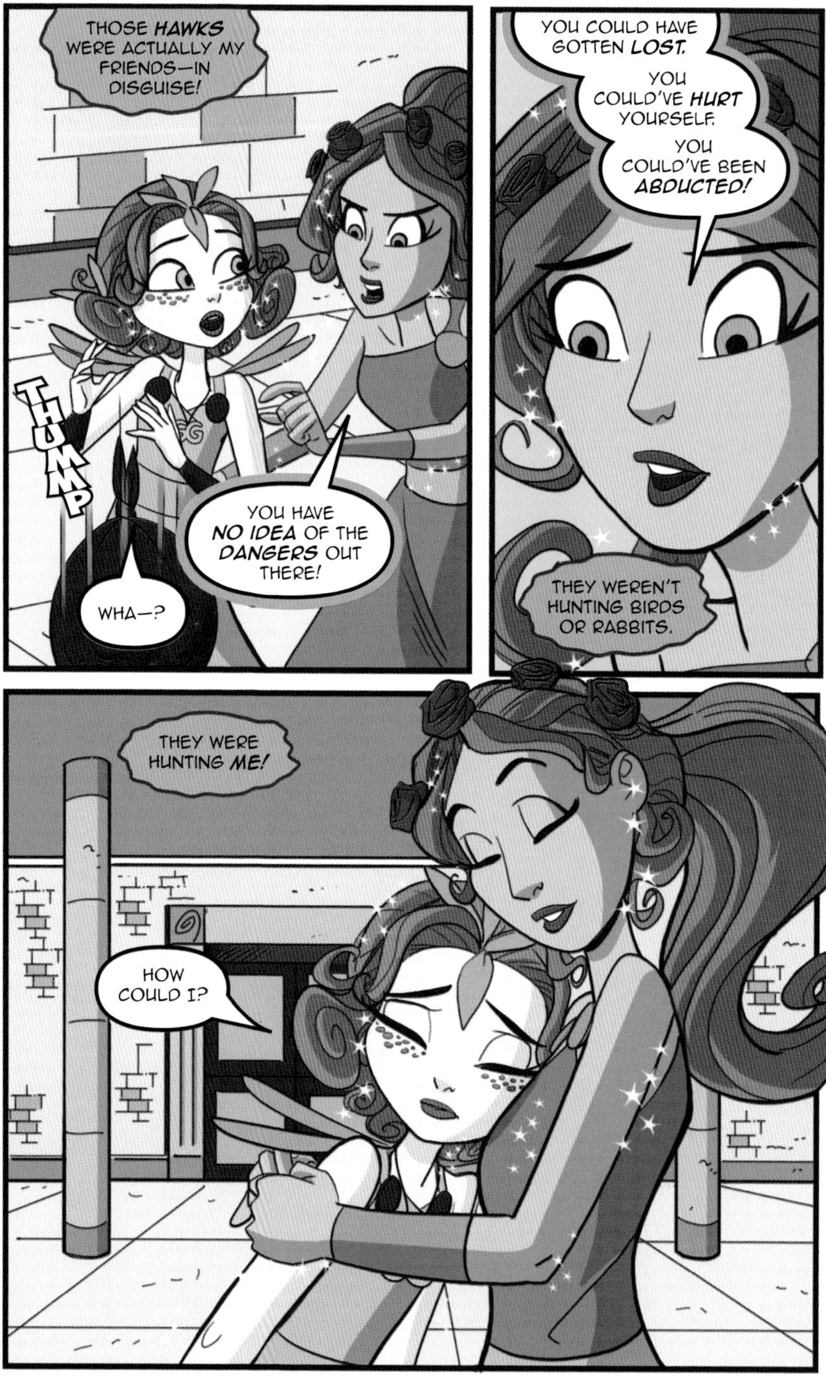
THOSE *HAWKS* WERE ACTUALLY MY FRIENDS—IN DISGUISE!
THUMP
WHA—?
YOU HAVE *NO IDEA* OF THE *DANGERS* OUT THERE!
YOU COULD HAVE GOTTEN *LOST.*
YOU COULD'VE *HURT* YOURSELF.
YOU COULD'VE BEEN *ABDUCTED!*
THEY WEREN'T HUNTING BIRDS OR RABBITS.
THEY WERE HUNTING *ME!*
HOW COULD I?

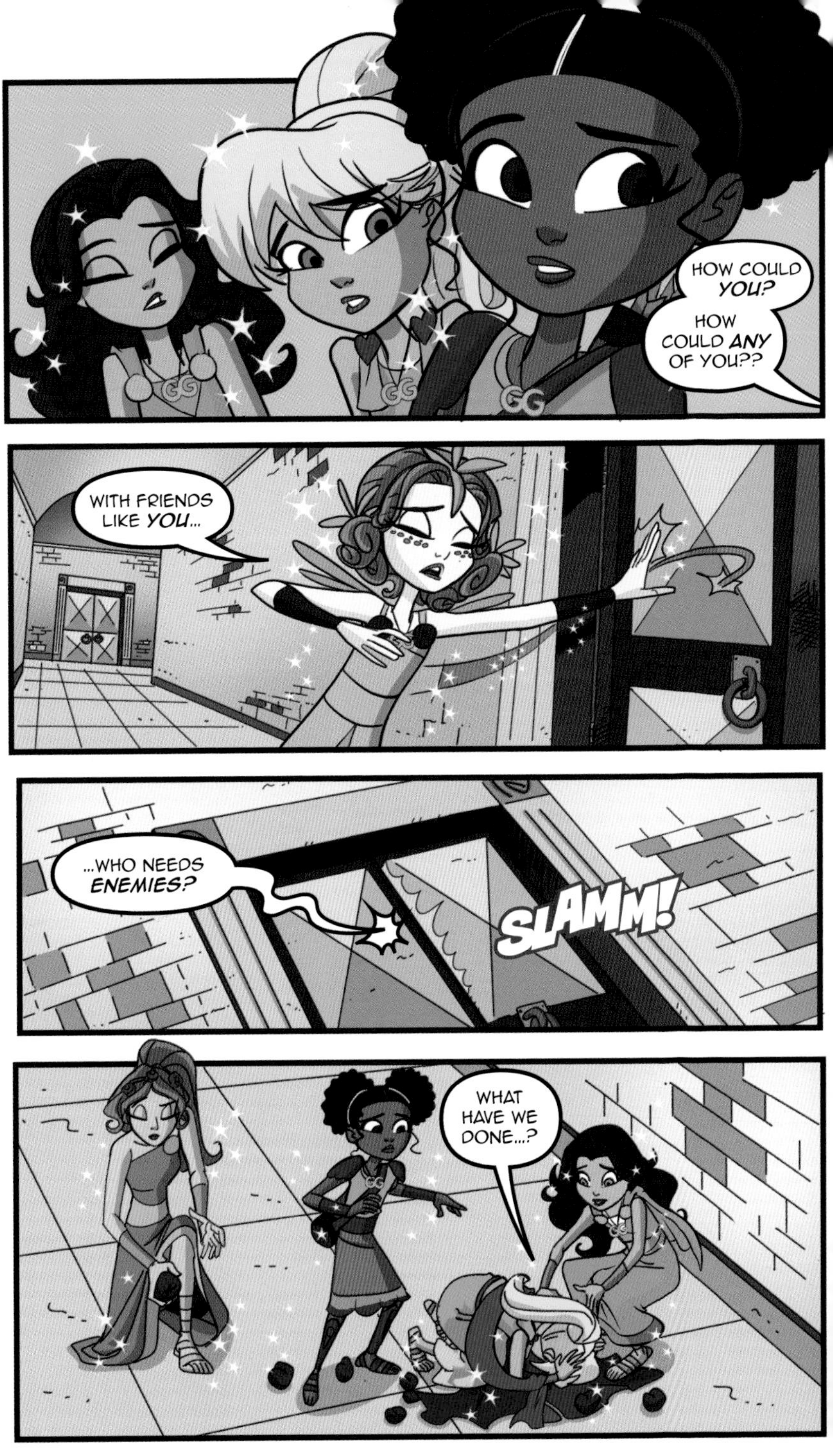
HOW COULD YOU?
HOW COULD ANY OF YOU??
WITH FRIENDS LIKE YOU...
...WHO NEEDS ENEMIES?
SLAMM!
WHAT HAVE WE DONE...?

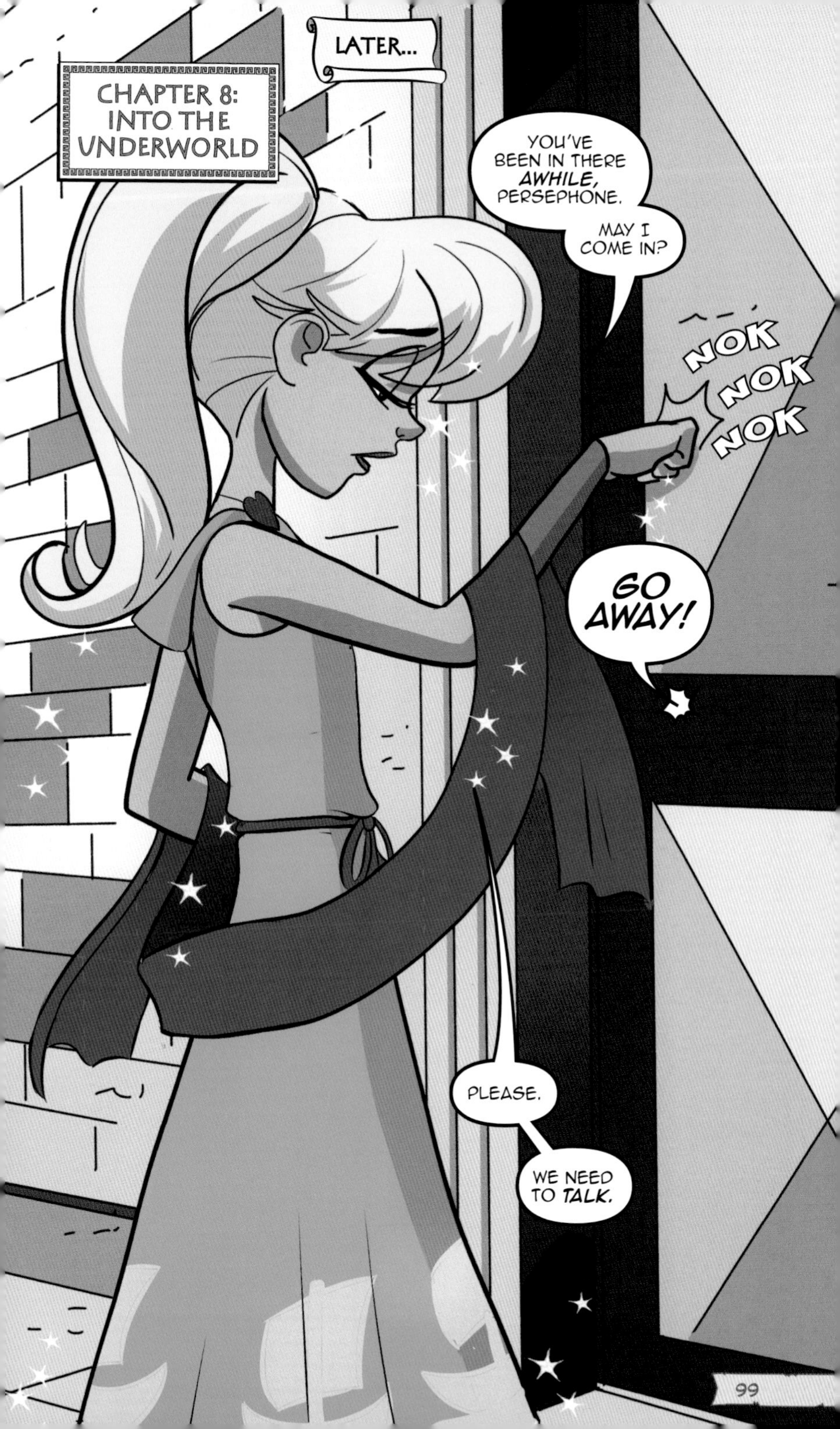

CHAPTER 8: INTO THE UNDERWORLD
LATER...
YOU'VE BEEN IN THERE AWHILE, PERSEPHONE.
MAY I COME IN?
NOK NOK NOK
GO AWAY!
PLEASE.
WE NEED TO TALK.

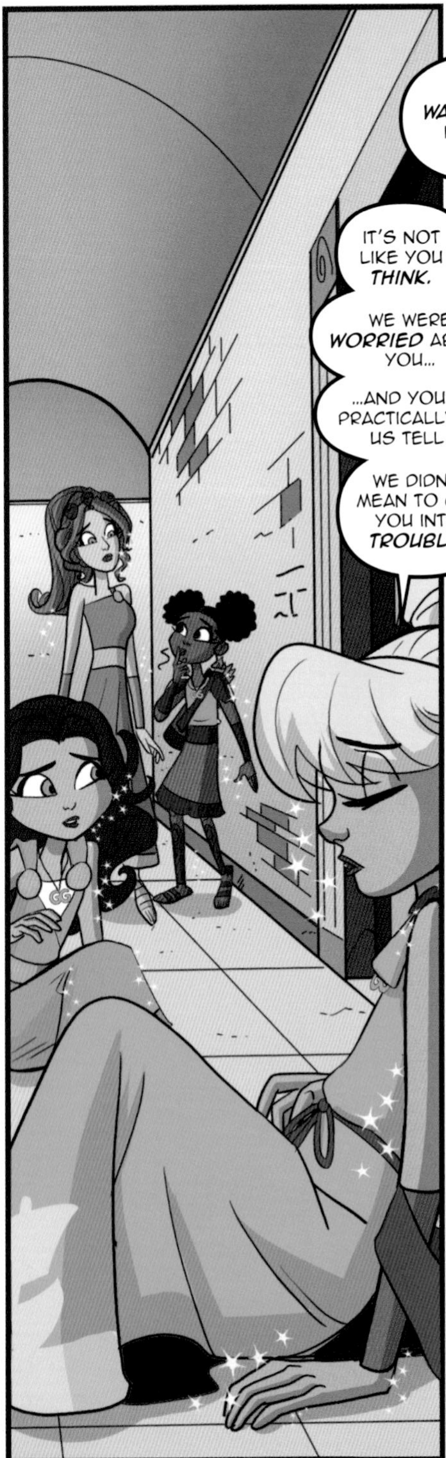
IT'S NOT LIKE YOU THINK.
WE WERE WORRIED ABOUT YOU...
...AND YOUR MOM PRACTICALLY MADE US TELL HER.
WE DIDN'T MEAN TO GET YOU INTO TROUBLE.

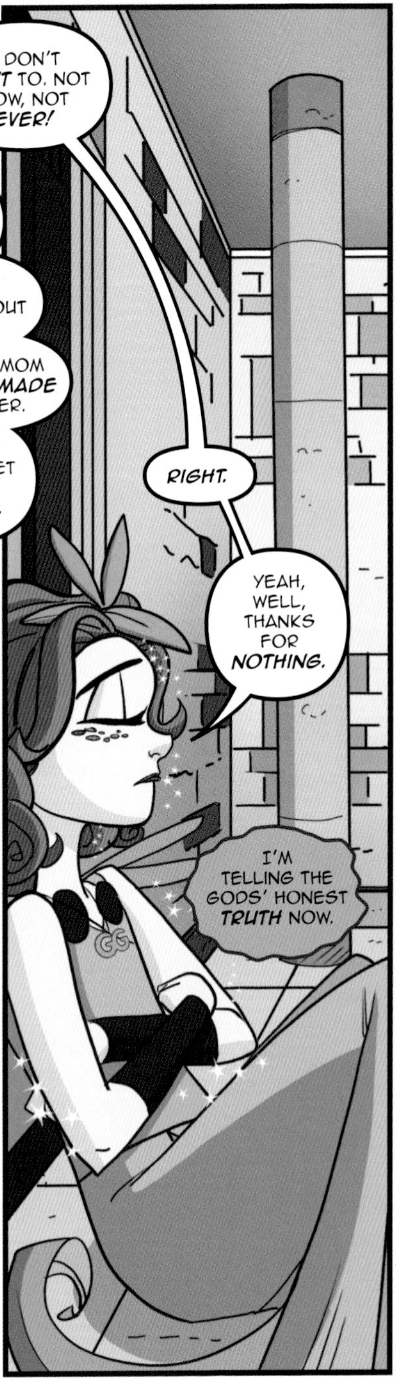
I DON'T WANT TO. NOT NOW, NOT EVER!
RIGHT.
YEAH, WELL, THANKS FOR NOTHING.
I'M TELLING THE GODS' HONEST TRUTH NOW.

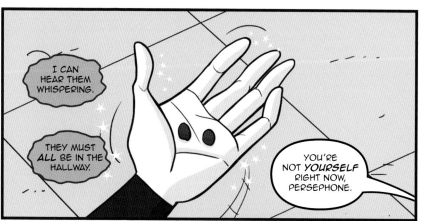

I CAN HEAR THEM WHISPERING.

THEY MUST *ALL* BE IN THE HALLWAY.

YOU'RE NOT *YOURSELF* RIGHT NOW, PERSEPHONE.

WE'LL TALK AT SCHOOL *TOMORROW...*

...AFTER YOU'VE *CALMED DOWN,* OKAY?

HAS ANYONE IN OLYMPUS OR EARTH HISTORY *EVER* CALMED DOWN BECAUSE SOMEONE *TOLD* THEM TO CALM DOWN?

WHOOPS!

OH! SORRY FOR THAT LOOSE *TILE,* DEAR.

I KEEP MEANING TO GET IT FIXED.

IT'S FINE!

"NOT YOURSELF," SHE SAYS.

APHRODITE HAS IT ALL *WRONG*.

THE PERSEPHONE THEY *KNOW* IS JUST PERSEPHONY...

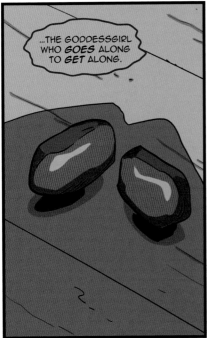

...THE GODDESSGIRL WHO *GOES* ALONG TO *GET* ALONG.

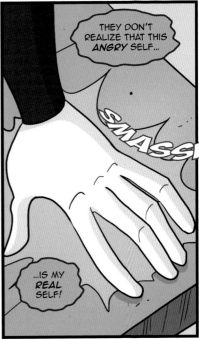

THEY DON'T REALIZE THAT THIS *ANGRY* SELF...

SMASSH

...IS MY *REAL* SELF!

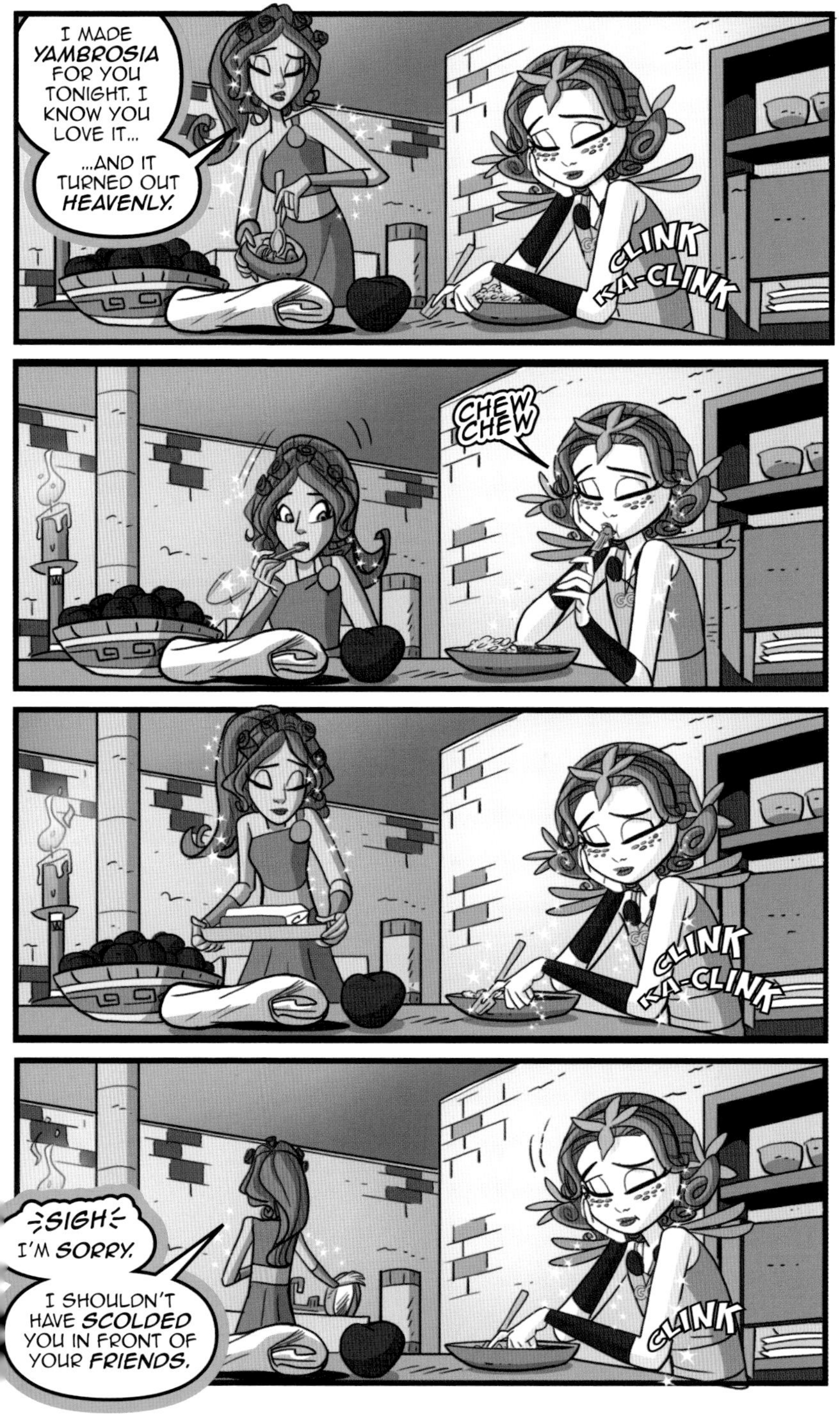
I MADE YAMBROSIA FOR YOU TONIGHT. I KNOW YOU LOVE IT...
...AND IT TURNED OUT HEAVENLY.
CLINK KA-CLINK
CHEW CHEW
CLINK KA-CLINK
=SIGH= I'M SORRY.
I SHOULDN'T HAVE SCOLDED YOU IN FRONT OF YOUR FRIENDS.
CLINK

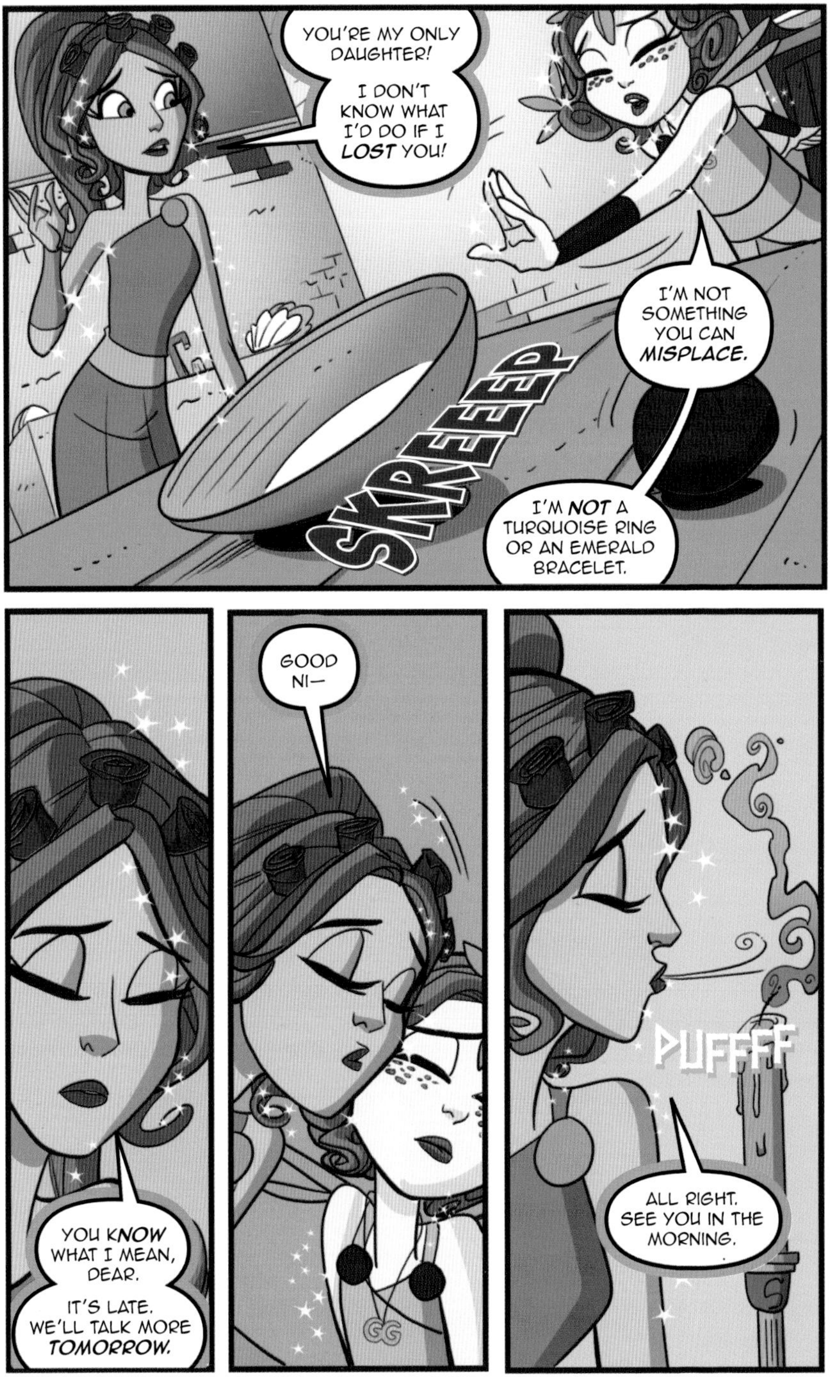
YOU'RE MY ONLY DAUGHTER!
I DON'T KNOW WHAT I'D DO IF I LOST YOU!
I'M NOT SOMETHING YOU CAN MISPLACE.
SKREEEP
I'M NOT A TURQUOISE RING OR AN EMERALD BRACELET.
YOU KNOW WHAT I MEAN, DEAR.
IT'S LATE. WE'LL TALK MORE TOMORROW.
GOOD NI—
PUFFFF
ALL RIGHT. SEE YOU IN THE MORNING.

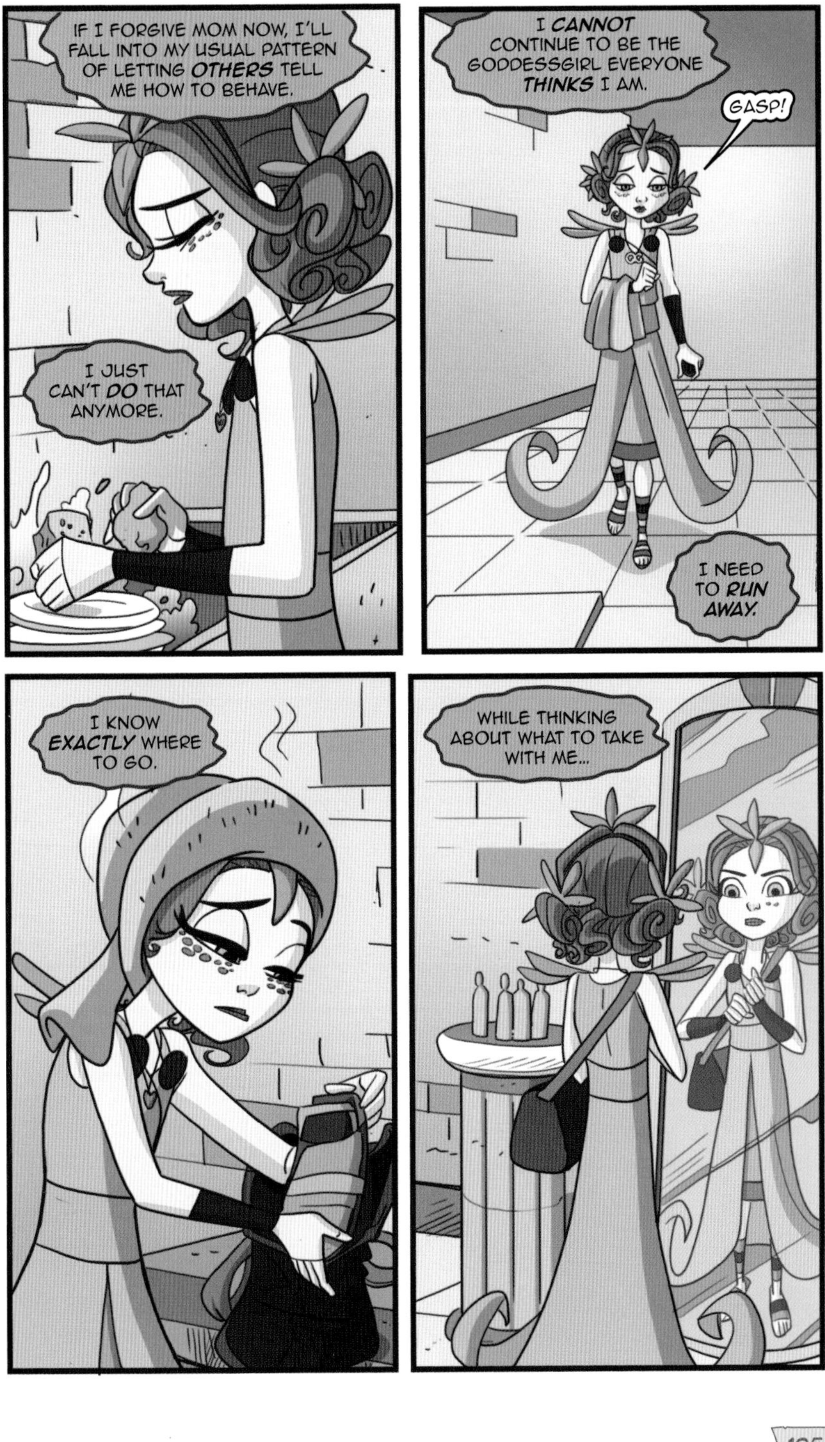
IF I FORGIVE MOM NOW, I'LL FALL INTO MY USUAL PATTERN OF LETTING *OTHERS* TELL ME HOW TO BEHAVE.
I JUST CAN'T *DO* THAT ANYMORE.
I *CANNOT* CONTINUE TO BE THE GODDESSGIRL EVERYONE *THINKS* I AM.
GASP!
I NEED TO *RUN AWAY.*
I KNOW *EXACTLY* WHERE TO GO.
WHILE THINKING ABOUT WHAT TO TAKE WITH ME...

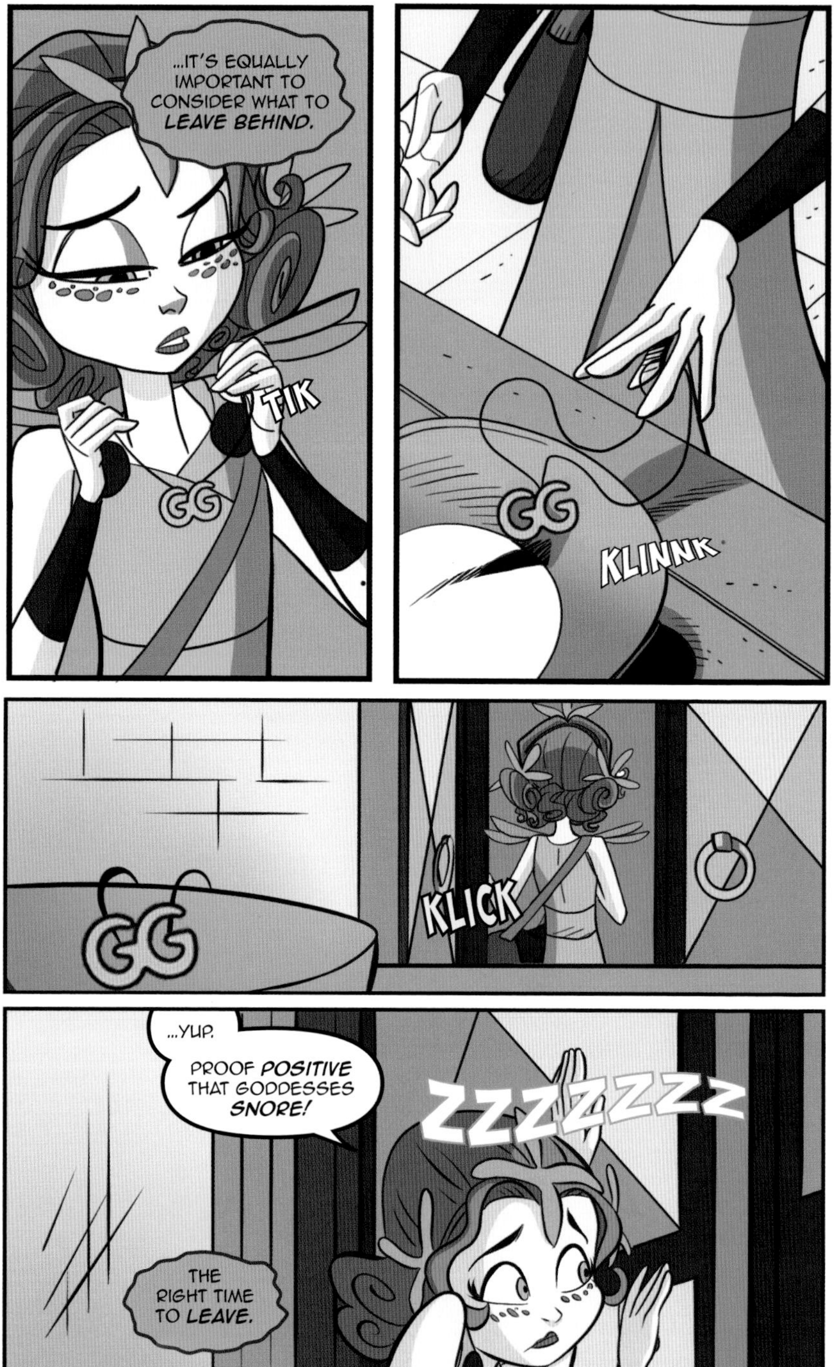
...IT'S EQUALLY IMPORTANT TO CONSIDER WHAT TO *LEAVE BEHIND.*
TIK
KLINNK
KLICK
...YUP.
PROOF *POSITIVE* THAT GODDESSES *SNORE!*
ZZZZZZZ
THE RIGHT TIME TO *LEAVE.*

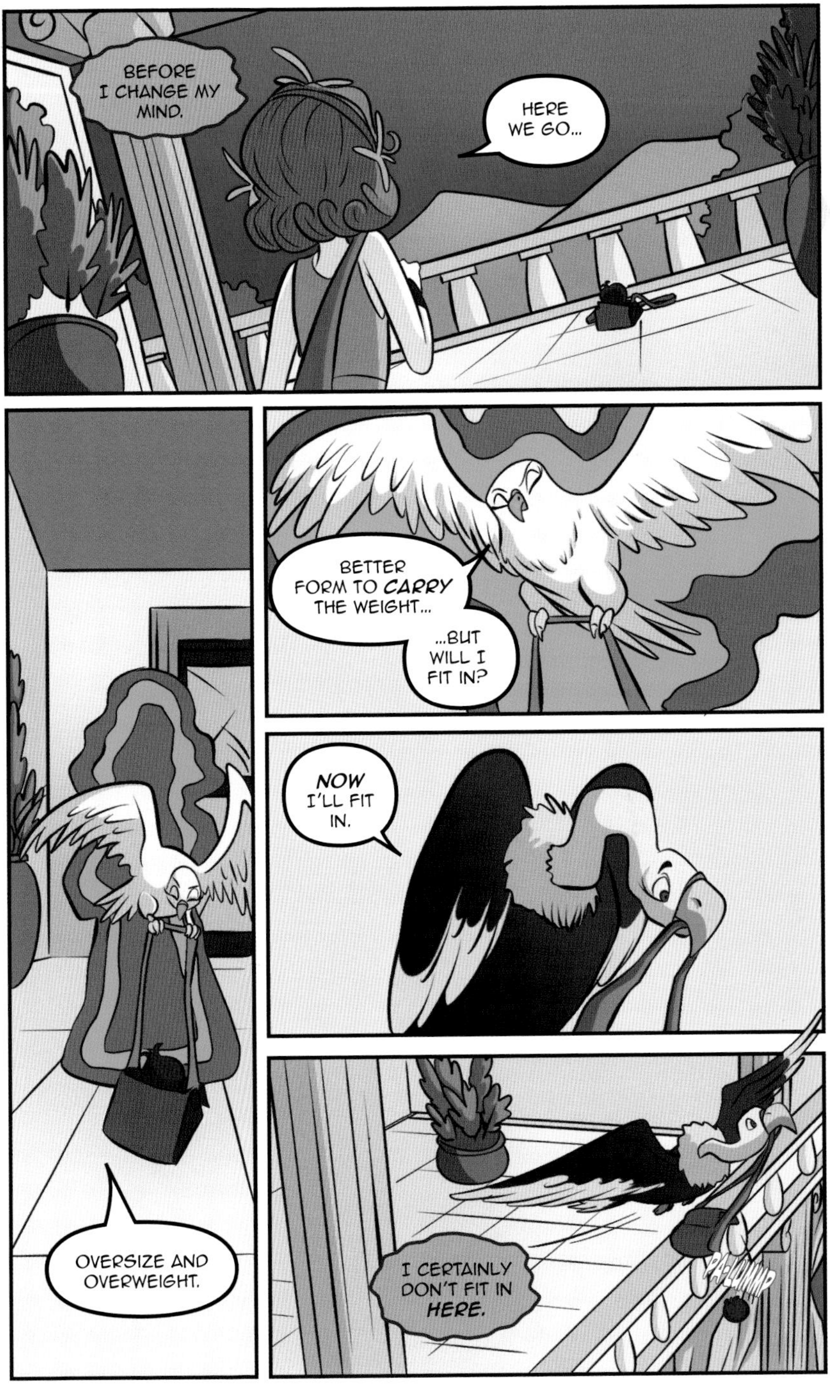
BEFORE I CHANGE MY MIND.
HERE WE GO...
BETTER FORM TO CARRY THE WEIGHT...
...BUT WILL I FIT IN?
OVERSIZE AND OVERWEIGHT.
NOW I'LL FIT IN.
I CERTAINLY DON'T FIT IN HERE.
PA-LUMMP

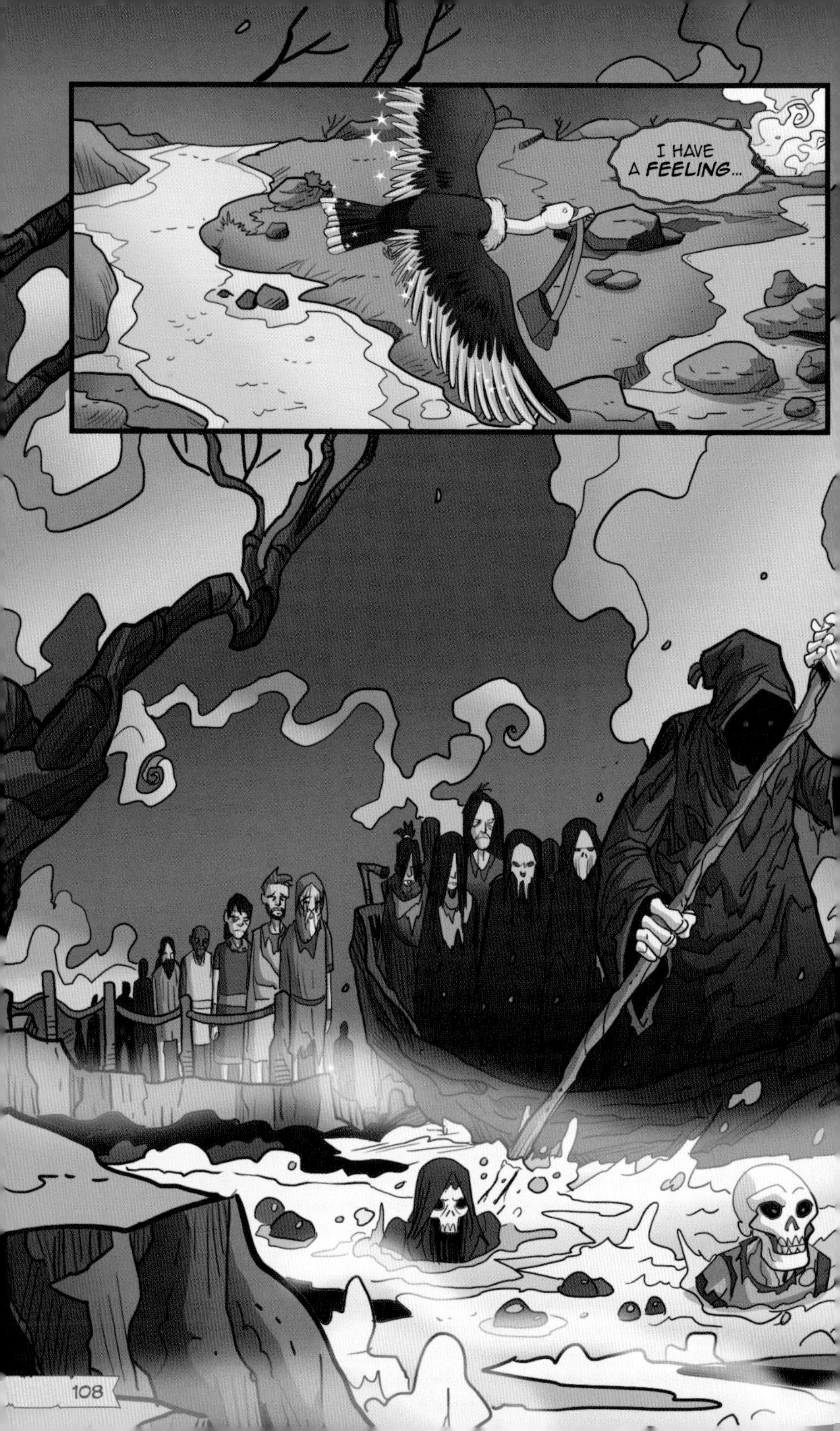
I HAVE A FEELING...

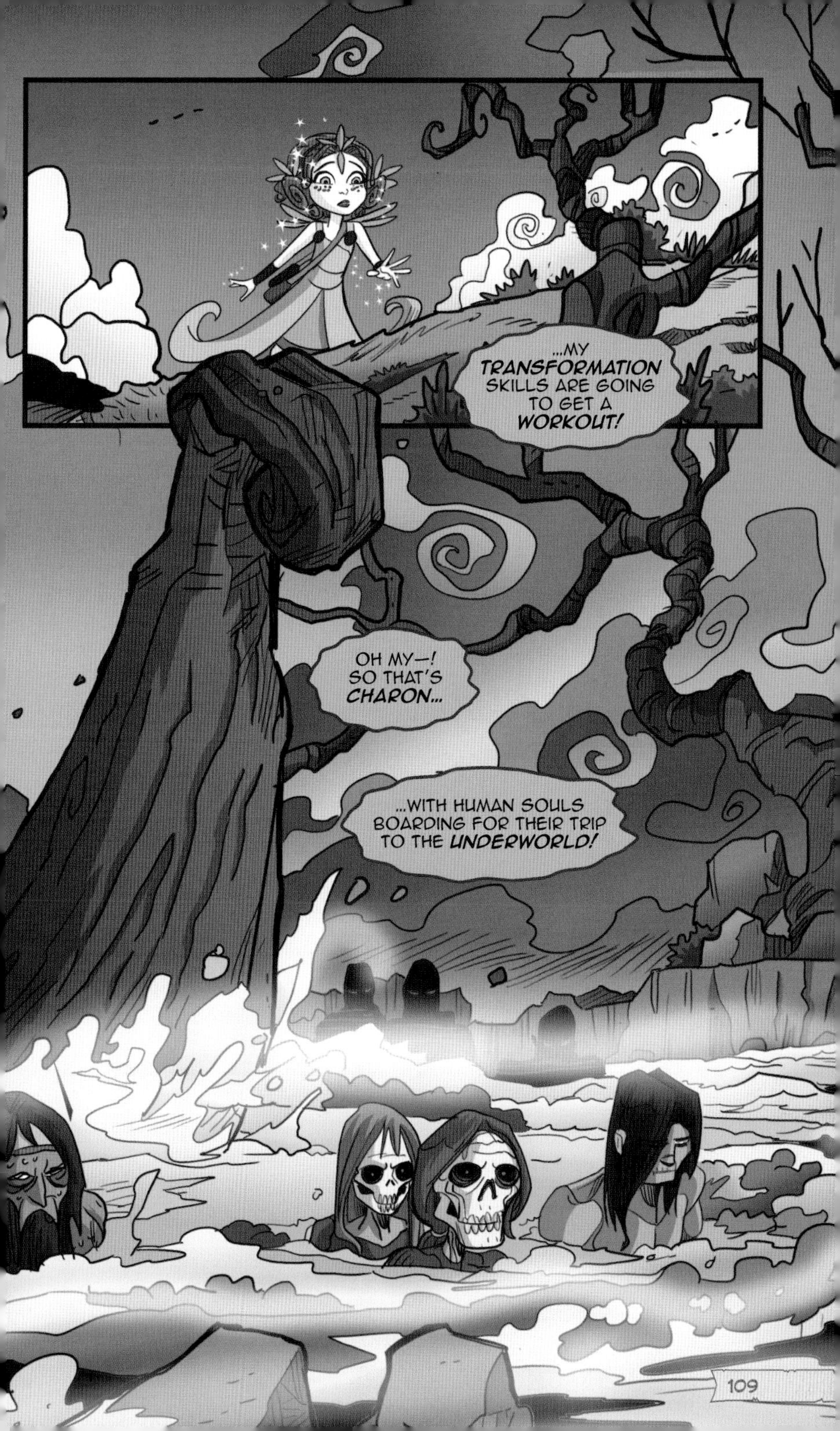
...MY *TRANSFORMATION* SKILLS ARE GOING TO GET A *WORKOUT!*
OH MY—! SO THAT'S *CHARON...*
...WITH HUMAN SOULS BOARDING FOR THEIR TRIP TO THE *UNDERWORLD!*

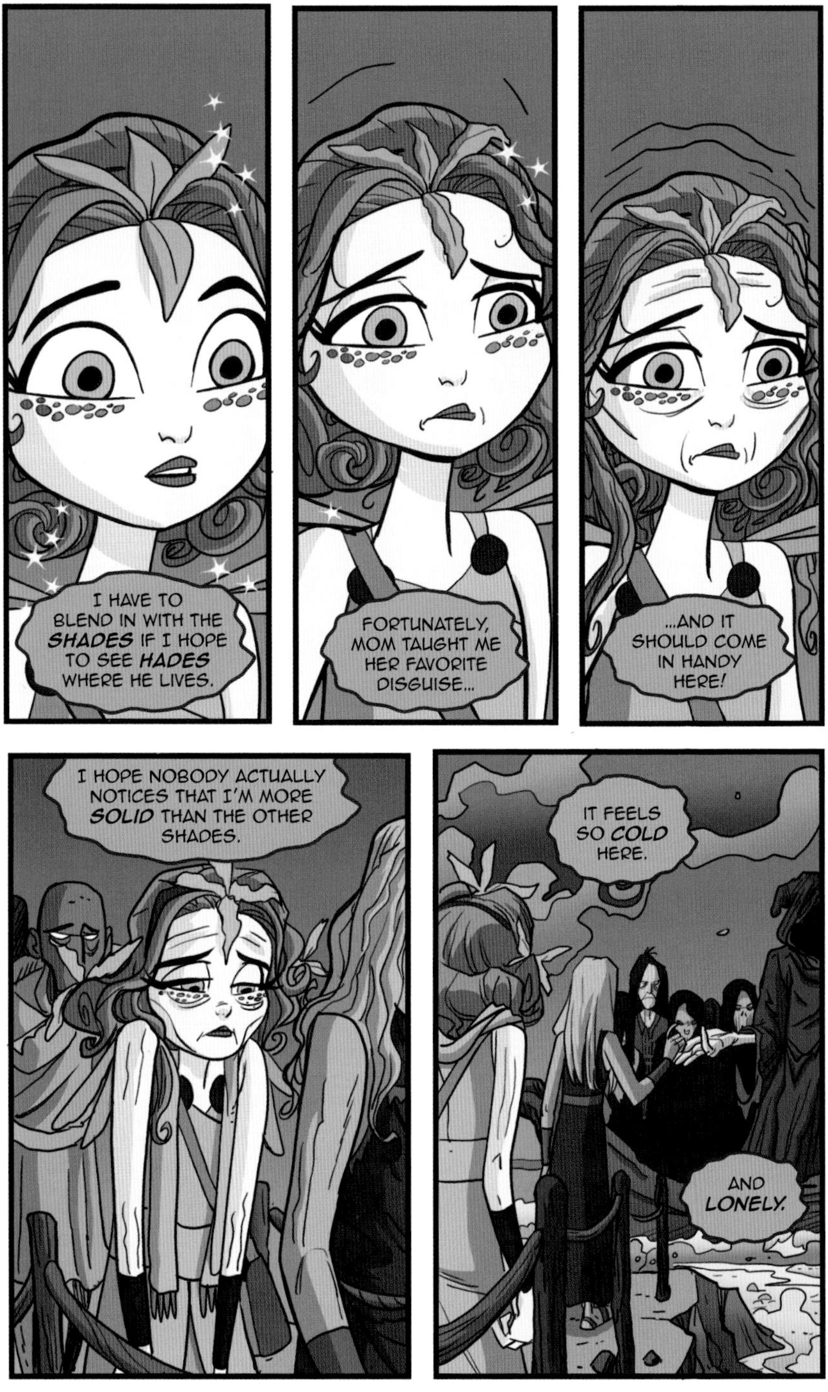
I HAVE TO BLEND IN WITH THE SHADES IF I HOPE TO SEE HADES WHERE HE LIVES.
FORTUNATELY, MOM TAUGHT ME HER FAVORITE DISGUISE...
...AND IT SHOULD COME IN HANDY HERE!
I HOPE NOBODY ACTUALLY NOTICES THAT I'M MORE SOLID THAN THE OTHER SHADES.
IT FEELS SO COLD HERE.
AND LONELY.

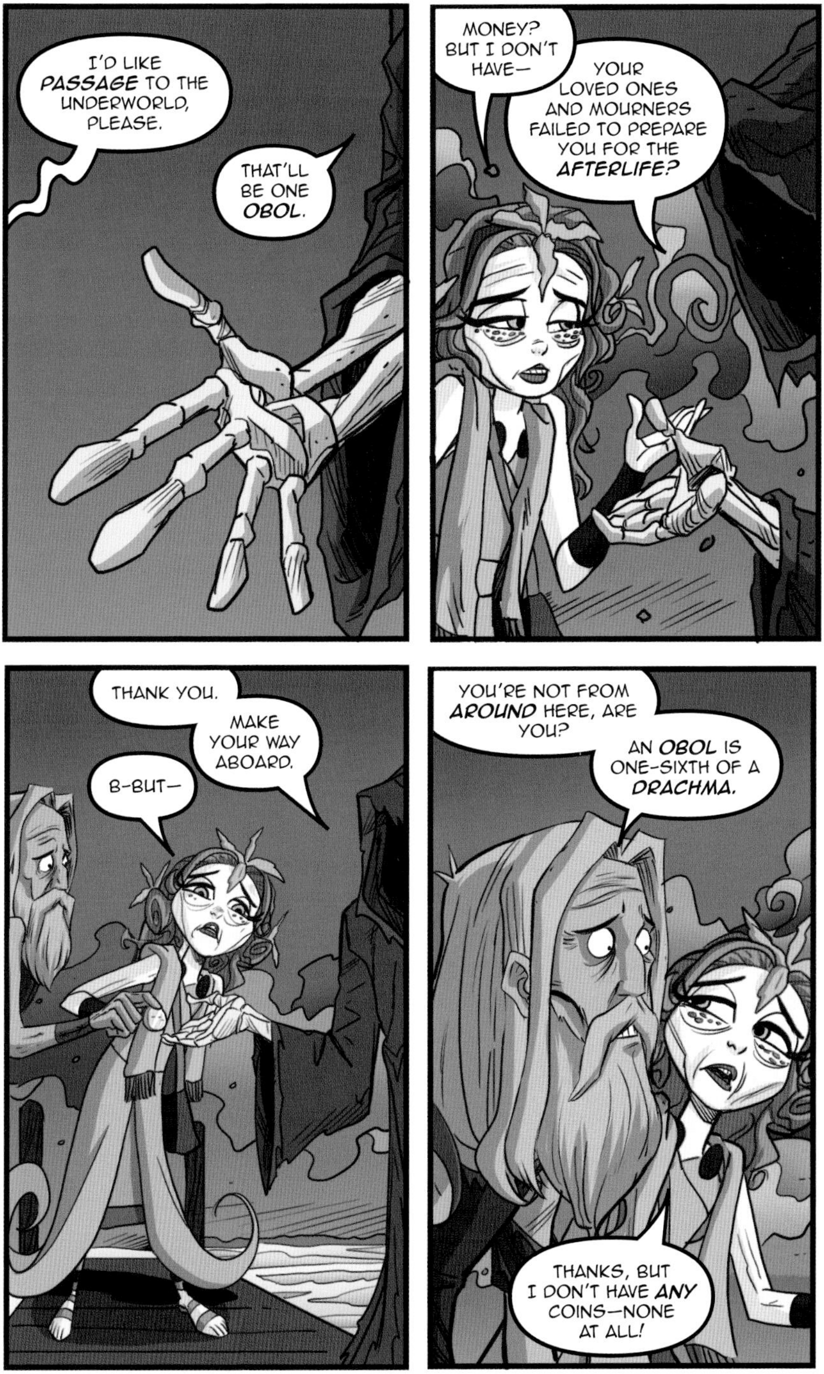
I'D LIKE PASSAGE TO THE UNDERWORLD, PLEASE.
THAT'LL BE ONE OBOL.
MONEY? BUT I DON'T HAVE—
YOUR LOVED ONES AND MOURNERS FAILED TO PREPARE YOU FOR THE AFTERLIFE?
THANK YOU.
MAKE YOUR WAY ABOARD.
B-BUT—
YOU'RE NOT FROM AROUND HERE, ARE YOU?
AN OBOL IS ONE-SIXTH OF A DRACHMA.
THANKS, BUT I DON'T HAVE ANY COINS—NONE AT ALL!

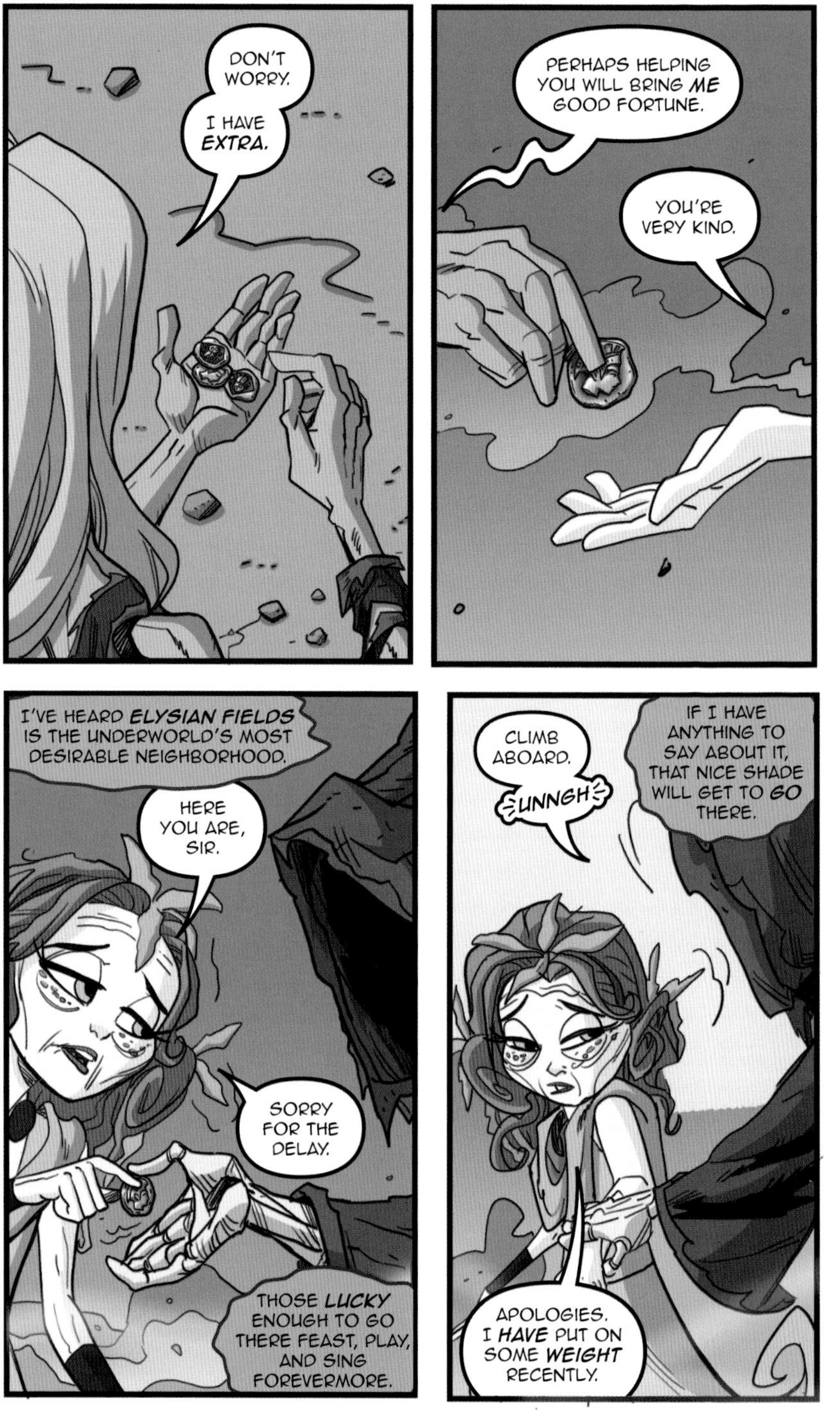
DON'T WORRY.
I HAVE EXTRA.
PERHAPS HELPING YOU WILL BRING ME GOOD FORTUNE.
YOU'RE VERY KIND.
I'VE HEARD ELYSIAN FIELDS IS THE UNDERWORLD'S MOST DESIRABLE NEIGHBORHOOD.
HERE YOU ARE, SIR.
SORRY FOR THE DELAY.
THOSE LUCKY ENOUGH TO GO THERE FEAST, PLAY, AND SING FOREVERMORE.
CLIMB ABOARD.
UNNGH
IF I HAVE ANYTHING TO SAY ABOUT IT, THAT NICE SHADE WILL GET TO GO THERE.
APOLOGIES. I HAVE PUT ON SOME WEIGHT RECENTLY.

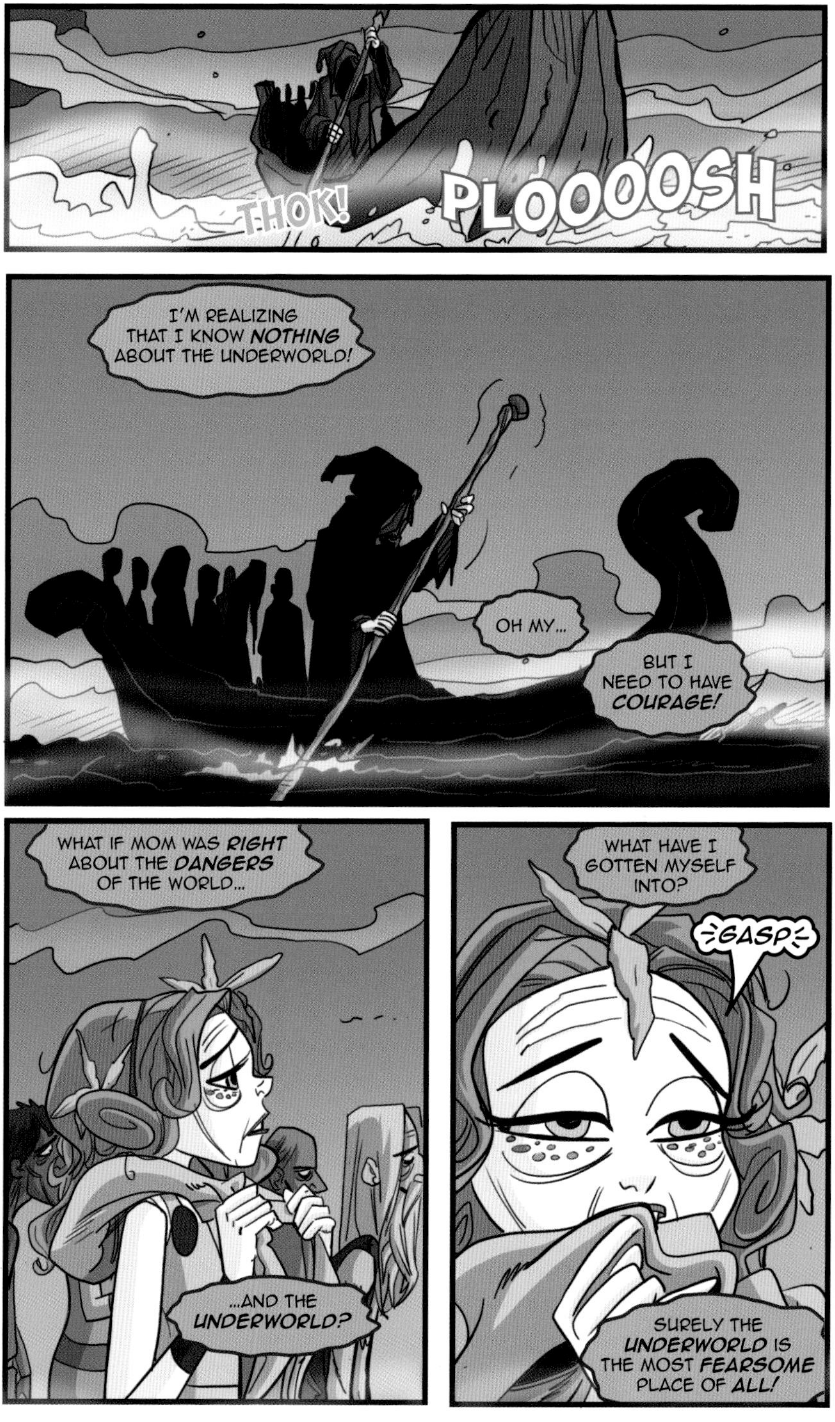
THOK!
PLOOOOSH
I'M REALIZING THAT I KNOW NOTHING ABOUT THE UNDERWORLD!
OH MY...
BUT I NEED TO HAVE COURAGE!
WHAT IF MOM WAS RIGHT ABOUT THE DANGERS OF THE WORLD...
...AND THE UNDERWORLD?
WHAT HAVE I GOTTEN MYSELF INTO?
GASP
SURELY THE UNDERWORLD IS THE MOST FEARSOME PLACE OF ALL!

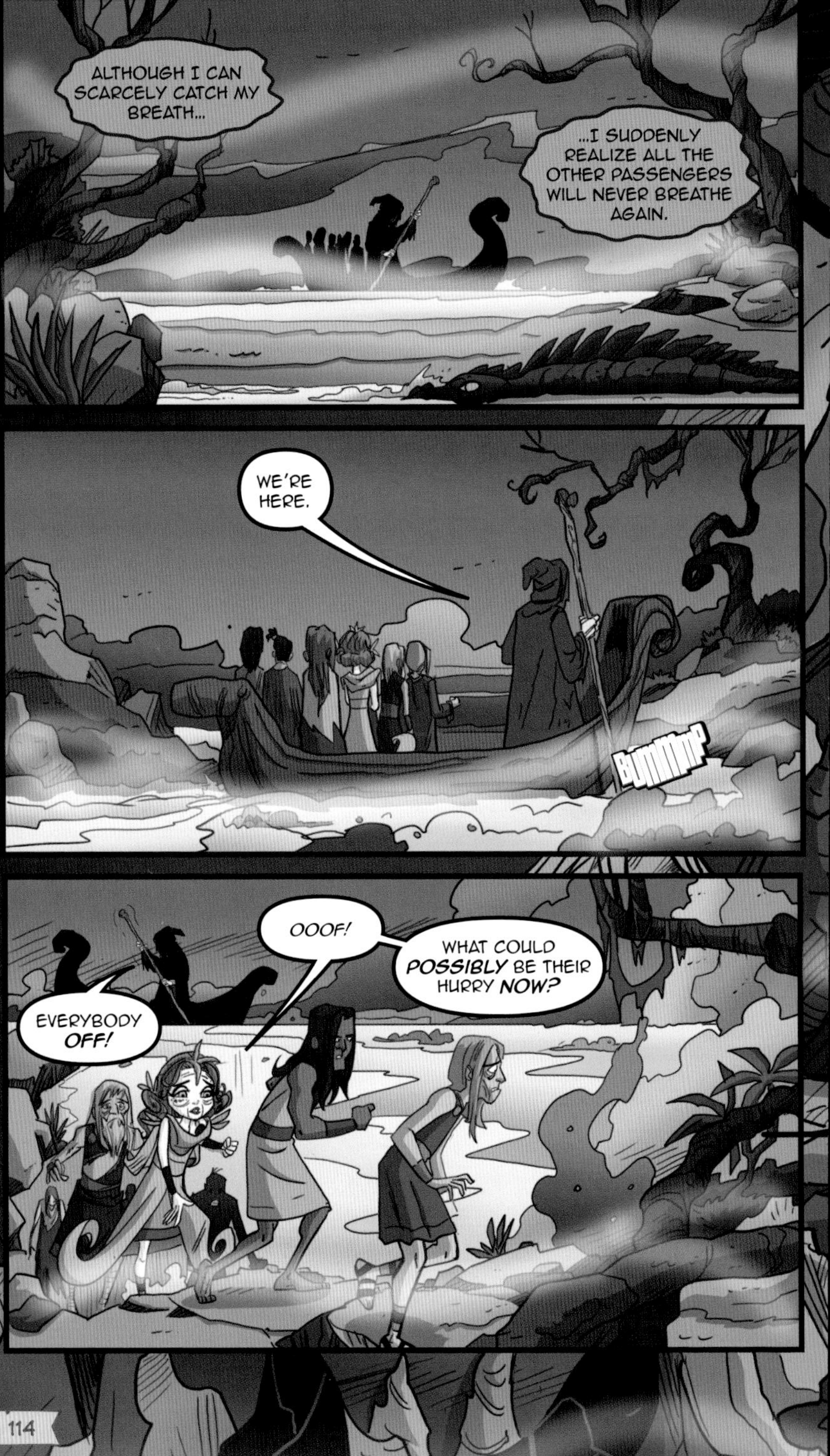
ALTHOUGH I CAN SCARCELY CATCH MY BREATH...
...I SUDDENLY REALIZE ALL THE OTHER PASSENGERS WILL NEVER BREATHE AGAIN.
WE'RE HERE.
BUMMMP
EVERYBODY *OFF!*
OOOF!
WHAT COULD ***POSSIBLY*** BE THEIR HURRY ***NOW?***

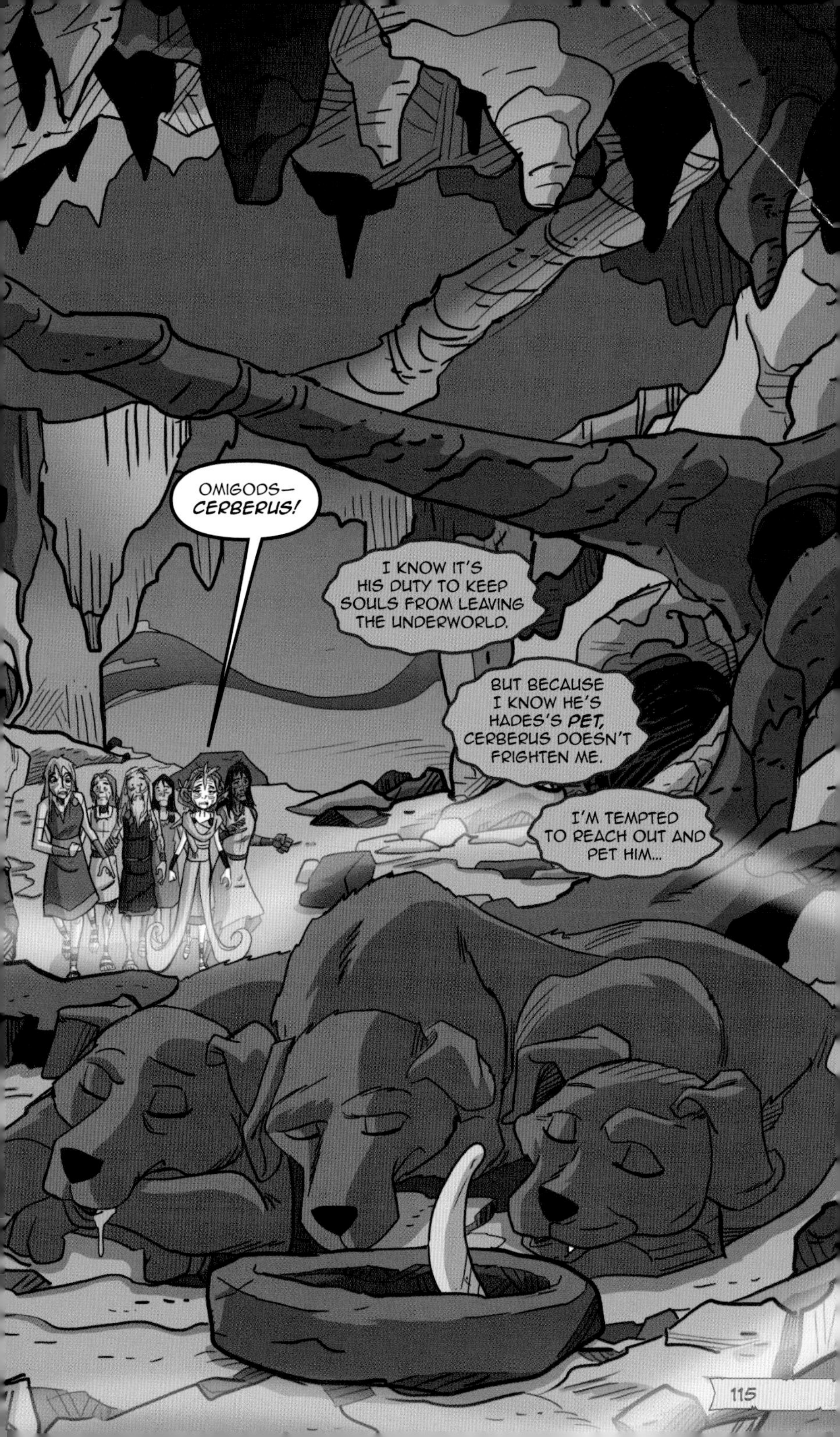
OMIGODS—
CERBERUS!
I KNOW IT'S HIS DUTY TO KEEP SOULS FROM LEAVING THE UNDERWORLD.
BUT BECAUSE I KNOW HE'S HADES'S *PET,* CERBERUS DOESN'T FRIGHTEN ME.
I'M TEMPTED TO REACH OUT AND PET HIM...

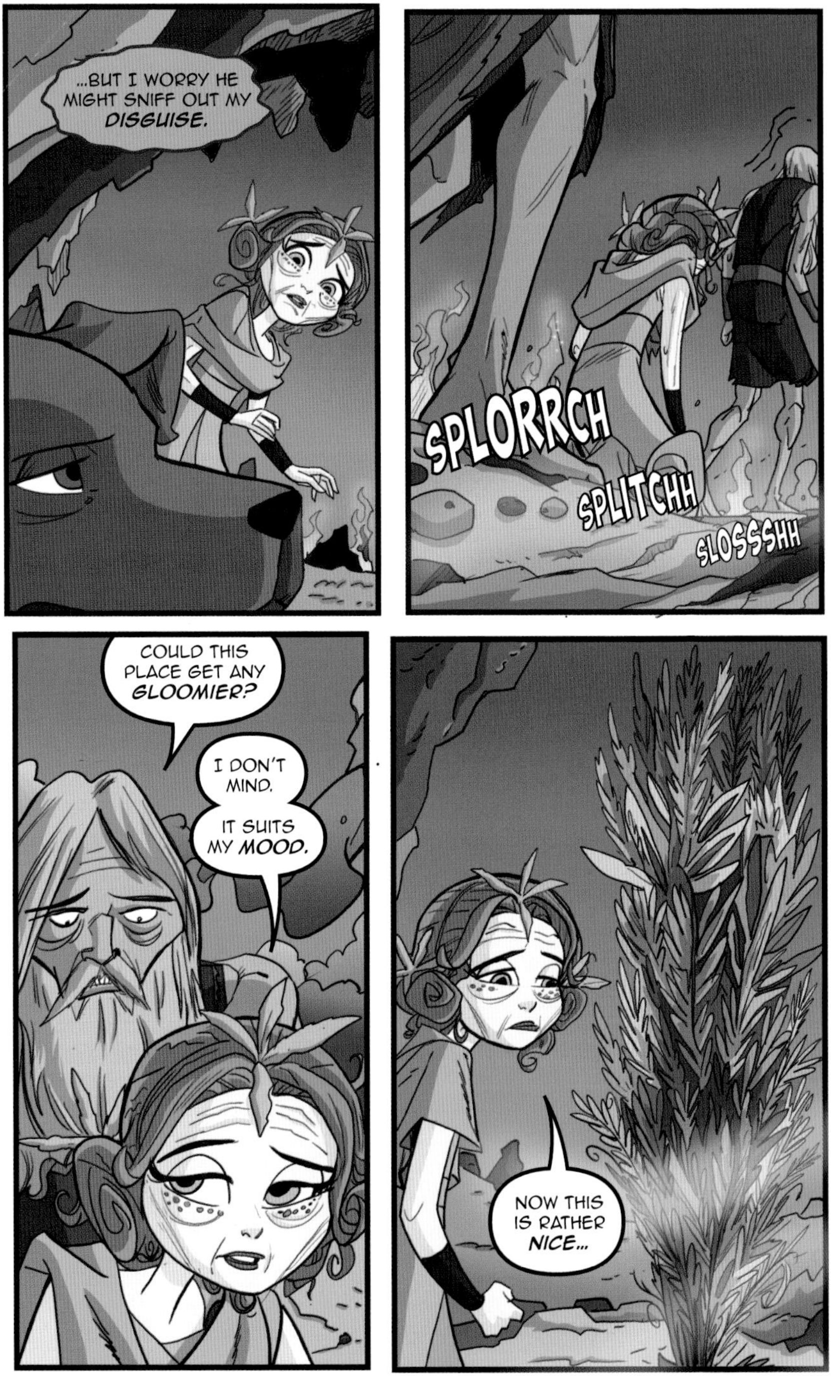
...BUT I WORRY HE MIGHT SNIFF OUT MY DISGUISE.
SPLORRCH
SPLITCHH
SLOSSSHH
COULD THIS PLACE GET ANY GLOOMIER?
I DON'T MIND.
IT SUITS MY MOOD.
NOW THIS IS RATHER NICE...

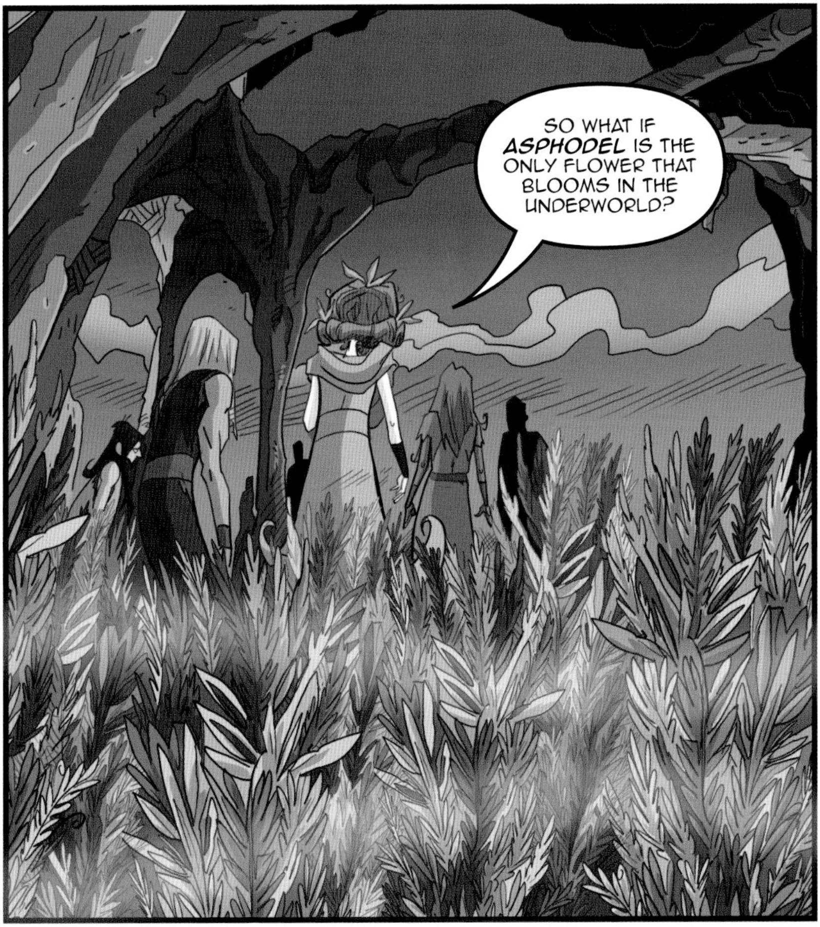
SO WHAT IF ASPHODEL IS THE ONLY FLOWER THAT BLOOMS IN THE UNDERWORLD?

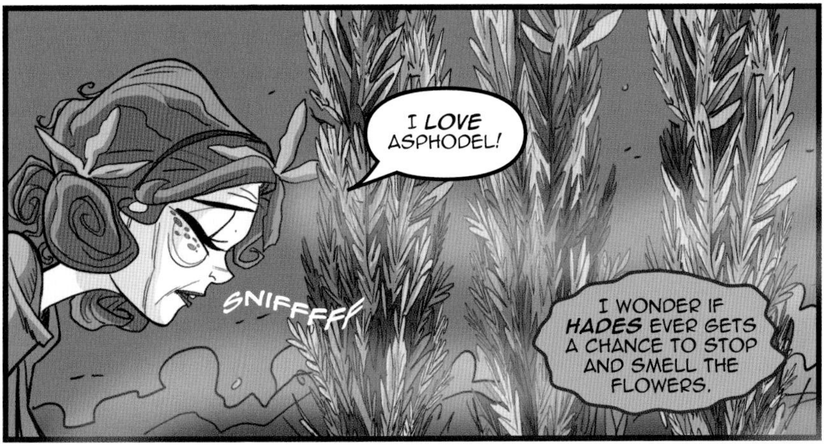
I LOVE ASPHODEL!
SNIFFFFFF
I WONDER IF HADES EVER GETS A CHANCE TO STOP AND SMELL THE FLOWERS.

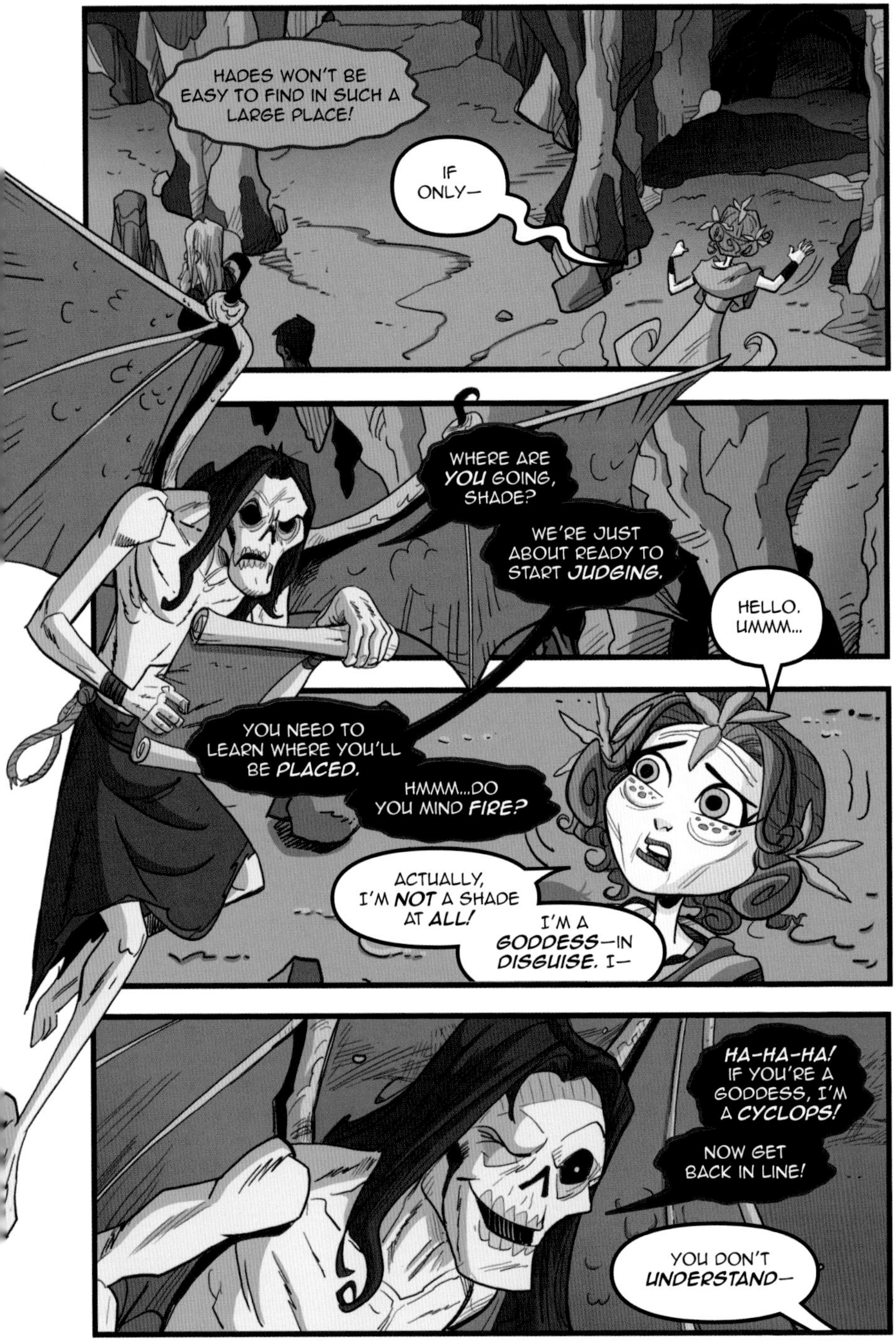
HADES WON'T BE EASY TO FIND IN SUCH A LARGE PLACE!
IF ONLY—
WHERE ARE YOU GOING, SHADE?
WE'RE JUST ABOUT READY TO START JUDGING.
HELLO. UMMM...
YOU NEED TO LEARN WHERE YOU'LL BE PLACED.
HMMM...DO YOU MIND FIRE?
ACTUALLY, I'M NOT A SHADE AT ALL!
I'M A GODDESS—IN DISGUISE. I—
HA-HA-HA! IF YOU'RE A GODDESS, I'M A CYCLOPS!
NOW GET BACK IN LINE!
YOU DON'T UNDERSTAND—

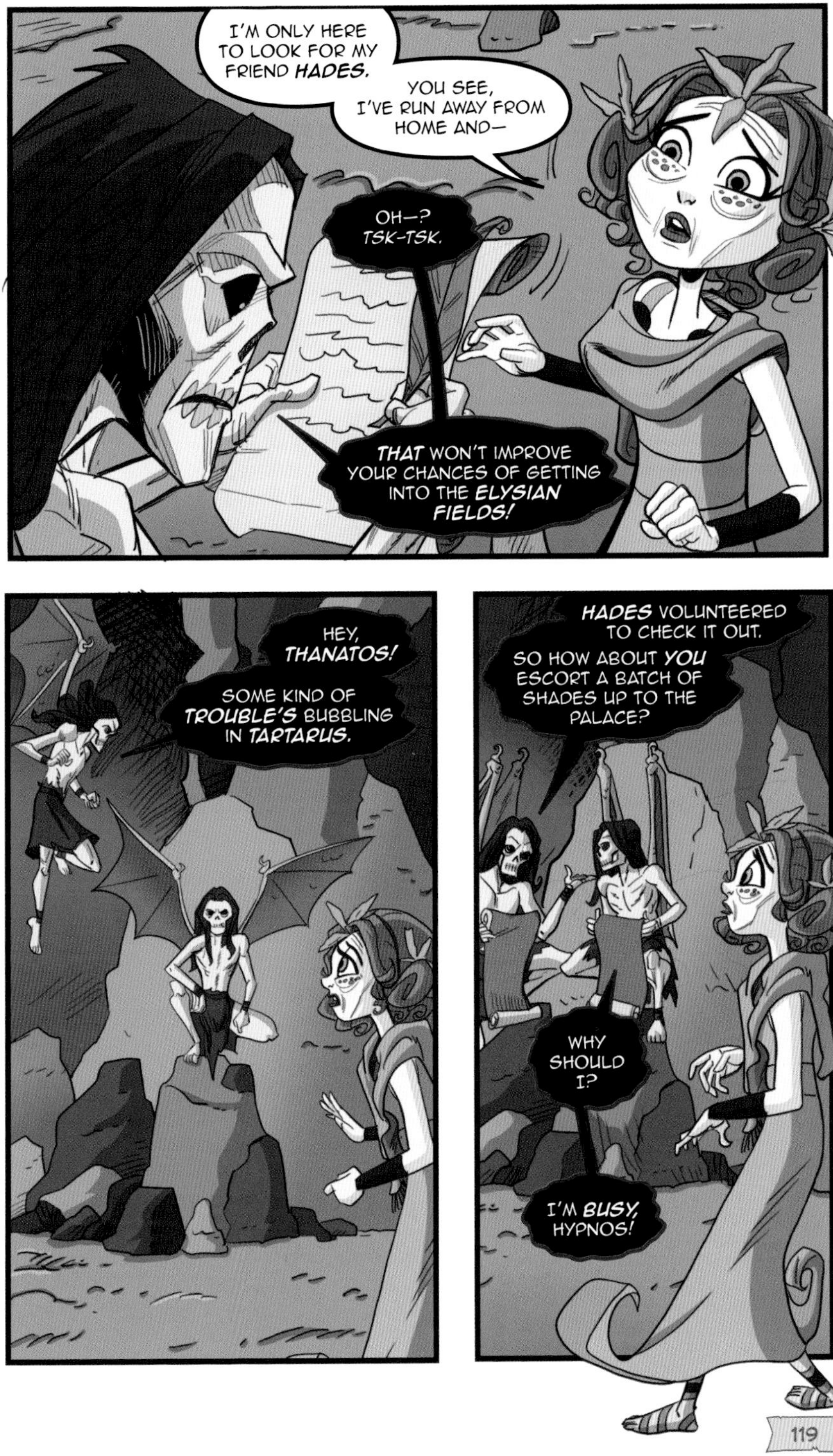
I'M ONLY HERE TO LOOK FOR MY FRIEND HADES.
YOU SEE, I'VE RUN AWAY FROM HOME AND—
OH—? TSK-TSK.
THAT WON'T IMPROVE YOUR CHANCES OF GETTING INTO THE ELYSIAN FIELDS!
HEY, THANATOS!
SOME KIND OF TROUBLE'S BUBBLING IN TARTARUS.
HADES VOLUNTEERED TO CHECK IT OUT.
SO HOW ABOUT YOU ESCORT A BATCH OF SHADES UP TO THE PALACE?
WHY SHOULD I?
I'M BUSY, HYPNOS!

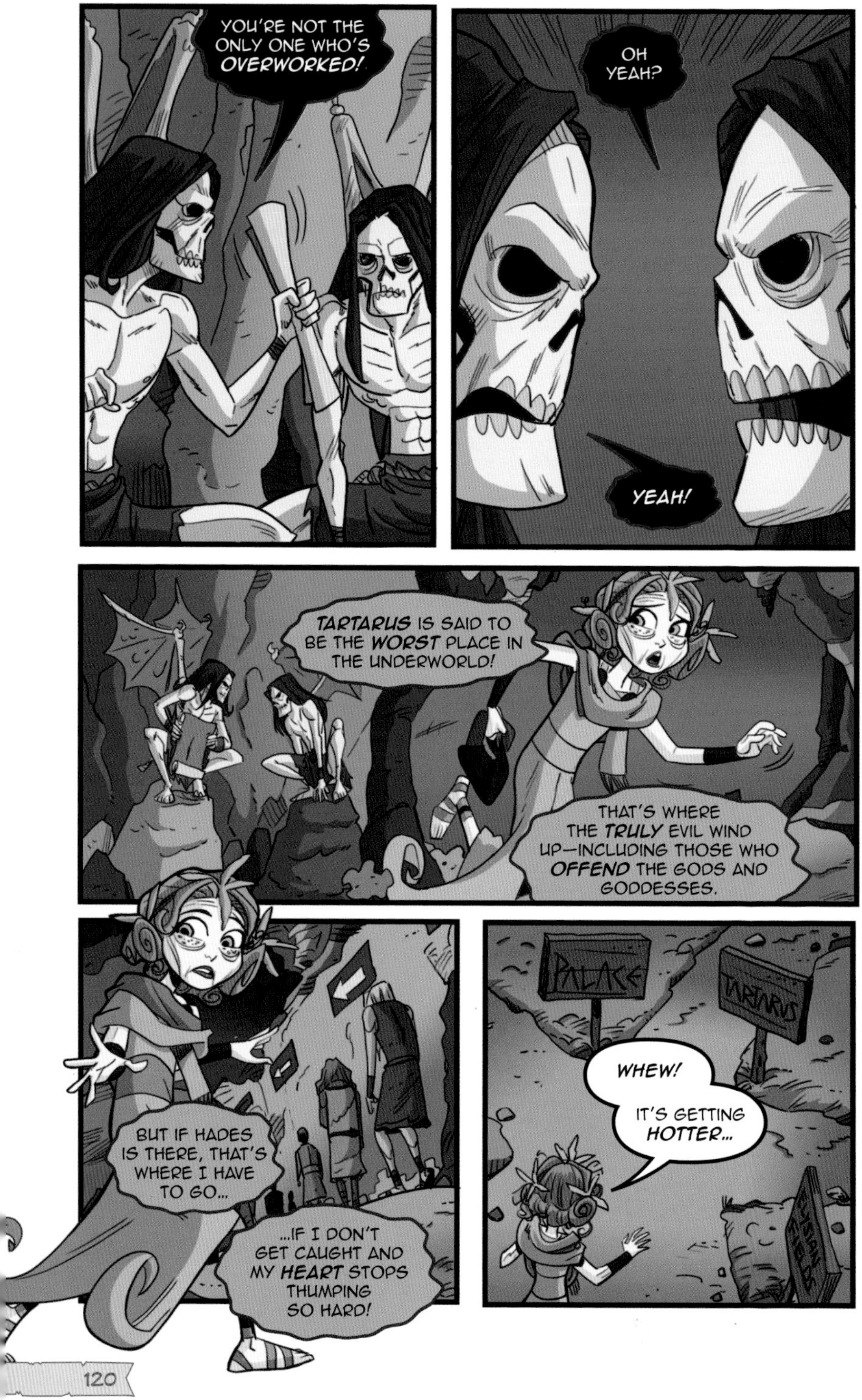
YOU'RE NOT THE ONLY ONE WHO'S *OVERWORKED!*
OH YEAH?
YEAH!
TARTARUS IS SAID TO BE THE *WORST* PLACE IN THE UNDERWORLD!
THAT'S WHERE THE *TRULY* EVIL WIND UP—INCLUDING THOSE WHO *OFFEND* THE GODS AND GODDESSES.
BUT IF HADES IS THERE, THAT'S WHERE I HAVE TO GO...
...IF I DON'T GET CAUGHT AND MY *HEART* STOPS THUMPING SO HARD!
PALACE
TARTARUS
WHEW!
IT'S GETTING *HOTTER*...

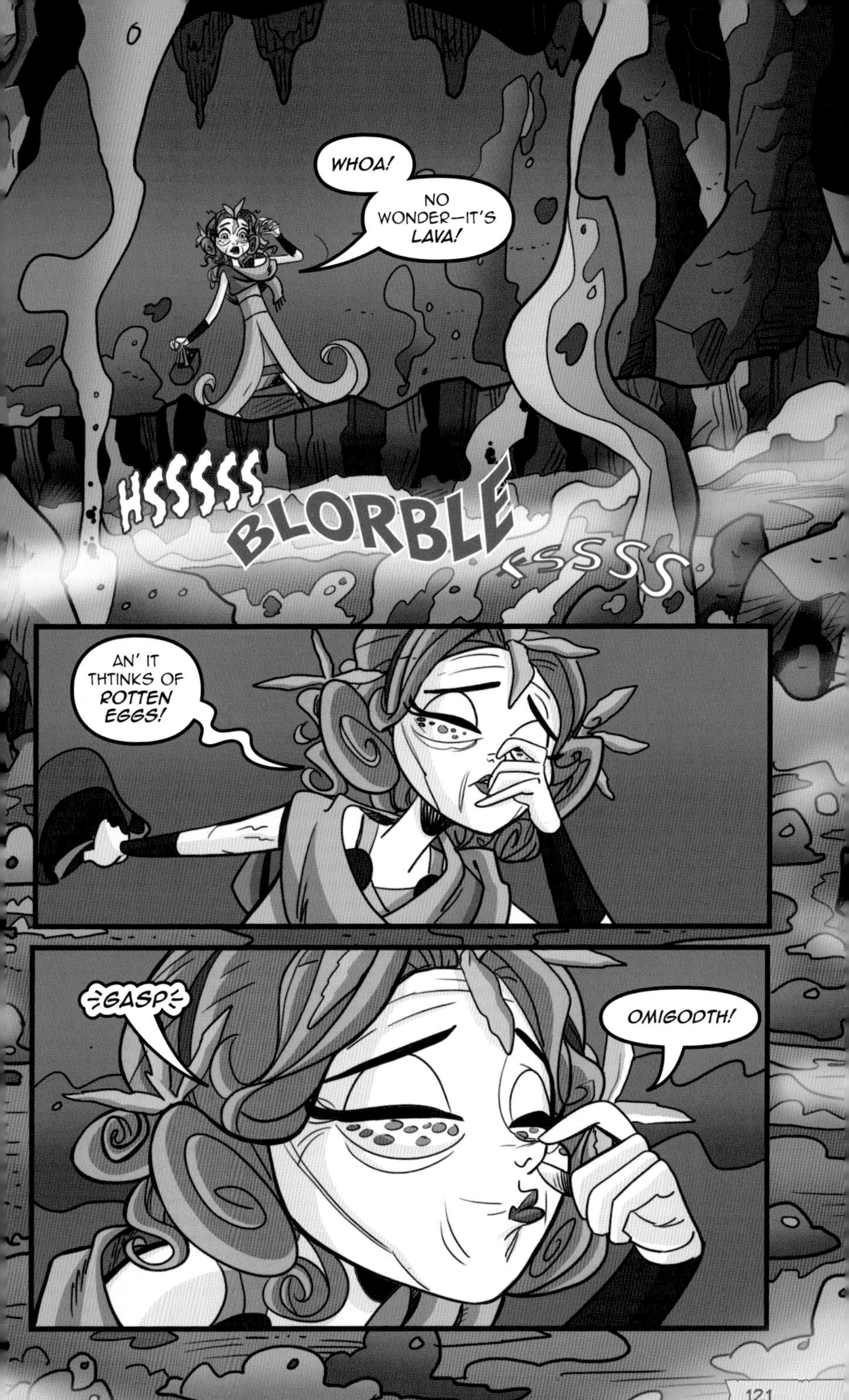
WHOA!
NO WONDER—IT'S LAVA!
HSSSSS
BLORBLE
SSSSS
AN' IT THTINKS OF ROTTEN EGGS!
GASP
OMIGODTH!

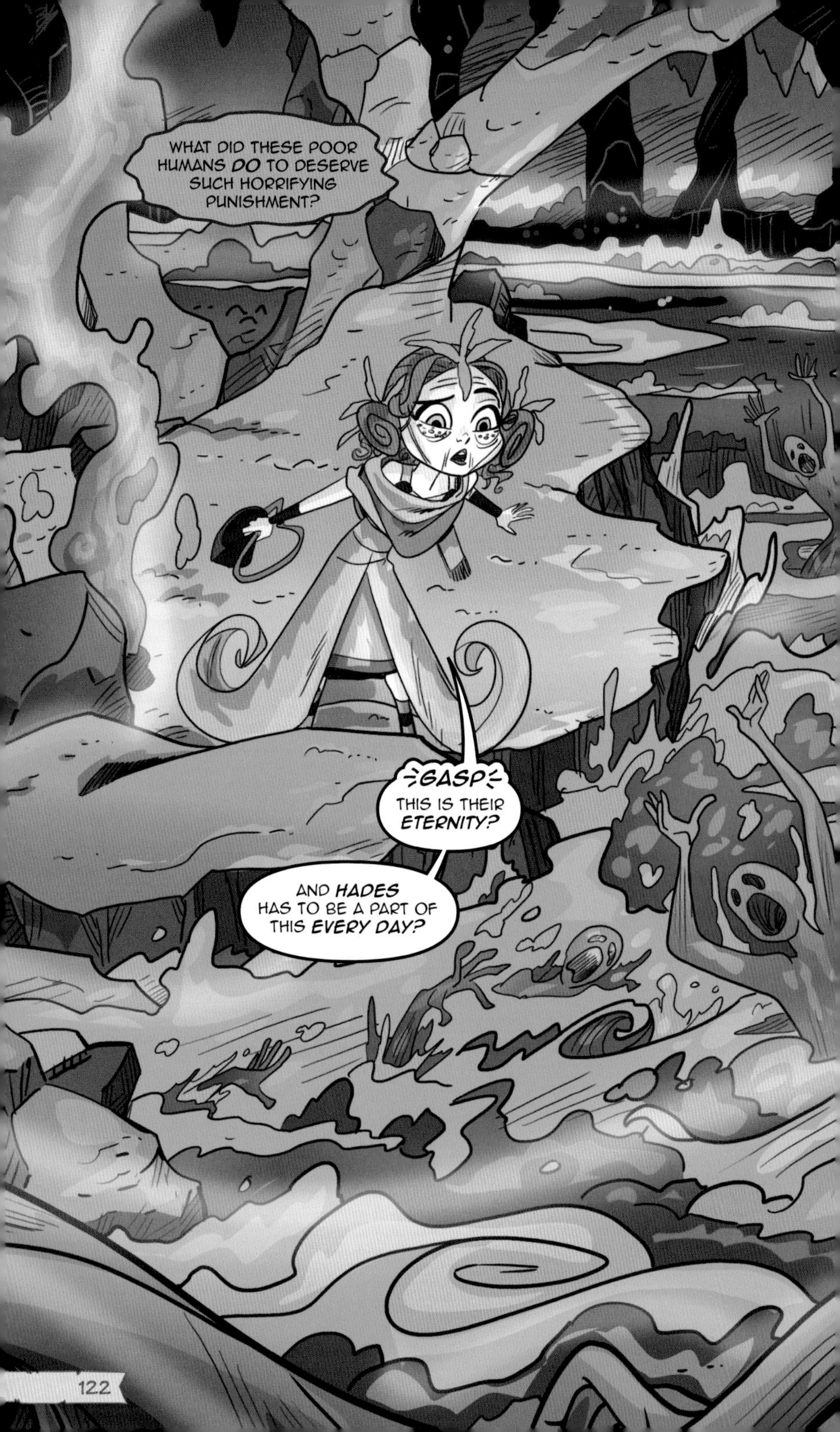
WHAT DID THESE POOR HUMANS DO TO DESERVE SUCH HORRIFYING PUNISHMENT?
GASP
THIS IS THEIR ETERNITY?
AND HADES HAS TO BE A PART OF THIS EVERY DAY?

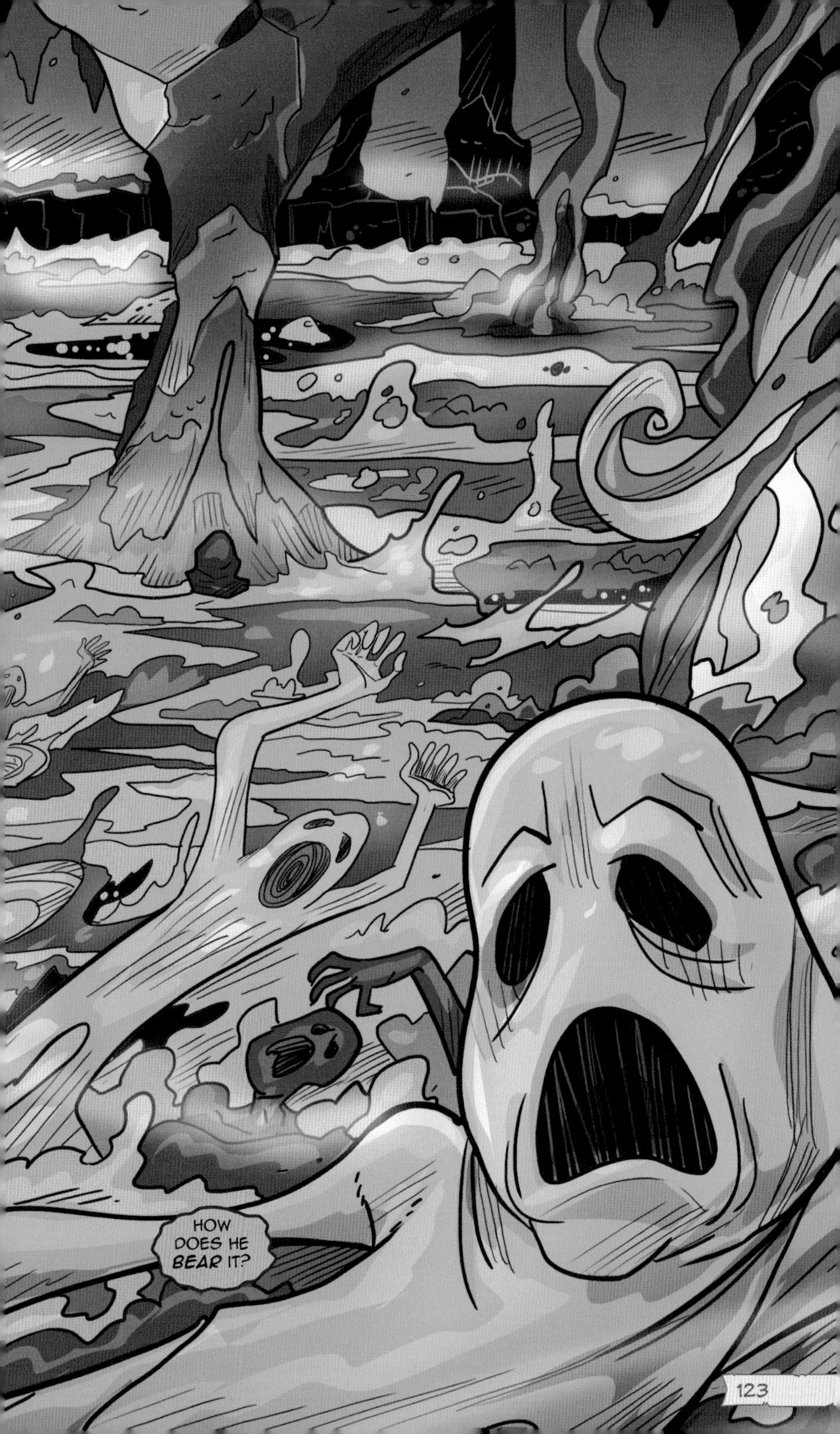
HOW DOES HE BEAR IT?

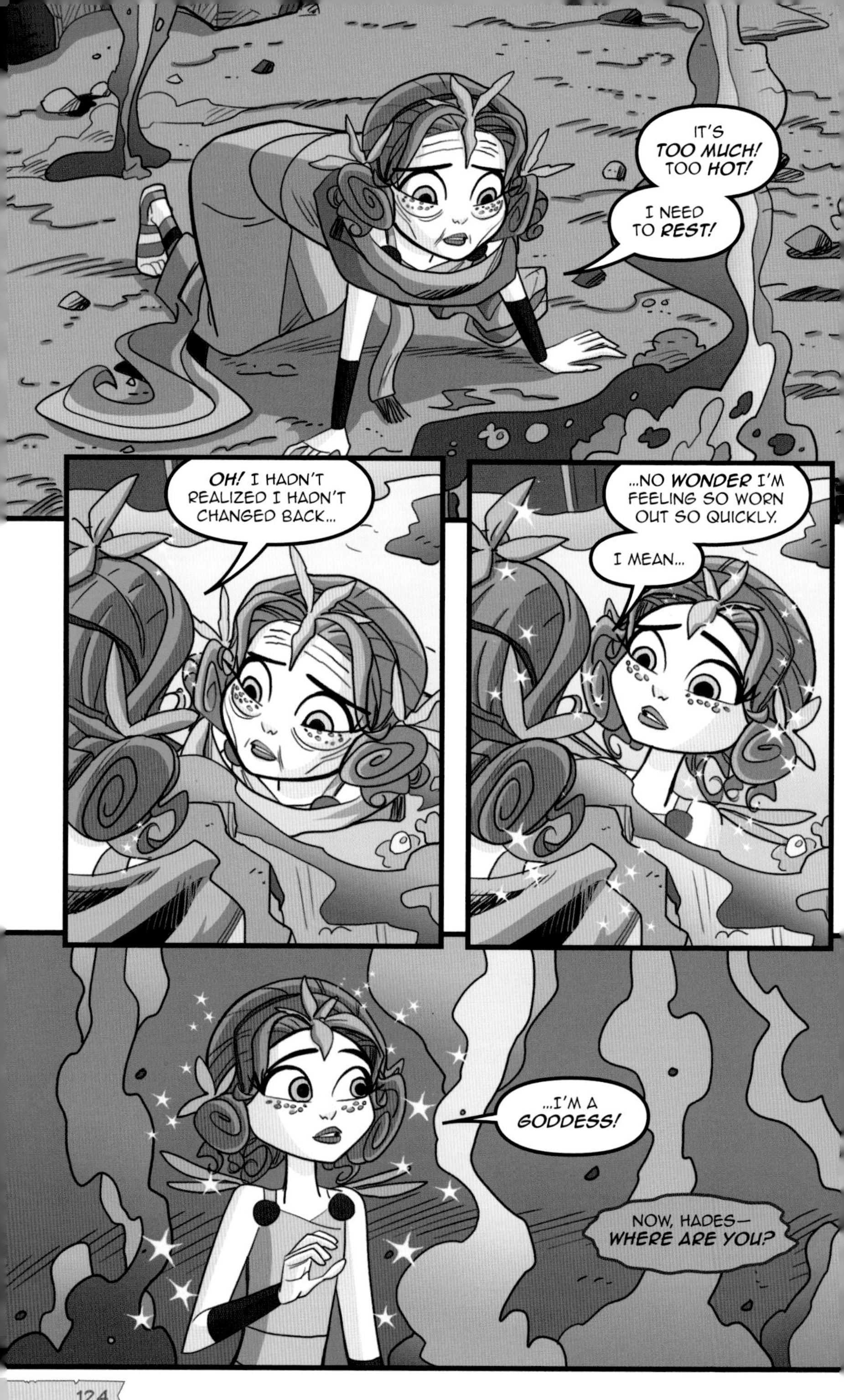
IT'S TOO MUCH! TOO HOT!
I NEED TO REST!
OH! I HADN'T REALIZED I HADN'T CHANGED BACK...
...NO WONDER I'M FEELING SO WORN OUT SO QUICKLY.
I MEAN...
...I'M A GODDESS!
NOW, HADES— WHERE ARE YOU?

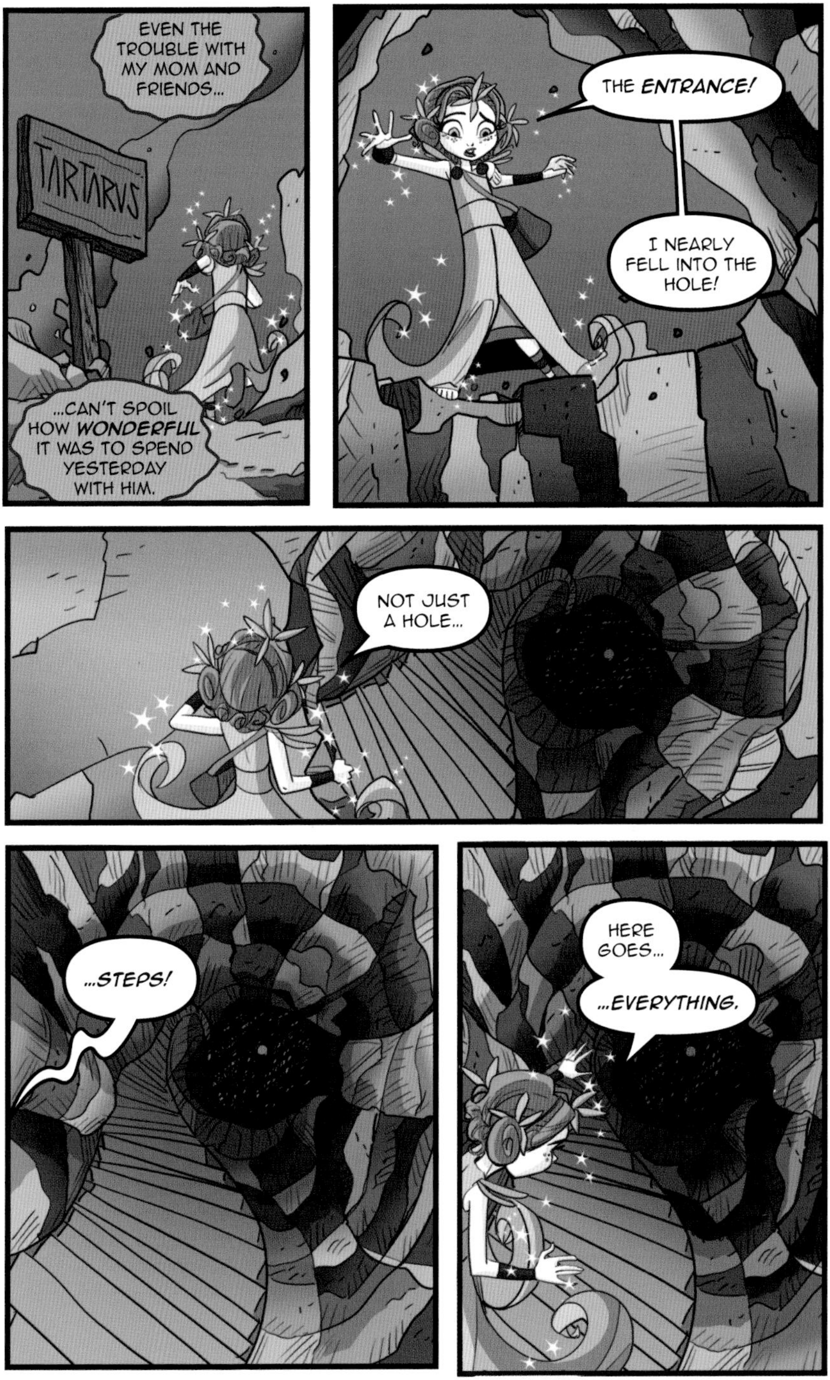
EVEN THE TROUBLE WITH MY MOM AND FRIENDS...
TARTARUS
...CAN'T SPOIL HOW WONDERFUL IT WAS TO SPEND YESTERDAY WITH HIM.
THE ENTRANCE!
I NEARLY FELL INTO THE HOLE!
NOT JUST A HOLE...
...STEPS!
HERE GOES...
...EVERYTHING.

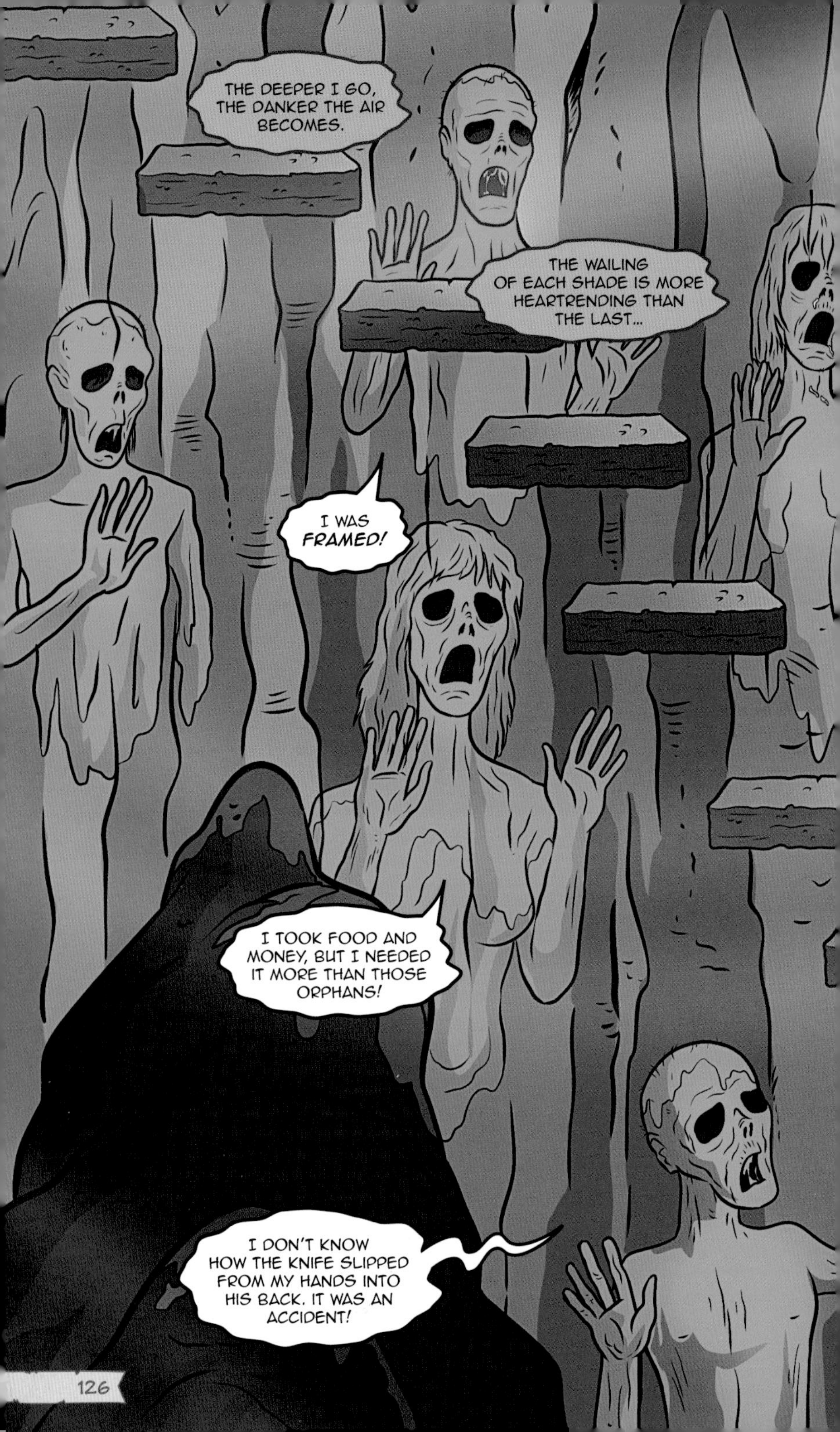
THE DEEPER I GO, THE DANKER THE AIR BECOMES.
THE WAILING OF EACH SHADE IS MORE HEARTRENDING THAN THE LAST...
I WAS *FRAMED!*
I TOOK FOOD AND MONEY, BUT I NEEDED IT MORE THAN THOSE ORPHANS!
I DON'T KNOW HOW THE KNIFE SLIPPED FROM MY HANDS INTO HIS BACK. IT WAS AN ACCIDENT!

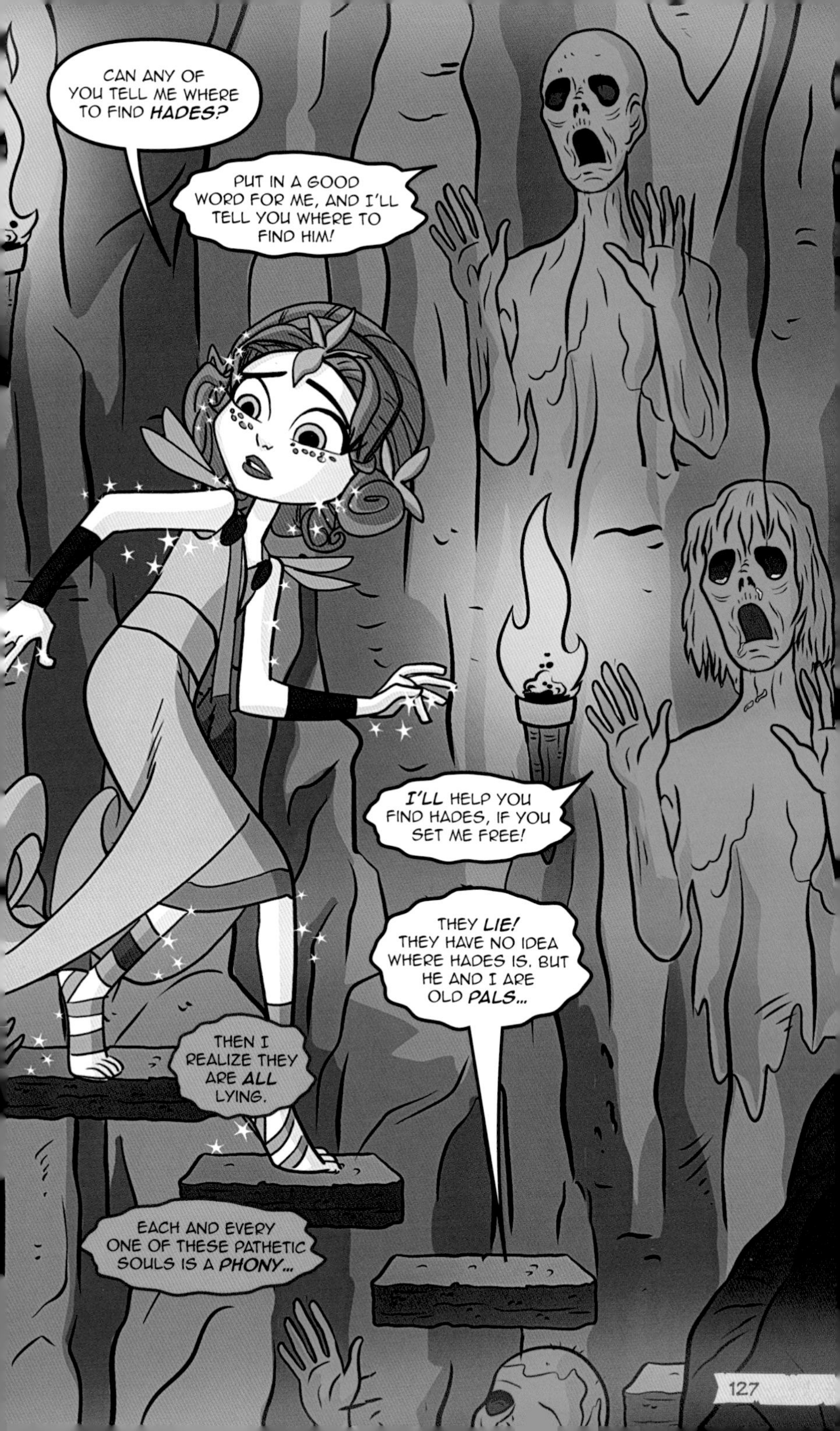
CAN ANY OF YOU TELL ME WHERE TO FIND HADES?
PUT IN A GOOD WORD FOR ME, AND I'LL TELL YOU WHERE TO FIND HIM!
I'LL HELP YOU FIND HADES, IF YOU SET ME FREE!
THEY LIE! THEY HAVE NO IDEA WHERE HADES IS. BUT HE AND I ARE OLD PALS...
THEN I REALIZE THEY ARE ALL LYING.
EACH AND EVERY ONE OF THESE PATHETIC SOULS IS A PHONY...

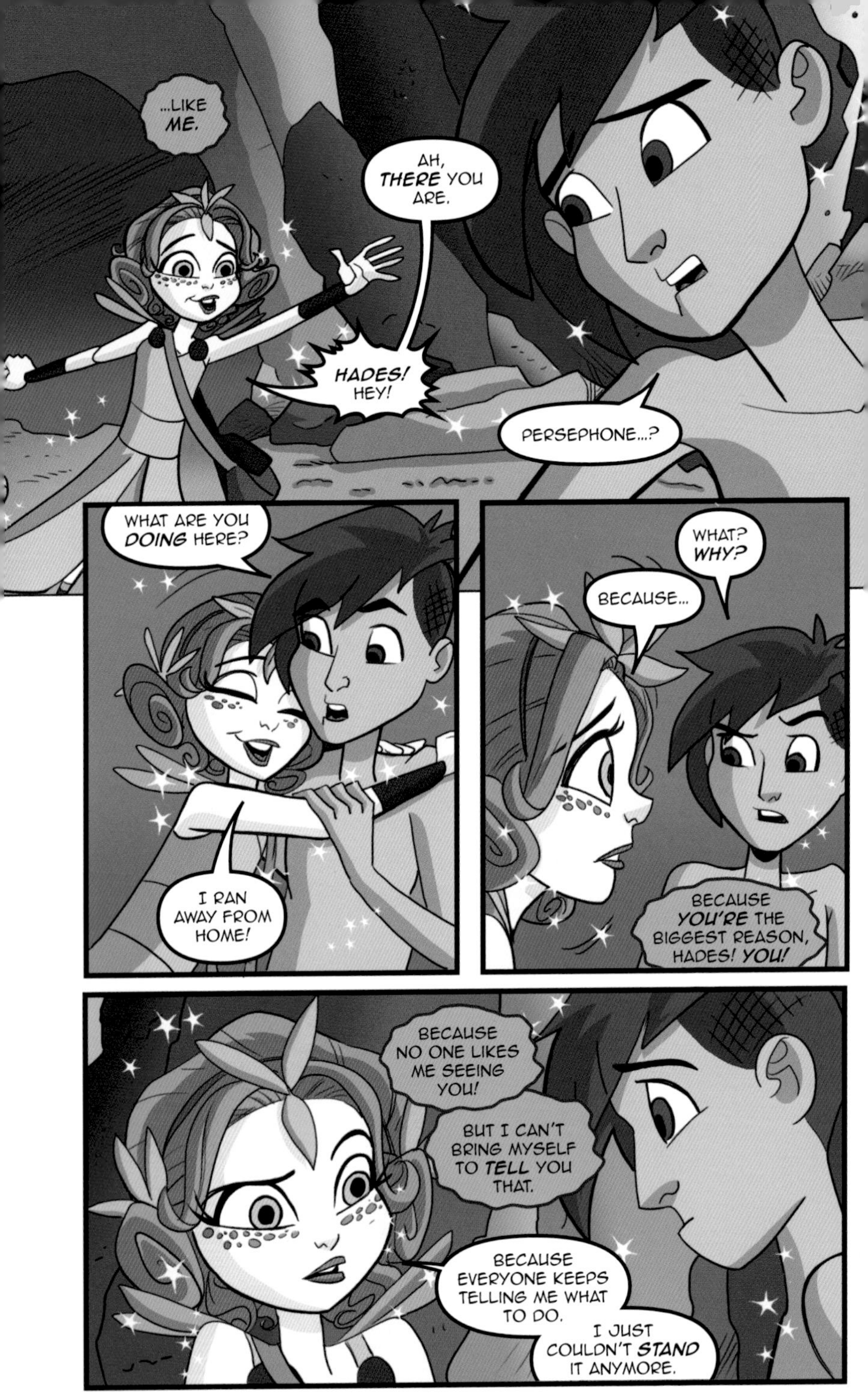
...LIKE ME.
AH, THERE YOU ARE.
HADES! HEY!
PERSEPHONE...?
WHAT ARE YOU DOING HERE?
I RAN AWAY FROM HOME!
WHAT? WHY?
BECAUSE...
BECAUSE YOU'RE THE BIGGEST REASON, HADES! YOU!
BECAUSE NO ONE LIKES ME SEEING YOU!
BUT I CAN'T BRING MYSELF TO TELL YOU THAT.
BECAUSE EVERYONE KEEPS TELLING ME WHAT TO DO.
I JUST COULDN'T STAND IT ANYMORE.

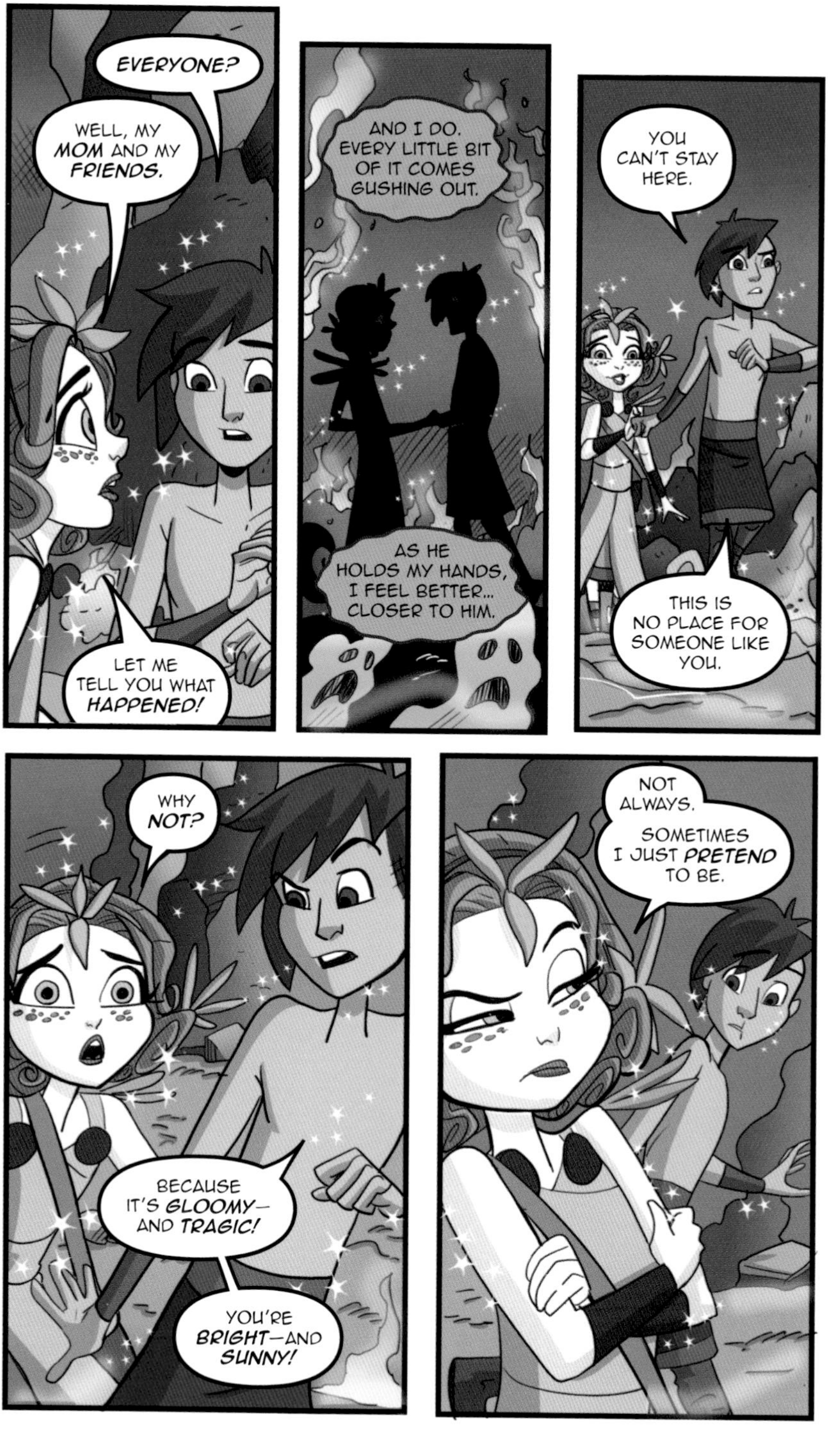
EVERYONE?
WELL, MY MOM AND MY FRIENDS.
LET ME TELL YOU WHAT HAPPENED!
AND I DO. EVERY LITTLE BIT OF IT COMES GUSHING OUT.
AS HE HOLDS MY HANDS, I FEEL BETTER... CLOSER TO HIM.
YOU CAN'T STAY HERE.
THIS IS NO PLACE FOR SOMEONE LIKE YOU.
WHY NOT?
BECAUSE IT'S GLOOMY— AND TRAGIC!
YOU'RE BRIGHT—AND SUNNY!
NOT ALWAYS.
SOMETIMES I JUST PRETEND TO BE.

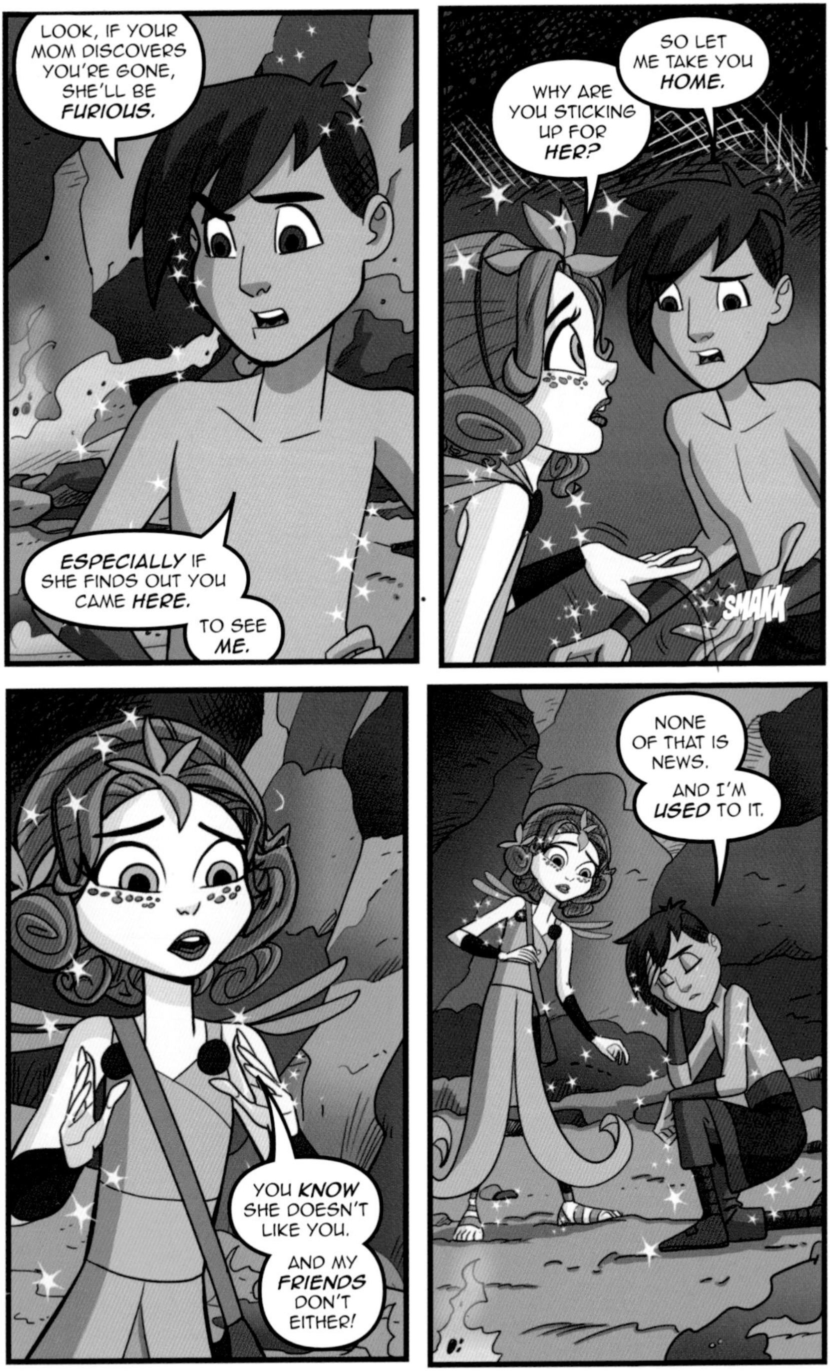

LOOK, IF YOUR MOM DISCOVERS YOU'RE GONE, SHE'LL BE FURIOUS.
ESPECIALLY IF SHE FINDS OUT YOU CAME HERE.
TO SEE ME.
WHY ARE YOU STICKING UP FOR HER?
SO LET ME TAKE YOU HOME.
SMAKK
YOU KNOW SHE DOESN'T LIKE YOU.
AND MY FRIENDS DON'T EITHER!
NONE OF THAT IS NEWS.
AND I'M USED TO IT.

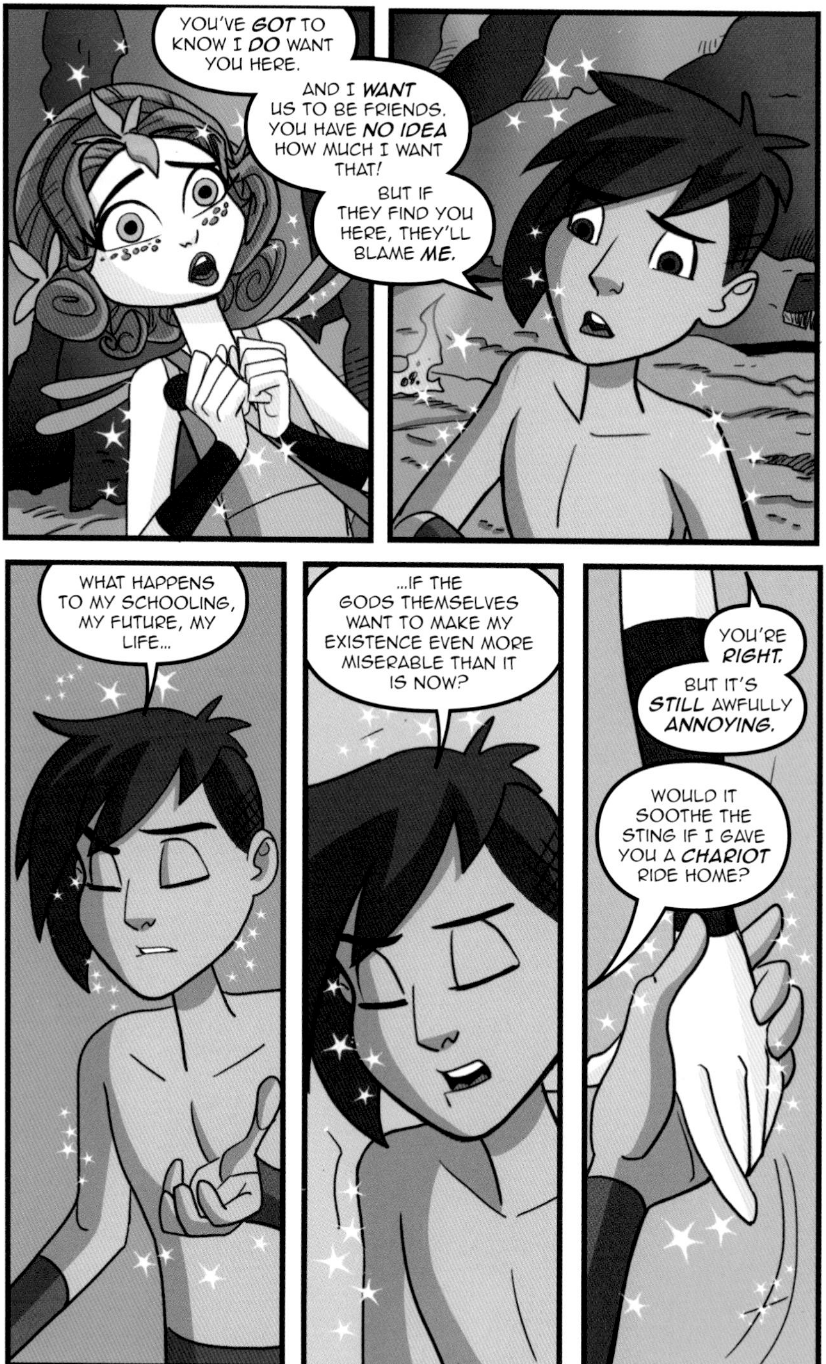
YOU'VE GOT TO KNOW I DO WANT YOU HERE.
AND I WANT US TO BE FRIENDS. YOU HAVE NO IDEA HOW MUCH I WANT THAT!
BUT IF THEY FIND YOU HERE, THEY'LL BLAME ME.
WHAT HAPPENS TO MY SCHOOLING, MY FUTURE, MY LIFE...
...IF THE GODS THEMSELVES WANT TO MAKE MY EXISTENCE EVEN MORE MISERABLE THAN IT IS NOW?
YOU'RE RIGHT.
BUT IT'S STILL AWFULLY ANNOYING.
WOULD IT SOOTHE THE STING IF I GAVE YOU A CHARIOT RIDE HOME?

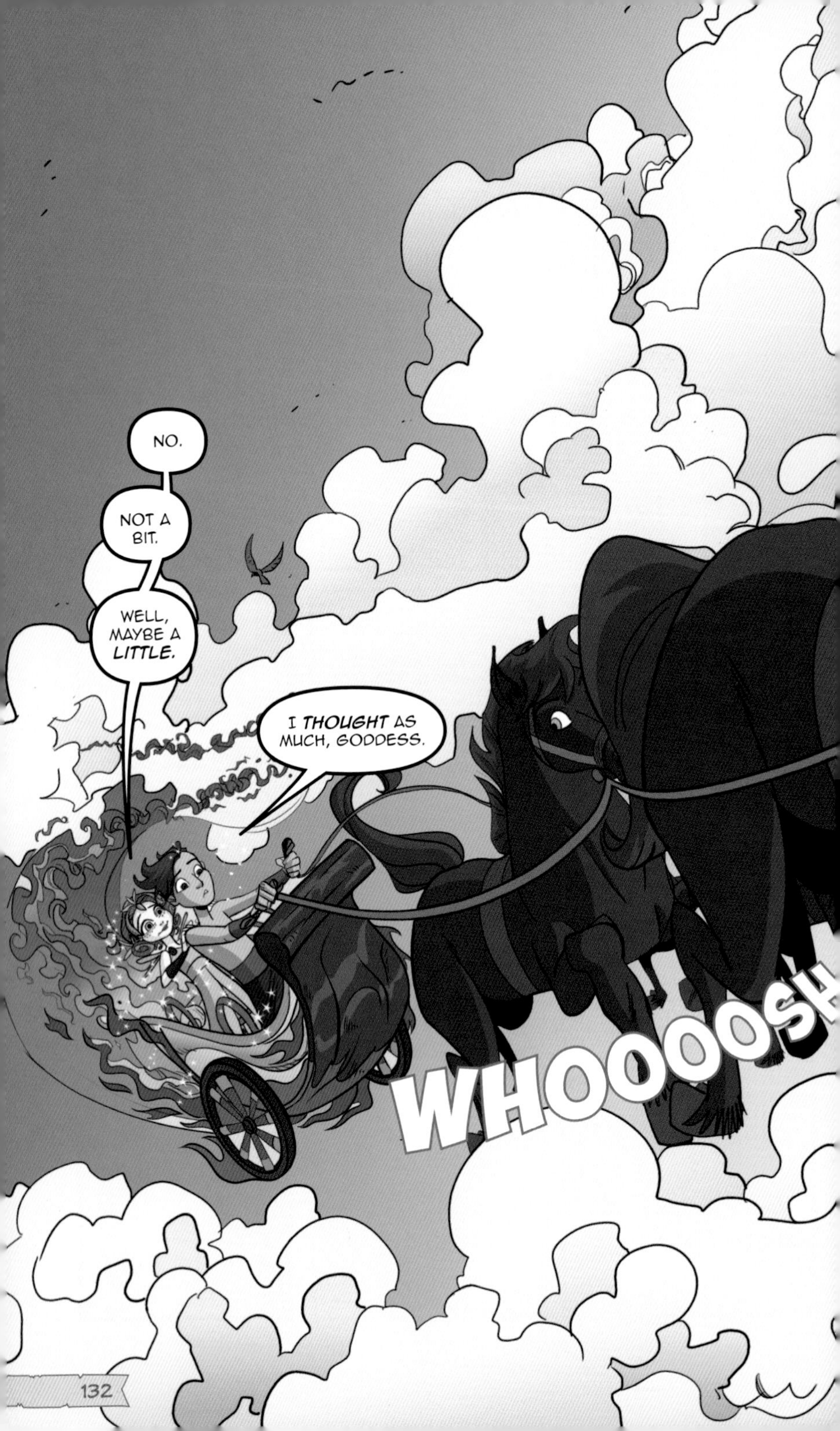

NO.
NOT A BIT.
WELL, MAYBE A *LITTLE.*
I *THOUGHT* AS MUCH, GODDESS.
WHOOOOOSH

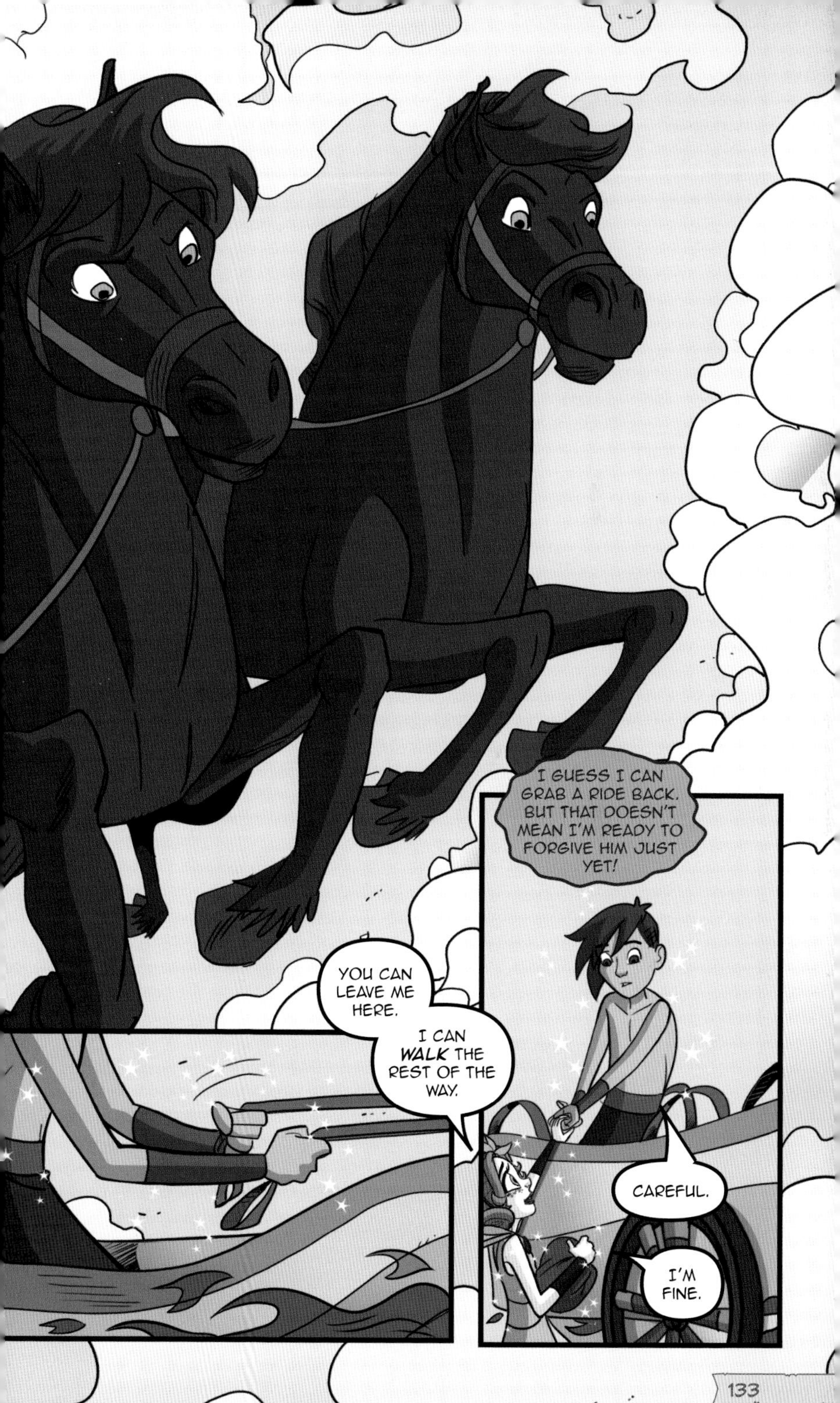
I GUESS I CAN GRAB A RIDE BACK. BUT THAT DOESN'T MEAN I'M READY TO FORGIVE HIM JUST YET!
YOU CAN LEAVE ME HERE.
I CAN WALK THE REST OF THE WAY.
CAREFUL.
I'M FINE.

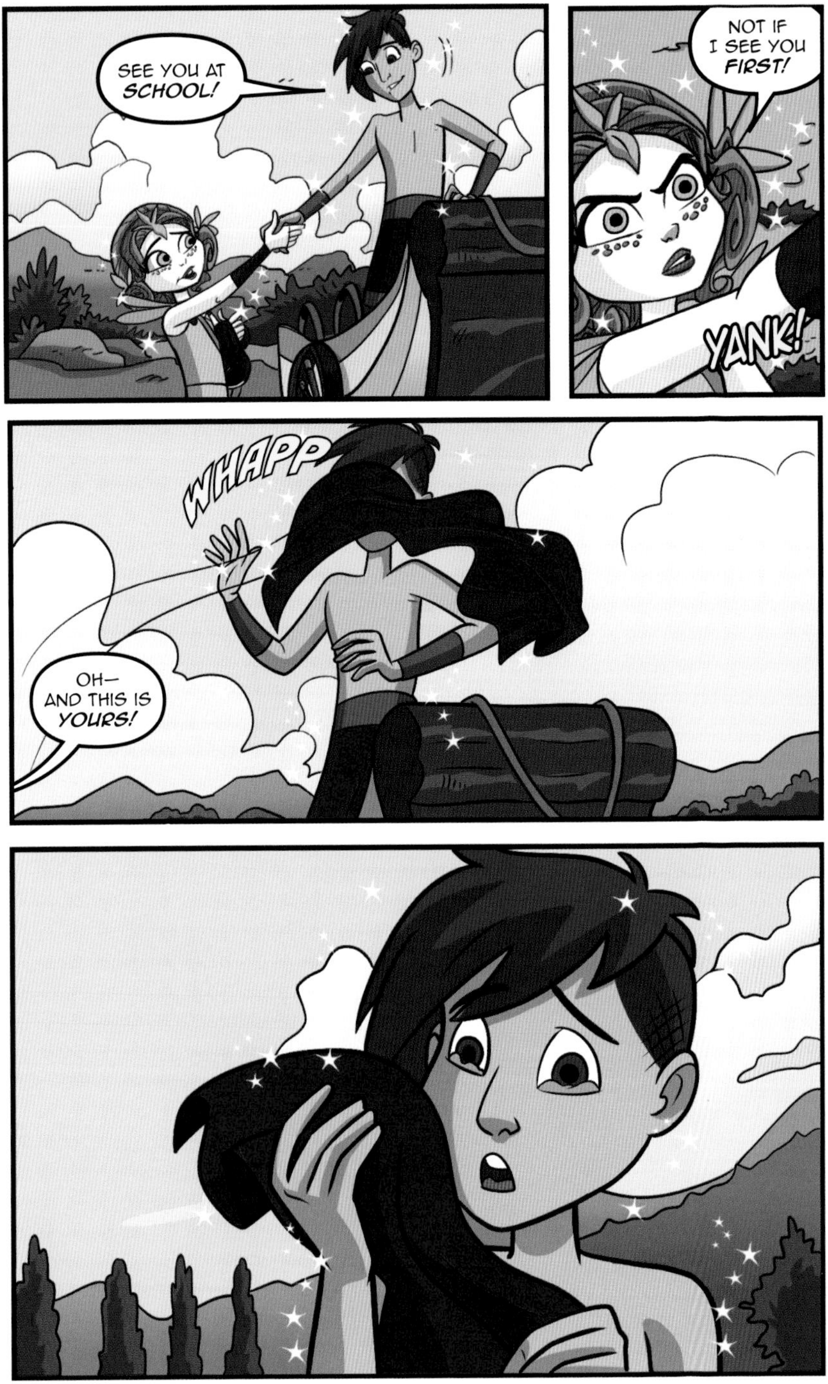
SEE YOU AT SCHOOL!
NOT IF I SEE YOU FIRST!
YANK!
WHAPP
OH— AND THIS IS YOURS!

CHAPTER 9: HOME AGAIN

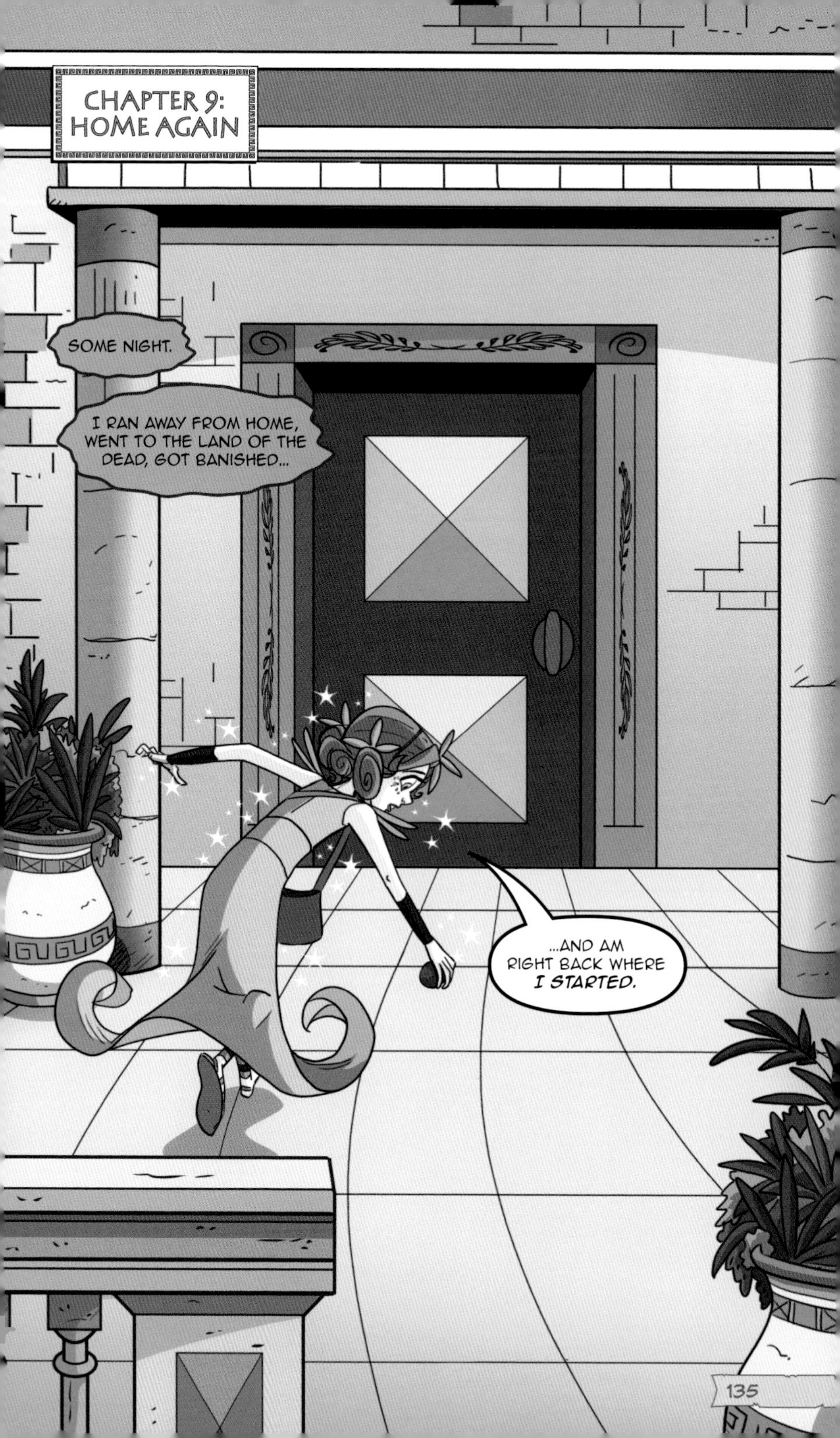
SOME NIGHT.
I RAN AWAY FROM HOME, WENT TO THE LAND OF THE DEAD, GOT BANISHED...
...AND AM RIGHT BACK WHERE *I STARTED.*

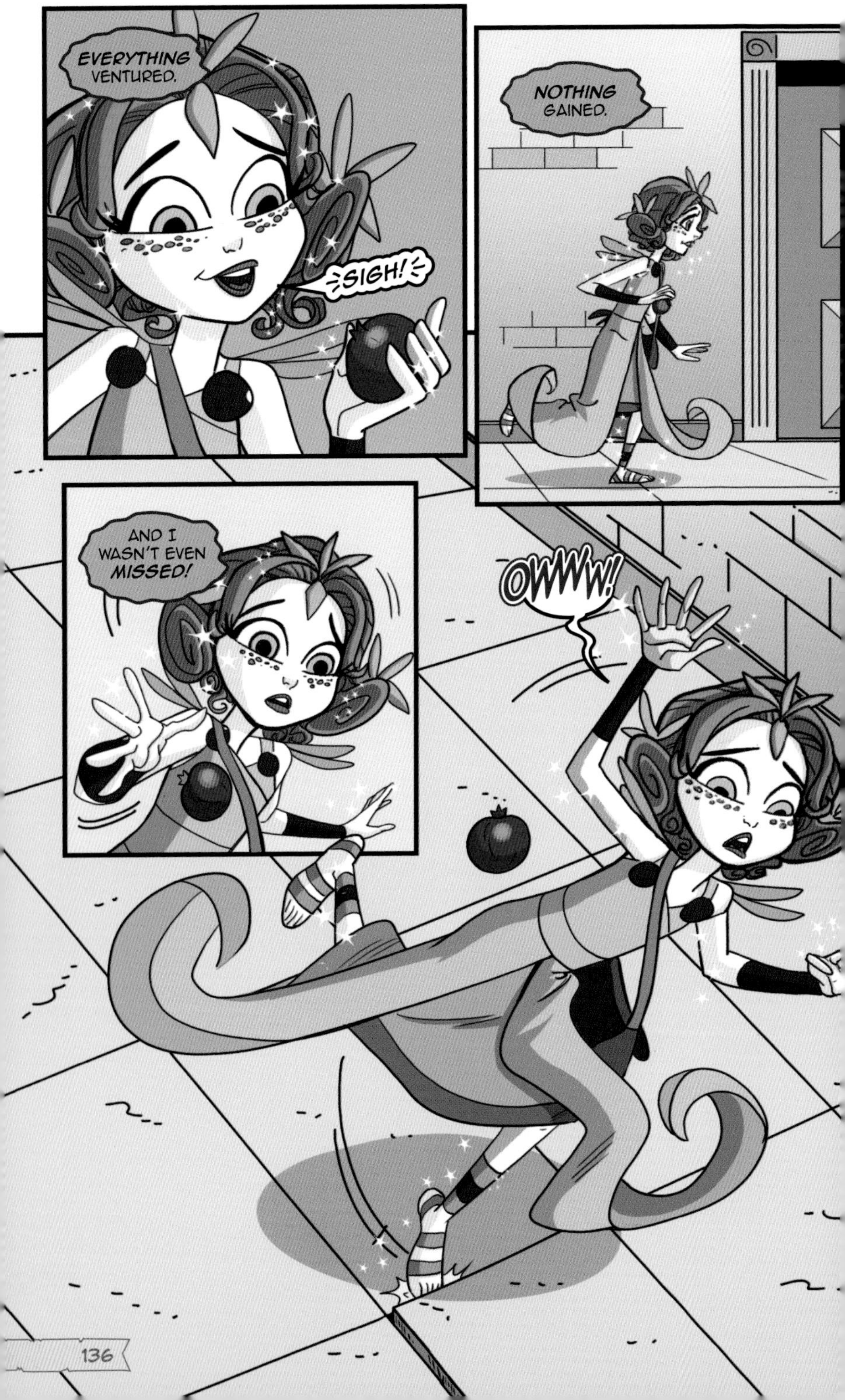
EVERYTHING VENTURED.
SIGH!
NOTHING GAINED.
AND I WASN'T EVEN MISSED!
OWWW!

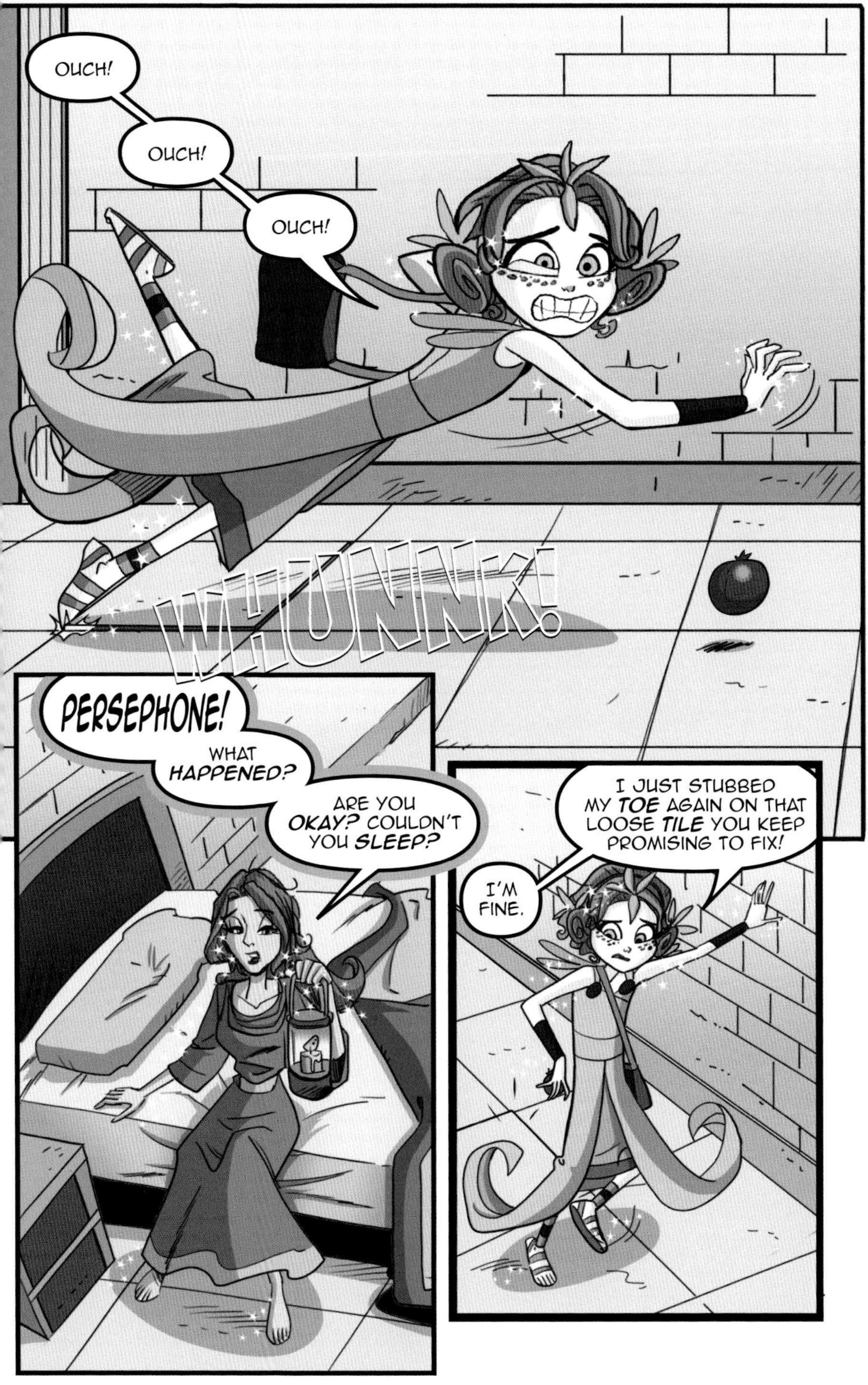

OUCH!
OUCH!
OUCH!
WHUNNK!
PERSEPHONE! WHAT HAPPENED?
ARE YOU OKAY? COULDN'T YOU SLEEP?
I'M FINE.
I JUST STUBBED MY TOE AGAIN ON THAT LOOSE TILE YOU KEEP PROMISING TO FIX!

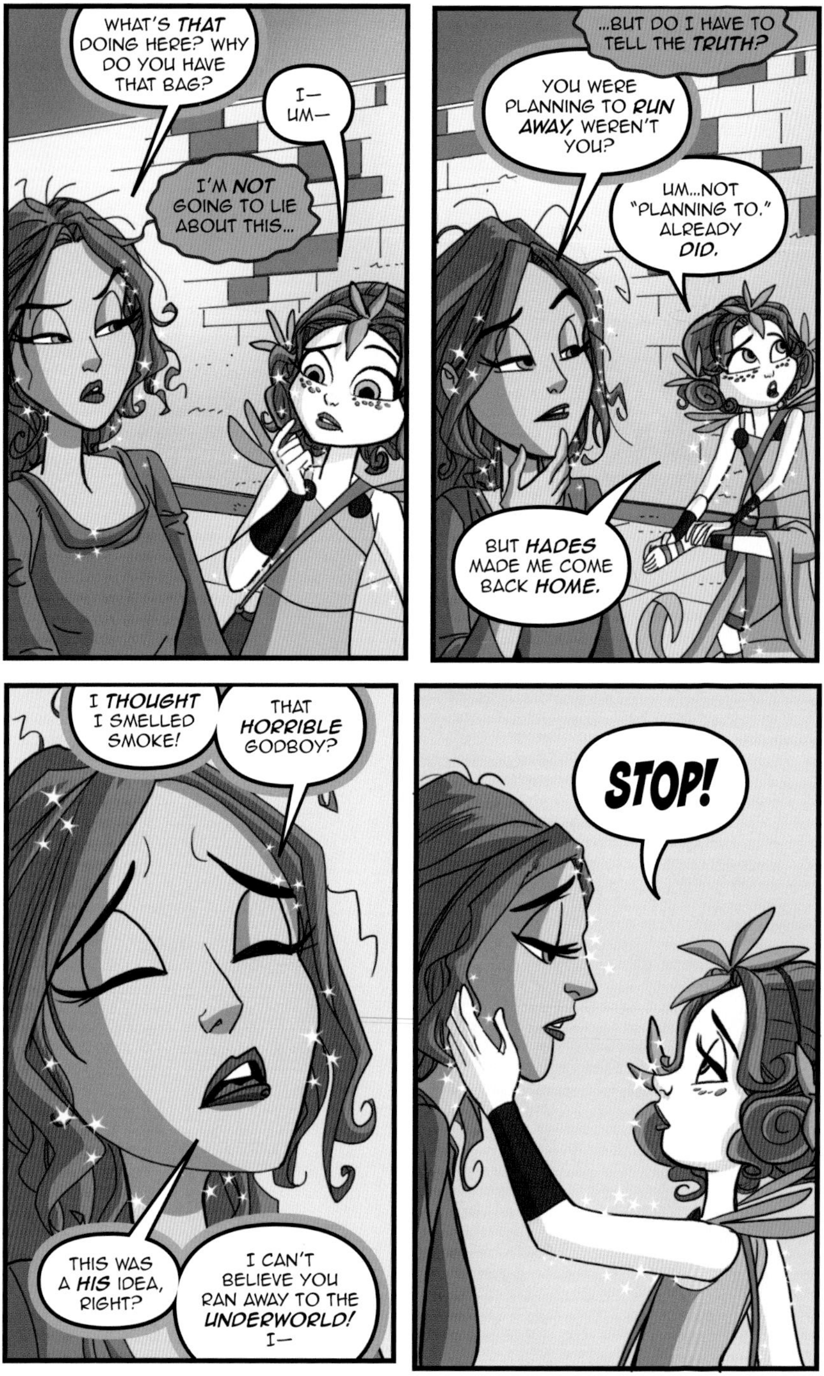
WHAT'S THAT DOING HERE? WHY DO YOU HAVE THAT BAG?
I— UM—
I'M NOT GOING TO LIE ABOUT THIS...
...BUT DO I HAVE TO TELL THE TRUTH?
YOU WERE PLANNING TO RUN AWAY, WEREN'T YOU?
UM...NOT "PLANNING TO." ALREADY DID.
BUT HADES MADE ME COME BACK HOME.
I THOUGHT I SMELLED SMOKE!
THAT HORRIBLE GODBOY?
THIS WAS A HIS IDEA, RIGHT?
I CAN'T BELIEVE YOU RAN AWAY TO THE UNDERWORLD! I—
STOP!

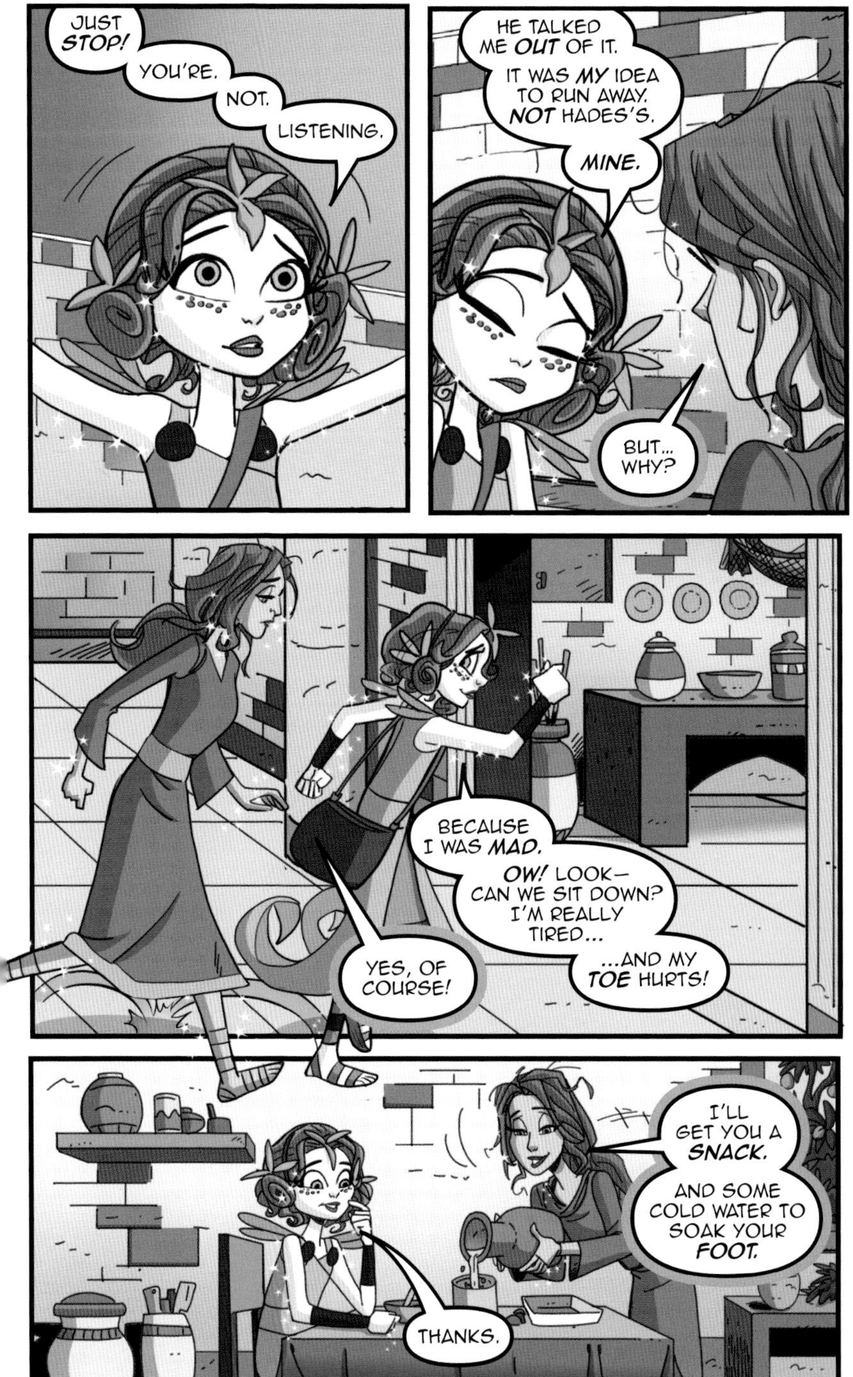
JUST STOP!
YOU'RE.
NOT.
LISTENING.
HE TALKED ME OUT OF IT.
IT WAS MY IDEA TO RUN AWAY. NOT HADES'S.
MINE.
BUT... WHY?
BECAUSE I WAS MAD.
OW! LOOK— CAN WE SIT DOWN? I'M REALLY TIRED...
YES, OF COURSE!
...AND MY TOE HURTS!
I'LL GET YOU A SNACK.
AND SOME COLD WATER TO SOAK YOUR FOOT.
THANKS.

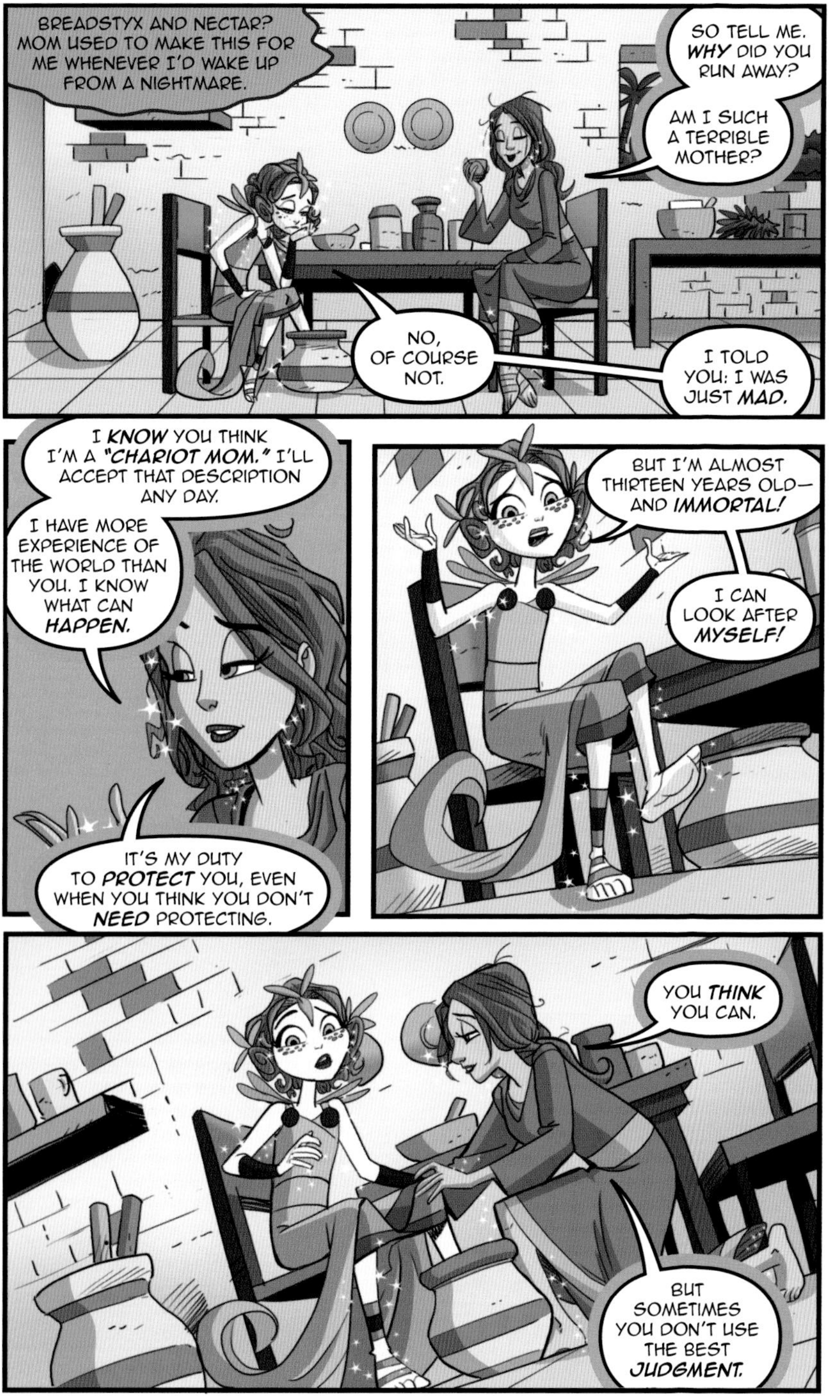
BREADSTYX AND NECTAR? MOM USED TO MAKE THIS FOR ME WHENEVER I'D WAKE UP FROM A NIGHTMARE.
SO TELL ME. WHY DID YOU RUN AWAY?
AM I SUCH A TERRIBLE MOTHER?
NO, OF COURSE NOT.
I TOLD YOU: I WAS JUST MAD.
I KNOW YOU THINK I'M A "CHARIOT MOM." I'LL ACCEPT THAT DESCRIPTION ANY DAY.
I HAVE MORE EXPERIENCE OF THE WORLD THAN YOU. I KNOW WHAT CAN HAPPEN.
IT'S MY DUTY TO PROTECT YOU, EVEN WHEN YOU THINK YOU DON'T NEED PROTECTING.
BUT I'M ALMOST THIRTEEN YEARS OLD— AND IMMORTAL!
I CAN LOOK AFTER MYSELF!
YOU THINK YOU CAN.
BUT SOMETIMES YOU DON'T USE THE BEST JUDGMENT.

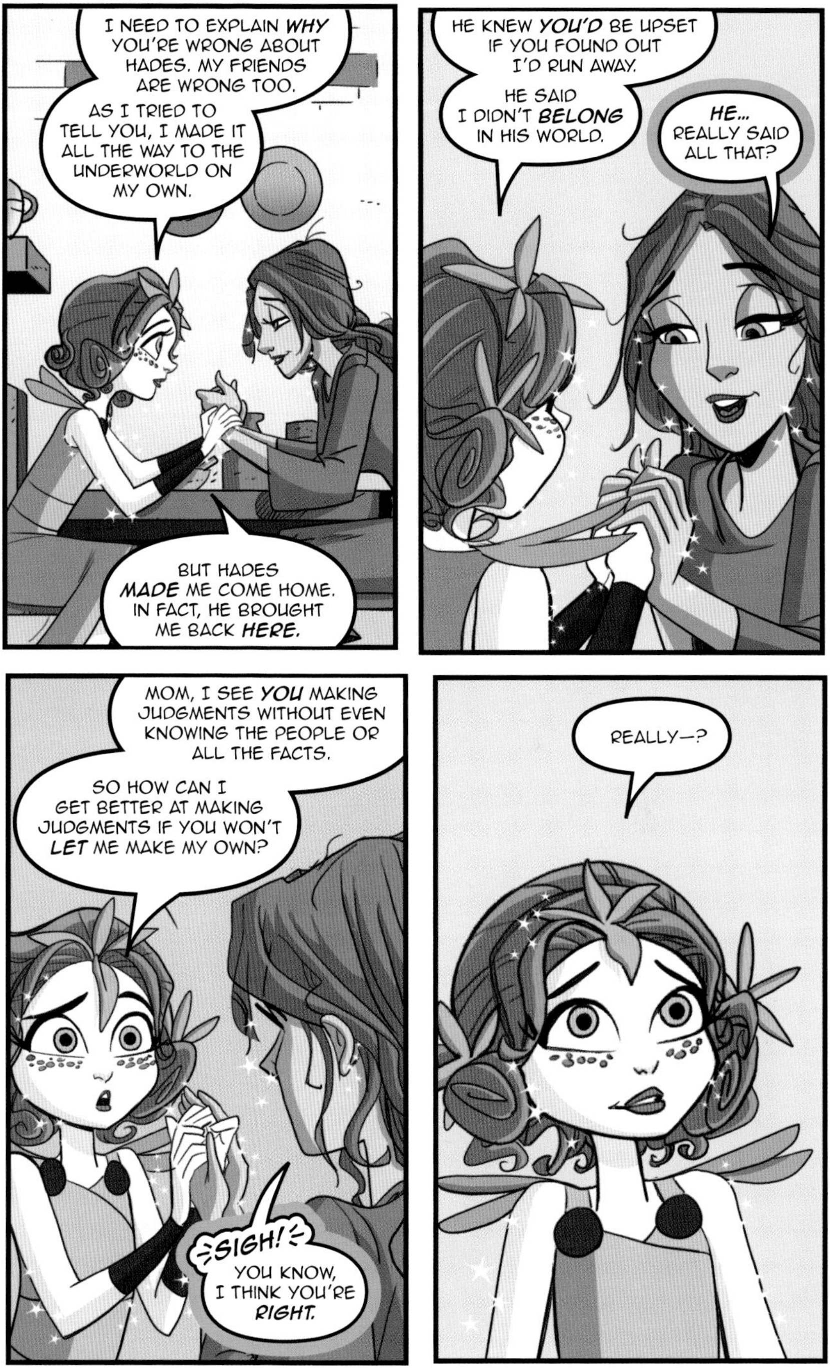
I NEED TO EXPLAIN WHY YOU'RE WRONG ABOUT HADES. MY FRIENDS ARE WRONG TOO.
AS I TRIED TO TELL YOU, I MADE IT ALL THE WAY TO THE UNDERWORLD ON MY OWN.
BUT HADES MADE ME COME HOME. IN FACT, HE BROUGHT ME BACK HERE.
HE KNEW YOU'D BE UPSET IF YOU FOUND OUT I'D RUN AWAY.
HE SAID I DIDN'T BELONG IN HIS WORLD.
HE... REALLY SAID ALL THAT?
MOM, I SEE YOU MAKING JUDGMENTS WITHOUT EVEN KNOWING THE PEOPLE OR ALL THE FACTS.
SO HOW CAN I GET BETTER AT MAKING JUDGMENTS IF YOU WON'T LET ME MAKE MY OWN?
SIGH!
YOU KNOW, I THINK YOU'RE RIGHT.
REALLY—?

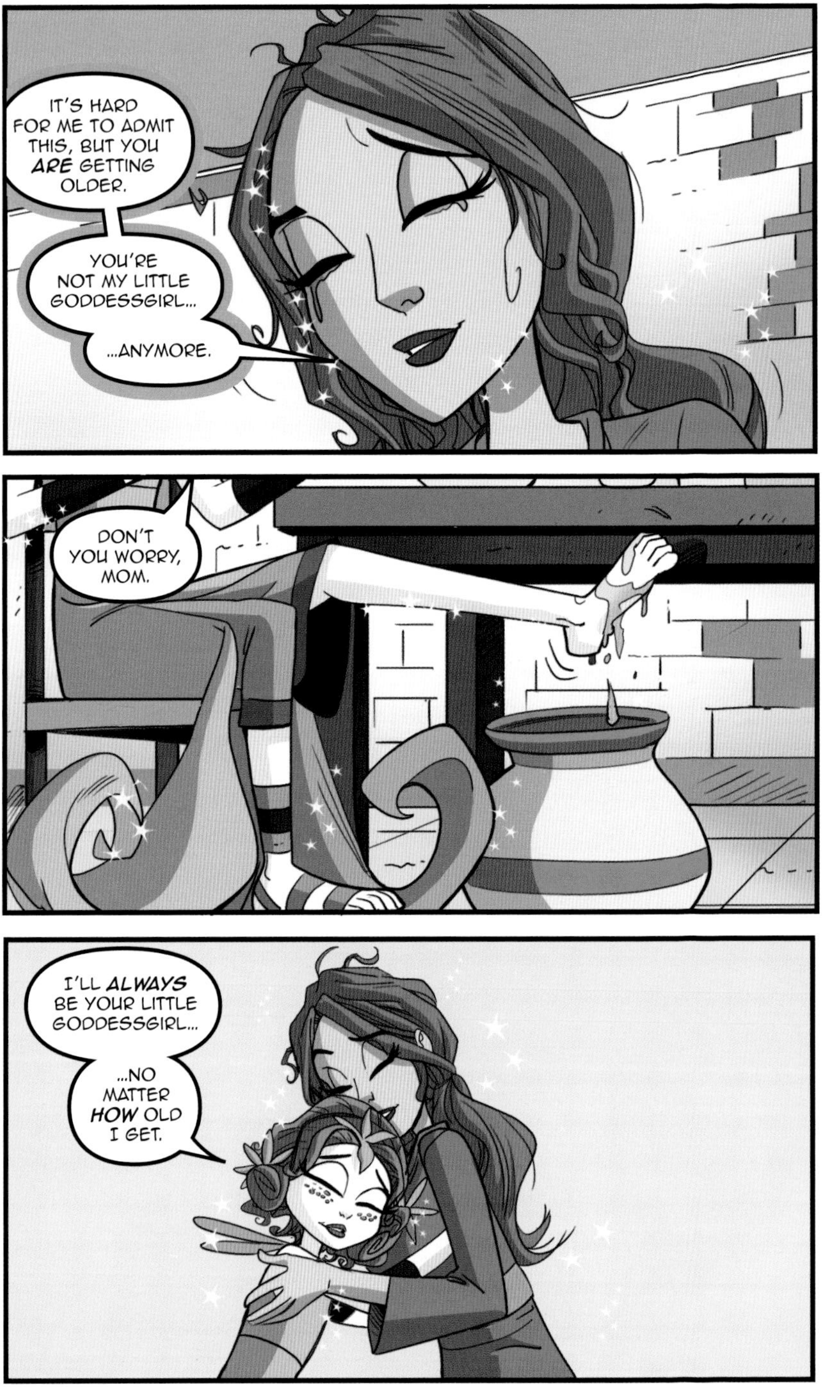
IT'S HARD FOR ME TO ADMIT THIS, BUT YOU ARE GETTING OLDER.
YOU'RE NOT MY LITTLE GODDESSGIRL...
...ANYMORE.
DON'T YOU WORRY, MOM.
I'LL ALWAYS BE YOUR LITTLE GODDESSGIRL...
...NO MATTER HOW OLD I GET.

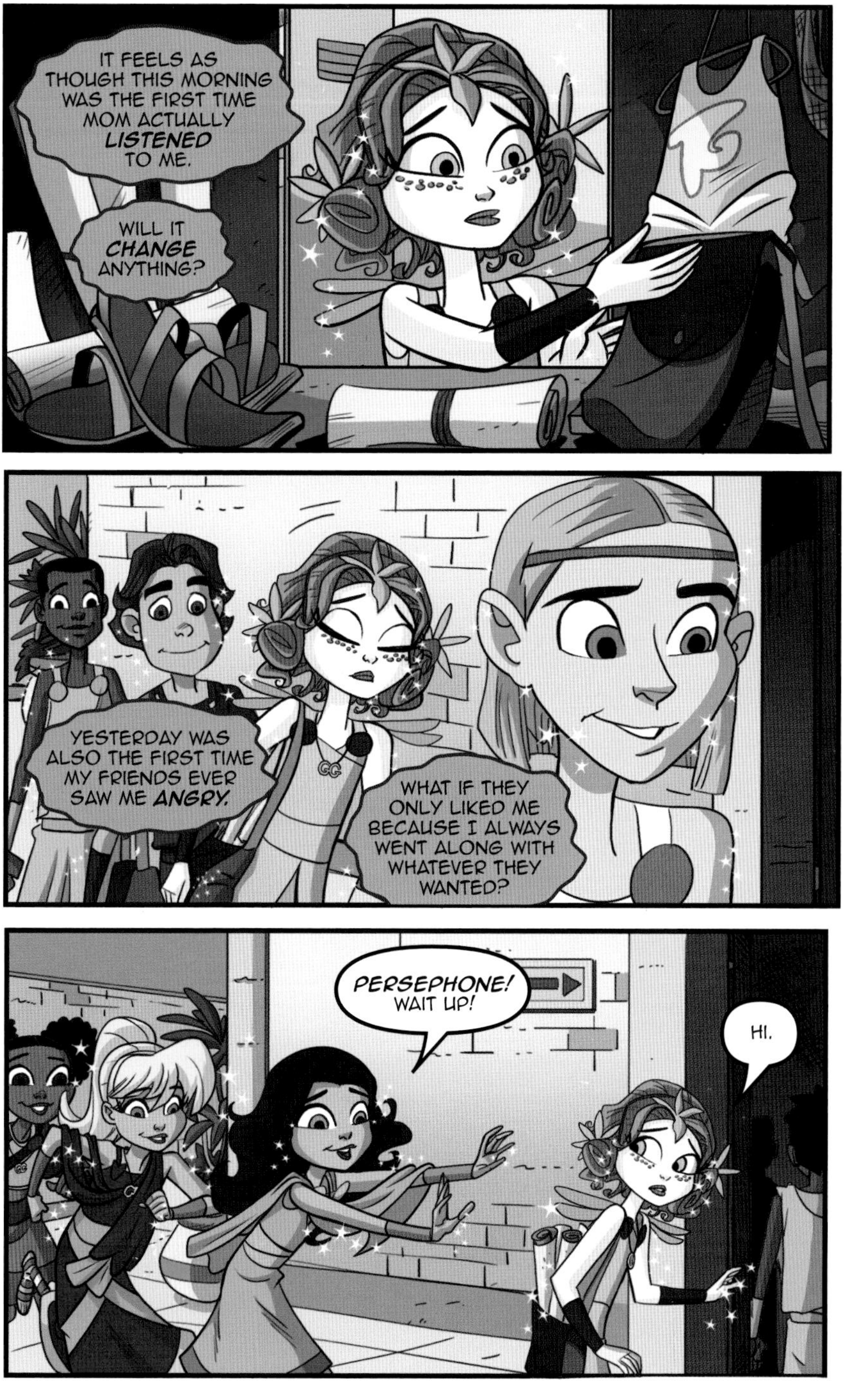
IT FEELS AS THOUGH THIS MORNING WAS THE FIRST TIME MOM ACTUALLY **LISTENED** TO ME.
WILL IT **CHANGE** ANYTHING?
YESTERDAY WAS ALSO THE FIRST TIME MY FRIENDS EVER SAW ME **ANGRY.**
WHAT IF THEY ONLY LIKED ME BECAUSE I ALWAYS WENT ALONG WITH WHATEVER THEY WANTED?
PERSEPHONE! WAIT UP!
HI.

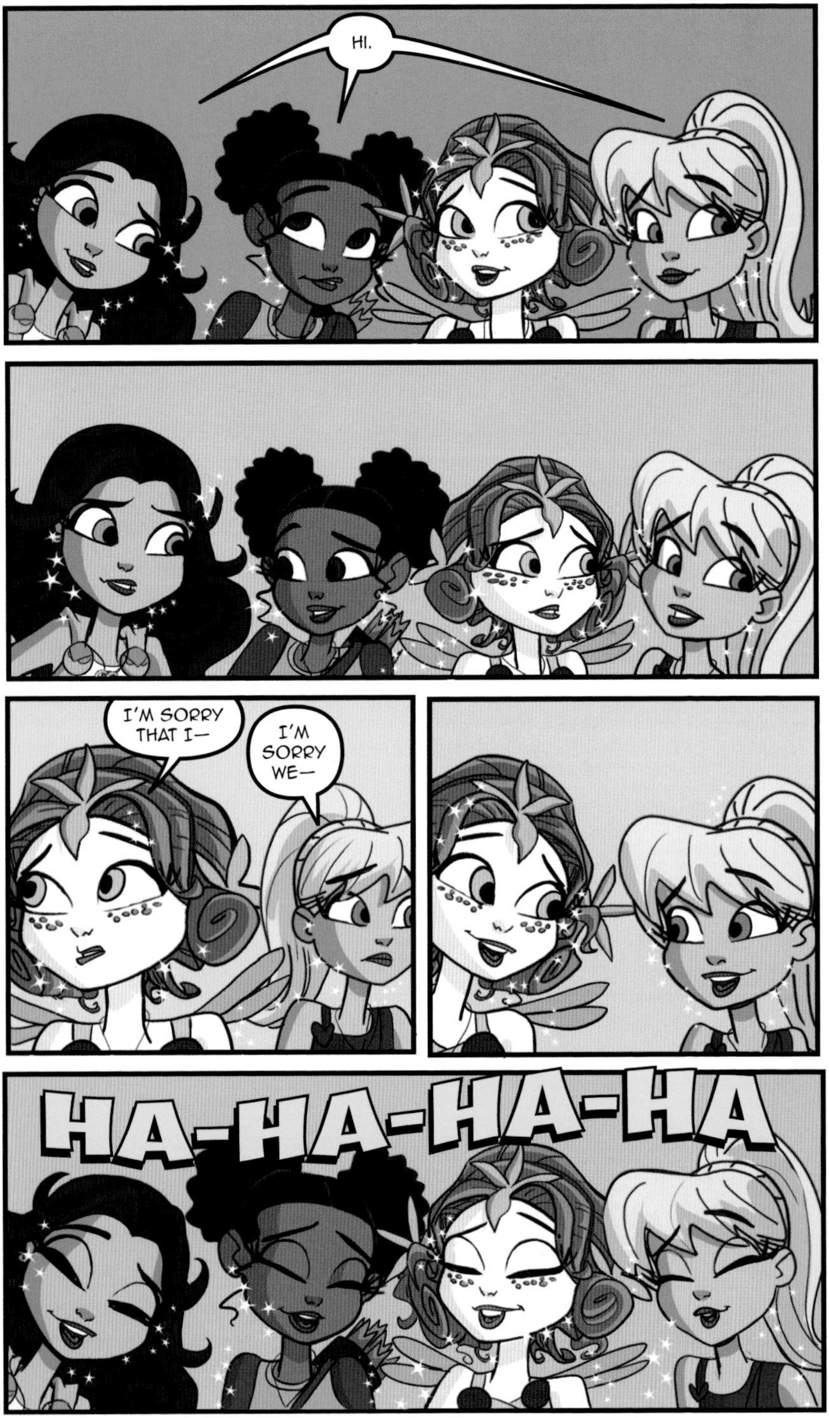
HI.
I'M SORRY THAT I—
I'M SORRY WE—
HA-HA-HA-HA-HA

I'M SO GLAD YOU'RE NOT *MAD* AT ME.

US TOO.

YEAH.

YEAH.

WOW. THEY... ABOUT WH... YESTERD...

ARE THINGS OKAY BETWEEN YOU AND YOUR MOM?

WE HAD A GOOD TALK LAST NIGHT...

THAT'S GREAT.

...*INCLUDING* MOM PROMISING TO FIX THE BROKEN *TILE* IN THE HALLWAY!

OUCH! THAT TILE TRIED TO TRIP *ME* UP YESTERDAY TOO.

I'VE NEVER *SEEN* YOU SO MAD BEFORE. DIDN'T KNOW YOU HAD IT IN YOU!

YOU ERUPTED LIKE A *VOLCANO*— A REAL MOUNT VESUVIUS!

I'M SORRY.

DON'T BE! DON'T YOU THINK *WE* GET ANGRY SOMETIMES TOO?

145

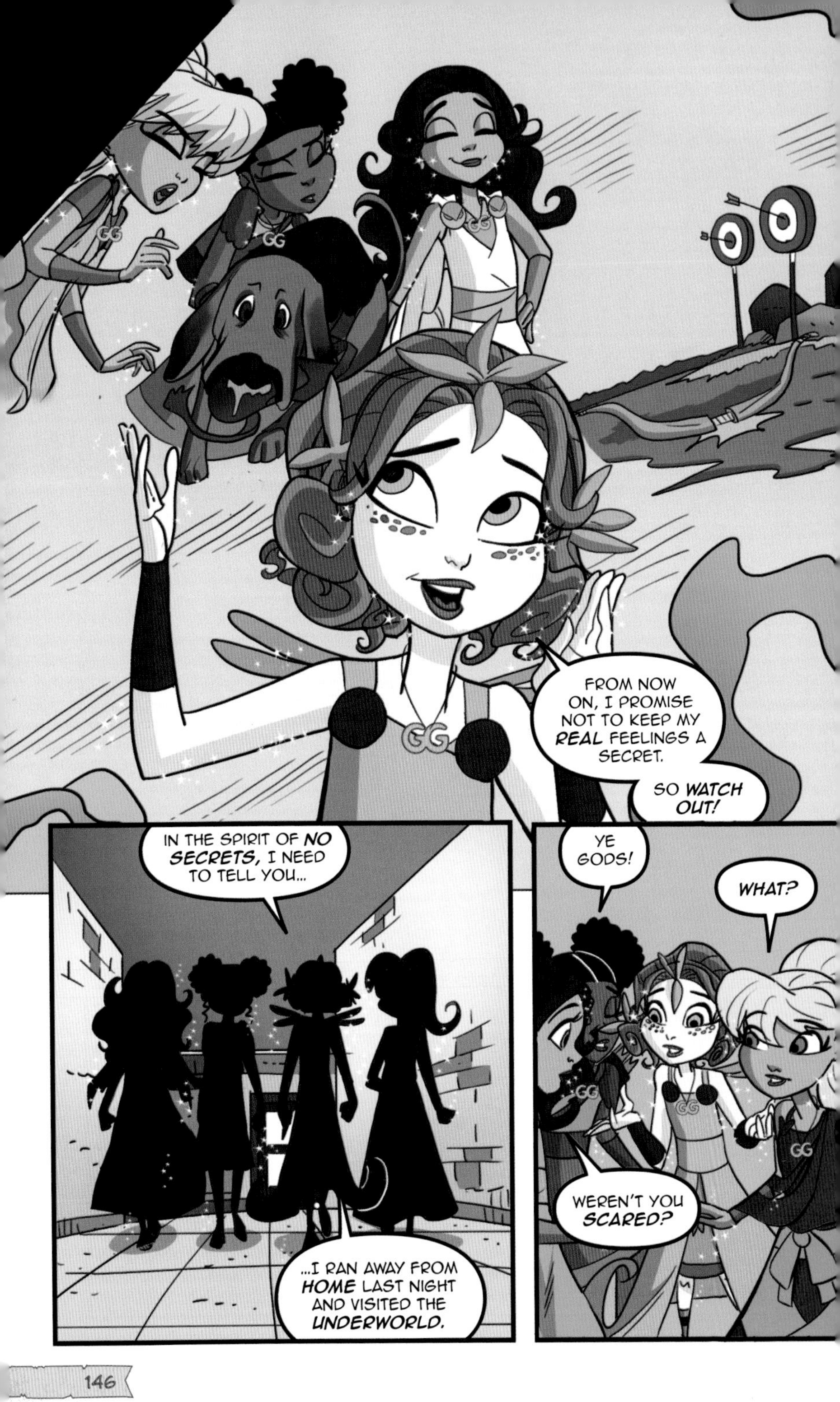
FROM NOW ON, I PROMISE NOT TO KEEP MY REAL FEELINGS A SECRET.
SO WATCH OUT!
IN THE SPIRIT OF NO SECRETS, I NEED TO TELL YOU...
...I RAN AWAY FROM HOME LAST NIGHT AND VISITED THE UNDERWORLD.
YE GODS!
WHAT?
WEREN'T YOU SCARED?

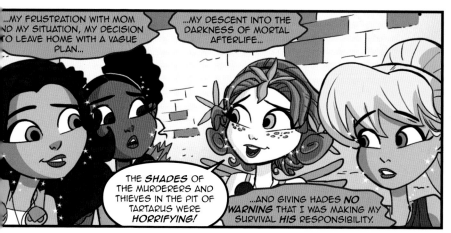

...MY FRUSTRATION WITH MOM AND MY SITUATION, MY DECISION TO LEAVE HOME WITH A VAGUE PLAN...

...MY DESCENT INTO THE DARKNESS OF MORTAL AFTERLIFE...

THE *SHADES* OF THE MURDERERS AND THIEVES IN THE PIT OF TARTARUS WERE *HORRIFYING!*

...AND GIVING HADES *NO WARNING* THAT I WAS MAKING MY SURVIVAL *HIS* RESPONSIBILITY.

SO BASICALLY HADES *BANISHED* YOU FROM THE UNDERWORLD??

YEAH. THOUGH IF HADES HADN'T RUSHED ME *HOME*, I WOULD'VE LIKED TO HAVE *SEEN* MORE—DESPITE MY FEAR.

YOU'RE BRAVER THAN ME, FOR SURE!

WOW, ME TOO! I WOULDN'T EVEN KNOW WHAT *OUTFIT* TO WEAR IN THE UNDERWORLD!

MAYBE SOMETHING *FIREPROOF.*

HA-HA-HA-HA

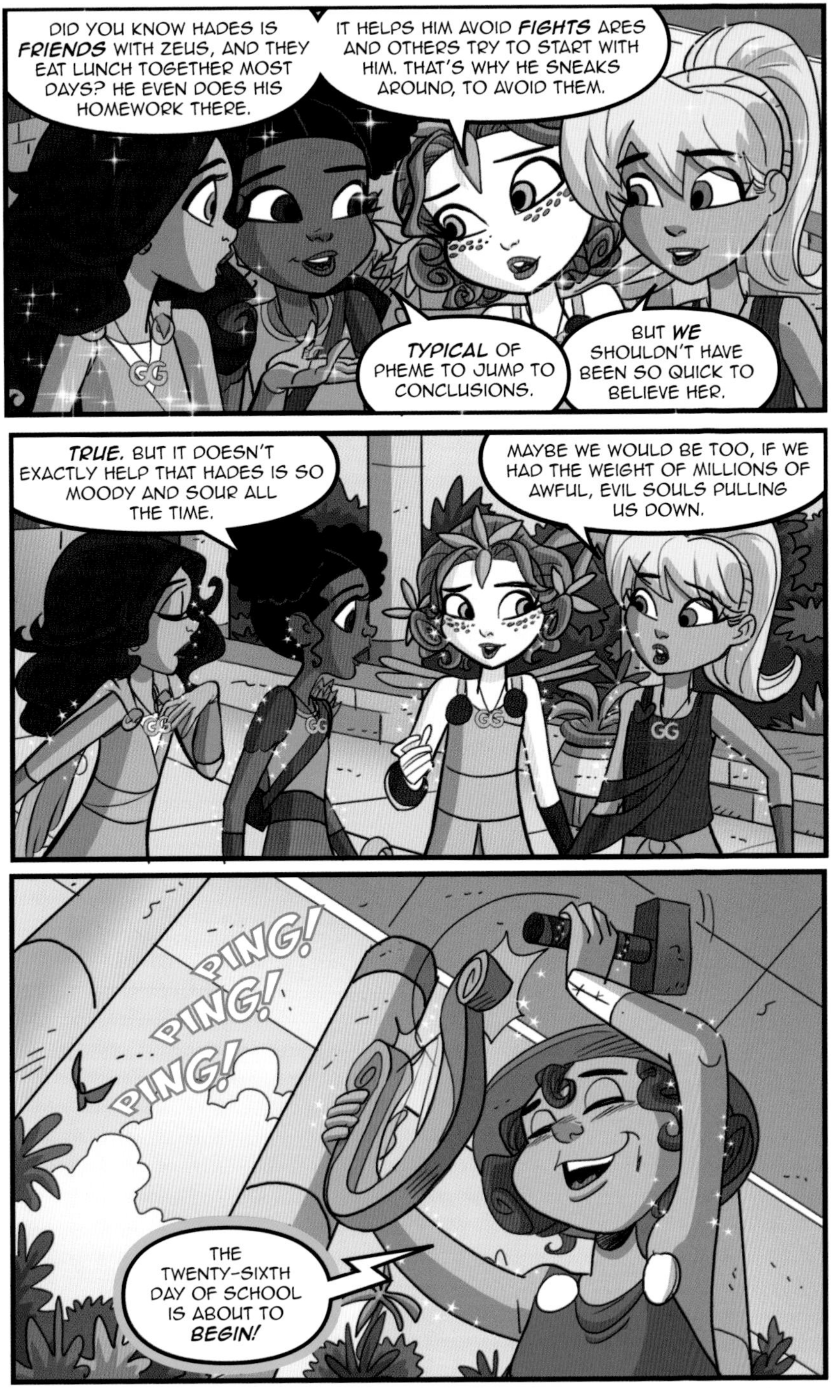
DID YOU KNOW HADES IS FRIENDS WITH ZEUS, AND THEY EAT LUNCH TOGETHER MOST DAYS? HE EVEN DOES HIS HOMEWORK THERE.
IT HELPS HIM AVOID FIGHTS ARES AND OTHERS TRY TO START WITH HIM. THAT'S WHY HE SNEAKS AROUND, TO AVOID THEM.
TYPICAL OF PHEME TO JUMP TO CONCLUSIONS.
BUT WE SHOULDN'T HAVE BEEN SO QUICK TO BELIEVE HER.
TRUE. BUT IT DOESN'T EXACTLY HELP THAT HADES IS SO MOODY AND SOUR ALL THE TIME.
MAYBE WE WOULD BE TOO, IF WE HAD THE WEIGHT OF MILLIONS OF AWFUL, EVIL SOULS PULLING US DOWN.
PING!
PING!
PING!
THE TWENTY-SIXTH DAY OF SCHOOL IS ABOUT TO BEGIN!

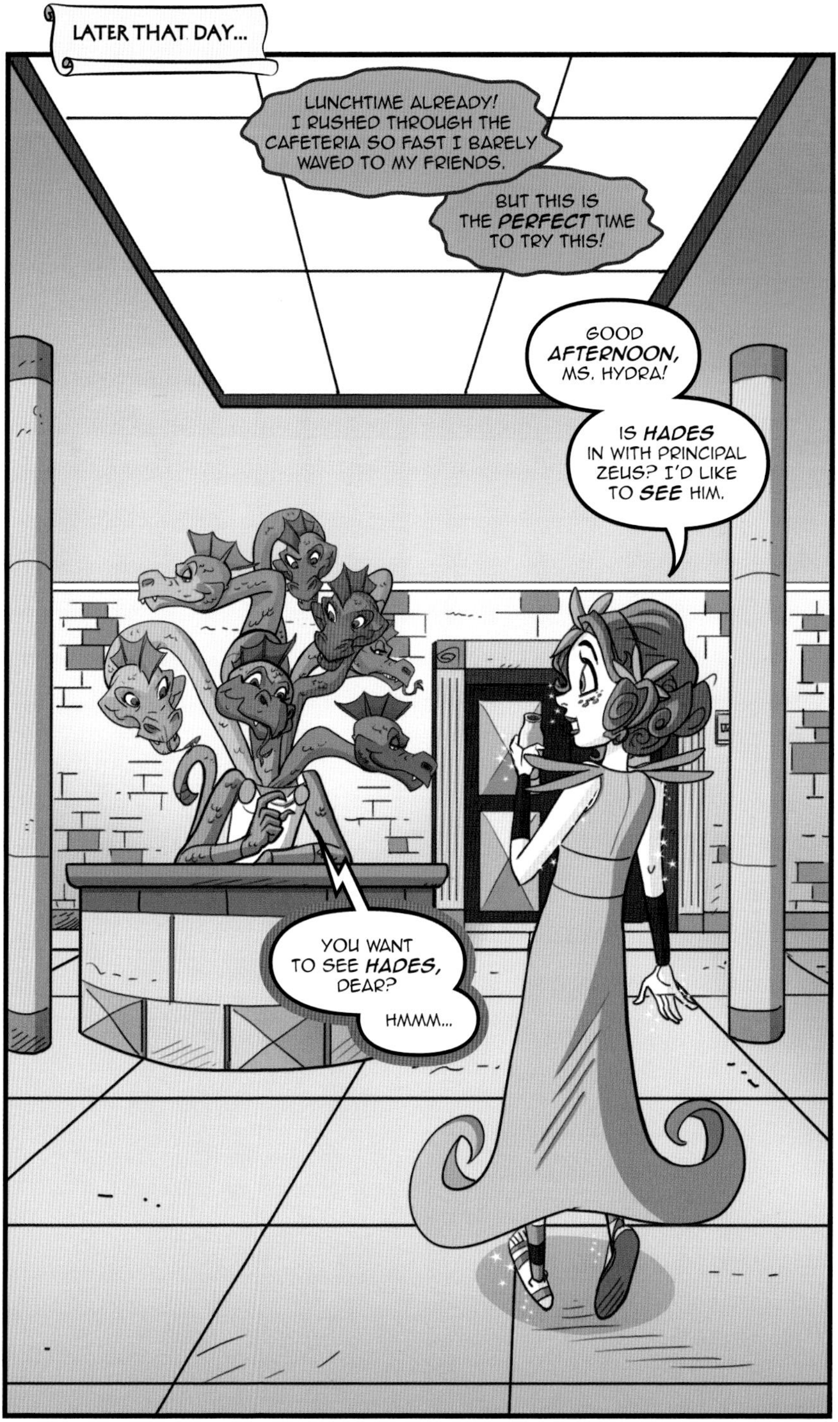
LATER THAT DAY...
LUNCHTIME ALREADY! I RUSHED THROUGH THE CAFETERIA SO FAST I BARELY WAVED TO MY FRIENDS.
BUT THIS IS THE *PERFECT* TIME TO TRY THIS!
GOOD **AFTERNOON,** MS. HYDRA!
IS **HADES** IN WITH PRINCIPAL ZEUS? I'D LIKE TO **SEE** HIM.
YOU WANT TO SEE **HADES,** DEAR?
HMMM...

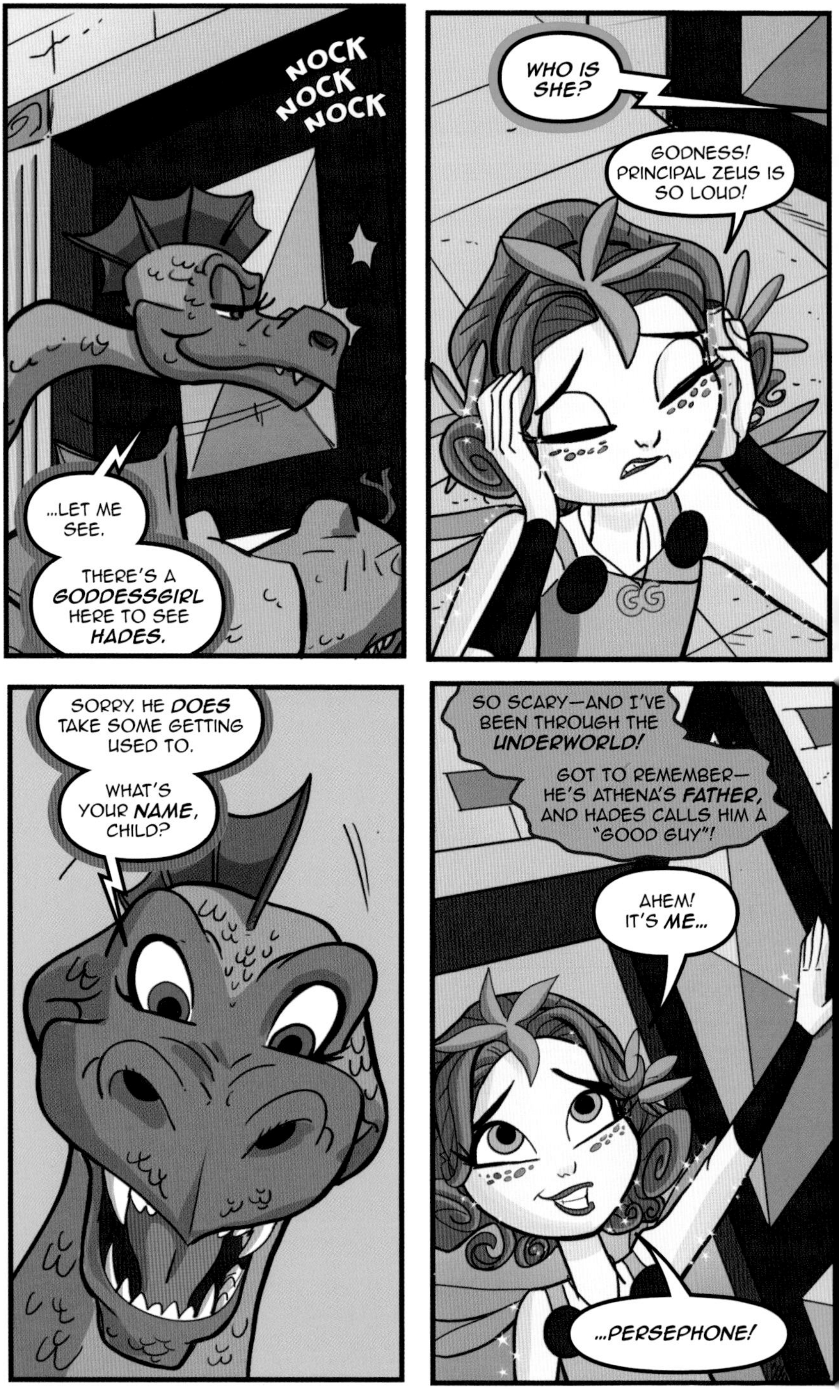
NOCK NOCK NOCK
...LET ME SEE.
THERE'S A GODDESSGIRL HERE TO SEE HADES.
WHO IS SHE?
GODNESS! PRINCIPAL ZEUS IS SO LOUD!
SORRY. HE DOES TAKE SOME GETTING USED TO.
WHAT'S YOUR NAME, CHILD?
SO SCARY—AND I'VE BEEN THROUGH THE UNDERWORLD!
GOT TO REMEMBER—HE'S ATHENA'S FATHER, AND HADES CALLS HIM A "GOOD GUY"!
AHEM! IT'S ME...
...PERSEPHONE!

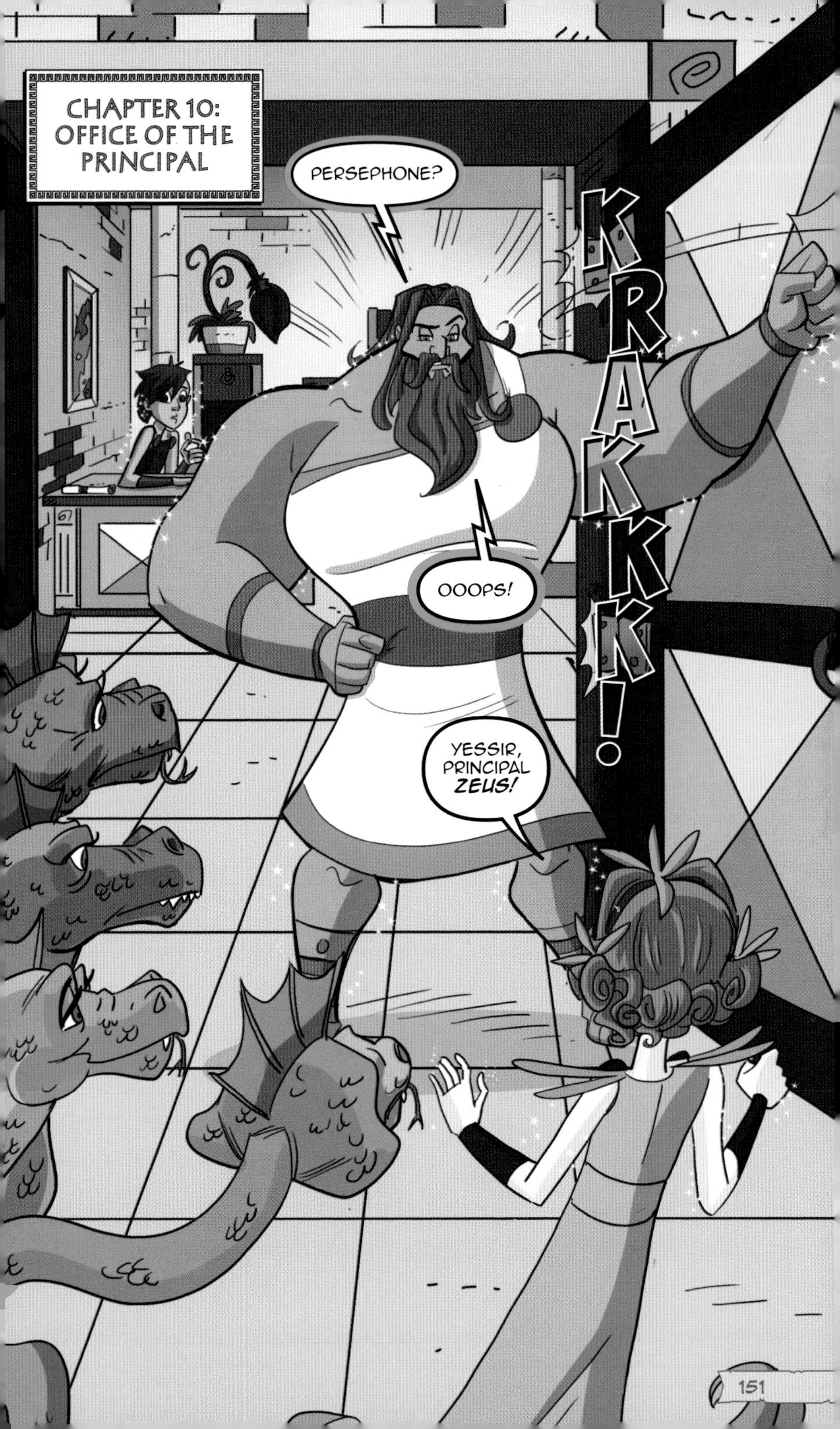

CHAPTER 10: OFFICE OF THE PRINCIPAL
PERSEPHONE?
KRAKKK!
OOOPS!
YESSIR, PRINCIPAL ZEUS!

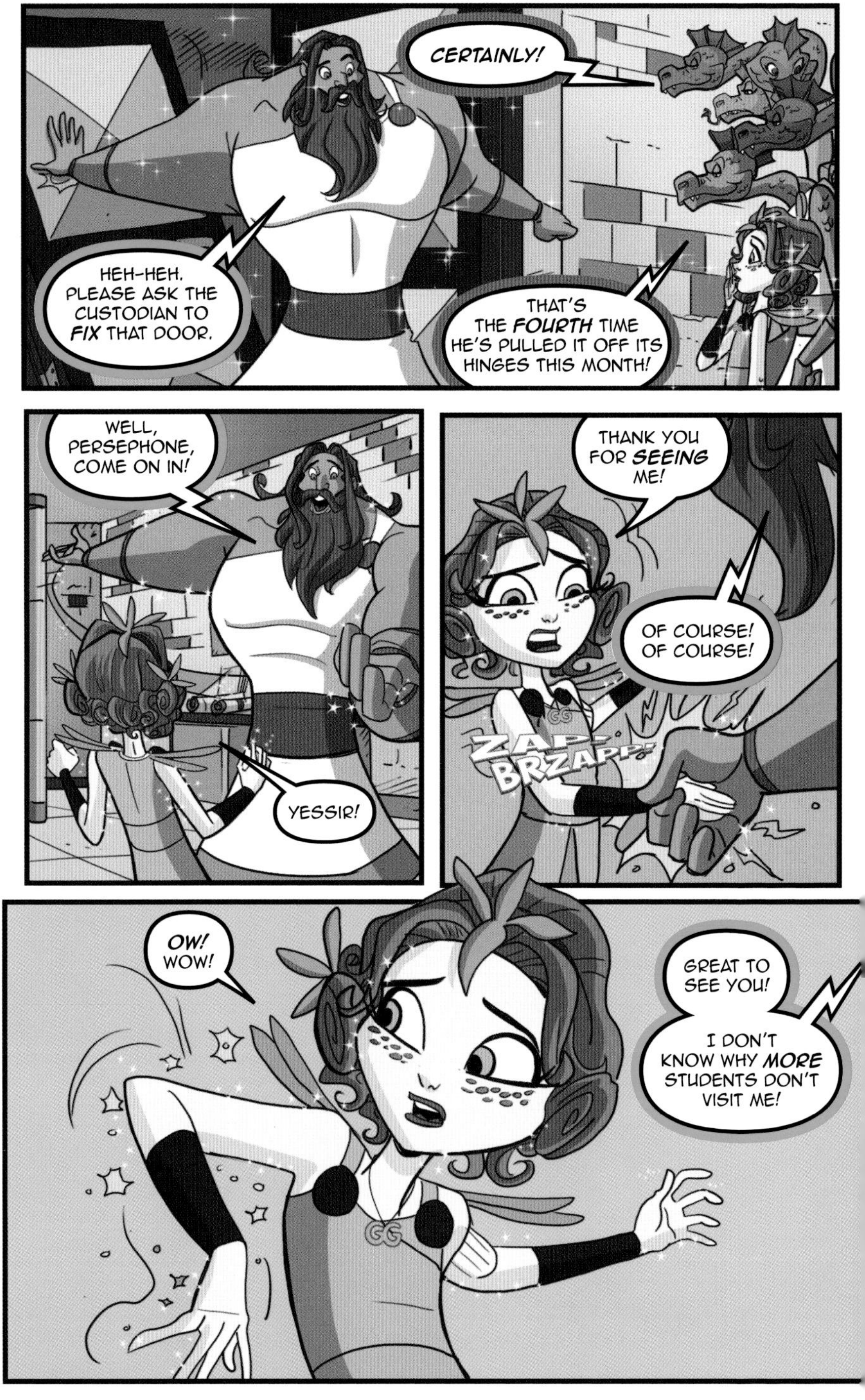
CERTAINLY!
HEH-HEH. PLEASE ASK THE CUSTODIAN TO FIX THAT DOOR.
THAT'S THE FOURTH TIME HE'S PULLED IT OFF ITS HINGES THIS MONTH!
WELL, PERSEPHONE, COME ON IN!
YESSIR!
THANK YOU FOR SEEING ME!
OF COURSE! OF COURSE!
ZAP! BRZAPP!
OW! WOW!
GREAT TO SEE YOU!
I DON'T KNOW WHY MORE STUDENTS DON'T VISIT ME!

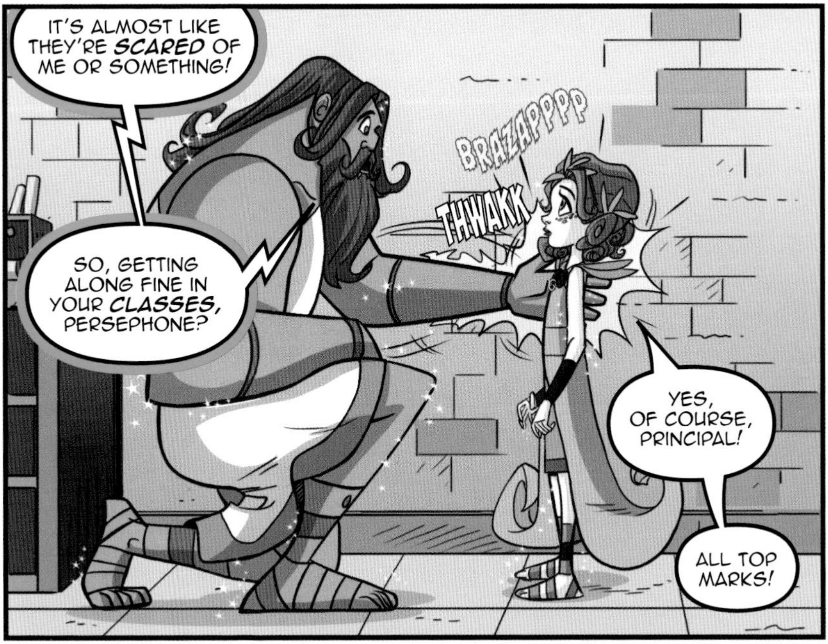
IT'S ALMOST LIKE THEY'RE *SCARED* OF ME OR SOMETHING!
SO, GETTING ALONG FINE IN YOUR *CLASSES,* PERSEPHONE?
BRAZAPPPP
THWAKK
YES, OF COURSE, PRINCIPAL!
ALL TOP MARKS!

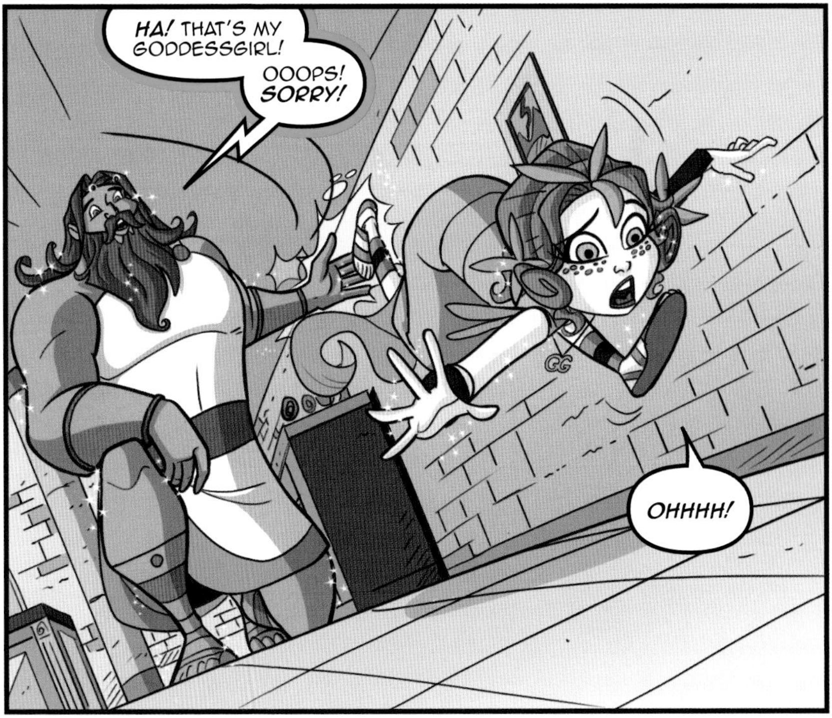
HA! THAT'S MY GODDESSGIRL!
OOOPS! *SORRY!*
OHHHH!

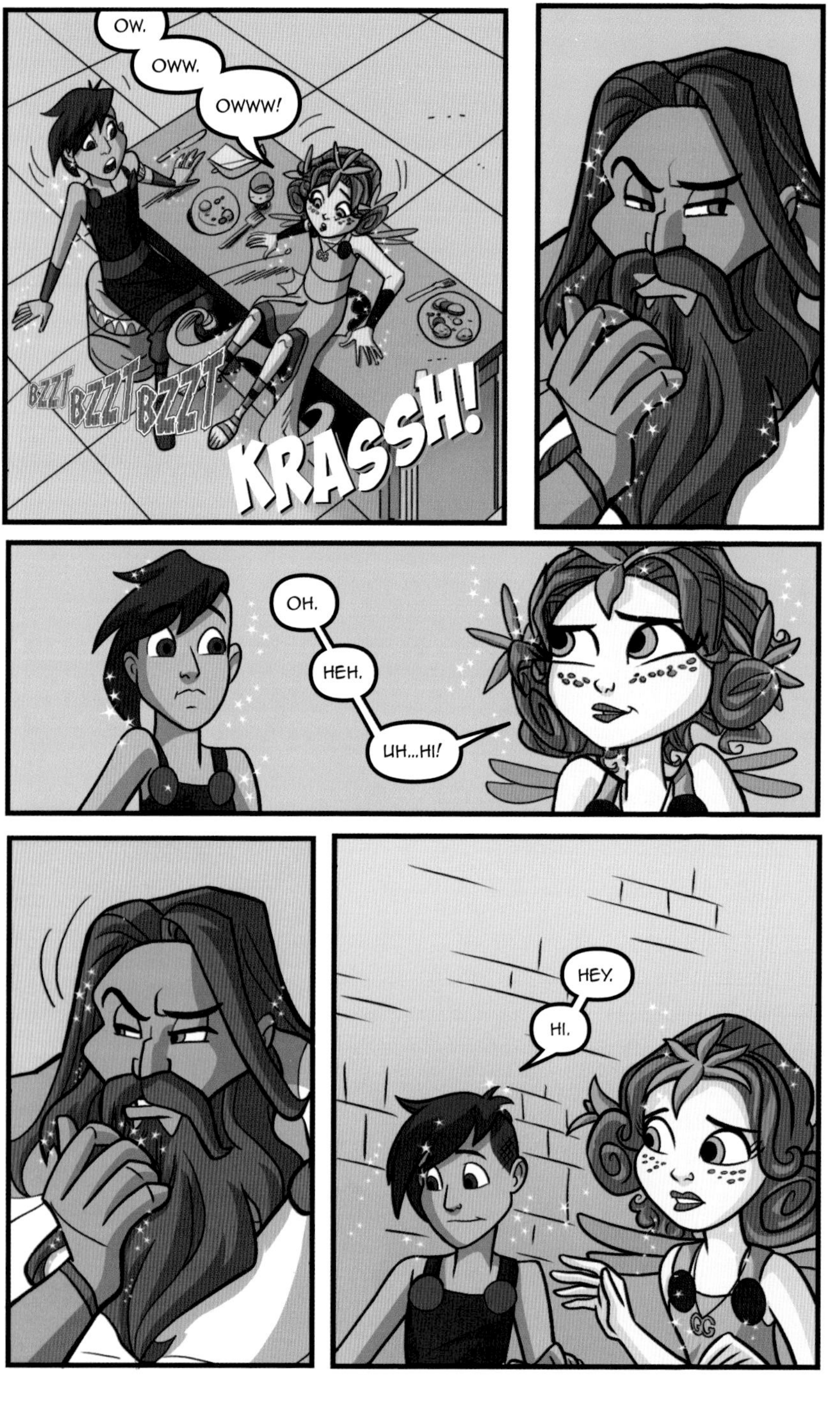
OW.
OWW.
OWWW!
BZZT BZZT BZZT
KRASSH!
OH.
HEH.
UH...HI!
HEY.
HI.

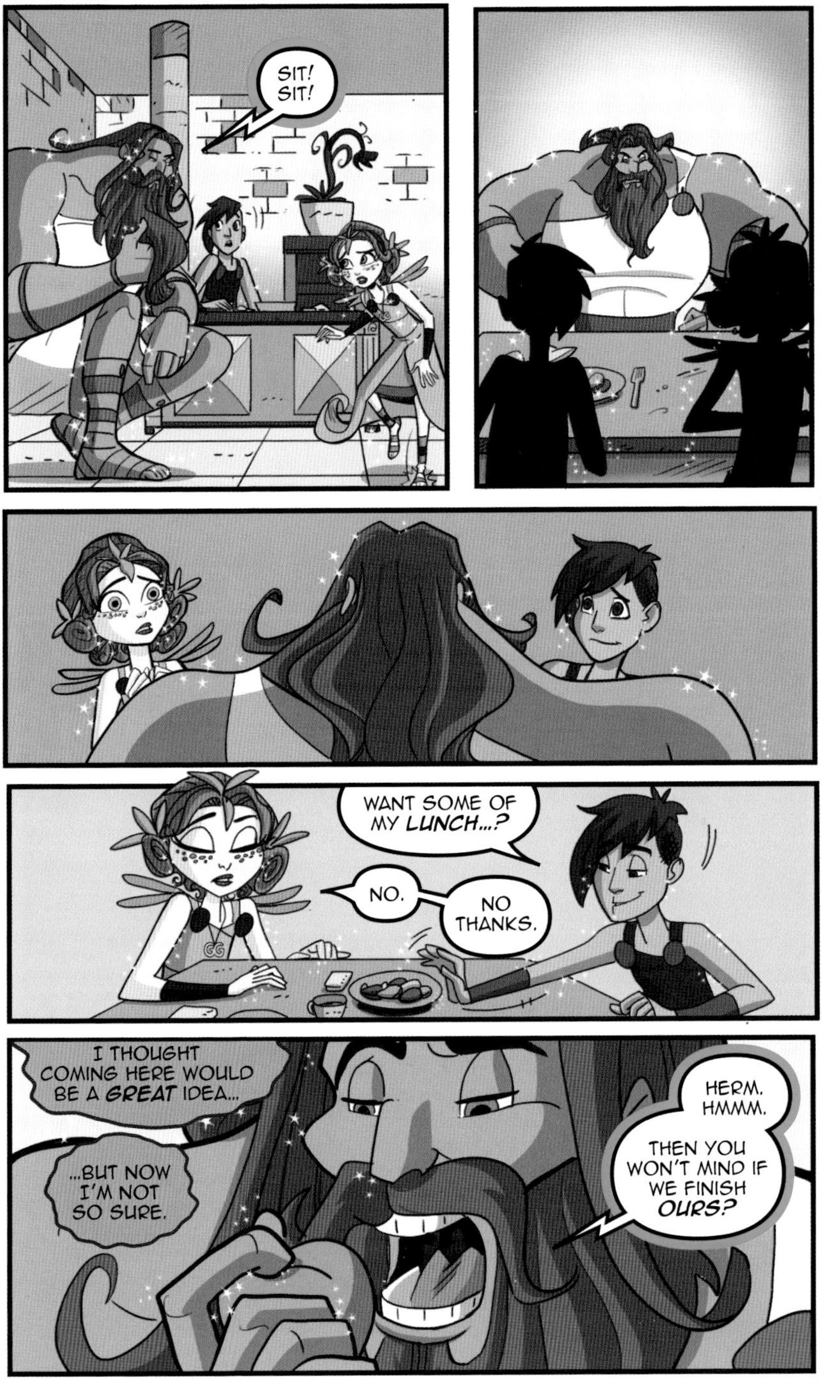
SIT! SIT!
WANT SOME OF MY LUNCH...?
NO.
NO THANKS.
I THOUGHT COMING HERE WOULD BE A GREAT IDEA...
...BUT NOW I'M NOT SO SURE.
HERM. HMMM.
THEN YOU WON'T MIND IF WE FINISH OURS?

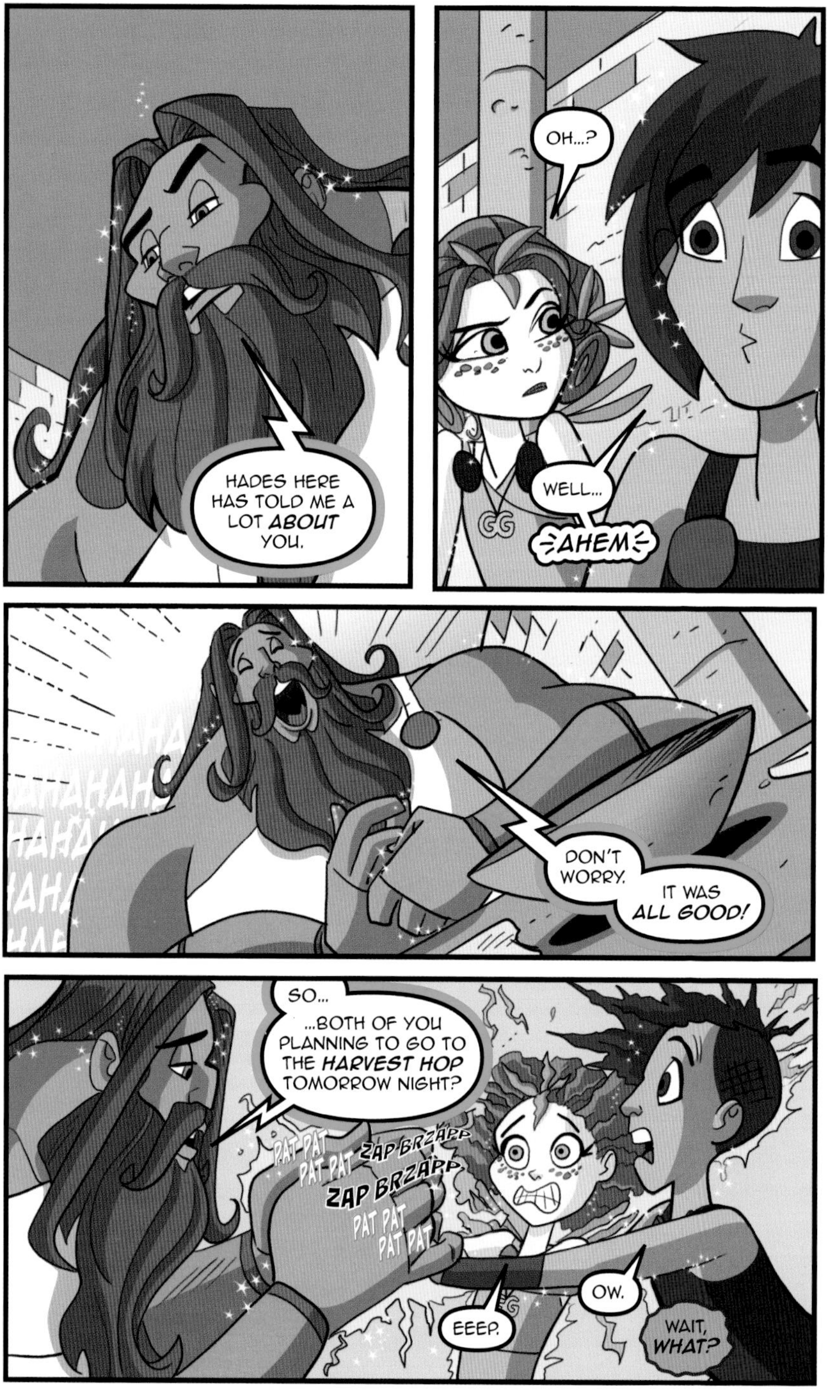
HADES HERE HAS TOLD ME A LOT ABOUT YOU.
OH...?
WELL...
AHEM
DON'T WORRY.
IT WAS ALL GOOD!
SO...
...BOTH OF YOU PLANNING TO GO TO THE HARVEST HOP TOMORROW NIGHT?
PAT PAT PAT PAT ZAP BRZAPP
ZAP BRZAPP
PAT PAT PAT PAT
EEEP.
OW.
WAIT, WHAT?

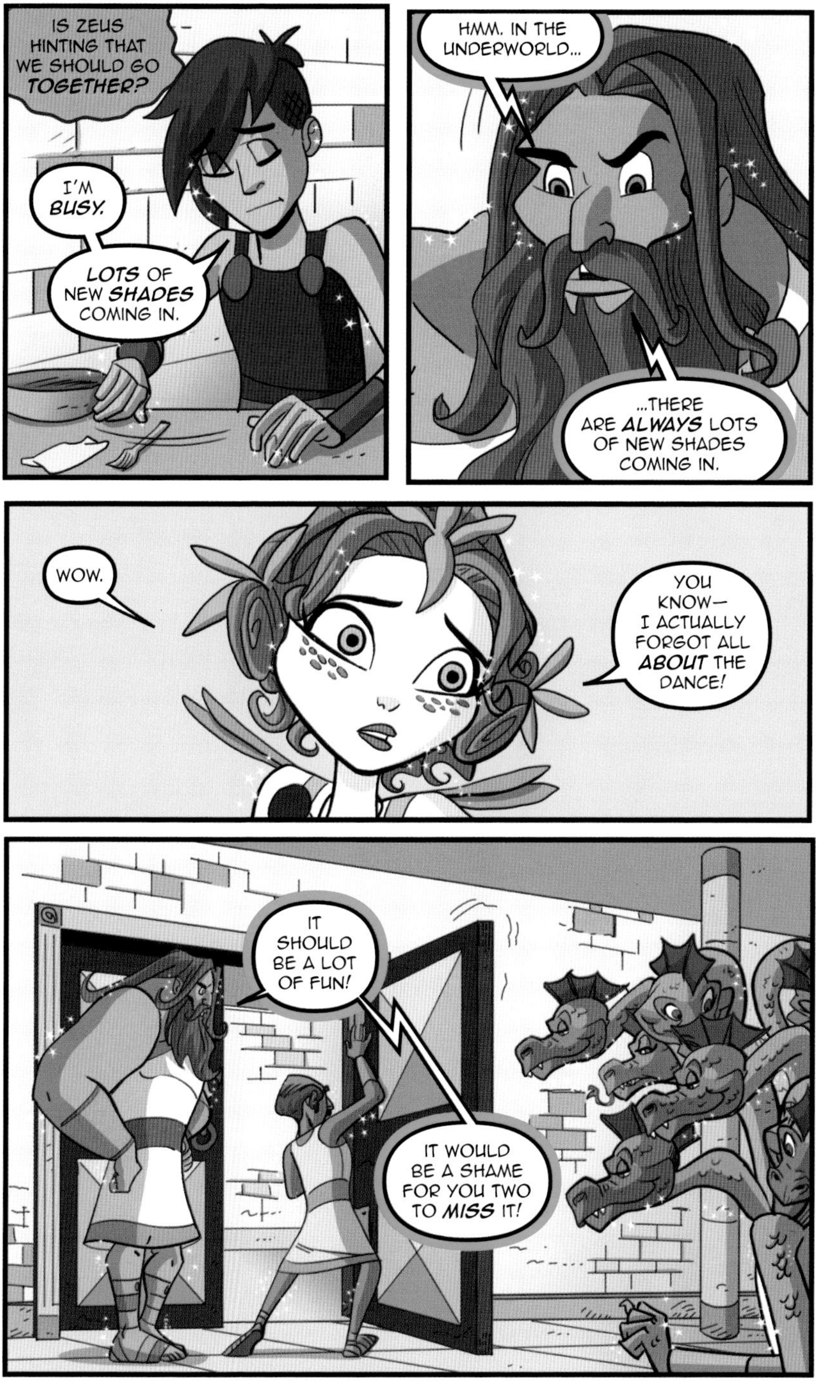
IS ZEUS HINTING THAT WE SHOULD GO TOGETHER?
HMM. IN THE UNDERWORLD...
I'M BUSY.
LOTS OF NEW SHADES COMING IN.
...THERE ARE ALWAYS LOTS OF NEW SHADES COMING IN.
WOW.
YOU KNOW— I ACTUALLY FORGOT ALL ABOUT THE DANCE!
IT SHOULD BE A LOT OF FUN!
IT WOULD BE A SHAME FOR YOU TWO TO MISS IT!

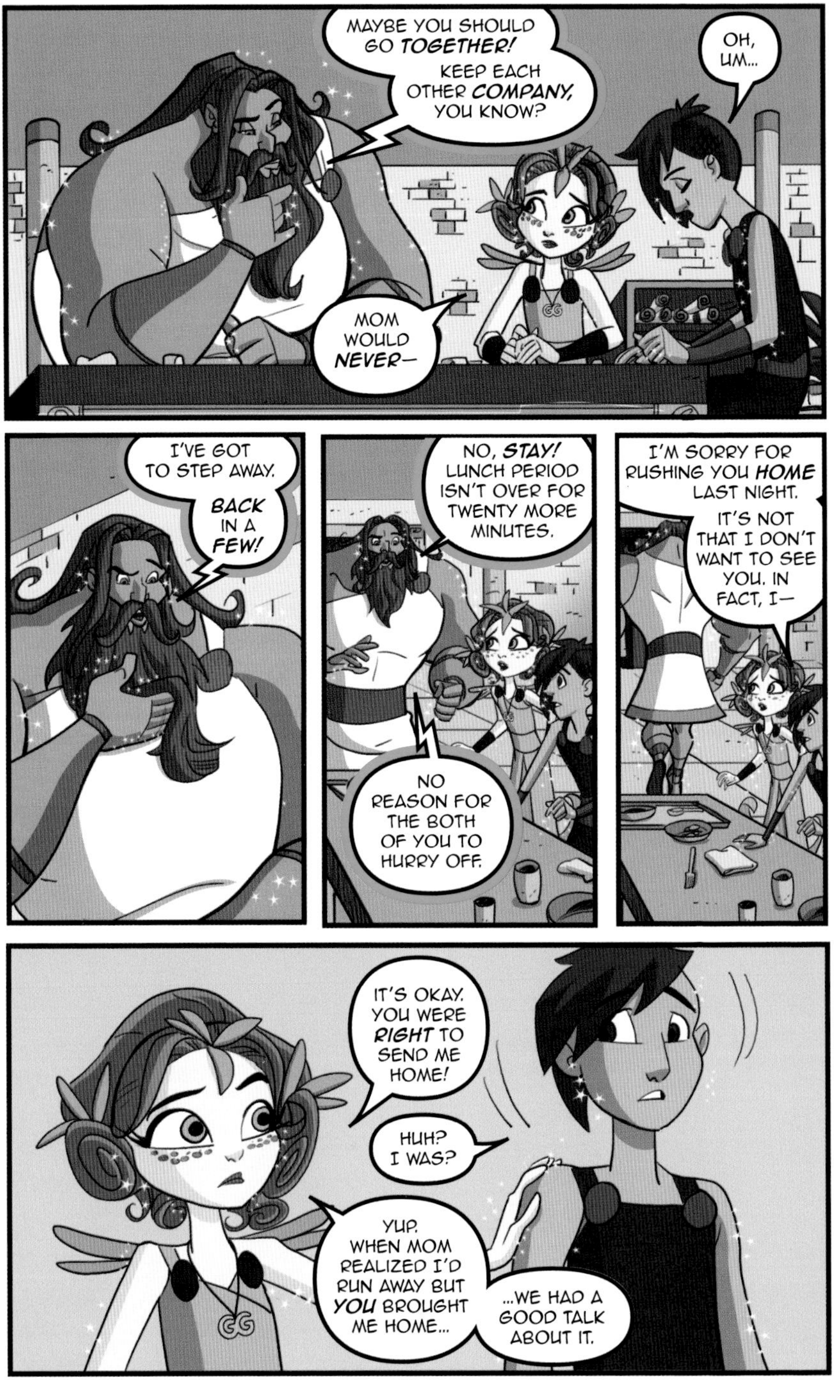
MAYBE YOU SHOULD GO TOGETHER!
KEEP EACH OTHER COMPANY, YOU KNOW?
OH, UM...
MOM WOULD NEVER—
I'VE GOT TO STEP AWAY.
BACK IN A FEW!
NO, STAY! LUNCH PERIOD ISN'T OVER FOR TWENTY MORE MINUTES.
NO REASON FOR THE BOTH OF YOU TO HURRY OFF.
I'M SORRY FOR RUSHING YOU HOME LAST NIGHT.
IT'S NOT THAT I DON'T WANT TO SEE YOU. IN FACT, I—
IT'S OKAY. YOU WERE RIGHT TO SEND ME HOME!
HUH? I WAS?
YUP. WHEN MOM REALIZED I'D RUN AWAY BUT YOU BROUGHT ME HOME...
...WE HAD A GOOD TALK ABOUT IT.

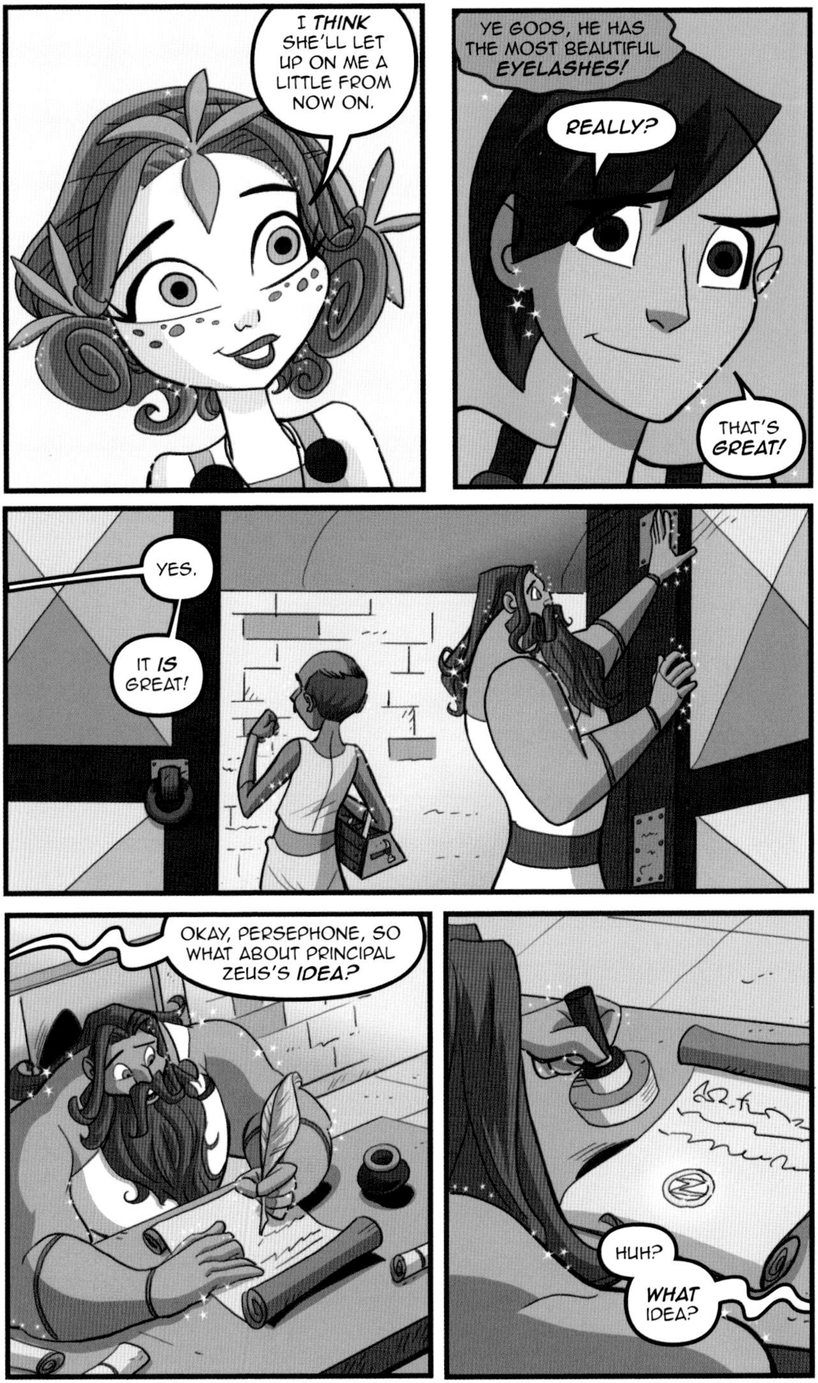
I THINK SHE'LL LET UP ON ME A LITTLE FROM NOW ON.
YE GODS, HE HAS THE MOST BEAUTIFUL EYELASHES!
REALLY?
THAT'S GREAT!
YES.
IT IS GREAT!
OKAY, PERSEPHONE, SO WHAT ABOUT PRINCIPAL ZEUS'S IDEA?
HUH?
WHAT IDEA?

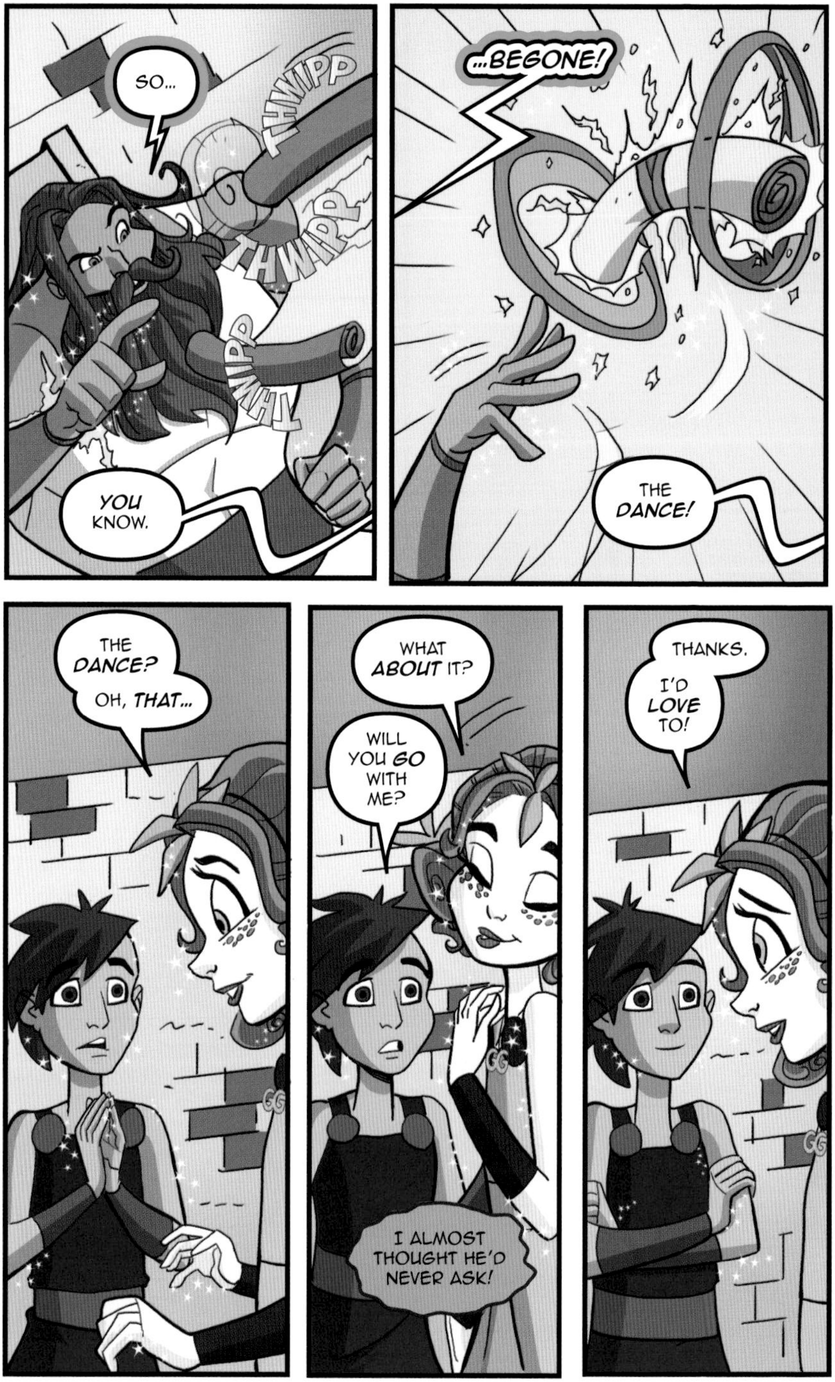
SO...
THWIPP
THWIPP
THWIPP
YOU KNOW.
...BEGONE!
THE DANCE!
THE DANCE?
OH, THAT...
WHAT ABOUT IT?
WILL YOU GO WITH ME?
I ALMOST THOUGHT HE'D NEVER ASK!
THANKS.
I'D LOVE TO!

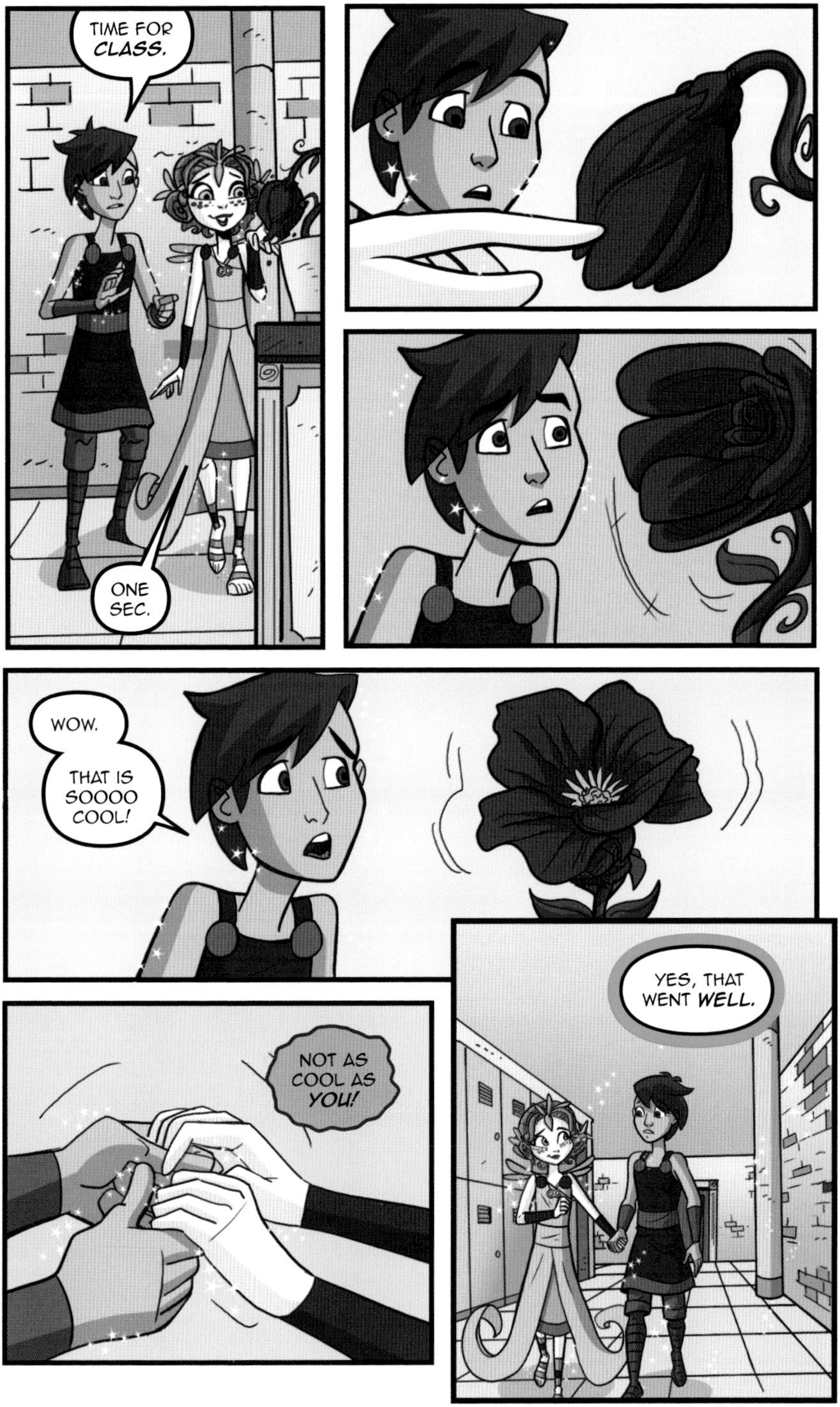
TIME FOR CLASS.
ONE SEC.
WOW.
THAT IS SOOOO COOL!
NOT AS COOL AS YOU!
YES, THAT WENT WELL.

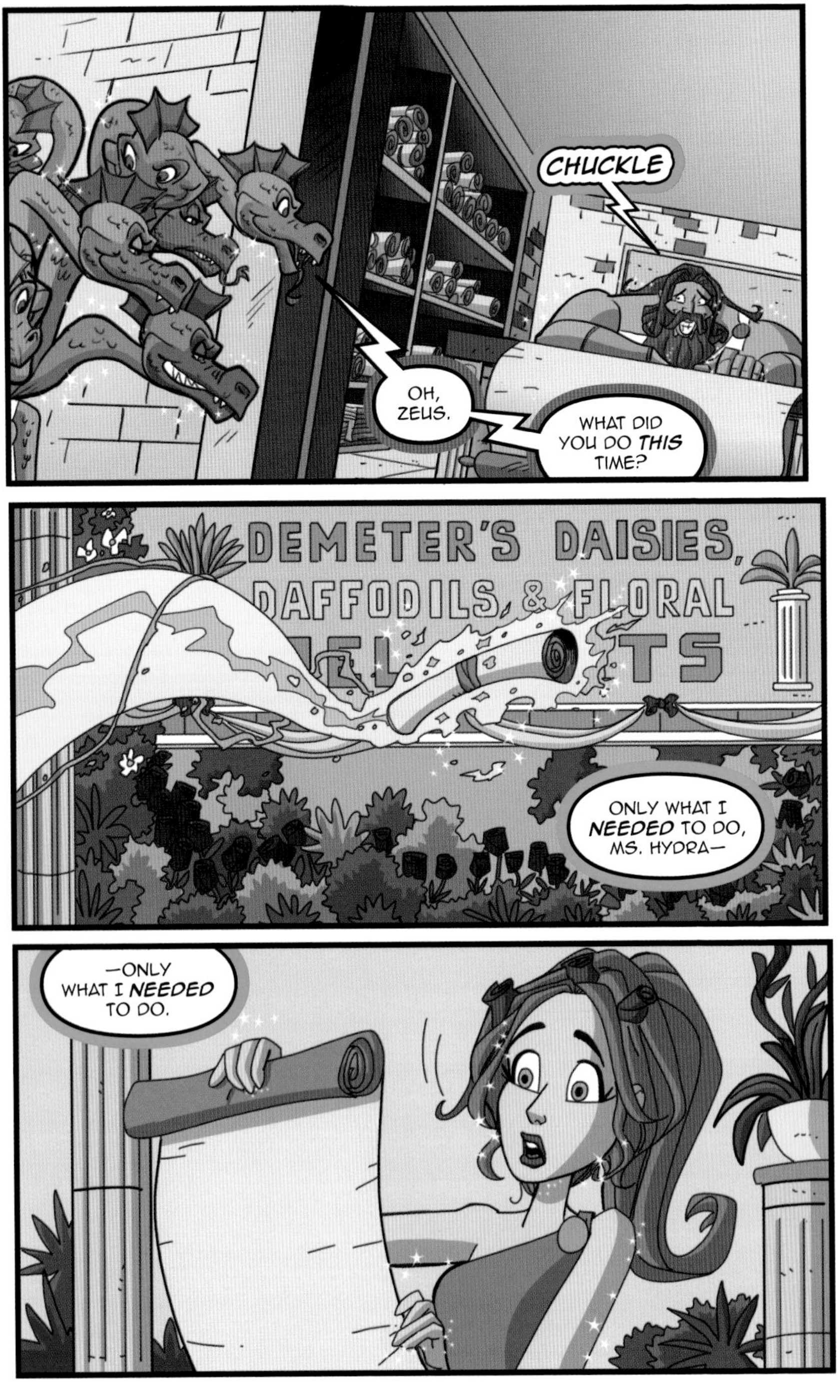
CHUCKLE
OH, ZEUS.
WHAT DID YOU DO *THIS* TIME?
DEMETER'S DAISIES, DAFFODILS, & FLORAL
ONLY WHAT I *NEEDED* TO DO, MS. HYDRA—
—ONLY WHAT I *NEEDED* TO DO.

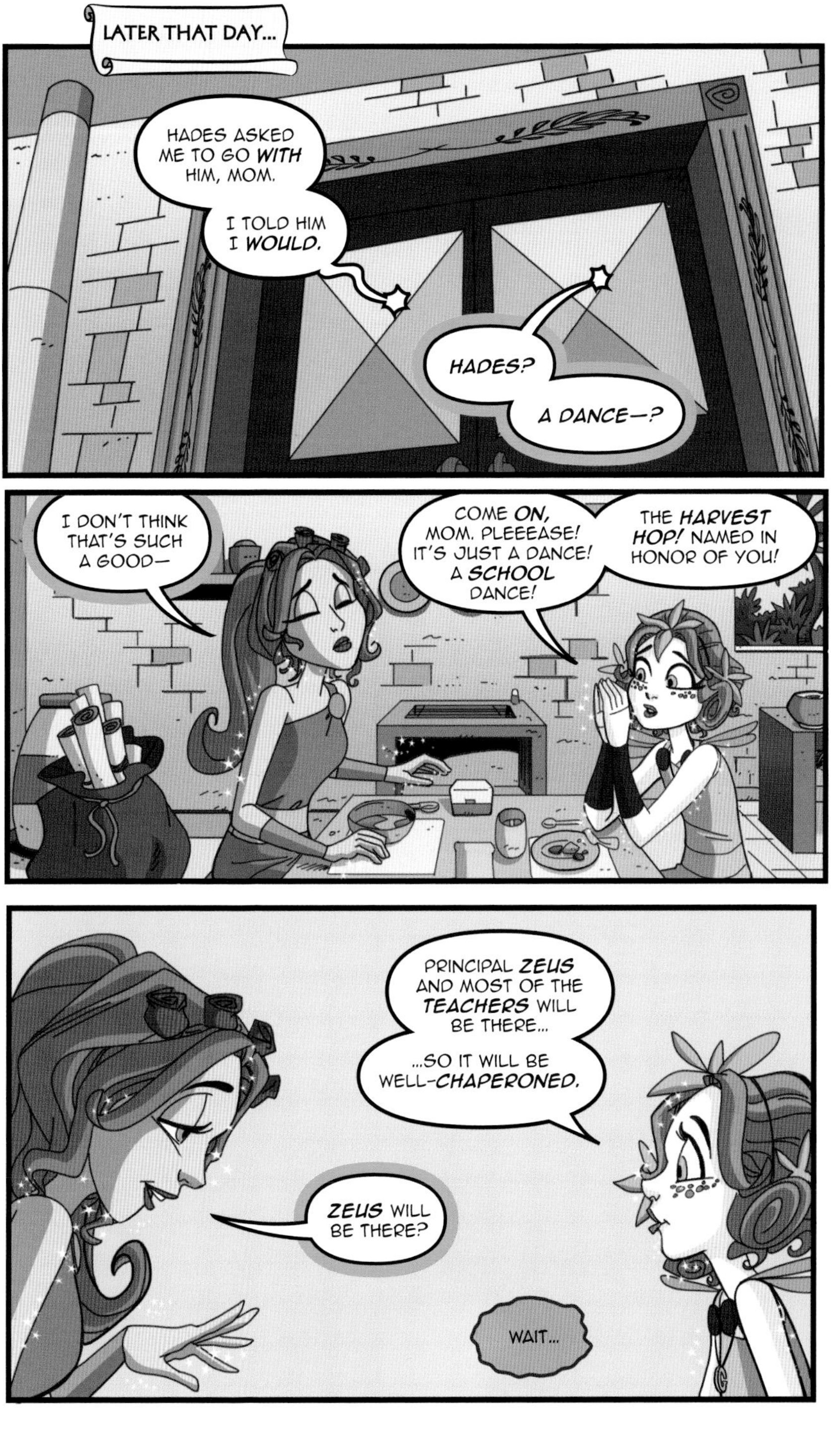
LATER THAT DAY...
HADES ASKED ME TO GO WITH HIM, MOM.
I TOLD HIM I WOULD.
HADES?
A DANCE—?
I DON'T THINK THAT'S SUCH A GOOD—
COME ON, MOM. PLEEEASE! IT'S JUST A DANCE! A SCHOOL DANCE!
THE HARVEST HOP! NAMED IN HONOR OF YOU!
PRINCIPAL ZEUS AND MOST OF THE TEACHERS WILL BE THERE...
...SO IT WILL BE WELL-CHAPERONED.
ZEUS WILL BE THERE?
WAIT...

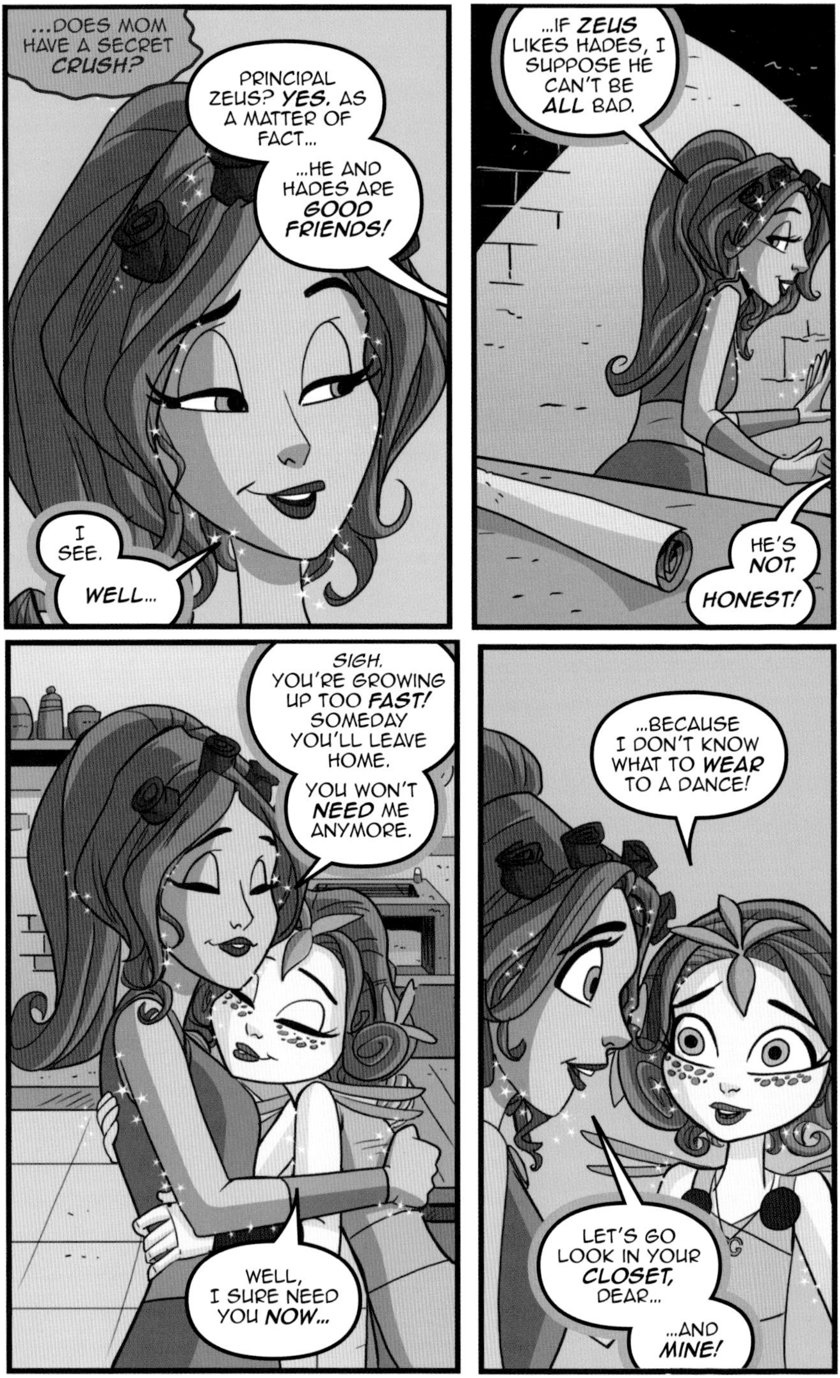
...DOES MOM HAVE A SECRET CRUSH?
PRINCIPAL ZEUS? YES. AS A MATTER OF FACT...
...HE AND HADES ARE GOOD FRIENDS!
I SEE.
WELL...
...IF ZEUS LIKES HADES, I SUPPOSE HE CAN'T BE ALL BAD.
HE'S NOT.
HONEST!
SIGH. YOU'RE GROWING UP TOO FAST! SOMEDAY YOU'LL LEAVE HOME.
YOU WON'T NEED ME ANYMORE.
WELL, I SURE NEED YOU NOW...
...BECAUSE I DON'T KNOW WHAT TO WEAR TO A DANCE!
LET'S GO LOOK IN YOUR CLOSET, DEAR...
...AND MINE!

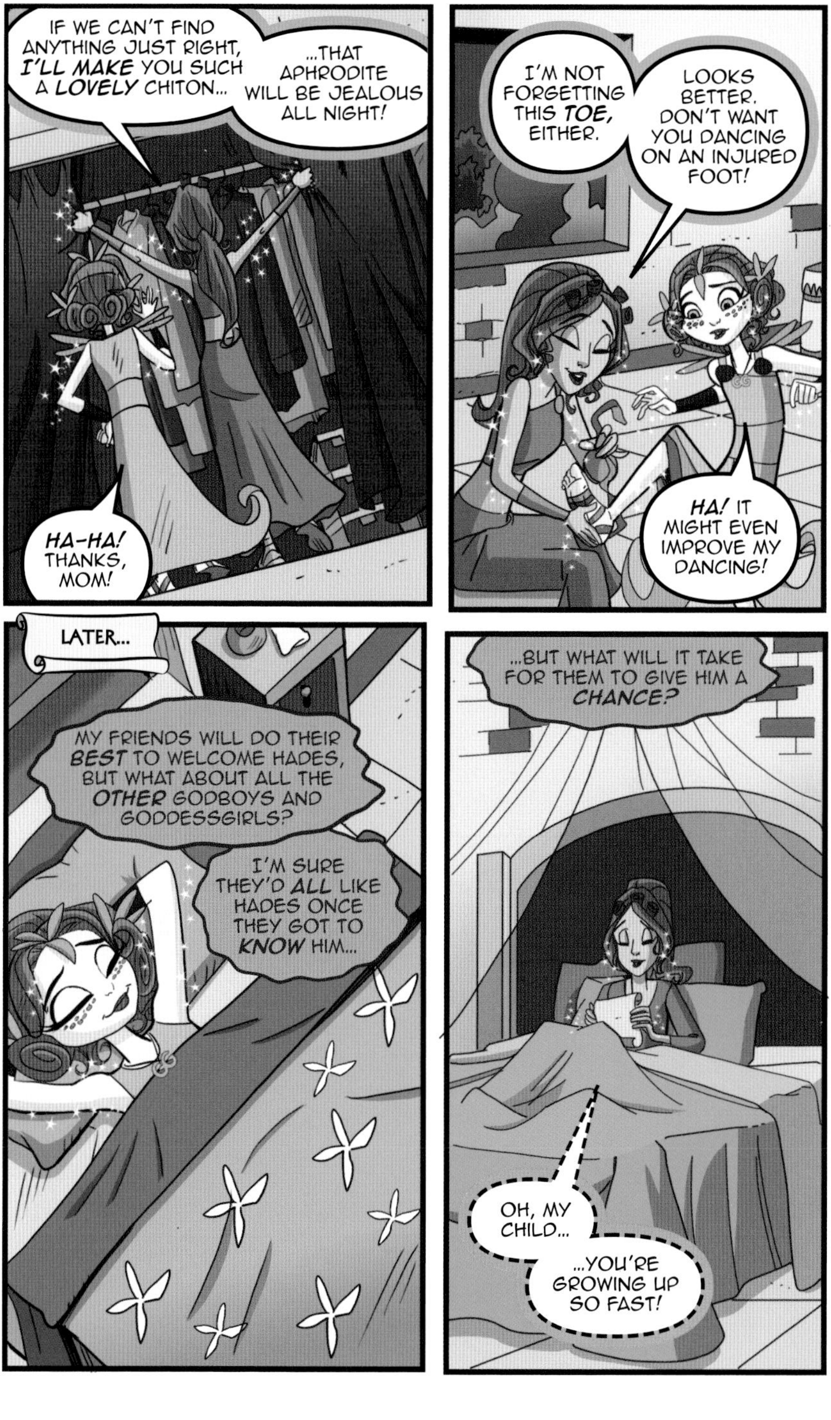
IF WE CAN'T FIND ANYTHING JUST RIGHT, ***I'LL MAKE*** YOU SUCH A ***LOVELY*** CHITON...
...THAT APHRODITE WILL BE JEALOUS ALL NIGHT!
HA-HA! THANKS, MOM!
I'M NOT FORGETTING THIS ***TOE,*** EITHER.
LOOKS BETTER. DON'T WANT YOU DANCING ON AN INJURED FOOT!
HA! IT MIGHT EVEN IMPROVE MY DANCING!
LATER...
MY FRIENDS WILL DO THEIR ***BEST*** TO WELCOME HADES, BUT WHAT ABOUT ALL THE ***OTHER*** GODBOYS AND GODDESSGIRLS?
I'M SURE THEY'D ***ALL*** LIKE HADES ONCE THEY GOT TO ***KNOW*** HIM...
...BUT WHAT WILL IT TAKE FOR THEM TO GIVE HIM A ***CHANCE?***
OH, MY CHILD...
...YOU'RE GROWING UP SO FAST!

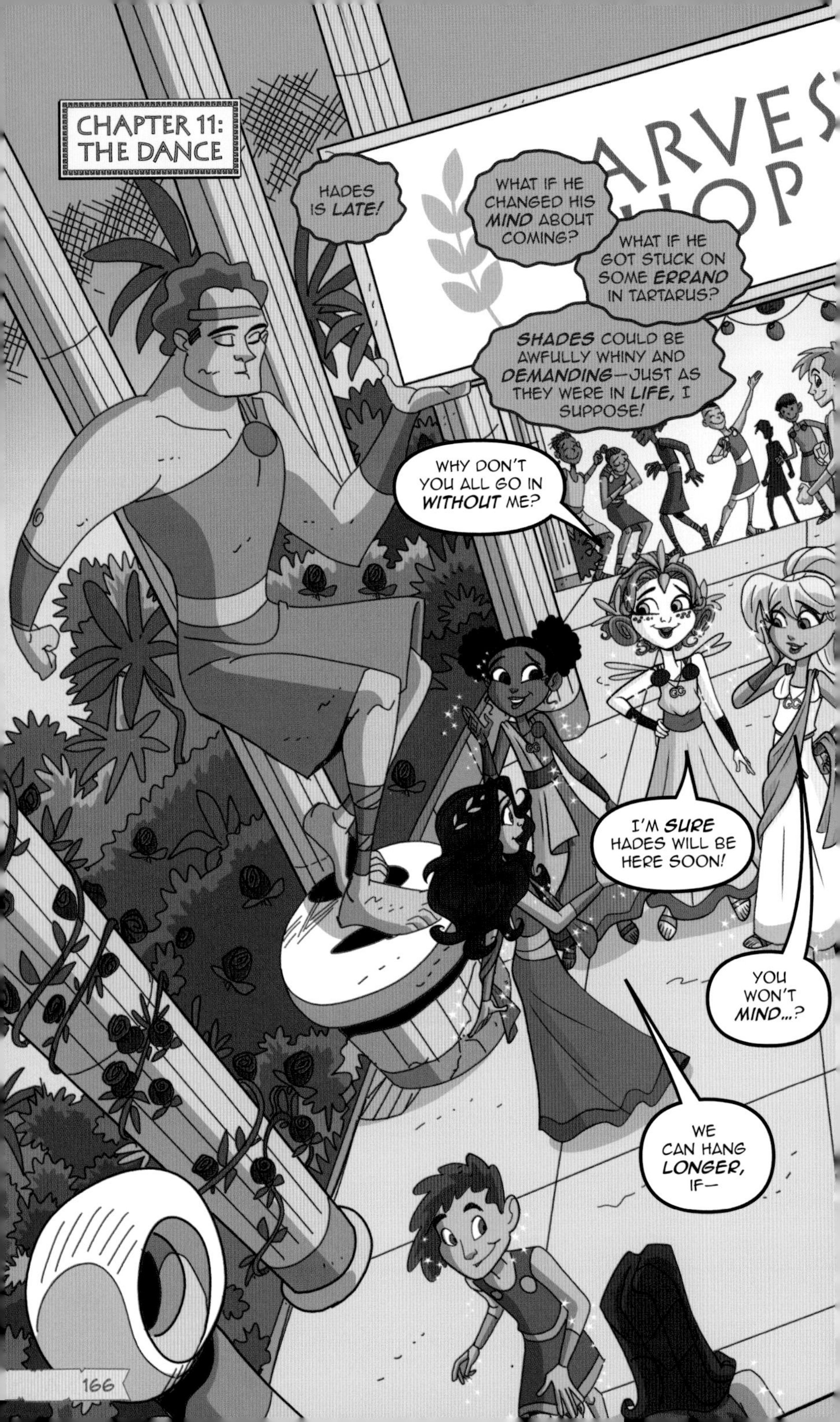

CHAPTER 11: THE DANCE
HADES IS LATE!
WHAT IF HE CHANGED HIS MIND ABOUT COMING?
WHAT IF HE GOT STUCK ON SOME ERRAND IN TARTARUS?
SHADES COULD BE AWFULLY WHINY AND DEMANDING—JUST AS THEY WERE IN LIFE, I SUPPOSE!
WHY DON'T YOU ALL GO IN WITHOUT ME?
I'M SURE HADES WILL BE HERE SOON!
YOU WON'T MIND...?
WE CAN HANG LONGER, IF—

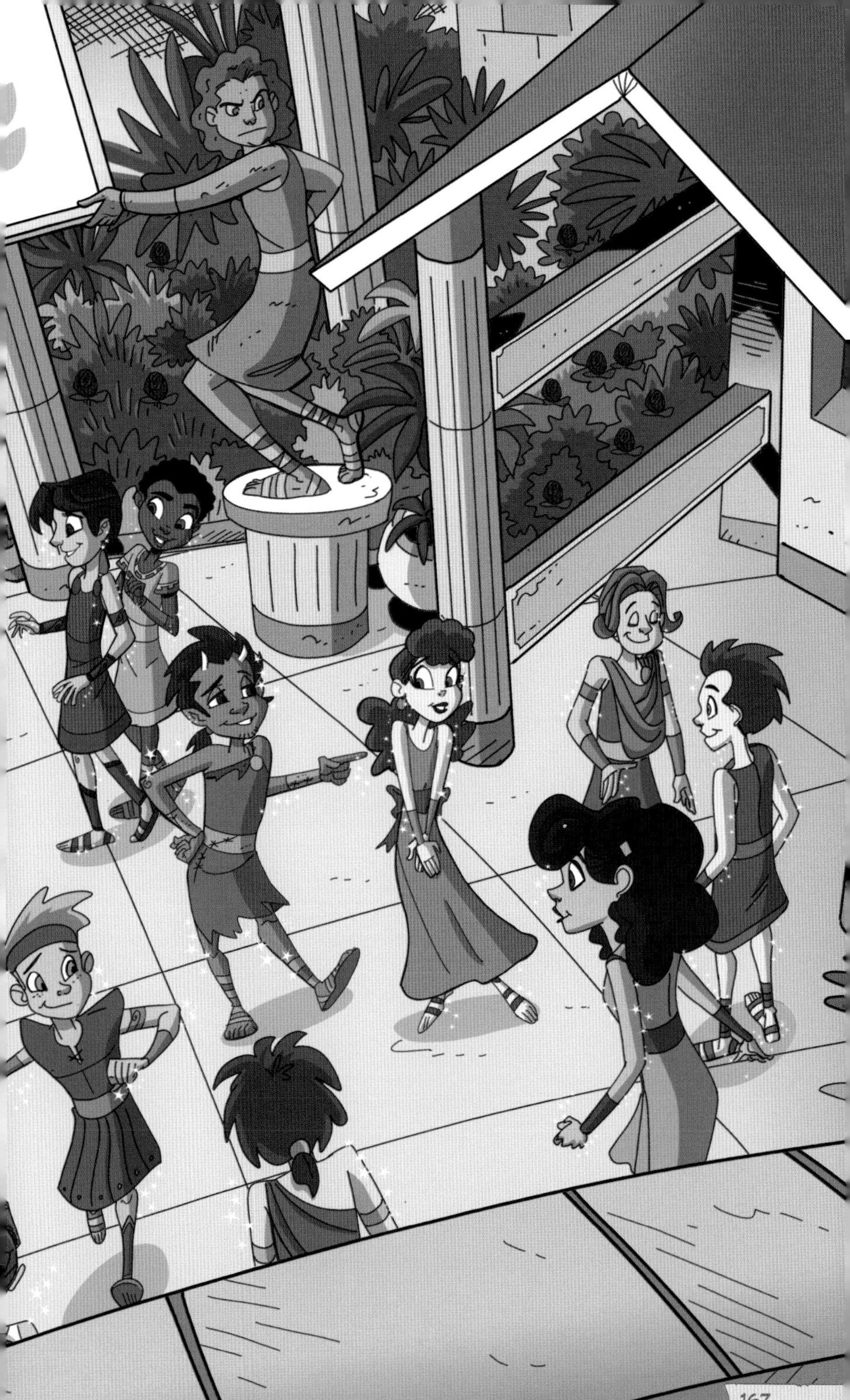

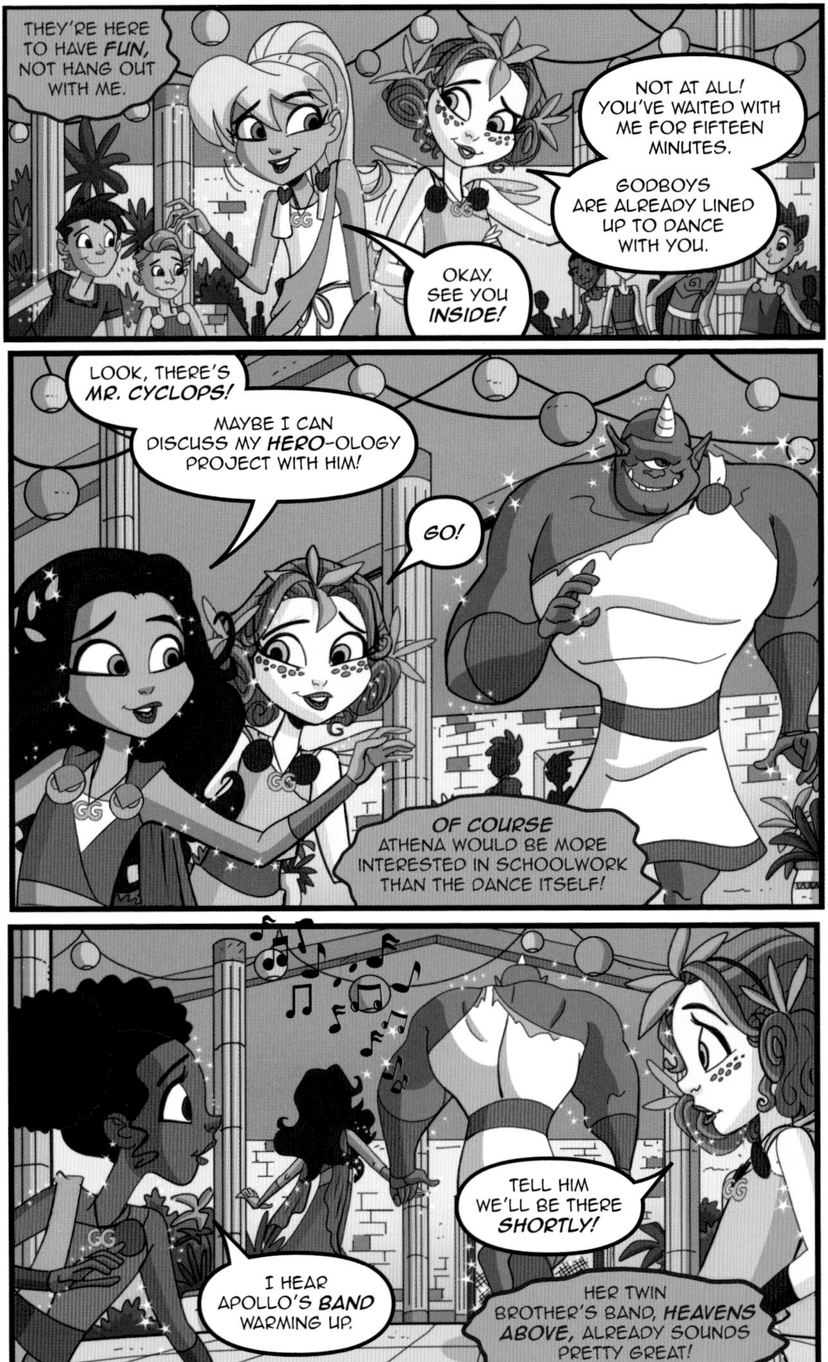
THEY'RE HERE TO HAVE FUN, NOT HANG OUT WITH ME.
NOT AT ALL! YOU'VE WAITED WITH ME FOR FIFTEEN MINUTES.
GODBOYS ARE ALREADY LINED UP TO DANCE WITH YOU.
OKAY. SEE YOU INSIDE!
LOOK, THERE'S MR. CYCLOPS!
MAYBE I CAN DISCUSS MY HERO-OLOGY PROJECT WITH HIM!
GO!
OF COURSE ATHENA WOULD BE MORE INTERESTED IN SCHOOLWORK THAN THE DANCE ITSELF!
I HEAR APOLLO'S BAND WARMING UP.
TELL HIM WE'LL BE THERE SHORTLY!
HER TWIN BROTHER'S BAND, HEAVENS ABOVE, ALREADY SOUNDS PRETTY GREAT!

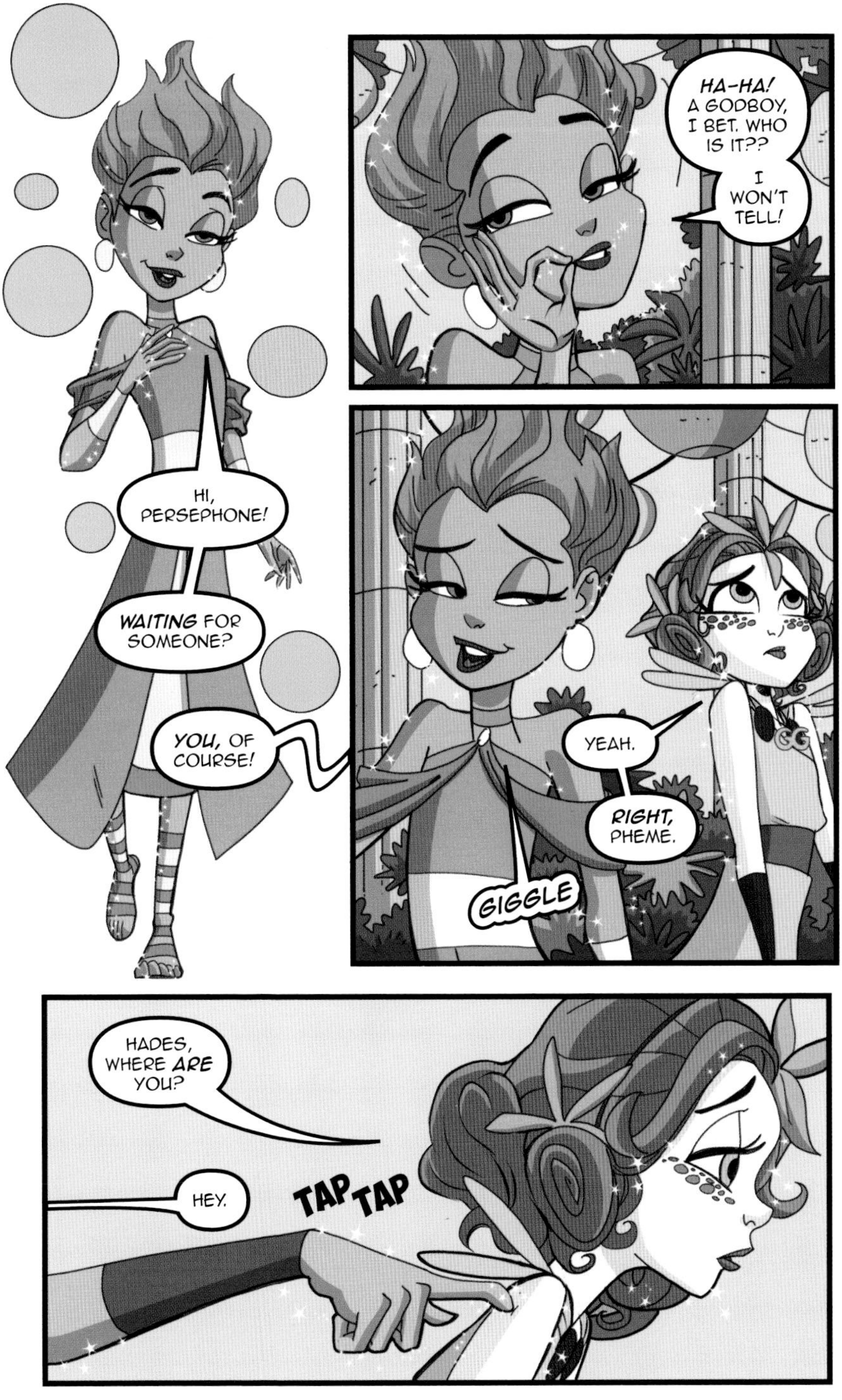
HI, PERSEPHONE!
WAITING FOR SOMEONE?
YOU, OF COURSE!
HA-HA! A GODBOY, I BET. WHO IS IT??
I WON'T TELL!
GIGGLE
YEAH.
RIGHT, PHEME.
HADES, WHERE ARE YOU?
HEY.
TAP TAP

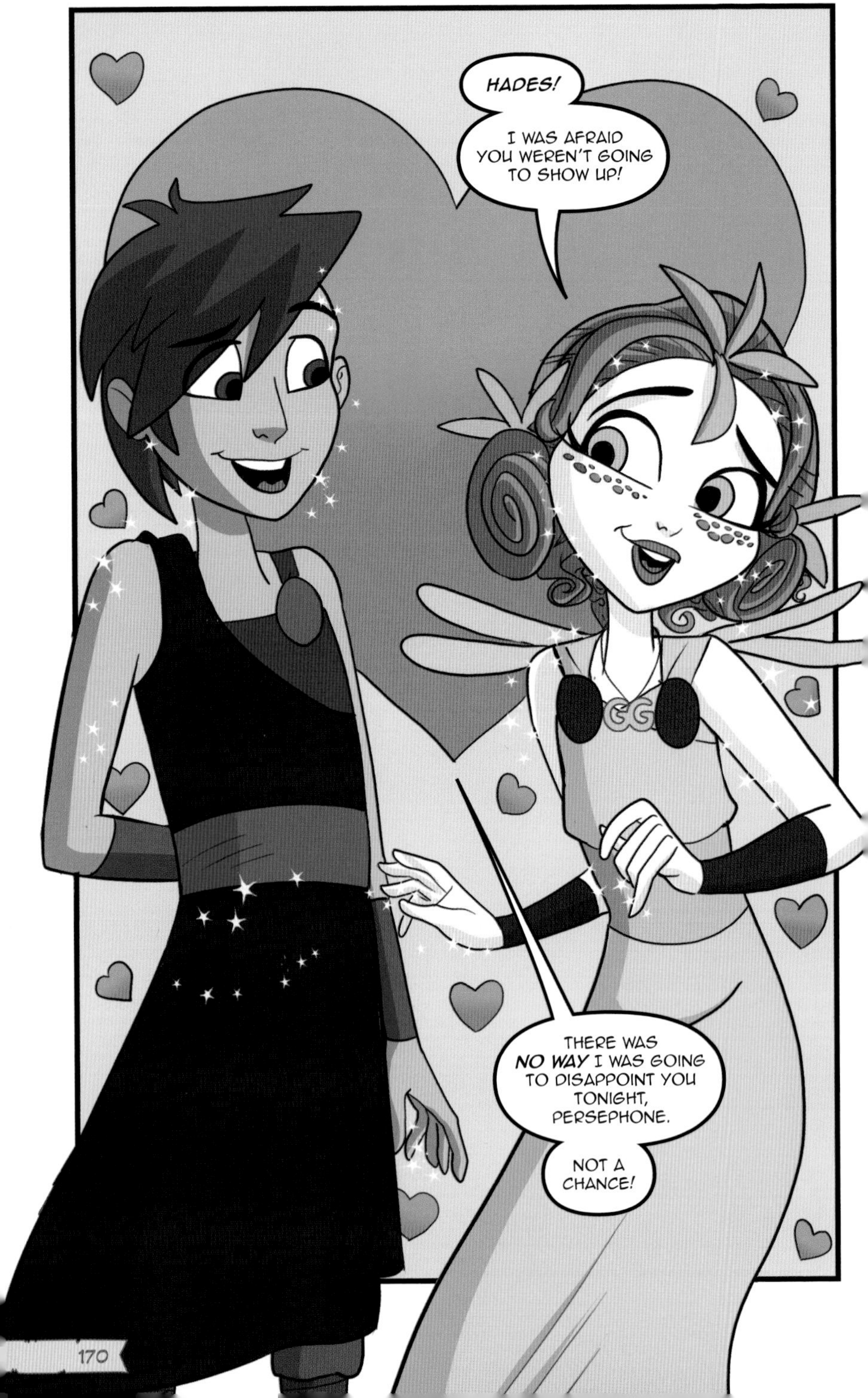
HADES!
I WAS AFRAID YOU WEREN'T GOING TO SHOW UP!
THERE WAS NO WAY I WAS GOING TO DISAPPOINT YOU TONIGHT, PERSEPHONE.
NOT A CHANCE!

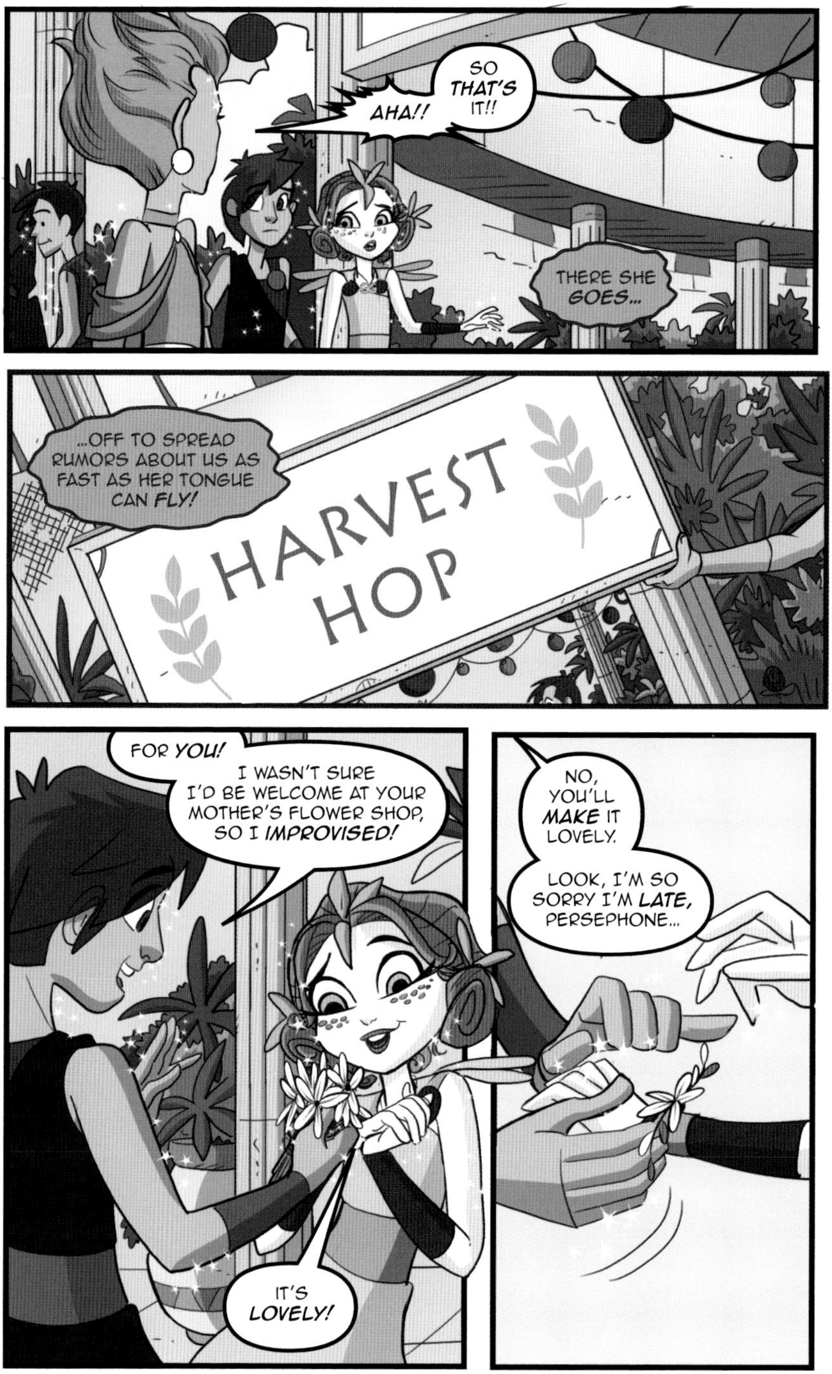
AHA!!
SO THAT'S IT!!
THERE SHE GOES...
...OFF TO SPREAD RUMORS ABOUT US AS FAST AS HER TONGUE CAN FLY!
HARVEST HOP
FOR YOU!
I WASN'T SURE I'D BE WELCOME AT YOUR MOTHER'S FLOWER SHOP, SO I IMPROVISED!
IT'S LOVELY!
NO, YOU'LL MAKE IT LOVELY.
LOOK, I'M SO SORRY I'M LATE, PERSEPHONE...

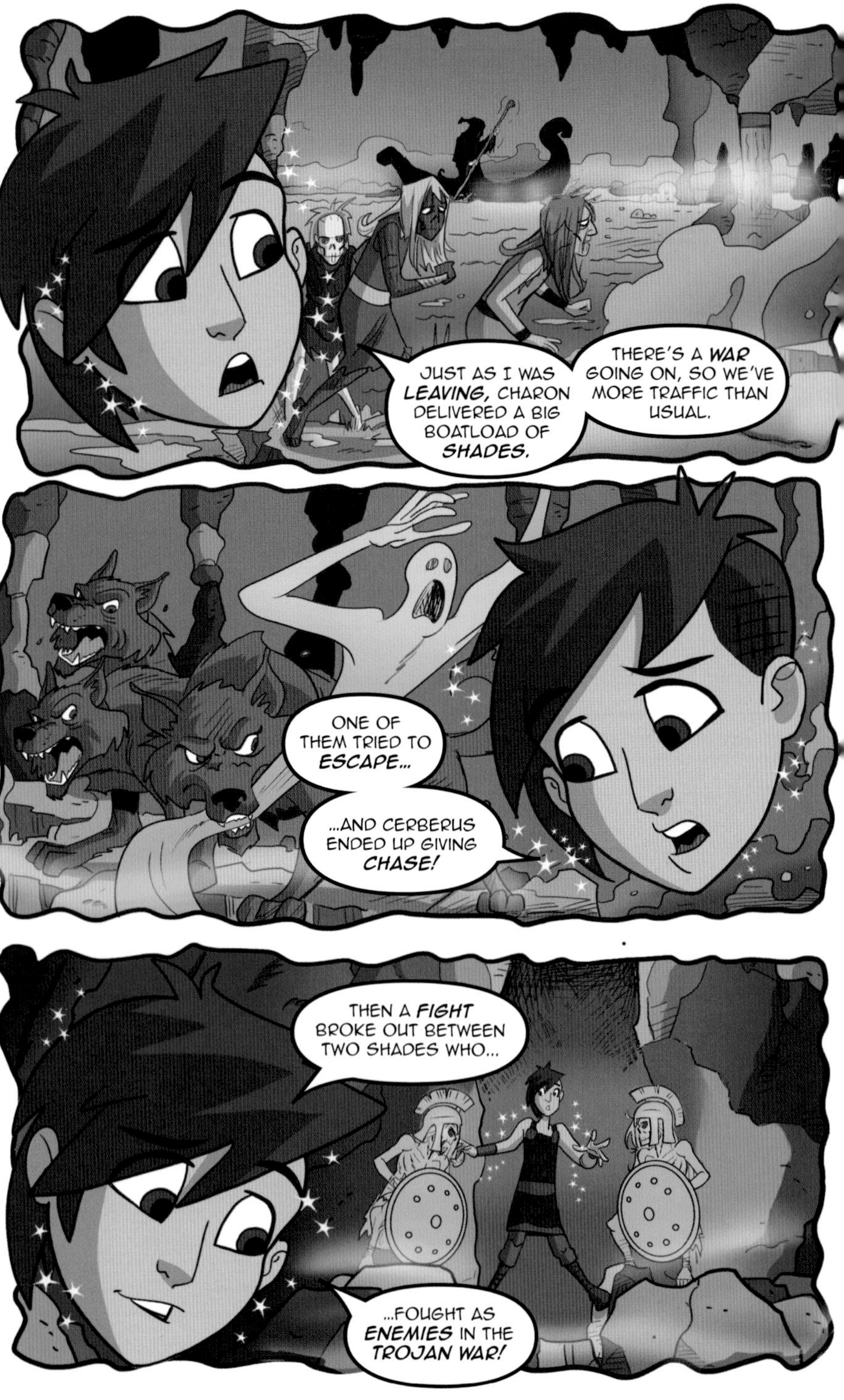
JUST AS I WAS LEAVING, CHARON DELIVERED A BIG BOATLOAD OF SHADES.
THERE'S A WAR GOING ON, SO WE'VE MORE TRAFFIC THAN USUAL.
ONE OF THEM TRIED TO ESCAPE...
...AND CERBERUS ENDED UP GIVING CHASE!
THEN A FIGHT BROKE OUT BETWEEN TWO SHADES WHO...
...FOUGHT AS ENEMIES IN THE TROJAN WAR!

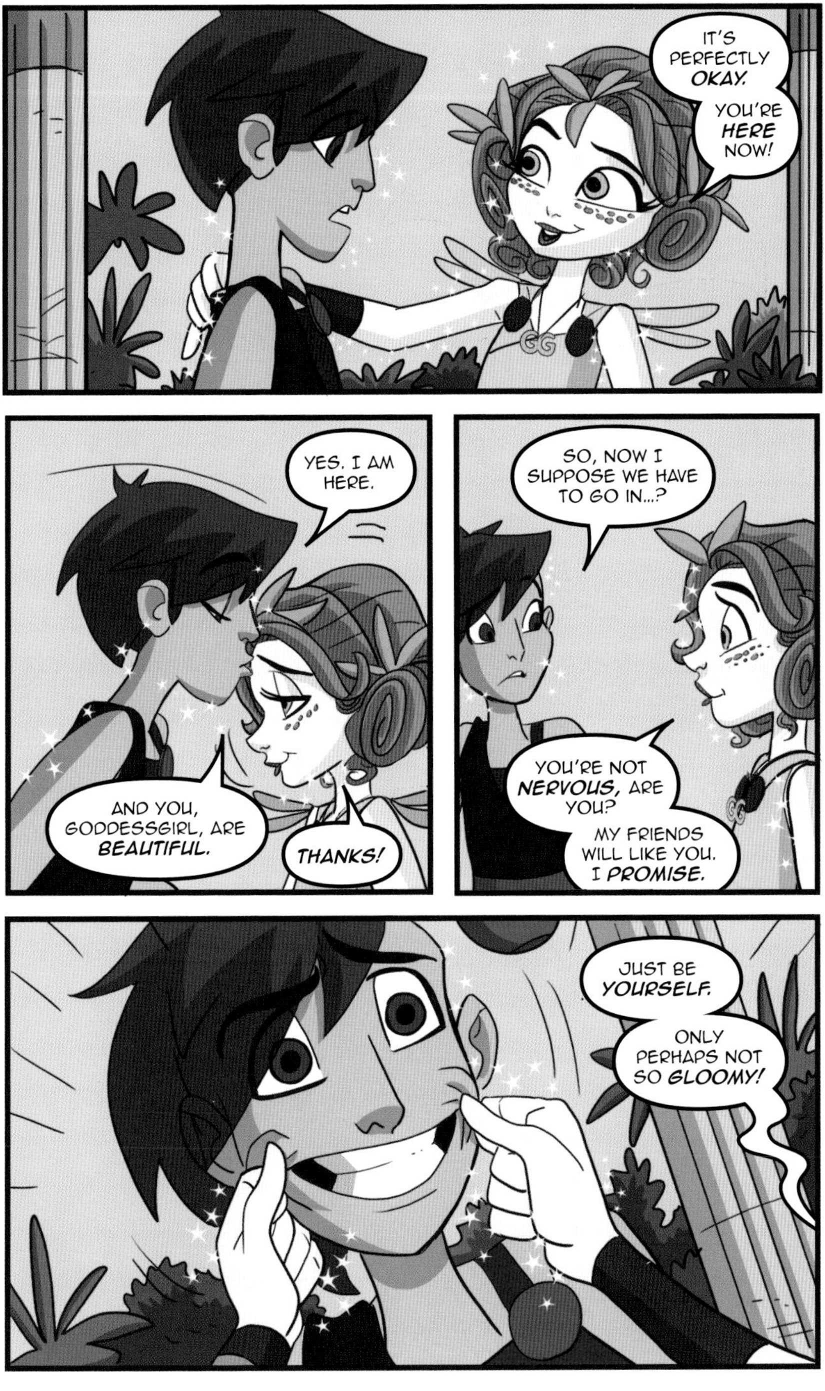
IT'S PERFECTLY OKAY.
YOU'RE HERE NOW!
YES. I AM HERE.
AND YOU, GODDESSGIRL, ARE BEAUTIFUL.
THANKS!
SO, NOW I SUPPOSE WE HAVE TO GO IN...?
YOU'RE NOT NERVOUS, ARE YOU?
MY FRIENDS WILL LIKE YOU. I PROMISE.
JUST BE YOURSELF.
ONLY PERHAPS NOT SO GLOOMY!

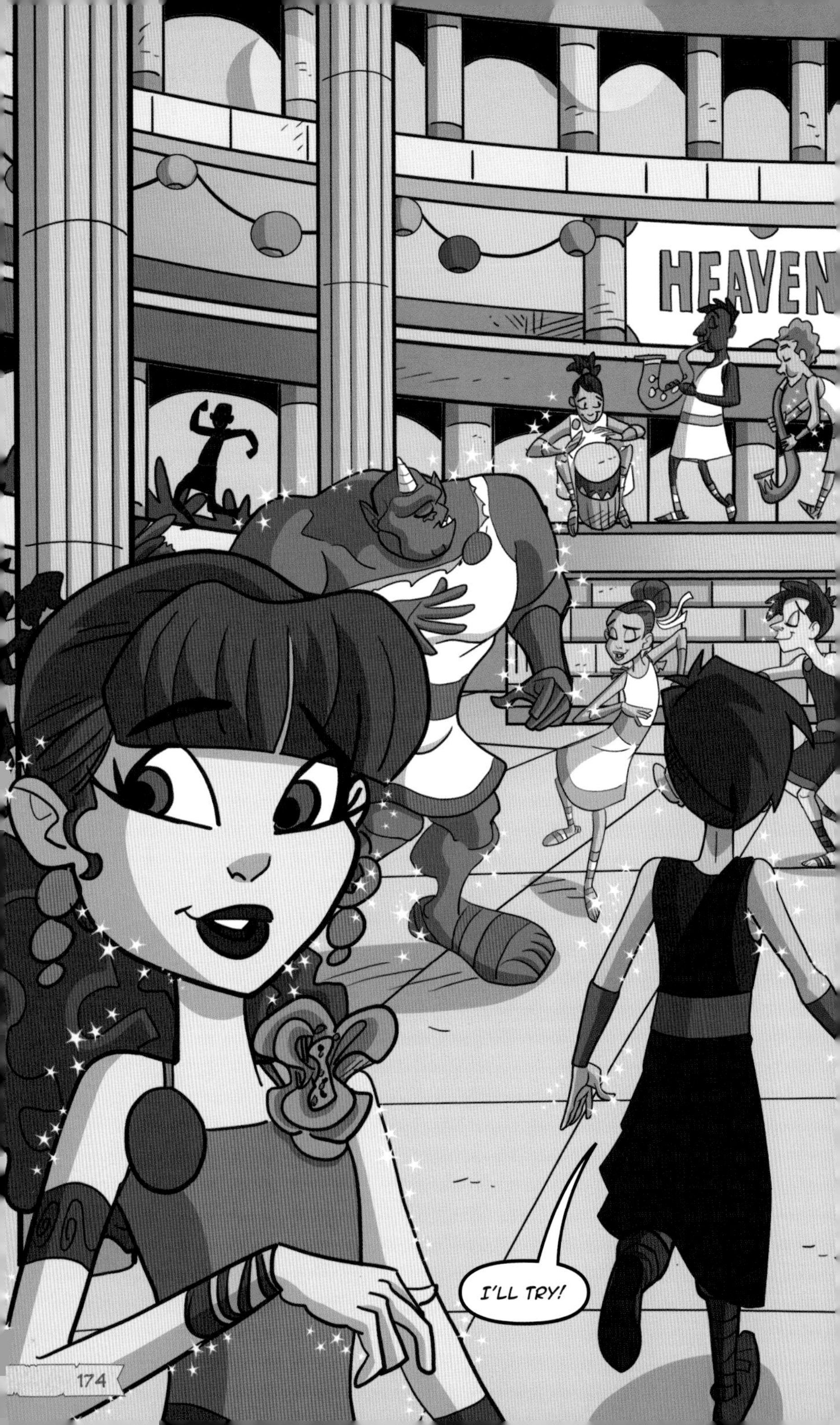
HEAVEN
I'LL TRY!

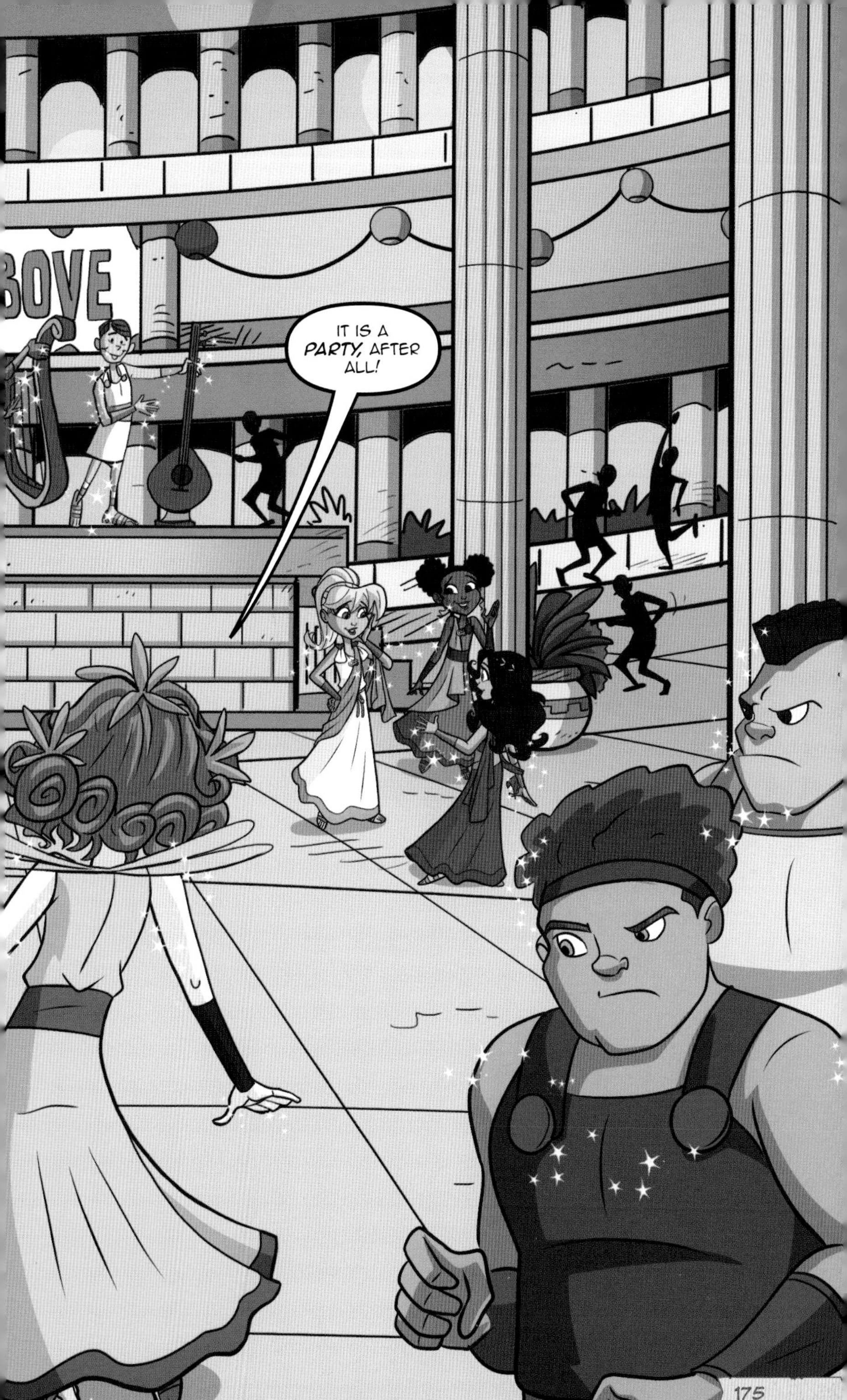
BOVE
IT IS A PARTY, AFTER ALL!

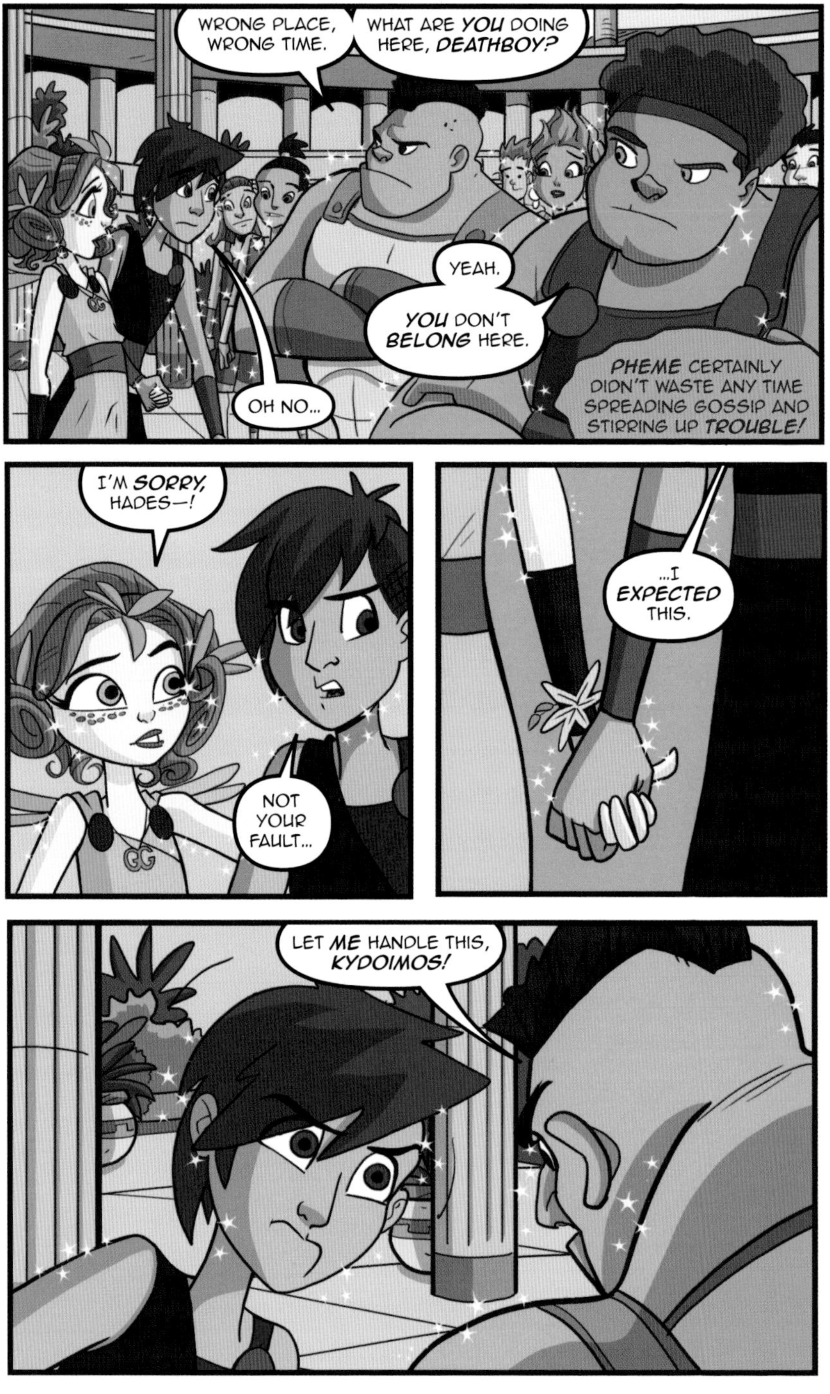

WHAT ARE YOU DOING HERE, DEATHBOY?
WRONG PLACE, WRONG TIME.
YEAH.
YOU DON'T BELONG HERE.
OH NO...
PHEME CERTAINLY DIDN'T WASTE ANY TIME SPREADING GOSSIP AND STIRRING UP TROUBLE!
I'M SORRY, HADES—!
NOT YOUR FAULT...
...I EXPECTED THIS.
LET ME HANDLE THIS, KYDOIMOS!

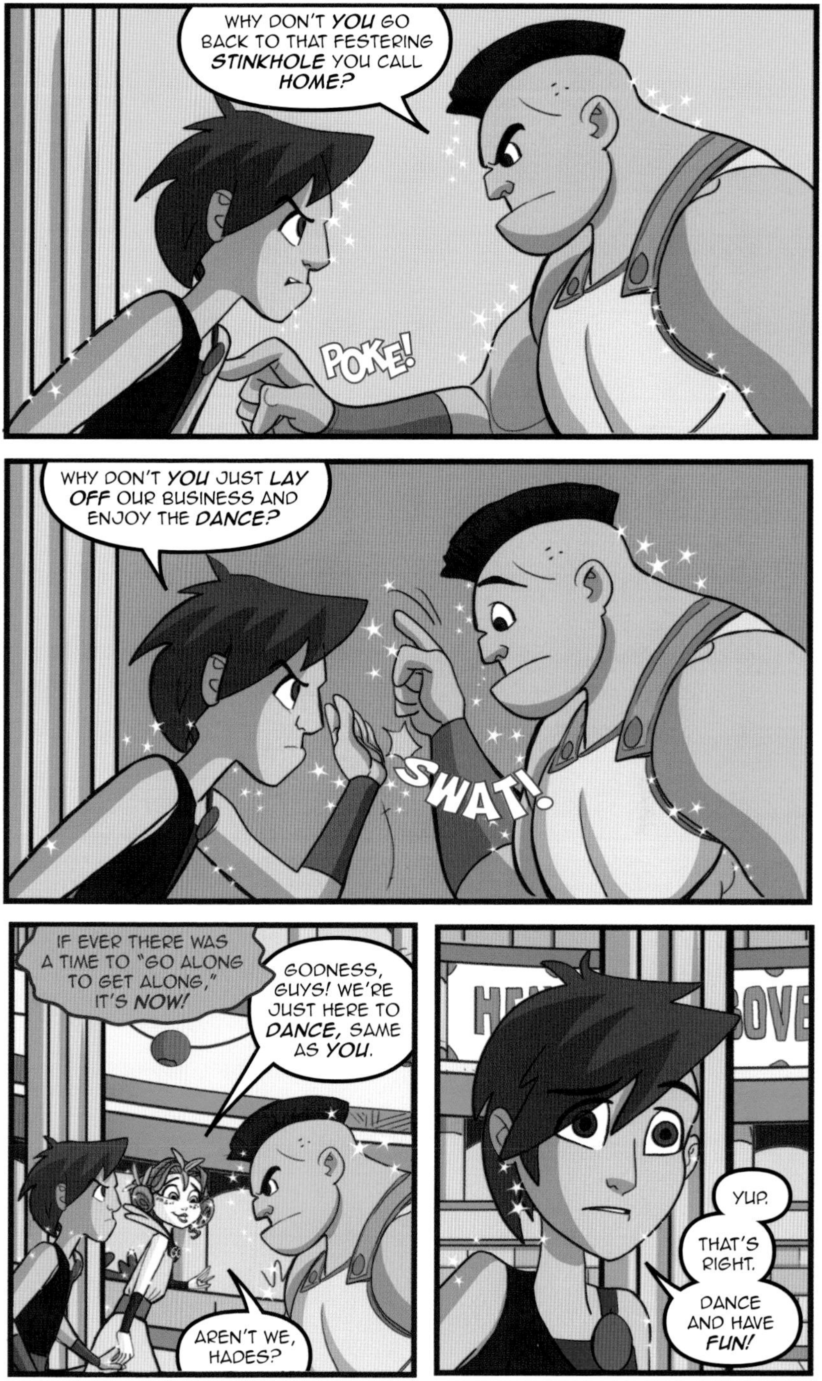
WHY DON'T *YOU* GO BACK TO THAT FESTERING *STINKHOLE* YOU CALL *HOME?*
POKE!
WHY DON'T *YOU* JUST *LAY OFF* OUR BUSINESS AND ENJOY THE *DANCE?*
SWAT!
IF EVER THERE WAS A TIME TO "GO ALONG TO GET ALONG," IT'S *NOW!*
GODNESS, GUYS! WE'RE JUST HERE TO *DANCE,* SAME AS *YOU.*
AREN'T WE, HADES?
YUP.
THAT'S RIGHT.
DANCE AND HAVE *FUN!*

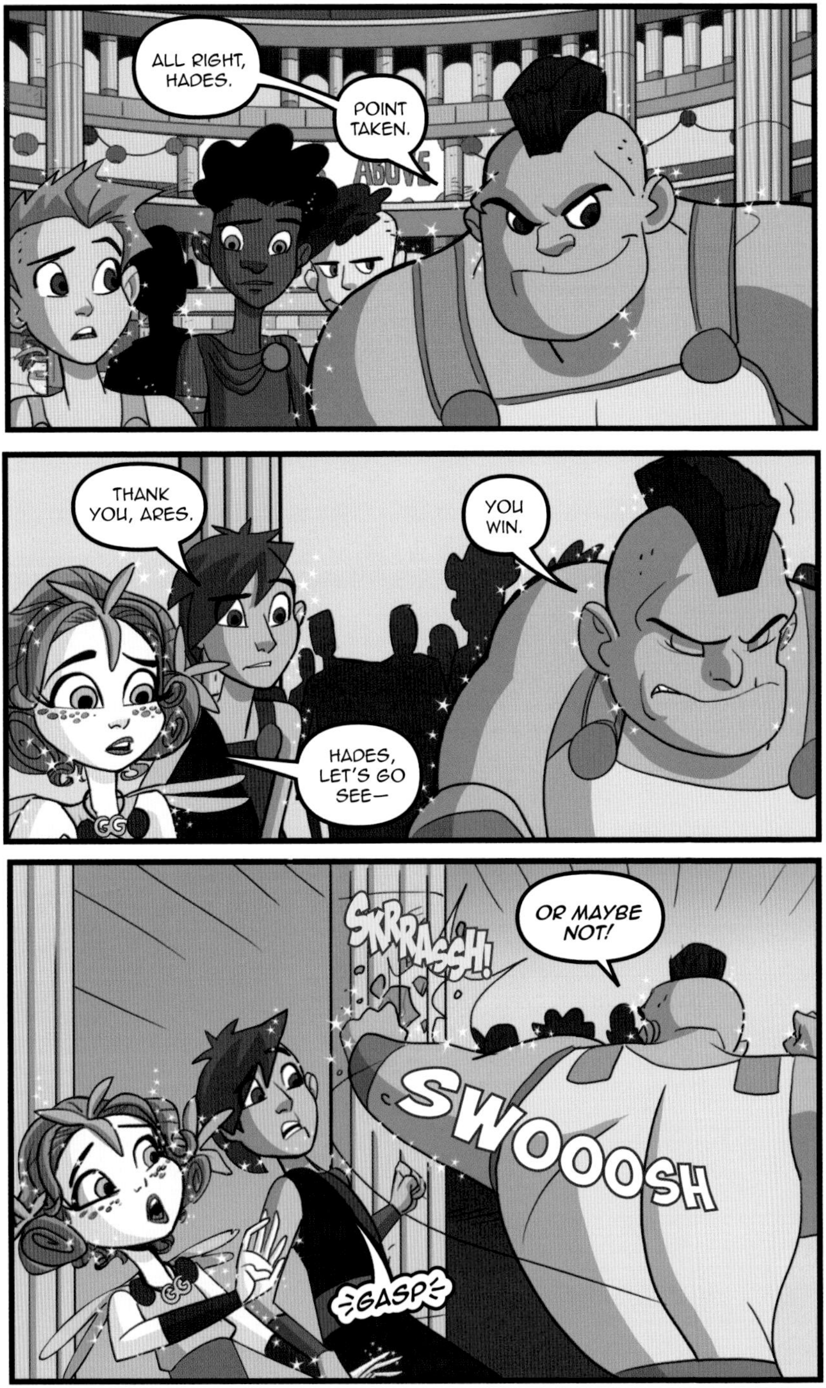
ALL RIGHT, HADES.
POINT TAKEN.
ABOVE
THANK YOU, ARES.
YOU WIN.
HADES, LET'S GO SEE—
SKRRASSH!
OR MAYBE NOT!
SWOOOSH
GASP
GG

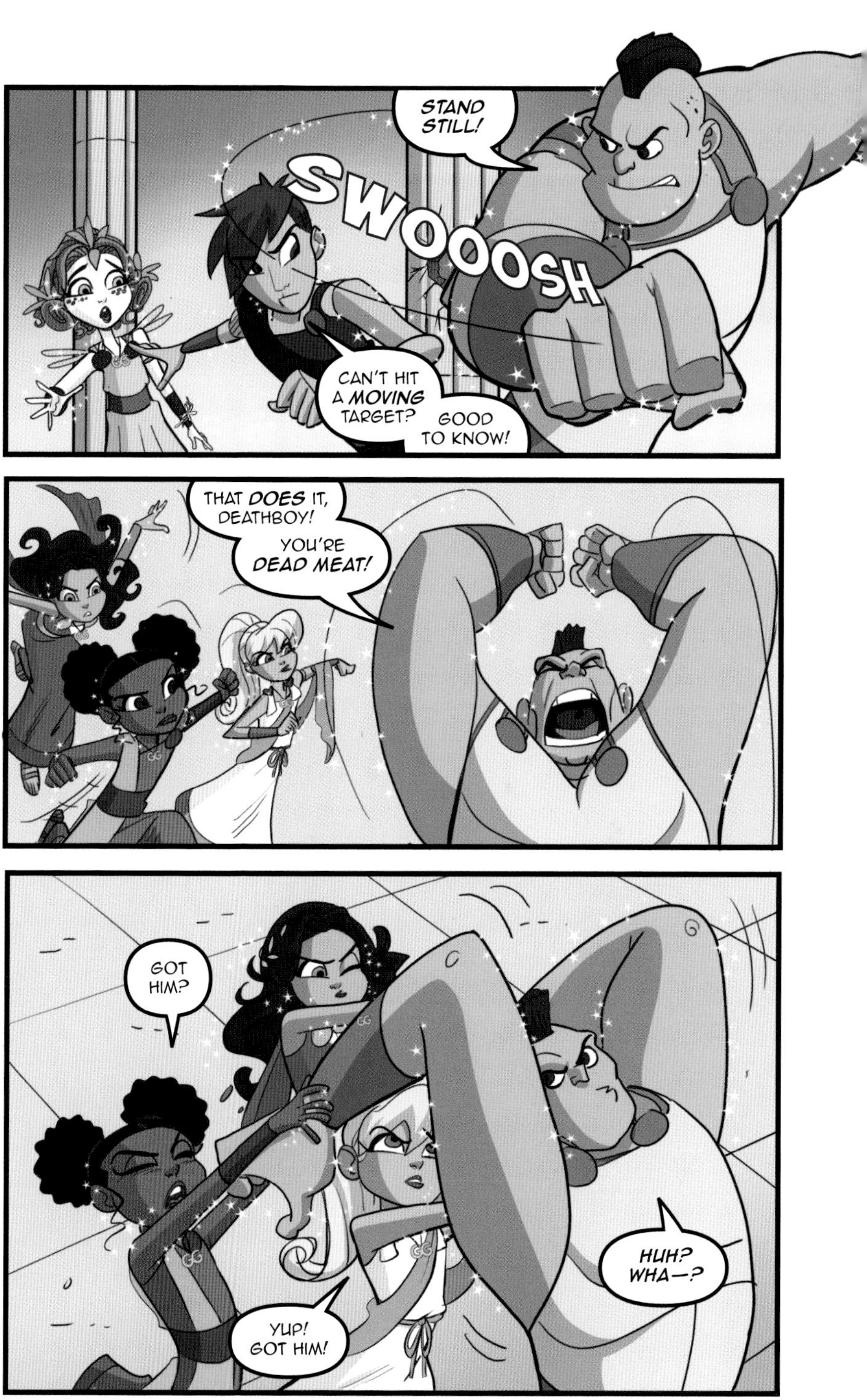
STAND STILL!
SWOOOSH
CAN'T HIT A MOVING TARGET?
GOOD TO KNOW!
THAT DOES IT, DEATHBOY!
YOU'RE DEAD MEAT!
GOT HIM?
HUH? WHA—?
YUP! GOT HIM!

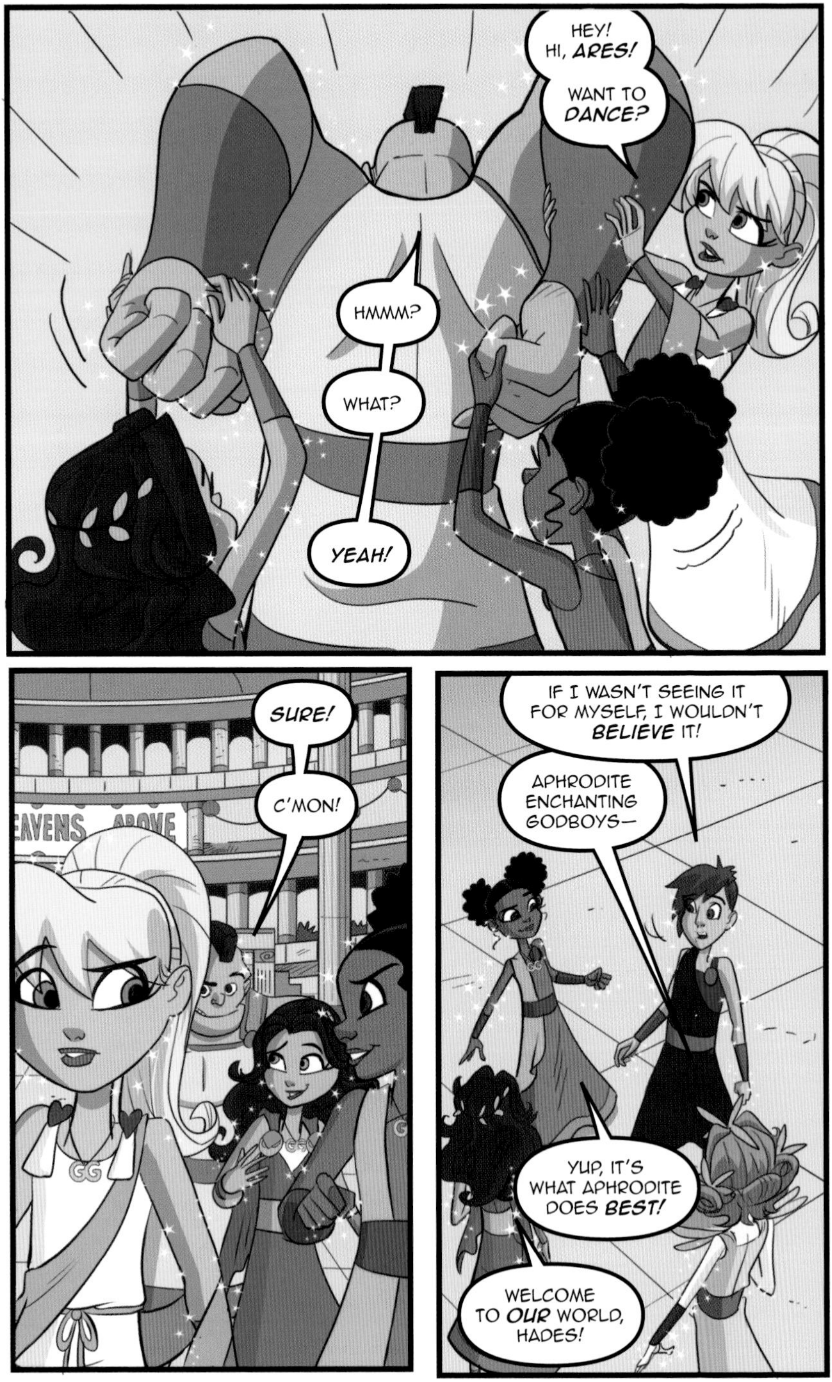
HEY!
HI, ARES!
WANT TO DANCE?
HMMM?
WHAT?
YEAH!
SURE!
C'MON!
EAVENS ABOVE
IF I WASN'T SEEING IT FOR MYSELF, I WOULDN'T BELIEVE IT!
APHRODITE ENCHANTING GODBOYS—
YUP, IT'S WHAT APHRODITE DOES BEST!
WELCOME TO OUR WORLD, HADES!

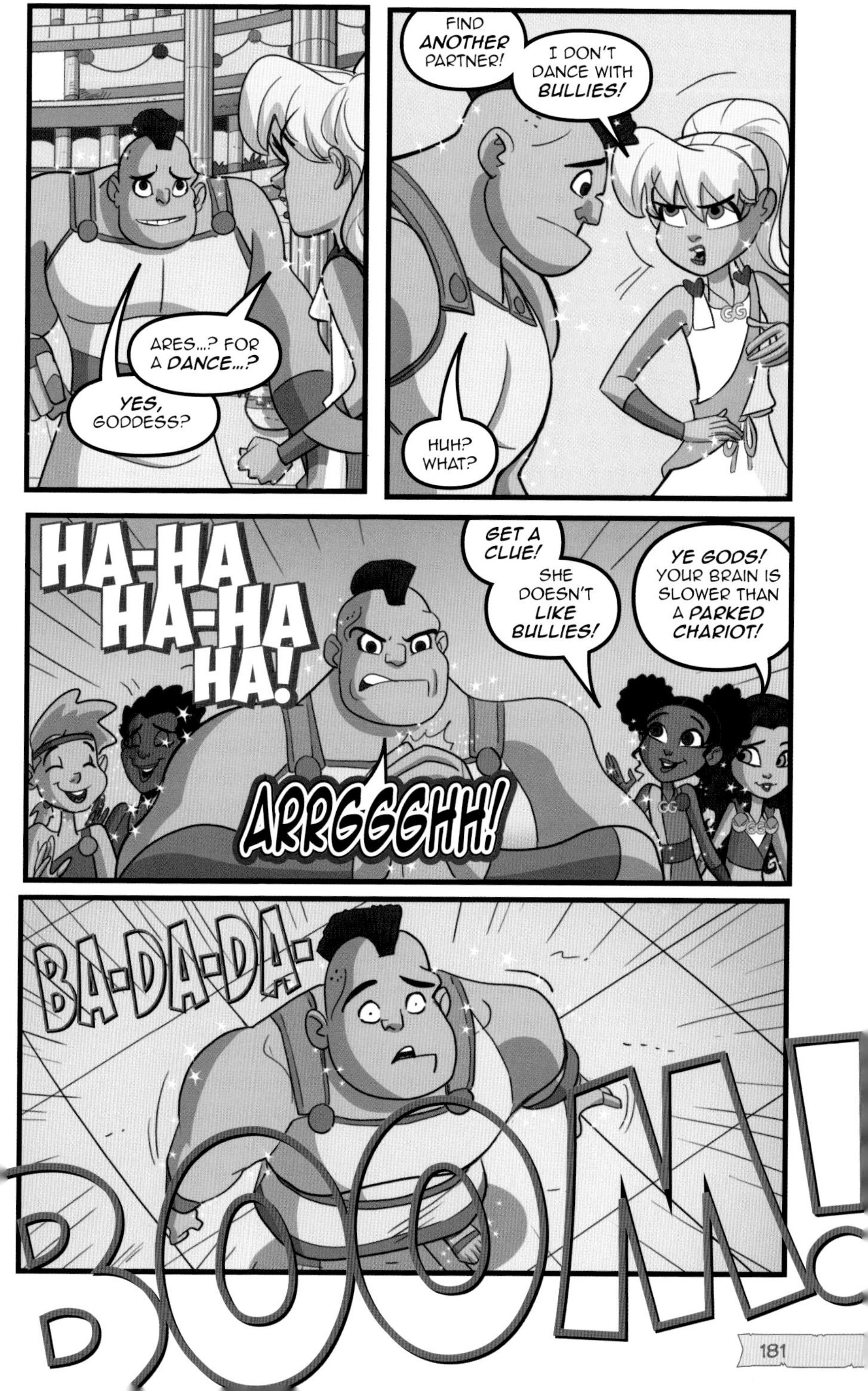

YES, GODDESS?
ARES...? FOR A DANCE...?
FIND ANOTHER PARTNER!
I DON'T DANCE WITH BULLIES!
HUH? WHAT?
HA-HA HA-HA HA!
GET A CLUE!
SHE DOESN'T LIKE BULLIES!
YE GODS! YOUR BRAIN IS SLOWER THAN A PARKED CHARIOT!
ARRGGGHH!
BA-DA-DA-
BOOOM!

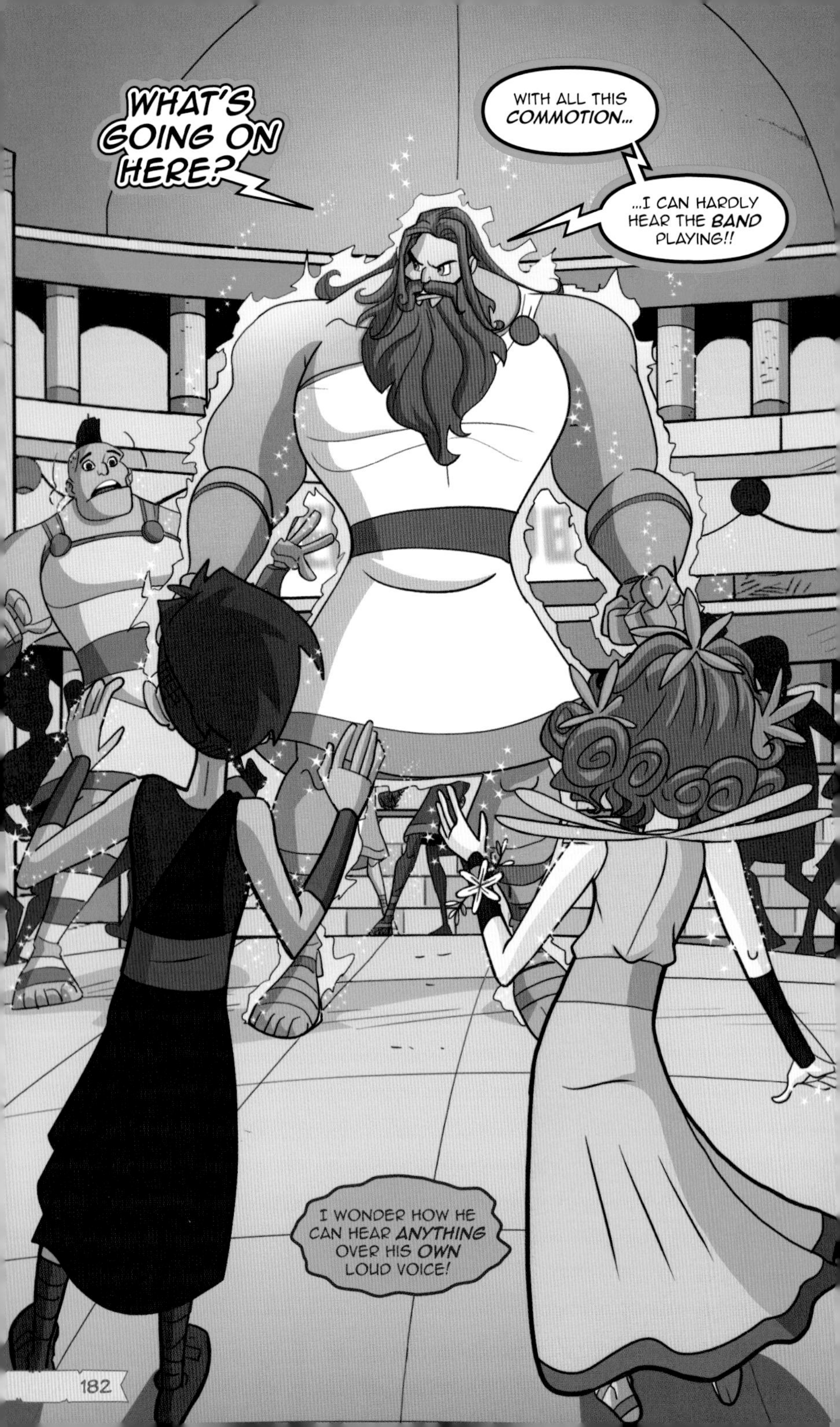
WHAT'S GOING ON HERE?
WITH ALL THIS COMMOTION...
...I CAN HARDLY HEAR THE BAND PLAYING!!
I WONDER HOW HE CAN HEAR ANYTHING OVER HIS OWN LOUD VOICE!

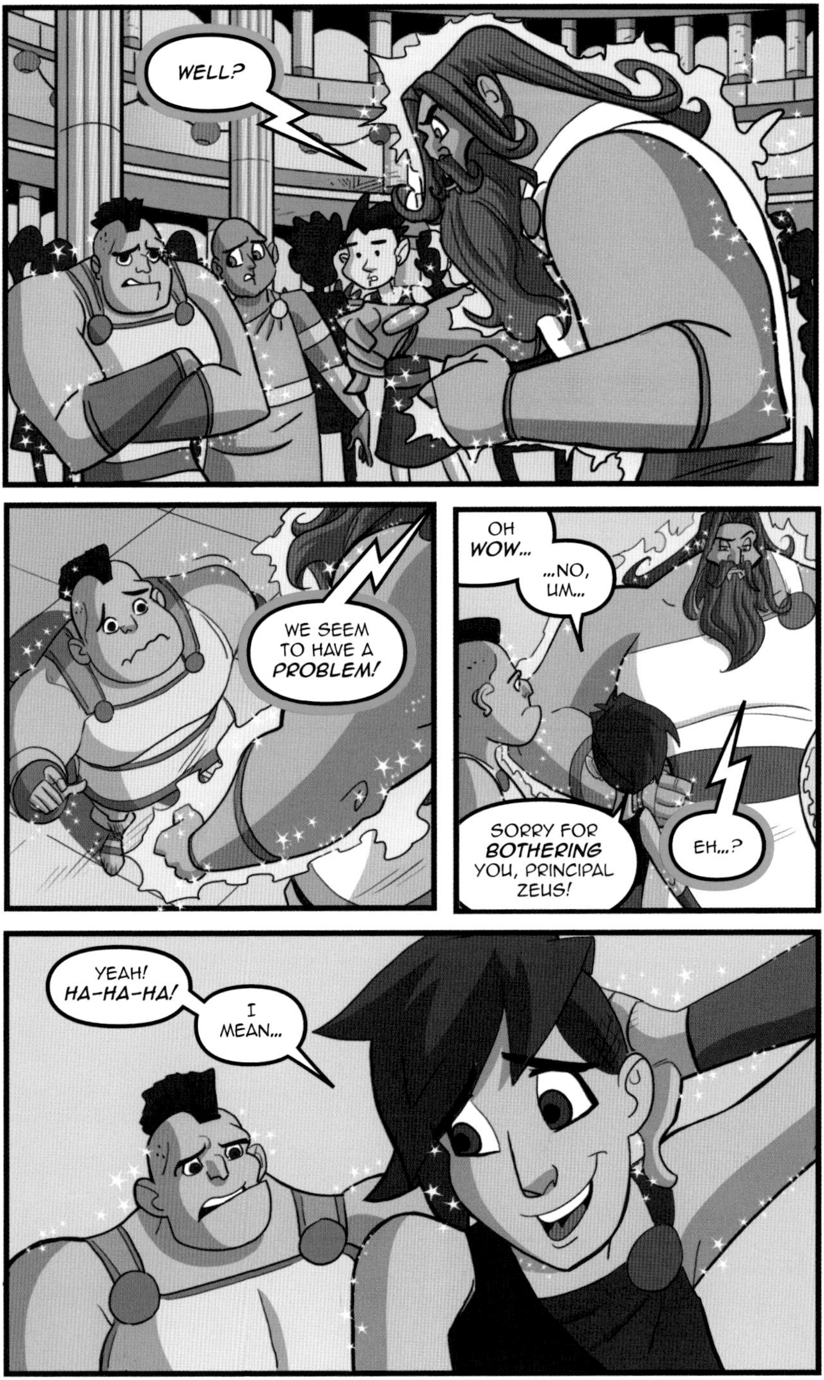
WELL?
WE SEEM TO HAVE A PROBLEM!
OH WOW...
...NO, UM...
SORRY FOR BOTHERING YOU, PRINCIPAL ZEUS!
EH...?
YEAH! HA-HA-HA!
I MEAN...

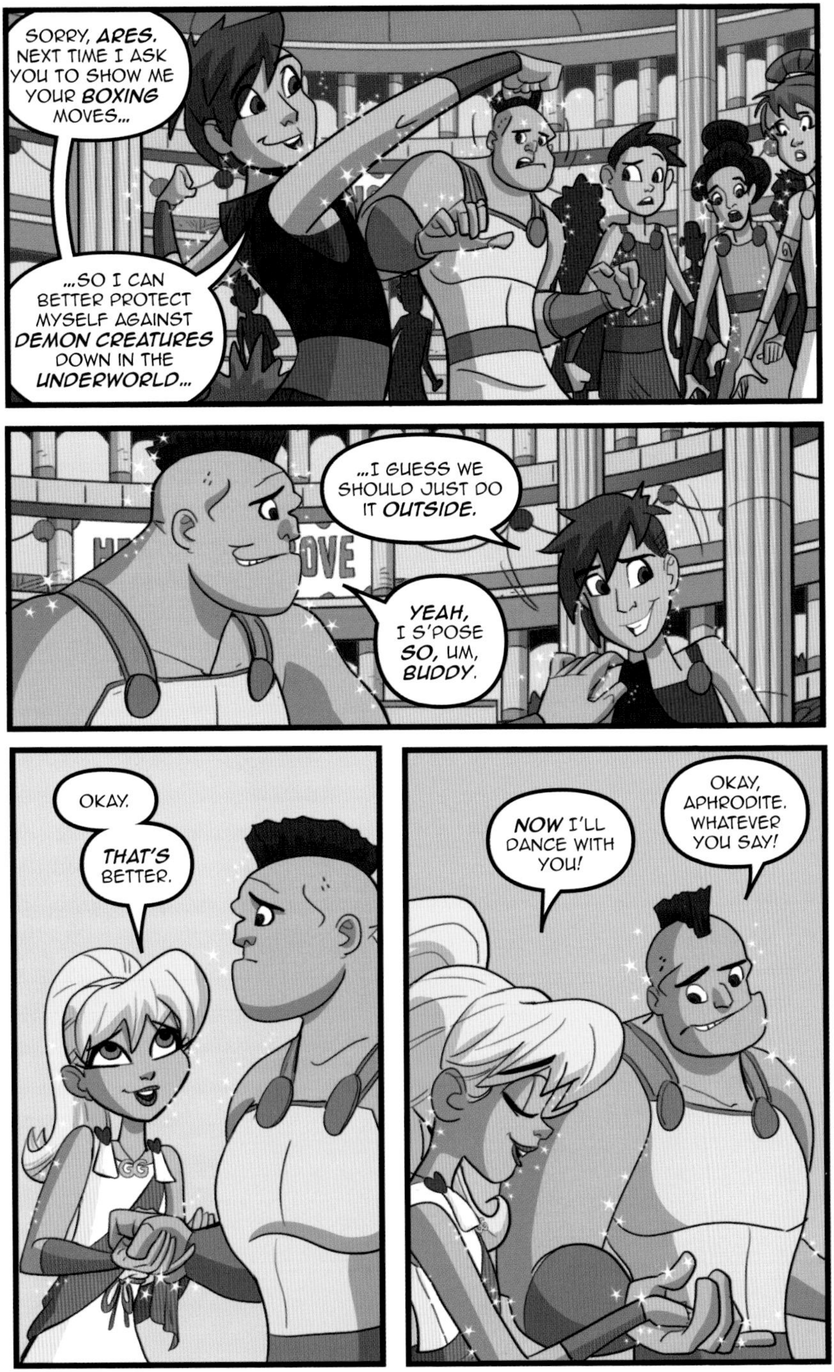
SORRY, ARES. NEXT TIME I ASK YOU TO SHOW ME YOUR BOXING MOVES...
...SO I CAN BETTER PROTECT MYSELF AGAINST DEMON CREATURES DOWN IN THE UNDERWORLD...
...I GUESS WE SHOULD JUST DO IT OUTSIDE.
YEAH, I S'POSE SO, UM, BUDDY.
OKAY.
THAT'S BETTER.
NOW I'LL DANCE WITH YOU!
OKAY, APHRODITE. WHATEVER YOU SAY!

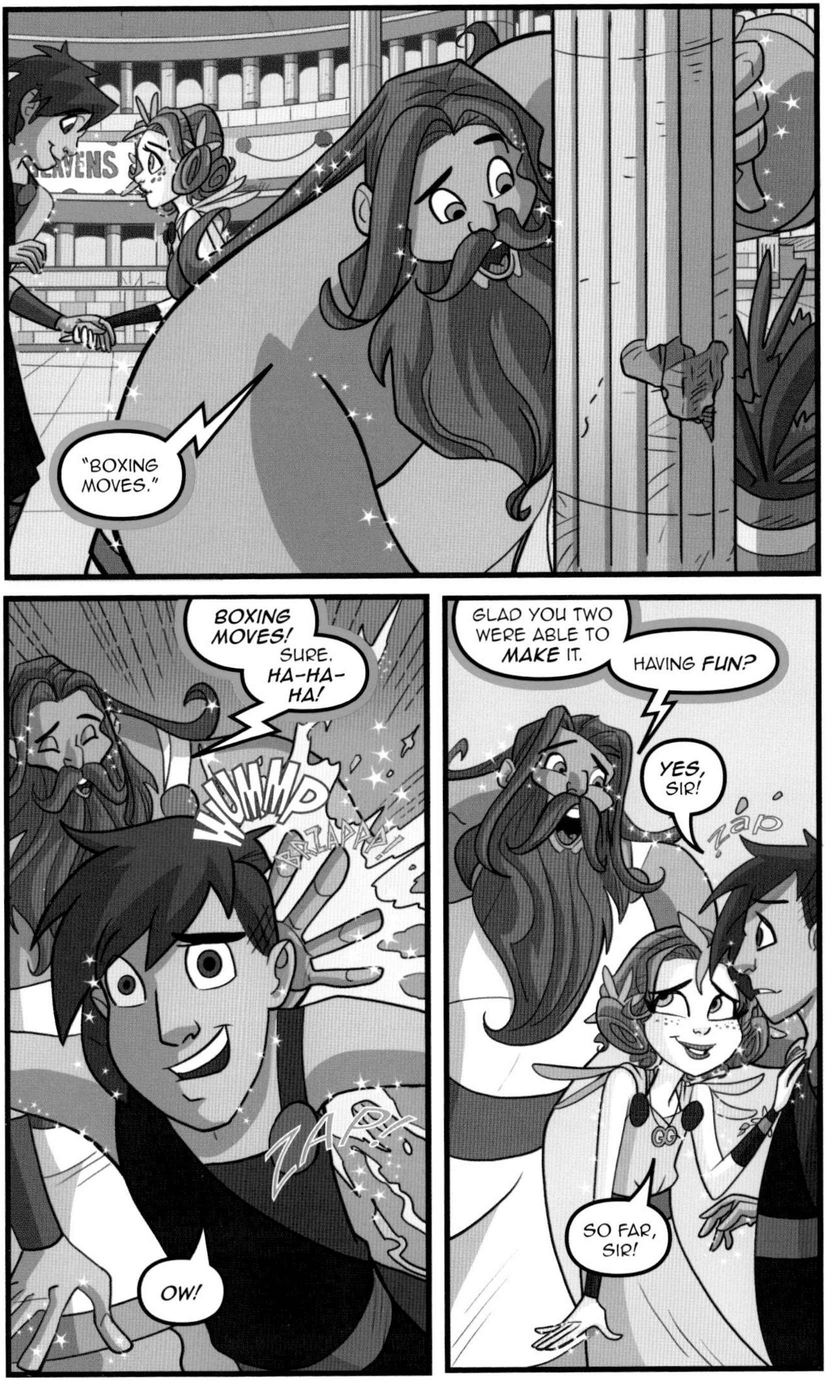

"BOXING MOVES."
BOXING MOVES! SURE. HA-HA-HA!
WUMMP
BRZAPPP!
ZAP!
OW!
GLAD YOU TWO WERE ABLE TO MAKE IT.
HAVING FUN?
YES, SIR!
ZAP
SO FAR, SIR!

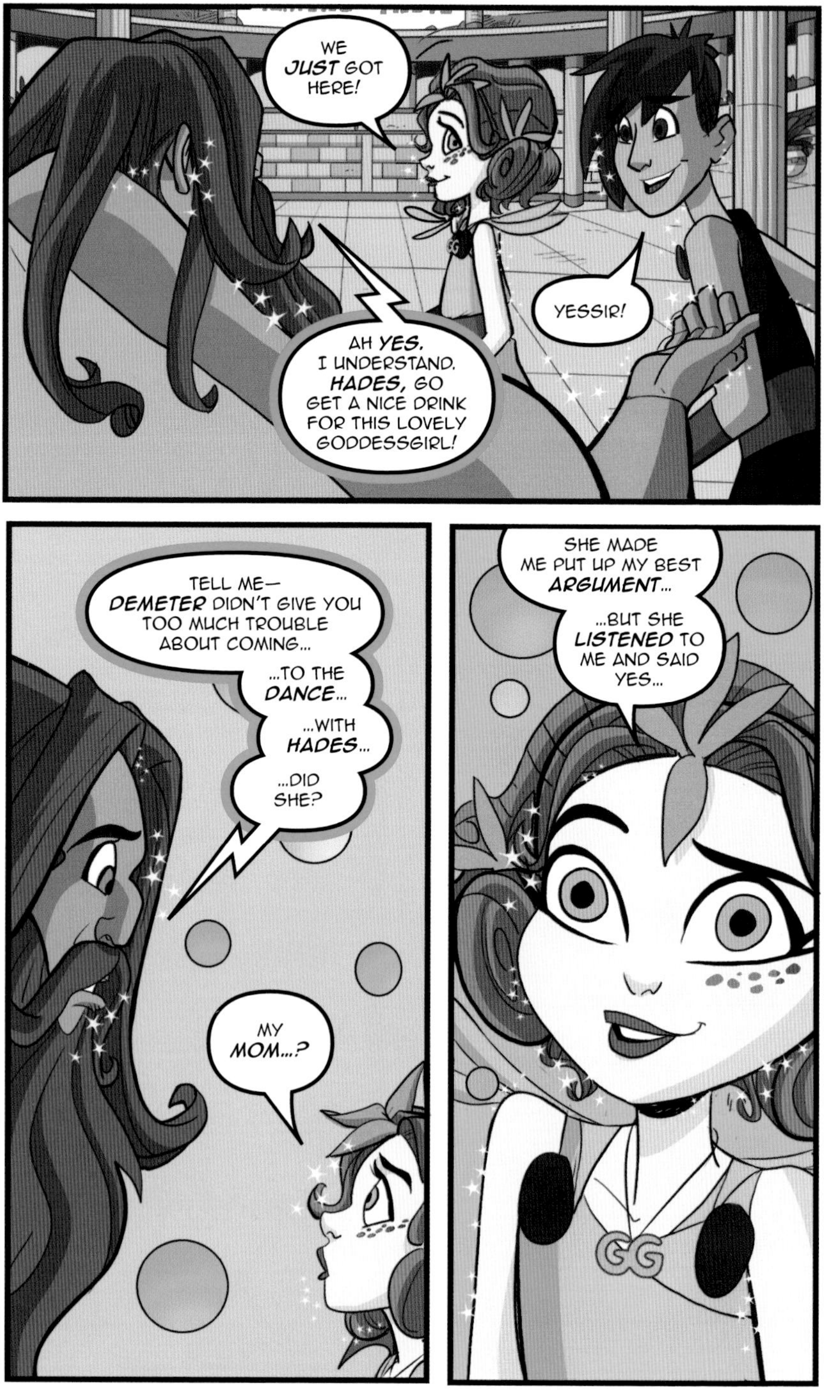
WE JUST GOT HERE!
AH YES. I UNDERSTAND. HADES, GO GET A NICE DRINK FOR THIS LOVELY GODDESSGIRL!
YESSIR!
TELL ME— DEMETER DIDN'T GIVE YOU TOO MUCH TROUBLE ABOUT COMING...
...TO THE DANCE...
...WITH HADES...
...DID SHE?
MY MOM...?
SHE MADE ME PUT UP MY BEST ARGUMENT...
...BUT SHE LISTENED TO ME AND SAID YES...

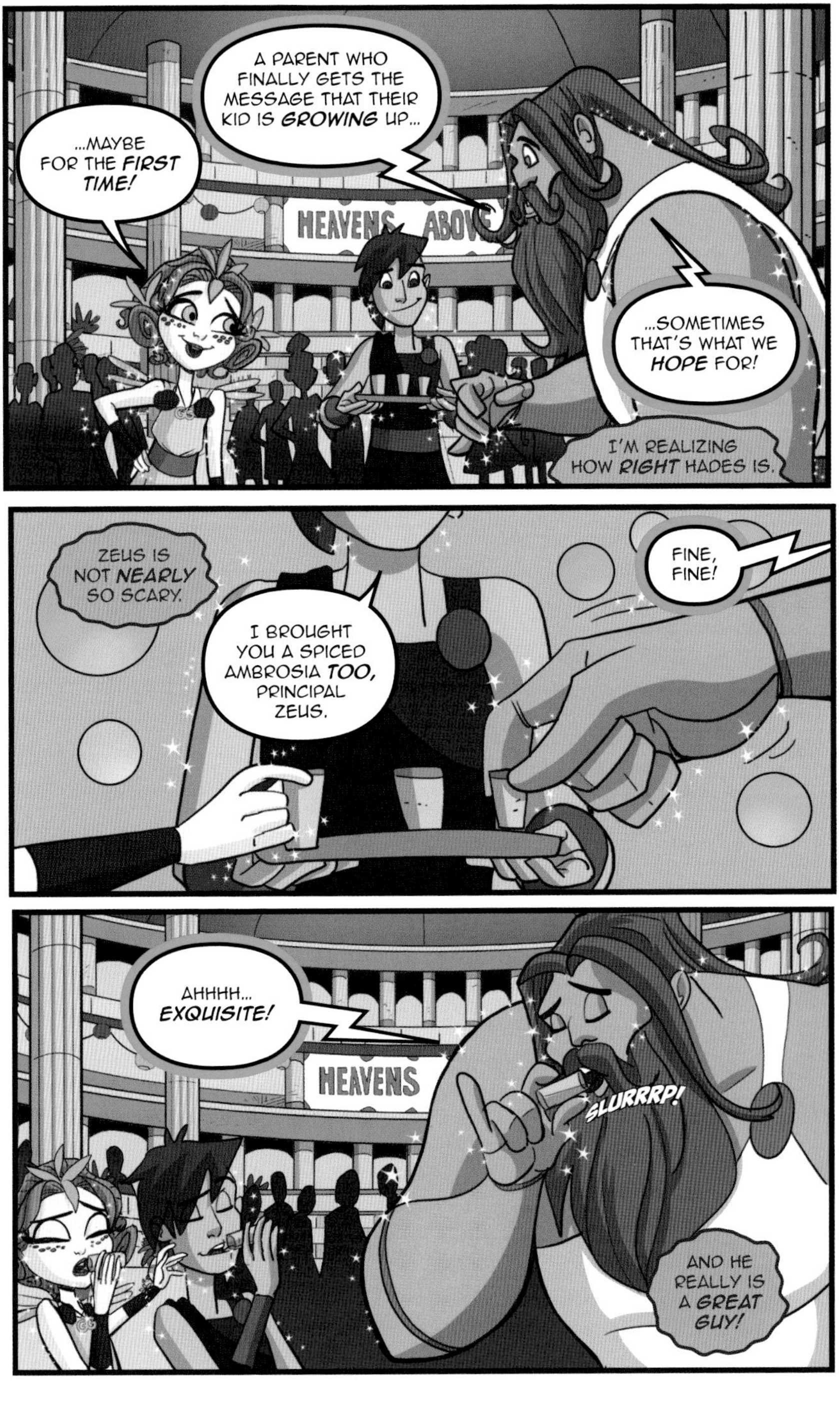
A PARENT WHO FINALLY GETS THE MESSAGE THAT THEIR KID IS GROWING UP...
...MAYBE FOR THE FIRST TIME!
HEAVENS ABOVE
...SOMETIMES THAT'S WHAT WE HOPE FOR!
I'M REALIZING HOW RIGHT HADES IS.
ZEUS IS NOT NEARLY SO SCARY.
FINE, FINE!
I BROUGHT YOU A SPICED AMBROSIA TOO, PRINCIPAL ZEUS.
AHHHH... EXQUISITE!
HEAVENS
SLURRRP!
AND HE REALLY IS A GREAT GUY!

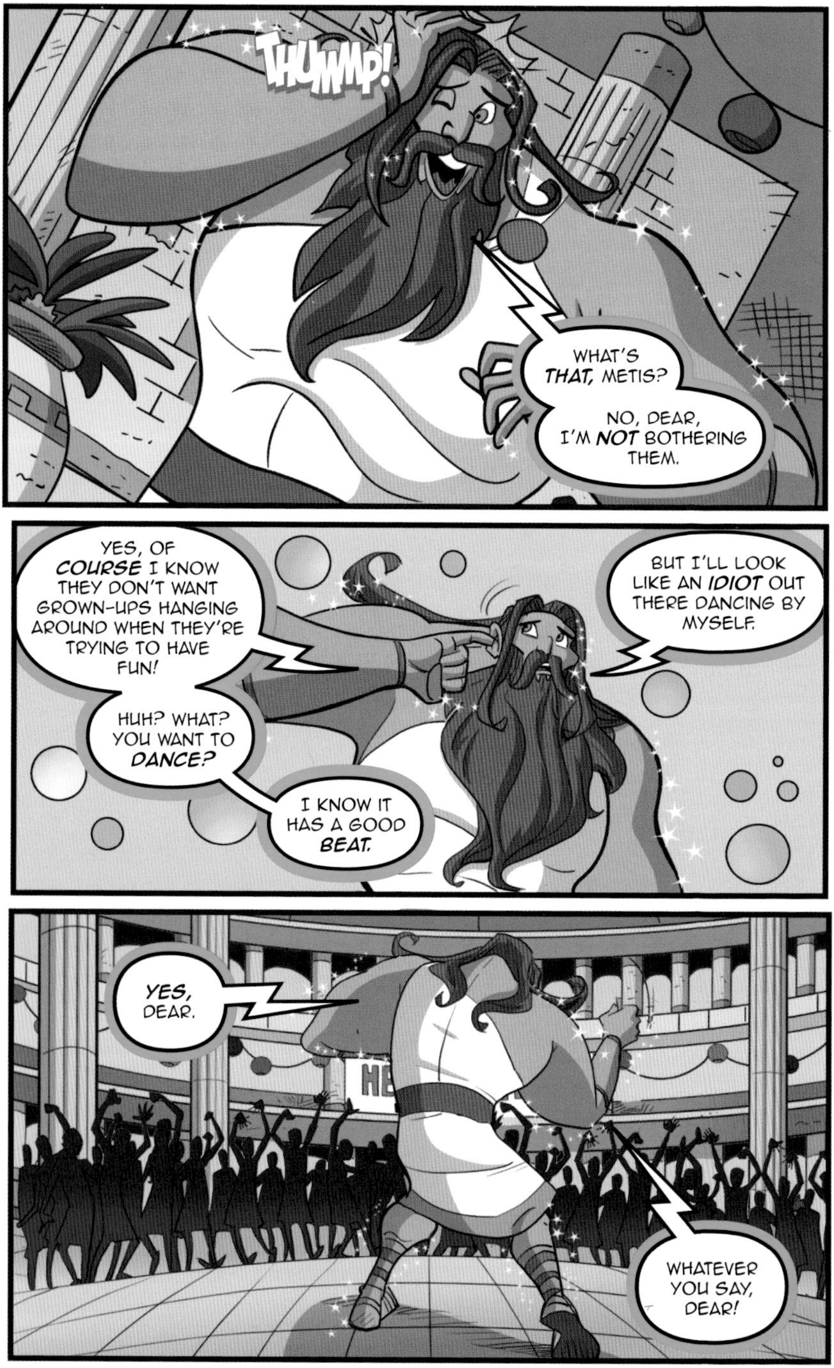
THUMMP!
WHAT'S THAT, METIS?
NO, DEAR, I'M NOT BOTHERING THEM.
YES, OF COURSE I KNOW THEY DON'T WANT GROWN-UPS HANGING AROUND WHEN THEY'RE TRYING TO HAVE FUN!
HUH? WHAT? YOU WANT TO DANCE?
I KNOW IT HAS A GOOD BEAT.
BUT I'LL LOOK LIKE AN IDIOT OUT THERE DANCING BY MYSELF.
YES, DEAR.
WHATEVER YOU SAY, DEAR!

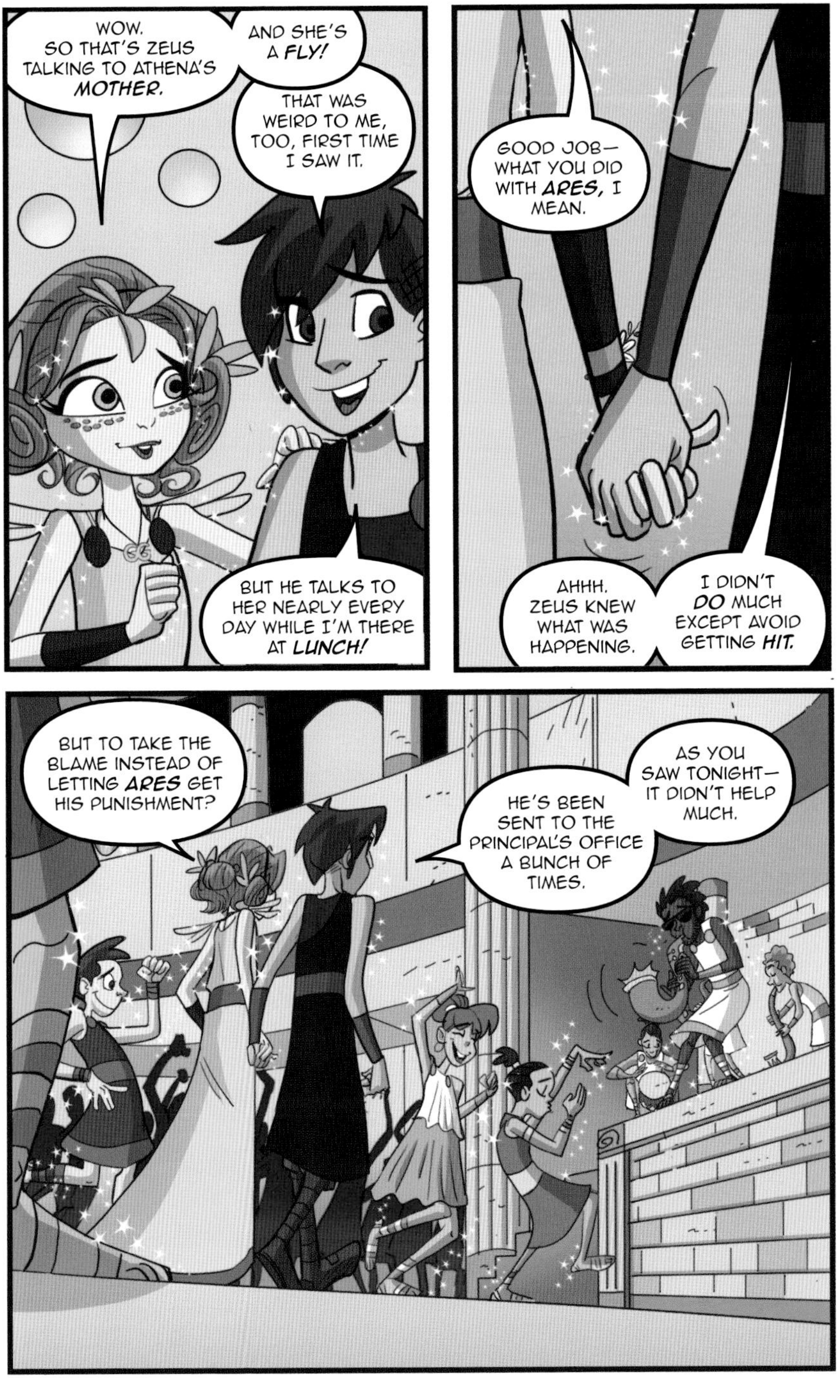
WOW. SO THAT'S ZEUS TALKING TO ATHENA'S MOTHER.
AND SHE'S A FLY!
THAT WAS WEIRD TO ME, TOO, FIRST TIME I SAW IT.
BUT HE TALKS TO HER NEARLY EVERY DAY WHILE I'M THERE AT LUNCH!
GOOD JOB— WHAT YOU DID WITH ARES, I MEAN.
I DIDN'T DO MUCH EXCEPT AVOID GETTING HIT.
AHHH. ZEUS KNEW WHAT WAS HAPPENING.
BUT TO TAKE THE BLAME INSTEAD OF LETTING ARES GET HIS PUNISHMENT?
HE'S BEEN SENT TO THE PRINCIPAL'S OFFICE A BUNCH OF TIMES.
AS YOU SAW TONIGHT— IT DIDN'T HELP MUCH.

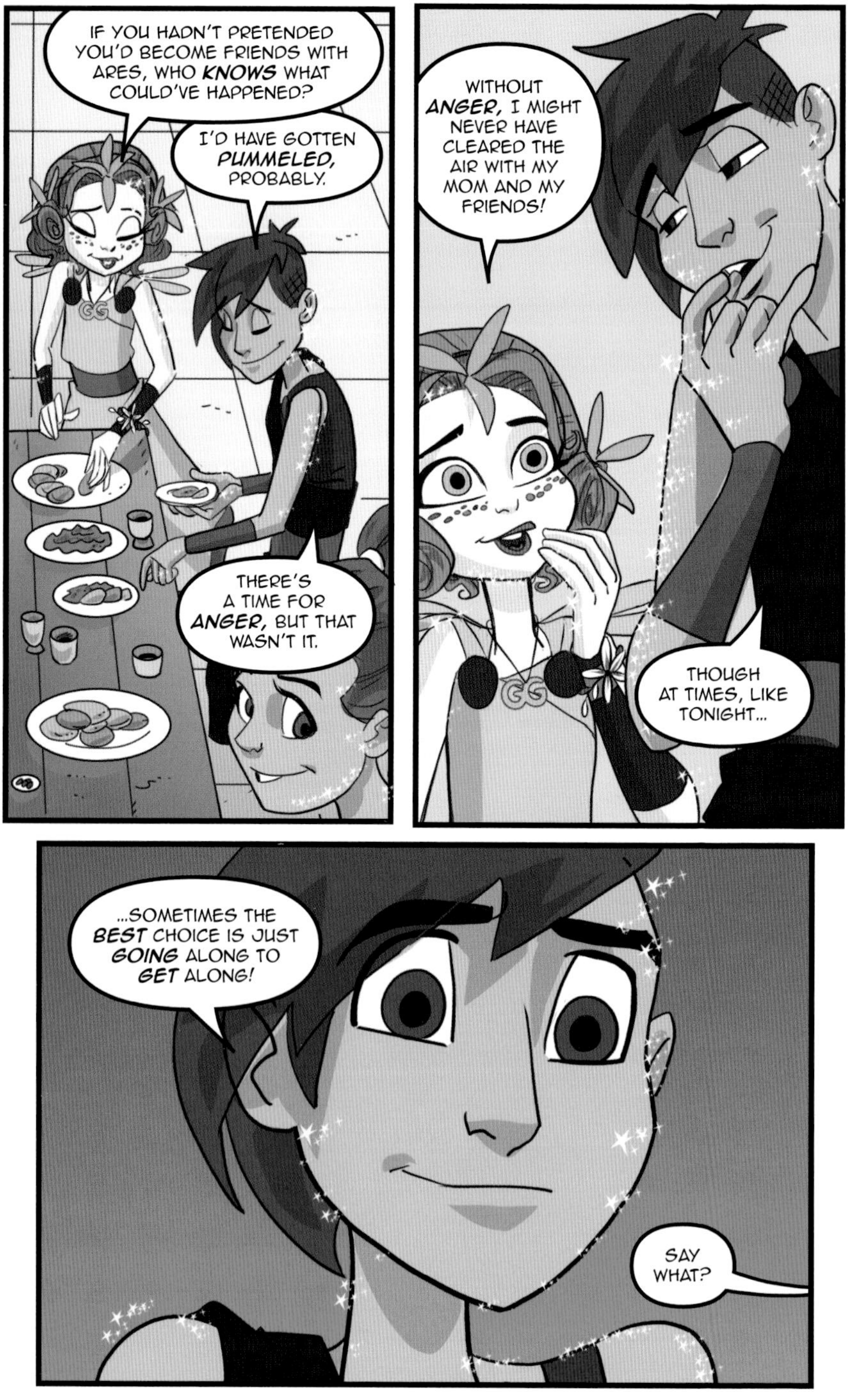
IF YOU HADN'T PRETENDED YOU'D BECOME FRIENDS WITH ARES, WHO KNOWS WHAT COULD'VE HAPPENED?
I'D HAVE GOTTEN PUMMELED, PROBABLY.
THERE'S A TIME FOR ANGER, BUT THAT WASN'T IT.
WITHOUT ANGER, I MIGHT NEVER HAVE CLEARED THE AIR WITH MY MOM AND MY FRIENDS!
THOUGH AT TIMES, LIKE TONIGHT...
...SOMETIMES THE BEST CHOICE IS JUST GOING ALONG TO GET ALONG!
SAY WHAT?

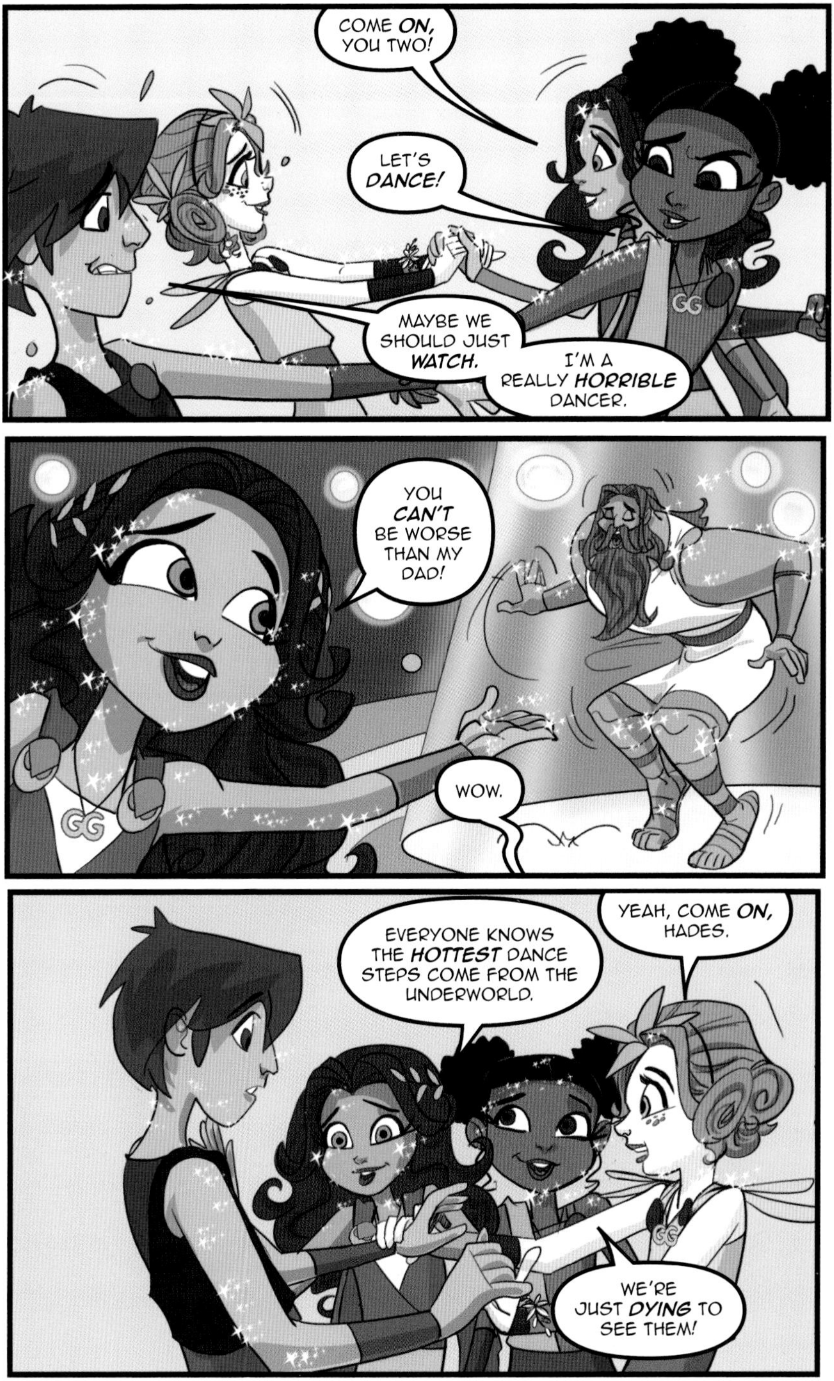
COME ON, YOU TWO!
LET'S DANCE!
MAYBE WE SHOULD JUST WATCH.
I'M A REALLY HORRIBLE DANCER.
YOU CAN'T BE WORSE THAN MY DAD!
WOW.
EVERYONE KNOWS THE HOTTEST DANCE STEPS COME FROM THE UNDERWORLD.
YEAH, COME ON, HADES.
WE'RE JUST DYING TO SEE THEM!

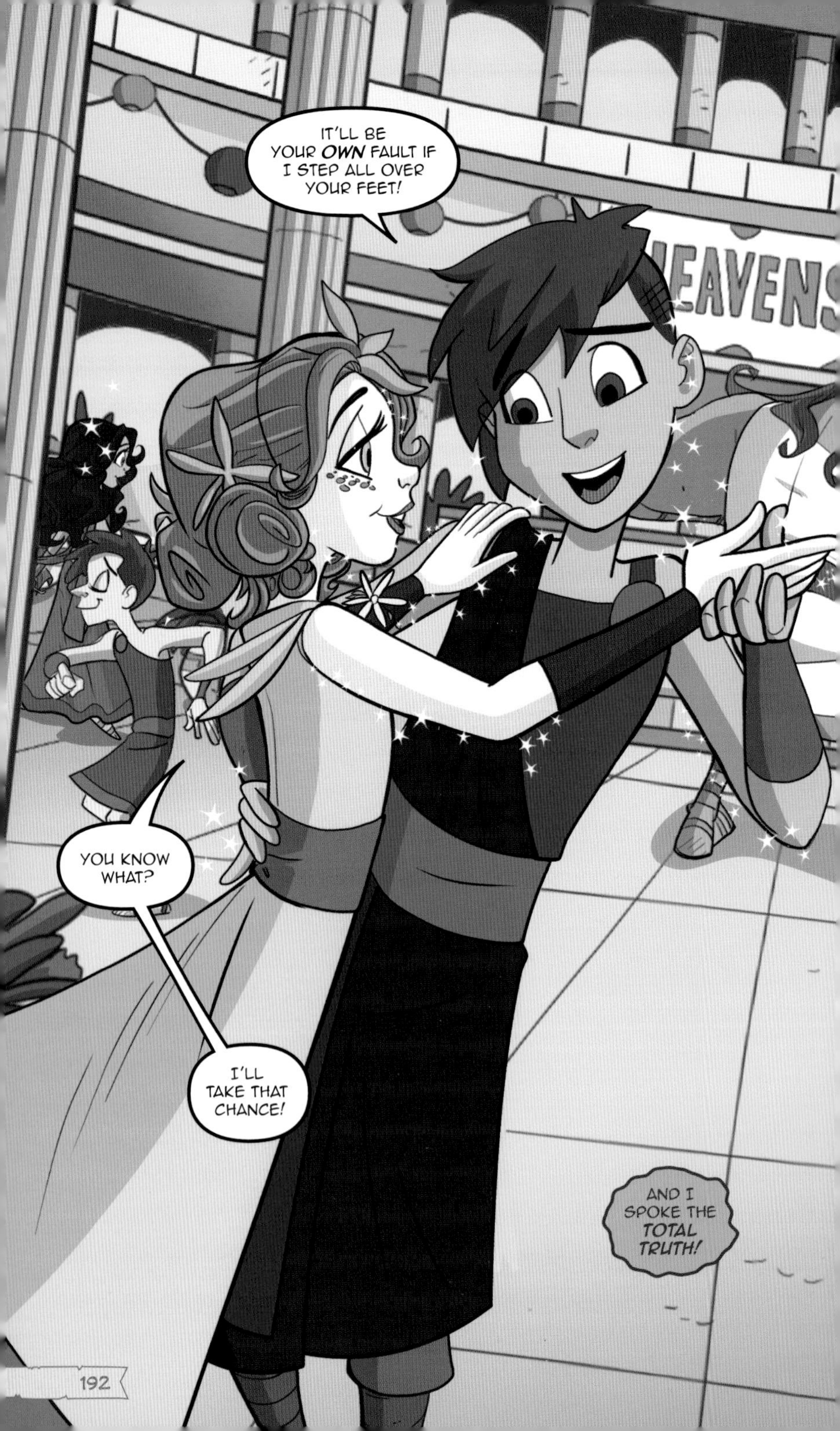
IT'LL BE YOUR OWN FAULT IF I STEP ALL OVER YOUR FEET!
EAVENS
YOU KNOW WHAT?
I'LL TAKE THAT CHANCE!
AND I SPOKE THE TOTAL TRUTH!